A Tale of Two Bubbas

D.Harold

ISBN-13: 978-0615796529
ISBN-10: 0615796524

Please visit www.dharold.com

Blue House / Magoo

Denver · St. Petersburg · Dubai

A Tale of Two Bubbas

D.Harold

Blue House / Magoo

A Tale of Two Bubbas

Contents

Introduction: Now and Then

It was the best of times, it was the worst of times; it was the hills of southern Kentucky in the late nineteen eighties. It was the age of chewing tobacco, it was not the age of anti-smoking ads, it was the epoch of Christianity past, it was the epoch of emerging post-modernism, it was the season of Dan Quayle, it was the season of big hair bands. It saw the emergence of paracute-pantaloons and the puzzlement of the cube of Master Rubick.

In recent times, it was the spring of Obama's Nobel Peace prize and the winter of Obama's troop escalation in Afghanistan. We had everything before us then, we have nothing before us now; we were all going direct to Heaven at that time, now we celebrate Kwanza, Channuka, and Festivus—in short, that period was not unlike the present period, except now we have the noisy authorities on MSNBC, CNN, CNBC, and FOX NEWS insisting on being received, for good or for evil—or both—in the superlative degree of empty talking heads wasting our time daily and nightly.

In the present period, there is a king of eloquent speaking ability and a queen with muscular shoulders on the throne in Washington, D.C. Back then there was Billy Ray King, holding a *Little Kings* as his wife held a lipstick-stained Marlboro in a disgusting dive bar in Coon Spit, Kentucky. In that time, it was clearer than an Elvis collectable plate that to the lords of the State went the Wonder Bread and Mrs. Paul's, and that things in general were settled forever.

- Book the First -

Total Recall

1

The Mail is Late...Again

It was a small artery off the Buckskin Trail that lay—on a late Friday night in November, 1988—before the first of the persons with whom this history has business. This artery lay, as to the driver, just beyond the outer limits of Grouse Gulch, as it lumbered up Shooter's Hill.

Toad kicked the truck's rear, took a piss, then walked two steps uphill in the mire by the side of the shoddy, and near worthless, mail truck. His wife hadn't bothered to get out of the vehicle to push.

Not because she didn't need the exercise (far from it—she was twenty years and a buck fifty pounds further along than Toad), but because the truck was on a hill, and there was mud, and there was all the mail and—blast it!—it was all so messy and heavy!

The truck had come to a stop three times that night before, engine dying, tires spinning uselessly in the mud, as if the danged thing had the mutinous intent of returning to the sub-station in Black Bear before Toad's rounds were complete.

W-D-40, a crowbar, a pair of pliers, in combination, had read that article of war which forbade such a purpose otherwise strongly in favor of that argument—that some brute vehicles simply needed to be read the riot act.

At least three times before, the truck had capitulated and returned to its duty. This time, however, being the fourth, even as her husband had taken it so slow and easy, and with his encouragements of "Whoo-Hoo!" when the tired old engine did tug, the truck had shaken violently, like an unusually emphatic horse, denying that the truck could be got up that hill.

They were stuck in mud. Going nowhere.

Outside the windshield, there was a steaming mist in all the hollows, and it had roamed in its forlornness up that hill, like an evil spirit, seeking rest and finding none. A clammy and intensely cold mist, it made its way through the air in ripples that visibly followed and overspread one another, as the waves of an unwholesome sea might do. It was dense enough to shut out everything but the light of the truck's headlights.

His hand on the driver's side door handle, Toad decided to take one more go at pushing them out, and walked round back to the hindquarters of the truck.

Two spectres plodding up the hill behind the mail truck were wrapped to the cheek-bones over their ears, and wore Timberlands. Not one of the two, and neither the spectres nor the husband, could have said, from anything he or she saw, what either of the other two was like; each was hidden under almost as many wrappers from the eyes of the mind as from the eyes of the body.

In those days, Coalmont County mailmen were suspicious of everyone, for anybody on the Buckskin Trail might be a robber or in league with robbers. That is why Toad brought no assistant with him except his wife; though depressed as the area around Coon Spit was, he was used to hucksters and charlatans coming up to him asking to help deliver the mail for a spell in exchange for some under-the-table green.

Postmaster Theodore Gabriel of Reams, Kentucky, who also oversaw the Black Bear sub-station, strickly forbade the practice, so the husband—on that Friday night in November, nineteen-hundred and eighty-eight, lumbering up Shooter's Hill, as he stood in the mud behind his truck, beating his feet, keeping an eye out on anyone or anything that might approach out of the mist—decided to contact his friend with a suped-up four-wheel-drive Cutlass to pull them out.

* * *

This story has its beginnings twenty-one years before the Year of the Death of Michael Jackson One: Sightings of the Virgin Mary on a Milk Dud were conceded in Coon Spit at that favored period, as at this.

That being said, for some inconsequential reason to the rest of this book, luckily for the Coon Spitters at that time, this period was mercifully free from the messages of fear and terror that had come lately to Coon Spit—and all of Coalmont County—from the mouths of yammering numbskulls by way of FOX NEWS; which, strange to relate, have proved less important to the human race than any communications yet received.

But enough of that for now. Let's take a moment and allow the reader introduction to the settings for this twisted tale of romance, barbarism and the baser aspects of globalization:

Coon Spit, Kentucky—A mid-size town less favored on the whole as to matters spiritual than her sister city of the crossbow and road-kill forty-five minutes across the holler by way of the Buckskin Trail.

Despite the guidance of her Christian pastors since that time, she entertains herself now with such inhumane achievements as *Grand Theft Auto 3*, in which a youth could have his hands cut off, his tongue torn out with pliers and his body burned alive, all because he had not kneeled down in the rain to honor a procession of dirty cops which passed within his view at a distance of some fifty or sixty yards.

But that is *now*. This story only concerns itself with *then*.

Grouse Gulch, Kentucky—In the small town of the crossbow and roadkill across the holler from Coon Spit, there was scarcely an amount of order and protection in the late nineteen eighties to justify much city-wide boasting.

In short: The police department sucked.

Daring burglaries by armed men, and highway robberies at rest areas took place in and around Grouse Gulch itself every night; families were cautioned to not go out of town without first removing their plastic-covered couches and all manner of Velvet Elvis, taking them to the nearest U-Store-It for security.

But the highway rest area mugger in the dark was a city councilman in the light, and, being recognized and challenged by his fellow councilman who stopped him in his character as the 'Toilet Paper Bandit,' gallantly shot him through the head and drove away.

Even the mail was waylaid by seven robbers for just a *Playboy* and Old Man Shifner's social security check; the vigilante councilman shot three dead with his crossbow before being shot dead himself by the other four, as the official police report later stated: 'For failure of a single crossbow to be any match for four punks with .22's,' unquote, after which the mail was gone through (and stolen) in peace by the punks *before* it was delivered.

In a somewhat related matter, that magnificent bastard, Otis Fielding, was held up at the Bell Buckling rest area for his social security check by one highwayman, who despoiled Otis of his clean shorts in the sight of all.

At the same time, prisoners in the jailhouse at Grouse Gulch fought battles with turkeys in a field out back, and the mayor himself probably wished he had the reformed blunderbuss Michael Vick to throw in among them, loaded with shot and ball, to break it all up.

All these things, and a thousand like them (that have no bearing whatsoever on our current story) came to pass in and close upon the dear old year one-thousand nine-hundred and eighty-eight.

* * *

Some moments before, the CB raido cord had been stretched way outside the truck, but presently, the husband had climbed back in to wait upon said contacted friend with the badass Cutlass.

Toad smiled that smile his wife Josephine knew, being with him long enough through the years.

The mail truck was in a less than congenial position on the side of the hill when the spectres approached. Fogged windows and metres of space between themselves and the truck prevented a clear deducement of the contents within.

Inside, and without earshot of the spectres, Toad called out, "One more pull and you got it, Jo...!"

Outside, having approached the stalled vehicle, one spectre leaned in and lightly rapped the back window, calling out softly "Hello?"

Inside, Jo gasped. "What time is it?"

"Oh My God!" ejaculated Toad as he ejaculated, then slumped over in a huff; looking at his watch. "Ten minutes past eleven," (huff, huff) "Why?"

"I think he's here!"

The mailman hadn't heard the men outside, but was startled to see shadows dancing on the misted window behind them. "Robbers?"

"Careful," a spectre whispered to his companion outside the vehicle, "They might be robbers inside!"

The passengers suspected the specters; the specters suspected the passengers, and they all suspected everybody else, and the husband was sure of nothing but that his mail truck, to which he could take an oath on two Testaments was not only not fit for the journey, but was also a worthless piece of shit.

Toad smacked the dashboard in disgust.

Postmaster Gabriel banged on the back window, now enlightened of his suspect. "Tsk, Tsk! And not atop of Shooter's Hill yet?"

The stillness consequent on the cessation of the

rumbling and rocking of the truck, added to the stillness of the night, making it very quiet indeed.

The hearts of the passengers beat loud enough perhaps to be heard; but at any rate, the quiet pause was audibly expressive of at least one man being out of breath, and holding that breath, and having his pulse quickened by expectation (and I think you know damn-well what I mean).

"Son-uv-a...!" Postmaster Gabriel sang out, as loud as he could roar. "Toad! Get out! I shall fire you! It's eleven o'clock at night for Chrissake!"

"Jo!" cried Toad in a warning way, wiping the front window with her sleeve.

"What you say, Toad?" Jo addressed him.

They both listened.

"I hear a motor coming. But it's not Jim's shitty-ass Cutlass!"

Jo and Toad began stepping from the vehicle as Postmaster Gabriel readied himself to light into Toad.

But Toad creaked his door and remained half in the truck and half out of it; Gabriel and his guest remained in the road below him. They all looked from Toad to Jo, from Jo to Toad, and listened.

Toad looked back and Jo looked back, and even the fearless leader Gabriel pricked-up his ears without contradicting.

The whine of the approaching engine suddenly checked, and with much splashing and floundering in the mud, a man's voice called out from the mist, "Is that the Black Bear mail?"

"Never-you-mind what it is!" Jo retorted, grabbing her rifle from the front seat. "What are you?"

"*Is* that the Black Bear *mail?*"

"Why do you want to know?"

"I'm looking for the Black Bear postmaster."

"It is I," Gabriel said.

"I'm looking for a man said to be with you. A Travis Templeton?"

The postmaster's companion whispered that it

was his name.

Jo and Toad eyed him distrustfully.

"Keep where you are," Jo called to the voice in the mist, "Because if I treat you to a kick in the testicles, they can never be set right in your lifetime!"

"Trip, answer him," Postmaster Gabriel said.

"What's the matter?" asked Travis 'Trip' Templeton, then, with mildly quivering speech. "Who wants me? Is it Jerry?"

"I don't like Jerry's voice, if it is Jerry," Jo growled under her breath. "He's hoarser than suits me, is Jerry."

Toad retorted, "He's probably got that there Eeds thing. Give the man a break."

"It's 'Aids,' you numb-nuts." corrected Jo.

"Templeton?" the messenger called out.

"What's the matter?"

"A message for you sent from over yonder."

"I know this messenger," said Trip, walking up next to the mail truck. "He may come close; there's nothing wrong."

"I hope there ain't, but I can't in tar'nation make sure of that." said Jo in rough soliloquy. "Hello You!"

"Well! And Hello You!" said Jerry, more hoarsely than before.

"You two *know* each other?" incredulated Toad.

"No...," said his wife haltingly, as if unsure of her answer, then she addressed the newcomer loudly: "Come on slowly! You hear me? And if you got a gun, don't let me see you goin' for it. I'm a devil at a quick mistake with my own gun, and when I makes one, you'll feel it where it hurts! So, now, let's look at you!"

The figure of a four-wheeler and its rider came slowly through the eddying mist, and came to the side of the mail truck, where the postmaster's companion stood.

The rider stopped, and casting up his eyes at Jo, handed the man a small folded paper.

The four-wheeler had nearly blown a gasket getting up the backside of that hill, and both wheeler and rider were covered with mud, down from the tires of the machine up to the ballcap of the rider.

"You!" called Trip to Jo, in a tone of quiet business confidence.

"My name's Jo, jackass! Not 'you'."

"Jo!"

The watchful wife, with her right hand at the stock of the rifle, her left at the barrel, and her eye on the four-wheelsman, answered curtly, "What?"

"There's no need getting your panties in a bunch. I own the Tall Tales strip club with the adjoining Cock-N-Bull Tavern. You must know Tall Tales in Grouse Gulch? I'm going to Coon Spit on business. And to drink Crown Royal. I may read this? I mean, may I read this? Goddamn, it's cold out here..."

"Sounds like you've been drinking already, Yoda. But what you lookin' for my permission fer? Go ahead, piss all over yourself, see if I care!"

Trip Templeton opened the note in the light of the mail truck headlights, and read—first to himself, and then aloud: "'Wait at Black Bear for Bunnie.' See, that didn't take long.... Jerry, say that my answer is 'Recalled To Honda, R.G.'"

Jerry started. "That's a bitch of a strange answer," said he, now at his most hoarse.

"Take that message back, and they will know that I received this as well as if I had written it myself. Good night."

With those words, Trip climbed into the mail truck; not at all assisted by the postmaster who followed him in.

Meanwhile, Jerry and Toad hooked a tow-rope to the bumper of the truck. The four-wheeler strained and tugged, and a last burst carried the mail truck to the summit of Shooter's Hill.

The engine breathed again as Jo popped the clutch on the descent.

Toad quickly jumped in the passenger side and

the truck lumbered on again, with heavier wreaths of mist closing round it as it began the descent.

Toad replaced Jo's rifle in its rightful place on the floor, then felt under the seat for their large collection of Smith and Wesson's.

"Toad," Jo said softly so only the two could hear, the roar of the mufflerless engine drowning out any communication sent to back.

"Hello, Jo..." said Toad irritatedly.

"Did you hear the message?"

"I did, Jo."

"What did you make of it, Toad?"

"Nothing at all, Jo."

"That's a coinky-dink, too," Jo mused, "for I made the same of it myself."

Jerry, left alone in the mist and darkness, dismounted meanwhile, not only to ease his spent four-wheeler, but to wipe the mud from his face and shake the wet off his high-rider cap brim, which might have been capable of holding half a gallon.

After standing a moment, uselessly shaking off his heavily-splashed arms, until the engine of the mail truck was no longer within hearing and the night was quite still again, he turned to ride down the hill.

"After that there, take me to the Skinned Hare over in Rabbit Grove, old lady, I won't trust your four wheels 'til I get you on the level," said this hoarse messenger, glancing at his ride. "'Recalled to Honda, R.G.' That's a bitch of a strange message! Much of that wouldn't do for you, Jerry! I say, Jerry! You'd be in a bitchin' bad way, if recalling to Honda was to become popular, Jerry!"

2

The Days of Anti-Psychotic Meds Having

Not Arrived Yet

A wonderful fact to reflect upon, that every human creature is constituted to be that profound secret and mystery to every other.

A solemn consideration, when one enters a small Kentucky hill town at night, that every one of those darkly clustered shacks and trailers encloses its own secret; that every beating heart and the hundreds of thousands of breasts that are there, is, in some of my imaginings—er, um, I mean, in some of *its* imaginings, as secret to the heart nearest to it.

Yeah, right. Not in this holler, my friend.

So with the three passengers and one driver shut up in the narrow compass of one lumbering old mail truck; they were mysteries to one another, as complete as if they had been in his or her own truck and six, or his or hers own truck and sixty, with the breadth of a manure-filled country-mile between them and the next.

The messenger rode back to his post at an easy speed, stopping often at bars by way to drink, but evincing a tendency to keep his own counsel, and to keep his high-rider hat cocked sideways on his head.

He had eyes that assorted very well with that decoration, being of the surface black, with no depth in the color of form, and much too near together—as if they were afraid of being found out in something singly, if they kept too far apart.

They held a sinister expression, under an old hat with a cock on it, a Cornish hen, and over a rusty muffler on his lap he had found laying solitary in the middle of Buckskin Trail five miles back.

When he stopped for a drink at The Skinned Hare Bar and Grill—complete with pink, shaved, blinking neon rabbit on the sign out front—he held the muffler with his left hand at the bar while he poured his liquor in with his right.

Then he'd look at the bartender and say, "Hey, you didn't give me nothin'!" To which the bartender took the rusty muffler and hit him over the head, bouncing him back out into the frigid night on his ass.

"No, Jerry, no!" said the messenger to himself, harping on one theme as he rode. "It wouldn't do for you Jerry. Jerry, you honest tradesman, it wouldn't suit your line of business! Recalled—! Bust me in the chops if I don't think he'd been a' drinkin'!"

Trip Templeton's message perplexed Jerry's mind to that degree that he was fain, several times, to take off his high-rider hat to scratch his head.

Except on the crown, which had been raggedly bald since nineteen, he had stiff black hair, standing jaggedly all over it, and growing down hill almost to his broad, blunt nose, giving off the effect of early Michael Bolton, and not in a good way. It was so much like a stack of barbed wire than a head of hair that the best of players at leap-frog might have declined him as being the most dangerous man in the world to go over, since you'd scratch your nut-sack as if on a scouring pad. Then again, if there were actually a place where grown men were playing leap-frog, they might also offer to do other things to him, or for him, in its stead.

But that is another matter.

While Jerry drove back over to Grouse Gulch with the message he was to deliver to the bouncer in his high chair at the door of Tall Tales (which included the Cock-N-Bull Tavern in back—for those who wanted to drink in abstention to the skin parade out front, but still wanted to get shit-faced in the grungiest dive in the county) who was to deliver it to greater authorities within, the shadows of the night took such shapes to

Jerry as arose out of his message, and took such shapes as to seemingly scare even his four-wheeler machine half to death, which seemed to be numerous because he could hardly keep her on the road.

Making incredibly slow time, the mail truck lumbered, jolted, rattled, and bumped upon its tedious way, with its four fellow-inscrutables inside. To whom, likewise, the shadows of the night revealed themselves, in the forms their dozing eyes and wandering thoughts suggested.

Tall Tales was making money as the last of the mail was being delivered, of that you can be assured. As the strip club owning passenger—with an arm drawn through a leather strap, which had been used earlier that night in an act by Bubbles Casanova—he did once in awhile playfully hit the next passenger with it, driving Gabriel into his corner of the backseat, whenever the truck got a special jolt.

Trip nodded with half-shut eyes, the truck's dome light dimly gleaming through them, and the bulky bundle of opposite passenger morphed into a stripper, and he did a great stroke of business.

The chug of the dying engine was the swish of one dollar bills. And more dollar bills were made in five minutes than at his competitor's along the highway, with its out-of-state and local customers.

Then the private rooms underground at Tall Tales, with such their valuable stores and secrets as were known to the passenger (and it was not a little that he knew about them), opened before him in his mind as he went in among them with the keys and a feebly working flashlight, and found everyone safe, and strong and sound and not-quite still, but spending lots of money, just as he had last seen them.

But, though the strip club was almost always with him, and though the truck (in a confused way, like the presence of pain under an opiate, though Toad and Jo and Gabriel were currently enjoying a fatty) and all its rickety failings were always with him, there was another current of impression that never ceased to run, all through the night.

Trip was on his way to dig someone out of a grave.

Now, which of the multitude of faces that showed themselves before him was the true face of that buried person the shadows of the night did not indicate; but they were all the faces of a man of five-and-forty years, and they differed principally in the passions they expressed, and in the ghastliness of their worn and wasted state.

Pride, contempt, defiance, stubbornness, submission, lamentation, succeeded on another; so did varieties of sunken cheek, cadaverous color, callused palms and emaciated fingers. But the face was in the one main face, and every head was prematurely ejaculated.

A hundred times the strip club owner inquired of this spectre:

'Buried how long?'

The answer was always the same: 'Almost eight years.'

'You had abandoned all hope of being dug out?'

'Long ago.'

'You know that you are recalled to life?'

'They tell me so.'

'I hope you care to live?'

'I can't say.'

'Shall I show her to you? Will you come and see her?'

The answers to this question were various and contradictory. Sometimes the broken reply was, 'Wait! She would kill me if I saw her too soon!'

Sometimes, it was given in a tender rain of tears, and then it was 'Take me to her.'

Sometimes it was staring and bewildered, and then it was, 'I don't know her. I don't understand.'

After such imaginary discourse, the passenger in his fancy would dig, and dig, and dig—now, with a spade, now with a great key, now with his hands—to dig this wretched creature out.

Got out at last, with earth hanging about his face and hair, he would suddenly fall away to dust.

The passenger would then start to himself, and lower the window, to get the reality of mist and rain on his cheek.

Yet even when his eyes were opened on the mist and the rain, on the moving patch of light from the headlights, and the hedge and the roadside retreating by jerks, the night shadows outside the truck would fall into the train of the night shadows within. The real Tall Tales and Cock-N-Bull Tavern, the real business of the past day, the real private rooms underground, the real four-wheeler sent after him, and the real message returned, would all be there.

Out of the midst of them, the ghostly face would rise, and he would accost it once again.

'Buried how long?'

'Almost eight years.'

'I hope you care to live?'

'I can't say.'

Dig—dig—dig—until an impatient movement from one of the three other passengers would admonish him to pull up the window, draw his arm through the leather strap, and speculate upon the three other forms, until his mind lost its hold of them, and they again slid away into the strip club and the grave.

'Buried how long?'

'Almost eight years.'

'You had abandoned all hope of being dug out?"

'Long ago.'

The words were still in his hearing as just spoken—distinctly in his hearing as ever spoken words had been in his life—when the weary passenger started to the consciousness of light from the passing Days Inn at Black Bear, and found that the shadows of the night were gone.

Trip lowered the window, and looked out at the Rising Sun liquor store. There was a ridge of plowed land, with a plow upon it where it had been left when the Amish couple who ran the Plow Horse Restaurant unyoked the live horses from the display out front; beyond that, a quiet coppice-wood, in which leaves of burning red and golden yellow still remained upon the trees, though it was tough to see that in the dark.

The earth was cold and wet, the sky was clear, and the moon shone bright, placid and beautiful.

"Eight years!" said the passenger, looking at the moon. "Gracious Creator of day! To be buried alive for eight years!"

"What?" Jo barked from the front seat.

"Nothing."

"Then back off the blunt some, ya jackass. You're spookin' me."

3

Distant Early Warnings

When the mail was finally successfully delivered in the course of the full-moon, the night manager of the Royal George Motor Lodge walked across the parking lot to the post-office sub-station at Black Bear on the other side of the lot.

He greeted the mail truck, as was his custom when they came in late. Which in winter, was more often than not.

The motel manager greeted the group with some flourish of ceremony (which Jo always thought was creepily gay), for a mail journey around Coalmont County in winter was an achievement to congratulate an adventurous traveler upon.

Toad parked the truck and he and Jo took off. But not before Gabriel thanked them for the 'J,' and in his current haze being higher than a kite, apologized to Toad profusely for yelling at him and firing him and promptly gave him his job back straight away, completing the usual winter mail carrying ritual.

Then Gabriel patted Trip on the back, walked to one of the more reliable mail trucks, and against postal service policy—in fact it was a felony, but he did not care—he drove it home.

By that time, there was only one adventurous traveler left to be congratulated; and he stood in the sub-station lot rubbing his forehead and looking at the moon.

"Will there be a taxi to Coon Spit tomorrow, Earl?"

"Yeah, Trip. If the weather holds and the roads hold tolerable fair. You be needin' a room tonight then?"

In exchange for when he was in want of, or in

need of, a night's stay unencumbered by legal tender while he was found to be in Black Bear and needing a comfortable place to recline his tired and oft worn out soul-conveyor, Trip would lock Earl in one of the private screening rooms downstairs in Tall Tales for hours on end without asking the least bit of recompense.

"Yep, 'spect so. I won't be needin' a bed right yet, Earl, but I could sure use a room, a clean toilet and some HBO."

"And then breakfast in the mornin', Trip? We got us a cont'netil breakfast of do-nuts and coffee at six in the a.m. By the way—you ever stay in our Boom-Boom Room? It's the new one the owner just put in. It's one of them fancy-shmancy thematic rooms, you know? You wanna see it? The owner keeps tellin' me, 'Show the fuckin' Boom-Boom Room! Hot water and a shower in the Boom-Boom Room! Pull off the men's boots for 'em in the Boom-Boom Room!'...er, uh, it even has one of them fake fireplaces in it..."

While Trip took up the pen attached to the plastic string and wrote a fake name and address in the guest ledger, the night manager squirmed as if suddenly really needing to piss and said: "When you gonna git a men's stripper night at yer stripper club there, Trip?"

"Every night's a men's stripper night, Earl," Trip said in a bored tone as he scratched out his information without looking up.

"Naw, I means a night when mens strip. But I'm not askin' for me—oh, no, I'm no homer-seckshul. It's just that I hear mens talkin' around this here motor lodge, and I git the 'pression that some of thems would like it."

"Not a chance in Hell, Earl."

"Why? Ya already got the name—Cocks-N-Balls."

"It's Cock-N-Bull, Earl, and besides, that's the bar in back, not the strip club out front. That's the name that came with the bar when I bought it. People didn't want it changed."

"I heard rumor that some homer-seckshul truck-ers from off the highway frequent the Cocks-N-Balls..."

"Earl! It's Cock-N-Bull, and like I said, there's not a chance in Hell we're gonna do a men's night, so cut it out! You know these backwoods hillbillies ain't ready for something like 'at yet. And as far as your truckers are concerned, what I don't know, I don't tell; just as long as they pay for their liquor and don't start no fights, everything's copesetic far as I'm concerned. I could care less about the rest."

"Copa-*what*?"

"Nevermind."

"Jes think about it, Trip. S'all I'm askin'."

Trip finished writing and looked up. "I thought about it, Earl, and the answer is still 'Hell no.' So don't bring it up again. And no, I don't want the Boom-Boom Room tonight—or whatever the fuck it's called—nor do I want to see it. Just give me a standard room if you'd please."

The Boom-Boom Room had an odd interest for the establishment of the Royal George in that although one kind of man was seen to go into it, all kinds and varieties of men came out of it.

Consequently, another night manager, male, and several Latino males in maid outfits, *and* the owner of the Royal George were all loitering outside the Boom-Boom Room by 'accident' and at various points be-tween the room and the front office, when a gentleman of sixty, usually formally dressed in a brown suit of clothes—pretty well worn, but very well kept, with large square cuffs and large flaps to the pockets—but now wearing nothing but a brown French maid's out-fit, passed along on his way to the Coke machine.

The vending alcove had no other occupant than the man in the brown maid outfit—save for a few moths.

From places unknown, the man pulled out change and was drawn before the Coke machine like one of the moths. As he stood, glowing in its shimmering light, having put the change in and now waiting for his Coke, he stood so still that he might have been sitting for one of those cheesy picture booth pictures you see at the county fair.

Very orderly and methodical he looked, he bent to retrieve his sodactic treat with a hand on each knee, and a loud watch ticking a sonorous sermon under the flap of his maid's smock, as though it pitted its gravity and longevity against the levity and evanescence of the bright glow of the Coke machine.

He had good legs, and was a little vain of it, for his brown stockings fit sleek and close, and were a fine texture; his shoes and buckles, too, though plain, were trim. He wore an odd little sleek crisp flaxen wig, setting very close to his head; which wig it is to be presumed, was made of hair, but which looked far more as though it were spun from filaments of silk or glass. His linen, though not of a fineness in accordance with his stockings, was as white as the tops of the waves that broke upon the *Hatfield and McCoy Wild Mountain Putt-Putt and Indoor Wave Pool Beach Resort* next door.

A face habitually suppressed and silent waited for the man before him to gather his ware, then stepped forward himself, lighted by the Coke machine, his moist bright eyes must have cost their owner, in years gone by, some pains to drill to the stern and composed expression of a strip club owner.

Trip had a healthy color in his cheeks, and his face, though lined, bore few traces of anxiety. But, perhaps the confidential strippers at Tall Tales were principally occupied with the cares of other people—*at least they better be*, the club owner thought.

But perhaps second-hand cares, like second-hand clothes, come easily off and on. But mostly off at Tall Tales—*at least they better be*, the club owner thought.

Back at his room, despite drinking a Coke an instant before so doing, Trip dropped off to sleep.

At that precise moment, a man named Jim with a piece-of-shit souped-up four-wheel-drive Cutlass walked to and fro in mud stained boots in a tucked away artery of the Buckskin Trail, calling out "Toad? Jo? Where the fuck ya'all at? Hey! Anybody out here...?"

* * *

A too early knock on the door by an inconsiderate maid, female this time, sputtering indiscriminate words in Spanish, roused Trip to his breakfast of cinnamon do-nuts and luke-warm coffee in the front office.

He pulled up a chair and said to Earl, who was still on duty, "I wish accommodation prepared for a young lady who may come here at any time today. She may ask for Travis Templeton, or she may only ask for a gentleman from Tall Tales strip club, or she might only ask for Trip. Please to let me know."

"Yer talkin' kinda funny Trip. You sleep ok las' night? I'm havin' trouble follwin' ya. What was that last bit?"

"Just let me know when the hot snatch I'm expectin' gets here!" barked Trip, actually having had too little sleep, no thanks to the late-night Coke and Cinemax on the TV in lieu of HBO.

Earl startled back a piece and said, "Let me try that fancy talk!"

Earl cleared his throat and put his hand on his heart (for some unknown reason) and said, "We have oftentimes the honor to entertain your gentlemen in their traveling backwards and forwards betwixt Grouse Gulch and Coon Spit. A vast deal of traveling, and discreet motel rooms needed, in Tall Tales' service to the community."

"Yes," Trip joined him in this reverie, since he was also slap-happy and hopped up on shitty lukewarm coffee. "We are quite popular to the Grouse Gulchians, as well as the Coon Spitians across the way. By the way," he rejoined, "loved the 'betwixt' Earl. That was really cool."

"Not much in the habit of needin' a room for yerself these days—if ya know what I mean—are ya Trip?"

"Not of late years. It is fifteen months since we—since I—came last from Tennessee."

"Came *from* Tennessee? Or came *in* Tennes—well, no matter. All that was ba'fore my time here. Ba'fore anyone's time here who still works in this shithole for that matter. The 'George was in other hands at that time."

"I believe so."

"Hell, I'd bet you Tall Tales was makin' money hand over fist—no pun intended, haw, haw—fifteen years 'go, not to menshun fifteen months 'go..."

"You might treble that, and say a hundred and fifty, yet not be far from the truth."

Earl looked at his friend. "Now jus' what the hell you sayin', Trip? Is that some sort of code or sump'in'?"

Trip smacked his cheeks hard. "I don't know, Earl. My brain's all jumbled. Been jumbled all morning. The hell you put in that coffee anyway? Rufies?"

"Indeed, sir!"

"Then pour me another cup, damn it! And be quick about it!"

Rounding his mouth and both his eyes, since he'd already had three cups himself, Earl stepped 'round the counter and shifted the coffee pot from his right hand to his left, poured, then dropped into a comfortable attitude, and stood surveying his guest—who sat cramming as many do-nuts into his mouth at one time as he possibly could while sloshing down coffee like there was no tomorrow.

When Trip had finished his 'breakfast,' he went out for a stroll through the putt-putt golf and beach dome next door, of the *Hatfield and McCoy* 'resort' variety.

The 'beach' was a desert of heaps of cess and

gravel tumbling wildly about, as the 'sea' did what it liked, and what it liked was destruction. The air among the 'beach' was so strong a noxious flavor that one might have supposed sick fish had been dipped in it, as sick people most likely went down to the twenty-four hour clinic after having been dipped in it themselves. Small tradesman who owned places such as this, but did no business whatsoever, sometimes unaccountably realized large fortunes and it was remarkable that nobody in the neighborhood understood it was merely a front for the laundering of drug money, as Trip was sure it most certainly was.

As the day declined into afternoon, and the air, which had been at intervals clear enough to allow the Waffle House to be seen down the street, the air had became again charged with mist and vapor.

Trip's thoughts seemed to cloud too.

When it was dark, pissed that he'd have to stay at the R.G. another night, he sat before the fake fireplace in the front office awaiting a pizza he'd ordered from Domino's.

When it finally arrived, it was so late and cold there was no charge and he gave no tip. Trip ate his dinner as he ate his breakfast, but this time in his room, his mind busily digging, digging, digging, in the cheese and red pepperonis.

But this time, without the rufies.

A bottle of good Mad Dog after dinner does a digger in the red peps no harm, otherwise than it has a tendency to throw the contents of his stomach out of itself.

Trip had been idle a long time and had just poured out his last shot of M.D. with as complete an appearance of satisfaction as is ever to be found in a middle-aged gentleman of a fresh complexion who owns a strip club and has got to the end of a bottle, when a rattling of car alarms spewed up the street, and something rumbled into the Royal George parking lot.

Trip set down his shot-glass untouched.

"This is Bunnie!" said he.

In a very few minutes, Earl knocked on Trip's door and announced that Bunnie had arrived from wherever it was they found her and would be happy as shit to see the gentleman from Tall Tales.

"So soon?" Trip told Earl with biting sarcasm. "Tell her I'll see her in her room."

Miss Bunnie had taken some refreshment at the Burger King down the road and required no food in addition, and was extremely anxious to see the gentleman from Tall Tales immediately, if it suited his pleasure and convenience.

The gentleman from Tall Tales had nothing left but to empty his glass with an air of stolid desperation, and followed Earl to Miss Bunnie's room.

It was a small, dank room, furnished in a funeral manner with black bedspreads and a dark, cigarette-burned table, including on the walls two oils of Elvis in Hawaii, among other velvets.

The obscurity was so difficult to penetrate that Trip supposed Bunnie to be for the moment not yet in the room, then he heard a flush of a toilet and saw ready to receive him a young lady of not more than seventeen in a black Motley Crue *Dr. Feelgood* concert Tee (in mint condition), and a black, pleather jacket and blue jeans, still holding her motorcycle helmet by its straps in her hand, one of which had a small tattoo of a bright red rose on its back, and the other, a blackened heart engraved with a combination of letters that when put together and slid over the gaze of the uninformed, they soon reveal to such a reader, 'The Angel of Death.'

As his eyes rested on the short, slight, pretty figure with the hellacious rack and a quantity of golden-dyed hair—on her head, of course—a pair of blue eyes blackened by too high a quantity of mascara met his own eyes with an inquiring look, and a forehead with a singular capacity (remembering how young and smooth it was) of lifting and knitting a double eyebrow ring on each side into an expression that as not quite one of perplexity, or wonder, or alarm, or merely of a bright fixed attention, though it included all these things, a sudden vivid likeness passed before him— well, without all the extraneous crap that now hung from the young lady's personage in places that seemed to take the threshold of pain to its outermost limits—of a child whom he had once held in his arms on a visit to that very motel, one cold time, when the snow drifted heavily and the toilet ran high.

This likeness passed away like a breath along the surface of a picture on the wall behind her, inside the frame of which, a hospital procession of Negro cupids, several headless and all cripples, were offering black baskets of Dead Sea fruit to black divinities of the feminine gender.

Upon seeing this, Trip bowed slightly toward the girl then nearly threw up in her face.

"What the hell is *that*!?"

"You like it?" the young woman squealed with delight. "I painted it myself! I wanted to hang it up in here to surprise you."

"Jesus Christ! Mission accomplished, then. But this is the *new* south, you fuckin' freak. We even have a black president now, for fuckssake. Just what kind of drugs were you on when you painted that?"

Trip retched a little into his shirtsleeve.

"No drugs, Trip. I've been clean for eight years, ever since...ever since...well, you know."

Trip nodded in acknowledgement.

He did know, and he coughingly navigated his way through a brief gagging spell.

"Anyway, I got the idea from a passage in a Charles Dickens novel I read in high school. It kinda stuck with me, you know. Was kinda hard to crowbar outta my mind."

"Who? What? Dickens? Isn't that the guy who wrote those cute fluffy stories about Christmas ghosts and little beggar children?"

"That'd be the one."

Trip dared look at the painting again. "What kind of a sick bastard was he?"

"Look, Trip, I know you didn't ask me to come here to talk about Dickens..."

"You're right. But I certainly had no idea you'd bring that painting. We'll burn it later."

Bunnie plopped down on the bed and patted the bedspread next to her. "Sit your ass down here, boy, and tell me how your doin'."

She said this in a very clear and pleasant young voice; a little foreign in its accent for these parts; but very little indeed.

"I'd like to kiss your hand, Bunnie," said Trip with manners practiced at an earlier time, "but those tattoos look fresh, and I don't want to make my lips black."

He took his seat.

Bunnie said: "I received a text message from a bartender at Tall Tales yesterday informing me that some intelligence—or discovery—"

"The word is not material, Bunnie. Either word will do."

"Geez. Fucking patience!"

"It's that painting, Bunnie! I think it's making me crazy..."

"...respecting the small property, very small, of my poor father, whom I never saw—so long dead—"

"The hell you babbling about?"

"My father."

"Well, you *did* see him, all the time when you were a little girl in fact, but the drugs and the drinking have probably wiped away your memory."

"Probably true. But since I have no memory of him, I miss him all the more, if you can understand that."

Trip moved on the bed, just enough to cause him to see around Bunnie and cast a troubled look toward the hospital procession of Negro cupids. *As if they had any help for anybody in the absurd baskets... What? I must be losing my fucking mind! Blast it that last bottle of Mad Dog!*

"...text message said it necessary I go to Coon Spit, there to communicate with a gentleman from Tall Tales so good as to come to Coon Spit for that purpose."

"Myself, I didn't make it to Coon Spit like I planned. A guy was showing me some property in the woods out on the edge of the county, when we got sidetracked by a broken down mail truck..."

"As I was prepared to hear."

"But how'd you know?"

"Earl told me. Just now."

"Oh."

"I couldn't find you anywhere in Coon Spit, Trip, so I had Jerry go out on his four-wheeler and...well, I guess you know the rest."

"So you understood the message 'Recalled to Honda, R.G.?"

"Not at first. I...well, Jerry, apparently thought by R.G. you meant Rabbit Grove, so I was told to go all the way over there instead."

"That explains why it took you so long to get here..."

"Yes, but please don't hold it against me! It was Jerry's idea, to go to Rabbit Grove. He thought you were sending me there to....well, it doesn't matter now. The Honda part of the message still makes no sense, but whatever...we're both here and together now, and that's the important thing...right, Trip?"

She reached up and touched the gray hair besides his temples, with a pretty desire to convey to him how much older and wiser he was than she.

She continued: "It was told me by the bartender at Tall Tales that a gentleman would explain to me the details of the reason for my coming here, and that I must prepare myself to find them of a surprising nature."

She scooted closer to him on the bed and gave her bra a heave. "I have done my best to prepare myself," she flipped her hair with her right hand, "and I naturally have a strong and eager interest to know what it is..."

"Whoa there, Pocahontas. Back it down a notch."

Trip jumped from the bed and after a brief pace of the carpet, pulled out a solitary Swisher Sweet (with the wax tip) and placed it behind his right ear. "Naturally, you want to know why you are here. Yes—I—It is very difficult to begin."

He did not begin, but, in his indecision, met her glance. The young forehead with the painful eyebrow piercings lifted itself into that singular expression—but it was pretty and characteristic, besides being singular—and she raised her hand, as if with an involuntary action she caught at, or stayed some passing shadow.

"Are you quite a stranger to me, Trip?"

"Am I not?" Trip opened his hands, and extended them outwards with an argumentative smile.

Between the eyebrows and just over the little feminine nose, the line of which was as delicate and as fine as it was possible to be, the expression deepened itself. She looked away and twiddled her hair between her fingers, focusing her search for any split ends caused by years of abuse at the hands of Miss Clairol.

Trip went on, as if in a trance, mesmerized by her long flowing locks:

"In your adopted county, I presume, I cannot do better than address you as a young, southern-fried piece of ass? Er, um...I-I didn't mean to say that...at least not out loud..."

She whipped her head around. "If you please!" she said, at once outraged and embarrassed.

"Bunnie, let's move this in a more productive direction. I am a man of 'business.' And I have a bit of 'business' to bring to your attention. That is why you are here. Think of me as nothing more than a mere robot; or a tool—truly, I am not much else."

"Awwww, does someone need a hug?"

"I will, with your permission, relate to you, Bunnie, the story of one of your customers....er, ab, da...one of *our* customers... our customers."

"Story? I love a good story!"

He seemed willfully to ignore her simpleton response, and added in a hurry, "Yes, *customers*; in the strip club business we usually call them 'horn-dogs.' As in, 'He was a fine Senator from South Carolina'; or he was 'a scientific gentleman'; or 'the greatest golfer to ever play the game'; or 'A doctor,' and so forth."

"You mean like a 'john'?"

"Why yes, a john. Thank you. Like Mr. Runyon, your father, a customer can be considered a john..."

Upon hearing this, any other woman in the world would have slapped Trip into next Tuesday, or at least made an effort to gouge out his eyeballs with a rusty fork; but Bunnie did neither. And he hadn't expected her to. After all, he hadn't said anything offensive, he was just stating the facts.

"Like Mr. Runyon, your father, the 'john' of whom I'm speaking was of ill repute in Coon Spit. I had the 'honor' of knowing him there. Let's call him—John Doe. Our relations were business relations..."

She gave him a sly look. *Yeah, right...*

"...but confidential..."

Of *course* they were...

"I was at that time in my family's *Gay Prairie* Double-Wide—and let me tell you, them Frenchies can make a damn fine D-Wide!"

He lost himself momentarily in the memory. "Yeah, I'd say at that time I was right about twenty years..."

"At *that* time? May I ask at *what* time, Trip?"

"I speak, Bunnie, of twenty years ago. He married a British whore of all things—and I was one of his wing-men. His affairs, like the many affairs of many other trailer-trash men and trailer-trash families, were entirely in the hands of Tall Tales. Seems no one was faithful to husband or wife, girlfriend or boyfriend, in those days. In a similar way I am, or I have been, the wing-man of one kind or other for scores of our customers. These are mere business relations, Bunnie; there is no friendship in them, no particular interest, nothing like sentiment. I have passed from one to another, in the course of my business life, just as I pass from one of your customers...er, ab, da...one of *our* customers...to another in the course of my business day. In short, I have no feelings; I am a mere tool. To go on—"

"But this is my father's story, Trip; and I begin to think"—the curiously roughened forehead was very intent upon him—"that when I was more or less left an orphan through my mother's barely surviving my father's beatings for two years, it was you who brought me to Grouse Gulch. I am almost sure it was you."

Trip took the hesitating tattooed hand that confidingly advanced to take his, and he put into it with some ceremony a Marlboro light.

He then conducted the young lady straight away from the room and out onto the balcony overlooking the parking lot (for they were on the second floor).

He restrained a stainless-steel ash can betwixt two cheap plastic chairs, then pulled the Swisher Sweet from his ear, and stood looking into her face as he lit them both with a fifty-cent lighter.

"Bunnie, it *was* I. And you will see how truly I spoke of myself just now, in saying I had no feelings, and that all the relations I hold with my fellow-creatures are mere business relations, when you reflect that I have never seen you since..."

"Relations? Well, I should say not! I was only three years old, you fuckin' freak. I don't need to *reflect* on that, as you say..."

"Indeed," he grimaced. "But may I continue?"

"Whatever..."

"No, instead of turning you over to be a ward of

the state, I made you a ward of the Tall Tales 'house' instead, and I have been busy with other 'business' of the Tall Tales strip club ever since. Relations, you say? *Meaningful* relations? I have no time for them, no chance for them! I pass my whole life, Bunnie, on turning a modest profit from the lives of other peoples' pleasure and pain, while making a complete mangle of my own."

After this odd description of his daily routine of employment, Trip mashed out his cigar in the ash can (which was most unnecessary since it had already burned way past the wax tip), and resumed his former attitude.

"Are you finished?" Bunnie barked. "Cuz all I gotta say is boo hoo for you! By the way, thanks for finally admittin' you were the one behind the Tall Tales '*house*'—as you so u-fimistically put it. Truly. I'm not being sarcastic. I always 'spected it was you, but never knew for sure. So thanks for takin' care of me all those years, Trip. And now that we're on that subject of the so-called 'house,' that reminds me—I ain't gonna sell no 'x' to that bitch over in Rabbit Grove no more," she snapped her fingers, "What's her name? Rhonda something...?(snap!) Rhonda Clorverfield! That's it. That bitch is jus' plain crazy! And if you're thinkin' of tryin' to make me sell to her, you can jus' plain shove it up your...."

"So, *Bunnie*," he strongly emphasized, "to change the subject to that of your regretted *father*. If your father had not died when he did..."

Her eyes blazed at him like fire.

"Don't be frightened! I'm not sure I like the way you're starin'..."

She grabbed both his shoulders and kneed him squarely in the balls.

"Pray," said Trip, at once hoarse and high-pitched in tone, "that my nuts may someday be separated from my tonsils. A good day to you...," and he fell to the concrete floor of the balcony in a thud.

When he came to, he was still in a heap on the balcony, his first sight the underside of two cheap plastic chairs, no human legs in sight to speak of. He brought his left hand up to the back of his chair, suddenly spying, and keeping a *very* close eye on, the supplicatory fingers in the chair beside that clasped him in so violent a knee-balling.

One hand on concrete and one hand on plastic seat, Trip kneeled on that balcony, coughed, and spit-up blood through the railing. Staring at the ground on which he had of late slumped for an indeterminate amount of ticks of the tocking clock, he wondered which of the germs from human excretions, dog droppings or animal carcass volunteered in subservience to belay other germs upwards his jowls on their way to such anticipated warm eye sockets and ear interiors, and which ones had opted for the less arduous route, and were, at this very moment in time, dancing a sweet Jig of Life and the hope of immortality—if not simple incubation—across his lips; playing all manner of 'Charades' and 'Red-Rover' inside such soggy hollows within the chasm of his darkened jowl.

Betwixt this and the continued undiminishment of Hiroshima's revenge having its way unrestrained in his crotchal area at this very moment in time, he could barely string together a complete sentence in his head, much less speak it thusly.

"...pray control your agitation—a matter of 'business.' As I was saying—"

Fingers drumming pleather at break-neck speed, Miss Bunnie had herself seated Native-American style on the chair, arms now folded tightly across her chest, a scowl on her face to wreck the space shuttle.

Her look so discomposed Trip that he stopped, wondered, slumped into his chair and began anew:

"As I was saying; if Mr. Runyon had not died; if he had suddenly and silently disappeared; if he had been spirited away (which wasn't out of the question since he lived his whole life on 'spirits') if it has not been difficult to guess what dreadful place, though no one named Art could trace him…"

"Huh?"

"Because it was tried once, but Art couldn't find him…"

"Oh."

"If he had an enemy in some acquaintance who could exercise a scheme that I in my own time have known the boldest people afraid to speak of in a whisper (so you know it must *really* be bad!); for instance, railroading someone on trumped up charges for the consignment of anyone to the oblivion of a prison for any length of time; if Mr. Runyon's wife had implored the mayor, his wife, the judge, the jury, and the religious folk around town for any news of his whereabouts, and been told to 'talk to the hand'—then the history of your father would have been the history of this unfortunate gentleman, our John Doe."

Bunnie was interested now. "Tell me more. And a little more clearly and direct if you could. You're freakin' me out with that crazy-talk."

"I will. I mean, I'm going to. You can bear it?"

"If you mean, '*Can you bear it*?,' then yes, Yoda, I can. I can bear anything but the uncertainty you leave me in at this moment."

"You're speakin' freaky too…"

"Touché."

"You speak collectedly, and you—*are* collected (though Trip kept a very close eye on her lest she take another shot at his man-grapes). A matter of business. Regard it as a matter of business—business that must be done…"

"Get on with it, Rain Man, cuz it's almost time for Wapner. Definitely almost time for Wapner…"

"Now if this doctor's wife, though a lady of great courage and spirit, even if she was a common West End whore, had suffered so intensely from this cause before her little child was born—"

"Ok, I'll play along with this shit-talk your talkin'.

This little child being a daughter, you mean?"

"A daughter. A-a—matter of business—"

"Stop saying that!"

"Don't be distressed, Bunnie," he folded up a leg between himself and a potential next strike.

Bunnie scowled. "I'm fixin' to jack you in the jewels again just for takin' so long to 'splain!"

"Bunnie, if the poor lady had suffered so intensely before her little child was born, that she came to the determination of sparing the poor child the inheritance of any part of the agony that she had known the pains of...."

"Yeah, yeah, because the old man bashed her in her cranium on a regular basis, go on..."

"...can you blame her for telling said child that her father was *dead*?"

He stood up and she made a motion toward him. He flinched but for unfounded reason. Because she knelt down before him.

"—No, don't kneel! In God's name why should you kneel to *me*?"

"If you don't know, then I probably shouldn't be down here! You once took care of me, so now I figure I'll return the favor..."

"But we're out of doors! On the balcony!"

"All the better!"

"Good lord... get up! What's the *matter* with you?"

"Sorry, I'm bored and all this crazy talk of 'business.' That and talk of my dead father has got me ancy for some strange."

"You're a sick individual, Bunnie, you know that?"

"Ha! Isn't that the first lady calling the president black!"

"Damn it, Bunnie! Enough with the racial crap! Anyway, they like to be called 'African-Americans' now. Didn't you know that?"

"Can I go now? This place sucks and your story blows."

"You'll be on your way soon enough, I assure you."

"*I assure you?* Woooo-hoo, look at Mr. Fancy pants again!"

"You got a smart mouth on you, you know that?"

"That's not what my teachers said…"

"Ok, look, let's go back inside before we cause an incident out here. Or at least, before *you* cause an incident."

She went in and took a seat on the bed, and he retired himself to the nasty, red vinyl chair next to a cigarette-burn splotched table, which smelled of an elephant's rear—the chair that is, not the table.

"Here's the dead skinny, Bunnie. You're mother gave you away at two years old to protect you from your father's abuse and the knowledge that he was a loser. She left you to grow up to be the bangin' hot mamma with the smokin' hot bod I see before me now, but without the dark cloud of your shit-eating father's life affecting you, and the concern over you that he was rotting away in some factory somewhere, or in some federal pen, taking it up the…."

"Ok! I get the picture." She leaned forward and placed her head in her hands, digesting the information. Then she looked up.

"You could've said all that in a fuck lot less words than you did, you know."

"But it wouldn't have been half as entertaining, don't ya think?"

"Well, you got me there." She grinned. "You know what? You're a fuckin' freak of nature, Trip. But you're a stand up guy in my book, in more ways than one in fact—three, that I can think of off the top of my—"

"Ok! Jeezus…"

Bunnie stood, Trip stood, and they engaged in a hearty handshake, and as if bound by some sudden, mysterious familial kinship. But their clasping hands lingered a little too long.

"Trip, dude, I'm glad we finally got to meet face to face. I really am."

Trip looked down, with an admiring tingle in his

crotchal region, at the flowing golden hair; he pictured himself taking her up on her earlier offer from the balc... *No! No! No! Focus! Back to business! Back to business...*

"You know that your parents had no great possessions..."

"No shit, Sherlock."

"...And that what they did have was stored away by your mother at the U-Store-It out on 59 to one day give to you, before the repo's raided the place and took everything."

"A lot of fucking good it did me..."

"I hate to say this, but there's been no new discovery, of money, or of any other property..."

"Well, isn't that just a fucking kick in the cunt..."

"....but—" Trip stopped. The expression in the forehead, which had so particularly attracted his notice, and which was now immovable, had deepened into one of pain and horror.

Still clasping her hand, he said, "Bunnie, I don't know how to say this. Your father has been—well, he's been found. He's alive. Greatly changed I've heard; maybe come to Jesus, if that's at all possible; almost a wreck, which I *know* is possible, though we should hope for the best. Anyway, he's still alive."

He felt a shiver run down her arm, transmitted at her wrist, and up into his.

She said: "But if he really is alive and come to Jesus, I am going to see his ghost! It will be his ghost—not him! And if he is still his *old* self...." She shuddered again.

"There, there!" said Trip in a fatherly tone, from whence it came, he knew not. "See now, see now! The best and the worst are known to you now. You are well on your way to the poor wronged ingrate, and, with a short ride in Hoss's pick-up through the holler, you'll soon be at his side!"

She repeated in the same sappy tone, sunk to a whisper: "I have been free, I have been happy, yet his ghost has haunted me forever!"

"Your father has been taken to the house of an old moonshiner over in Coon Spit, and we are going there: I, to identify him if I can: you, to restore him to life, love, duty, rest, comfort, or to smack his tired old ass right into Thursday—whatever you think is best. Oh, and one more thing: He was found under another name, Ichabod Drury Jabunknus."

"*What?*"

"His own name, Paul Runyon, had been long forgotten, or concealed. Even I, and everyone at Tall Tails avoid calling him by that name. As to the events that caused him to change his name, all my authority in the matter is wrapped up in the one line, 'Recalled by Honda.' Anyway, it'd be best not to talk about it, and just move his old-ass out of Coon Spit as fast as we can."

Perfectly still and silent, and not even sitting again on the bed; her eyes open and fixed upon him, and with that last expression looking as if it were carved and branded into her forehead, so close was her grip on his hand, that he feared she would again try to detach his berries from the stick, and he called out loudly for assistance, frozen deathly still in place.

"Earl! Help!"

In his agitation, Trip observed coming through the door a pale freckled fiery red-head of unflattering weight and figure; flowing, silky red scarf addressed to her cranium in the manner of Little Steven cira 1985 and dressed in some extraordinarily tight-fitting spandex to make even the largest of Middle Eastern pack-mules recoil at its public presentation.

A wild looking woman!

And not at all the opposite of unattractive, coming into the room in advance of Earl and soon settling the question of the potential detachment of Trip's nuts from their satchel by the teen seen before him, the fiery red-haired beast laid a brawny kick to Trip's gut using the whole force of one leg and a high-heeled whore sandal attached to her left trotter, sending Trip flying back against the rear wall, to which the offensive painting of Negro cupids fell from its roost and bashed him unabashedly on his crown, ripping the picture to threads and causing blood to trickle down into his left eye.

I think that was a man! was Trip's breathless reflection, simultaneous to the wall having knocked the living snot—and wind—right out of him.

"Why, look at you!" bawled the red-haired fiery bitch to the bewildered faux-blonde in the middle of the room. "Why don't you go fetch your things instead of standin' there starin' at me? Am I so much to look at? Am I? You ain't no lesbo, are you? No, I s'pose not. So why don't you go fetch your things? I'll let you know later if I need you to do anything down there for my kitty-kitten. In the meantime, I'm going to pour some smelling salts, cold water, and vinegar down this poor bastard's throat. That ought to do him in for permanent!"

There was an immediate retrieval of these restoratives from God-only-knows-where from the red-head's spandex ensemble stretched painfully and without the benefit of mercy to the very limits of its elastic boundaries—then pushed one step further.

She went over and softly kicked Trip in the hindquarters, her whore-heels connecting with a soft *mush* sound as she mockingly referring to him as 'My precious!' and gave him the bird in his stoic, and temporarily unbreathing, face.

She flipped her greasy, scraggly, crimping ironburnt Clairol-ravaged red hair to one side of her shoulder with great pride and care and straddled him with her two mountoonous tree-trunks (to which Trip made the ghastly mistake of looking up and being greeted to an image never, ever, *ever* to be burned-out from the inside of his cranial cavity without the aid of a nuclear blast).

"You! Hey you with the brown pile in your shorts!"

red-hair yelped indignantly, still straddling him. "Couldn't you tell her what you had to tell her in much less time and without frightening her to death? Look at her with her pretty face and cold hands. You call that being a respectable pimp? You're disgraceful!"

Trip was so exceedingly disconcerted by a question so hard to answer, that he could only look on, at a mere distance—mercifully this time, with much feebler humility and sympathy, while the strong woman— having had recently banished Earl from the room under penalty of *'never being able to remove this red stilt from your goddamned penile-ravaged bee-hind!'*— walked over and hugged the child, laying her soft blond head on the red-haired woman's big pillowy man-shoulder.

"I hope she will do well now," squeaked Trip.

"No thanks to you if she does, brown pants!" She turned to Bunnie. "Awwww, my darling pretty…"

"I hope," said Trip, after another pause of feeble sympathy and humility, "that you will accompany Bunnie and me to Coon Spit?" He couldn't believe what he'd just said. The blast to the wall must have shaken loose more than a little feces.

"Not likely, fuck-stick!" replied the strong woman. "If God ever intended me to wedge my big-ass up into them stupid pick-up trucks with the huge-ass tires you jackasses run all over these hills, you think he would've invented corn dogs and Twinkies? I should say not!"

This being another question hard to answer, Trip withdrew his consideration of it.

4

The Liquor Store

A large shipment of 40 oz.'s and wine coolers had been dropped and broken in the parking lot of Saint Antwan's Liquors and Beer.

The accident had occurred when Delbert hit a rut with the back left tire whilst pulling into Antwan's parking lot. He flipped the faulty non-secured latch on the back of the beer truck to an insecure position, opened the back-sliding door with a violent metallic outburst, and spilled the shipment to the pavement like so many crushed walnut shells.

"Shit!" Delbert's work companion cursed, "Get the fuck outta here! Go! Go! Go!"

And squealing tires could be received upon minute cartilages vibrating a quarter of a mile away as the truck beat away from that lot like a juvenile committing his first act of public property defacement.

Instantly, all manner of bug, beetle, and roach—rodents, birds and squirrels included—suspended their business, or their idleness (which is quite normal for animals in winter), after running in an opposing way from the initial roar of bottles crashing, turned and ran to the spot to lap at the wine and swill.

The rough, irregular potholes of the gravel lot—designed one might have thought to expressly maim all creatures who attempted to navigate it—was now filled with Lilliputian lakes, and were soon laced with jostling life forms—mostly birds—with a rate of success or failure of alcoholic consumption mostly depending on the creature's size.

Other animal forms on the fringes devoted themselves to shards of glass that, as fortune would have it, still held a bit of product somewhat intact.

The shrill laughter of children playing on the playground up the street resounded while this game lasted. When the swill was gone, however, and the places it had just been were slurped clean, there was a little roughness among the creatures and much playfulness, because they were all drunker than skunks—a reference to which two socially refined skunks at the scene would've taken great offense.

But strangely enough, though many creatures in the lot found themselves side-by-side with natural predators, also being drunk as skunks as they were, there was a special companionship in the revelry, an observable inclination on the part of everyone to join some other one, which led, especially among the birds and beetles—and others with an extremely low tolerance for alcohol—to frolicsome embraces, shaking of wings and antennae, and to the larger rodents a joining of claws and a dancing together, a half-dozen or so in tight semi-circles.

But these demonstrations ceased as suddenly as they had broken out. Ants scattered to their anthills, birds made for the highest electrical wires, rodents scurried back to the storage-locker when men with heavy coats, matted locks and cadaverous faces came walking forth upon the lot from the opposite direction of the playground, and a gloom gathered on the scene that appeared more natural than sunshine—which isn't saying much, since this was southern Kentucky in winter after all.

Saddened eyes from drooping countenances roamed the wreckage of their beloved sustainer, and looking one to the other, each man could barely fathom the mindset of the bungler that allowed such heinous act to transpire.

"Dat's jus' a damn shame, losin' all dat liquor! I bet Barge is pissed!"

The 40 oz.'s were Black Label, and the wine-coolers Seagram's, which had stained the liquor store lot, which resided smack on the Coon Spit corporation limit.

Saint Antwan's parking lot had stained many a hand, too, and many a face, and many a naked foot and even a few Air Jordan's, when folk would stumble out of their cars, shit-faced and three sheets to the wind, looking to purchase an extra drop of ambrosia to sail them forth upon the River Styx. These men had sawed-off shotguns, and left red marks on the foreheads—arms, legs, and backs included—of the women who nursed their children.

And now that the clouds had settled on Saint Antwan's, the darkness of it was heavy—cold, dirt, sickness, ignorance and want. These Lords in waiting in the parking lot, waiting for the store to open, waiting on the saintly presence of the store owner to open the fucker so they could purchase their Mad Dog and Bourbon—nobles of zero power all of them; they were the last in line in every conceivable way.

They were samples of a people that had undergone a terrible grinding and re-grinding at the Coon Spit Mill, just like they did in the fabulous 'mill' of fermentation in who's parking lot the two men currently stood, which ground old people young again, if only for a night, and if only in their minds.

The homeless shivered all over Coon Spit, passed out in most every doorway, looking in every window, crotch's tingling with every garment that the wind blew up.

The Coon Spit Mill, which had worked them down, was the mill that grinds young people old; the mills 'children' had ancient faces and grave voices from too much whiskey and Moonshine; and upon them, and upon grown faces, and plowed into every furrow of age and coming up afresh, was the sign—Hunger.

Hunger was prevalent everywhere. Hunger was pushed out of the tall houses, in the wretched clothing that hung upon poles and lines; Hunger was patched into them with straw and rag and wood and paper; Hunger was repeated in every fragment of the small modicum of firewood that The Man sawed off for them; Hunger stared down from the smokeless chimneys, and stared up from the filthy street that held a number of 1976 Gremlins among its refuse of outdated rust-buckets. Hunger was the inscription on Peterman's (empty) Bakery shelves, written into every small loaf of his scanty stock of bread; and at the butcher shop, where even dead dogs were now offered for sale. Hunger rattled its dry bones among the roasting chestnuts in the turned cylinder out in front of the Ace Hardware store; Hunger was even spread despite a sale on Ruffles Potato Chips at the Rexall Drug, no doubt fried with some reluctant drops of oil knowing they were being sent to such a godforsaken, financially depressed town.

Coon Spit was a series of narrow winding streets, full of offense and stench, with other narrow winding streets diverging, with people in rags and having drank too many nightcaps—and all smelling of shit and one too many nightcaps—and all visible things with a brooding look upon them that looked ill.

In the haunted air of the people there was yet some wild-beast thought of the possibility of turning against the city council of Coon Spit. Depressed and slinking though they were, eyes of fire were not wanting among them; only compressed lips, white with what they suppressed; nor foreheads knitted in the likeness of the gallows-rope they mused about inflicting on the city councilmen (and women), and one particular banker.

The shop signs were all grim illustrations of Want, for the merchants had not even the money to advertise themselves properly. The butcher's sign showed a poorly painted scrag of meat; the baker, a coarse mock-up of a loaf of bread. The crude liquor store sign portrayed two people drinking with bubbles floating above their heads (very unprofessional) and the store's patrons croaked to each other about the scanty measures of the thin selection of wines and beers.

Nothing was represented in a flourishing condition, save for the Slim Jim's and the weapons. The packaging of the Slim Jim's was sharp and bright, and the gun store's stock was murderous.

The town was so depressed, in fact, that only one family had cable TV.

Can you believe it?

But t'weren't for long since the time was to come when the gaunt scarecrows of that region watched the cable guy, in their idleness and hunger, so long as to conceive the idea of how to steal cable, and hauled up men to the tops of the telephone poles by ropes and pulleys, undercover of darkness, to provide others with such service, free of charge, greatly improving their condition.

But, the 'time' was not to come yet; and every wind that blew over Coon Spit shook the rags of the scarecrows in vain, for the birds, fine of song and feather, took no warning, and why should they?...they're only birds.

The liquor store was a cinder-block affair, better than most others in the county in appearance and degree (if you can believe that) and the master of the liquor store had arrived and stood outside it, in a yellow raincoat over green britches, looking out across what remained of his lost 40 oz.'s and wine-coolers.

"Hey guys," he greeted the two 'nobles' solemnly.

"Hey, Barge. Look what happened. Fuck."

"Well, it's not my affair," said he, with a final shrug of the shoulders. "Them fuckers from the distribution center did it. Let them bring another shipment."

There, his eyes happpened to catch a tall joker across the street, writing up his own joke on Aunt Helen's house with his pants at his ankles.

The owner of Saint Antwan's Liquors and Beer called to him across the way: "Say there, Skeeter! What do you do there?"

The fellow smiled a toothless grin and pointed to

his uncovered 'joke' with immense satisfaction, as was often the way with his tribe.

He was attempting to piss his name on the side of Aunt Helen's paint-peeled porch. It missed its mark too, and completely failed as was also often the way with his tribe—the flap of his jacket having hung down, receiving the entirety of the whiz, deflecting the greater portion of it back onto his shoes.

"Goddamn! What now?" the store owner muttered under his breath. "Are you out of your fuckin' mind, Skeeter?" said he, crossing the road and obliterating Skeeter's forehead with a handful of mud, packed for the purpose of knocking him senseless.

"Why do you feel the need to always piss in public, Skeeter? Is there—tell me you!—can you really find no bathroom around here to piss in? What about that old Photomat you used to own in the mall parking lot? It's still there, sitting empty, you know. Why don't you go piss in there?"

In his expostulation, the store owner dropped his mudless hand (perhaps out of kindness, perhaps from accident) upon the joker's jacket.

The joker rapped it with his own, took a nimble spring upward, and came down in a fantastic dancing attitude, with one of his stained shoes jerked off his foot and into his hand, shaking it in the store owner's face.

A joker of an extremely, not to say wolfishly, practical character, he looked now, under these circumstances not at all in a manner he used to, a manner that made his foregone Cherokee ancestors proud.

"Jesus! Put your shoe back on. Put it back on!" barked the liquor store owner. "What's the matter with you, Skeeter? Why don't you call Winnie and have her come pick you up?"

With that advice, the store owner wiped his mud-soiled hand upon the joker's jacket—quite deliberately, as having dirtied the hand on Skeeter's account, and said "That's what you get for tryin' to piss on Aunt

Helen's porch..."; and then re-crossed the road and entered Saint Antwan's Liquors and Beer.

The liquor store owner's given Christian name was Eldridge, with the fortunate surname of Debarge, so when pop star El DeBarge came on the scene in the 1980s his mother nearly crapped herself with glee since mama loved El from afar with a passion only reserved for the most libidinous exploits of one late-twentieth century American president; turning up the music so loud for the entire block to hear as she danced and weaved around the house—straining to keep her weave from becoming spoilt—as she cleaned the house, an occasion that t'weren't to be found too much in excess.

Eldridge Debarge, the unfamous and obscure man, was a no-necked, marshmallow-looking chunk of thirty. He should have been of a hot temperament, for, although it was a bitter day, he wore only the raincoat, and carried a hoodie slung over his shoulder. His shirt-sleeves were rolled up, too, and his brown arms were bare to the elbows. Neither did he wear anything more on his head than his own jheri-curled short dark hair. He was a dark man altogether, with good eyes and a good bold breadth between them.

It also helped against the cold that he was not in lack of breadth; or girth. Practically since day one he found himself of plump frame and buxom stature earning him many a ridicule among elementary school puerile ne'er do wells especially fond of one particular appellative play-on taunt, "Look out! Here comes Da-bridge *and* Dabarge!"

Neither did he once look back fondly on one unfortunate incident occurring in the third year of his grades, whereupon the teacher asked the pupils, "What are the four major food groups?"

Eldridge, being possessed of a superlatively serious and studious disposition at that point in his young, homo-sapiatic journey, raised his hand and replied in all manner of seriousness: "Let's see, d'eres

Eggo waffles, corn-dogs and mash, Slim Jim's and oh, yeah, Sprite!"

Eldridge's face grew increasing hotter as the children, as well as the educator, chortled and carried on without restraint, throwing the lad of innocence into such confusion from having merely answered truthfully to the very foods his mama was disposed of supplying him; nothing more, and nothing less.

However, out of the ignominy of that day, his legacy was cemented for all time as a purveyor of all things edible—rubbish foods as well as the (extremely) rare haut-cuisine; and his appellation was forever designated for all time by the simple moniker: 'Barge.'

The only other name this man has ever been recognized by is the one he used to sign his name on the papers for the bank loan of the purchase of the liquor store eight years past; 'Eldridge Dabarge.'

Mandy Debarge, his lily-white wife, having long completed her ritual intake of cannabis in the couples' massive, and massively ancient, Lincoln Town Car when they pulled up, at present sat behind the counter of the store as Barge came in.

Mandy Debarge was a stout woman of about his own age, with a lazy eye that seemed to look at nothing and everything at the same time; large sausage-like fingers heavily ringed, a drooping face, strong features; she was a horrible praticioner of manners. There was a character about Mandy Debarge from which one might have predicted that she did not often make mistakes against herself in any of the reckonings over which she presided.

Mandy Debarge being sensitive to cold, as all women are, was wrapped in rabbit fur and had a quantity of bright-pink bandanna wrapped around her head, though not to the concealment of her large earrings. She wore thigh-high black velvet boots which she never took leave of, replacing them as needed by an open account with Payless Shoes down the street; until four months ago when the store closed and she was forced to secure her boots from an online distributor, teaching herself the use of 'The Interwebs'; a debacle which nearly saw herself and her husband put into the ground.

Since childhood, Mandy had walked with such an exaggerated swivel of the hips that upon entering the pubescent-era of life's journey she absolutely displaced many a young boy of his cranial faculties (among other fluids).

Many thought it was the boots that caused her to walk in such a manner. Others simply called her 'boy crazy' and 'a whore' and charged her with doing it on purpose, stating that she was 'as horny as New York City at rush hour.'

Mandy had worked at Saint Antwan's Liquor Store since the youthful age of 12 by special permit of the Coon Spit city council. At that time, one Pastor Jennings of the respected First Congregational Baptist Church of Coon Spit sat on the council, and needed someone to faithfully replenish his communion coffers (and his own glass) with the imported French wines he so dearly loved—that, and to watch Mandy's hips in that exaggerated swivel coming down the sanctuary, something which he also so dearly loved.

The fact that Pastor Jennings' only daughter was also married to Judge Cornrow's son (the heir to the mayor's throne one day) also didn't hurt in the securement of such an underage work permit.

Mandy had been pregnant nearly every day of her life since the first egg fallopian'ed down her tube. Her mantra had always been, "There's always room for one more." To which her less-than-bright senior high school boyfriend once replied, "Not in there, there ain't! I'd bet if I checked right now, Bobby-Lee Franklin still'd be in there!'

'I meant babies, Dick-Stick! Babies!' was her caustic reply.

Luckily for Mandy, and later for her husband, there was an emerging market for blond haired babies in China. Some of her babies weren't born blond, of course (the odds of that significantly decreasing since she got married to Barge), but if they weren't born that way, she'd simply dye the hair and send them on their way. *It's them chinks problem now*, Mandy'd reason, to which a more level-headed and reasonable adult in the room, usually her husband, would say, "You know, you really shouldn't use the word 'Chinks' no more. They don't like it."

'Who gives a shit?' was her caustic reply.

Presently, Mandy slurped noisily on a Kentucky Fried Chicken leg before her, but laid it down temporarily to pick her teeth with a modified emory board.

Thus engaged, with her right elbow supported by her left hand, Mandy Debarge said nothing when her 'Lord' came in, but she coughed a hack that sounded like the devil himself were rising from the depths of her bowels.

This, in combination with the lifting of her painted eyebrows over heavily bright-blue eye-shadow, portrayed the oft discerned expression of not giving a flying-fuck; an expression that right now suggested to her husband that he would do well to look around the shop among the customers for any 'new customer' (read: undercover cops and shoplifters) who may have dropped in while he stepped out to accost Skeeter across the street.

The liquor store owner walked his way through his store and accordingly rolled his eyes about, until they rested in a far back corner upon two young unbearably beautiful blondes sporting sun-tanned bikini-clad bodies playing cards and drinking Captain Morgan with huge smiles plastered on eager faces.

In another corner, Barge came upon two middle-aged men playing dominoes in three-piece suits merrily sipping away on Ripple; but as Barge rounded the corner to make his way back up front, he took notice of three 'actual' men behind the counter lengthening out a short supply of wine directly into their mouths.

"Git your stinkin' asses away from those taps!" Barge bellowed at the perpetrators, all young men he knew. "Ya'all know them's samples are for the customers! Real customers, not jack-off delinquents like you!"

"Damn," Baby Magic declared. "Why you gotta be so harsh, Barge?"

"I *do* gotta be harsh, Baby M. And you too, Clocker. And you, DeWayne. Ya'all know I can't afford to be givin' away no liquor to nobody in these times. Business is bad enough as it is and it's only gonna get worse after they...after they...."

"Don't say it, Barge!" suggested Clocker, "Den it won't come true!"

Barge released a tension filled exhale, and allowed his shoulders to slump.

"Hey, Barge," called out DeWayne. "Who 'Saint Antwan' anyway?"

"Don't you mind about that, DeWayne. Jus' mind your *own* fuckin' business."

When Barge passed behind the counter, he gave the three degenerates a violent shove from the taps and took notice of a middle-aged gentleman and a young lady who had entered his store when he was making rounds in the back to be sure no one had stolen, or defaced, his cardboard cutout advertisements.

The middle-aged man said, "This is our man."

Barge immediately thought, *Do I know you?* but he feigned not to notice the two strangers and fell into discourse with the triumvirate of dickheads who were previously freely drinking from the counter taps.

"How goes it Harlan?" said Baby Magic to Barge. "Was that spill in the parking lot today the whole shipment, you think?"

"Every drop, Harlan," answered Barge.

When this interchange of Christian name was effected, Mandy Debarge, picking a tooth with her makeshift teethpick, coughed up a piece of chicken skin and raised her drawn-on eyebrows another time.

"It is not often," said Clocker, addressing Barge,

"that many of these miserable beasts around here know the taste of liquor, or of anything but French Fries from Mickey D's and maybe a piece of KFC Popcorn Chicken, or some such shit like that. Ain't that so Harlan?"

"It is Harlan," returned Barge.

At this second interchange of the Christian name, Mandy, still using her toothpick with profound composure, squirted a bit of chicken skin onto the counter from between two long-since rotted teeth, and raised her drawn-on eyebrows once more.

The last of the three was about to have his say, but as he threw back a now empty drinking vessel, Barge suddenly realized DeWayne had snagged a Miller Lite off a shelf and downed it without reimbursement.

Barge smacked the offender hard on the lips sending the bottle smashing to a thousand pieces on the concrete floor. "Dang it, Bro! Did I *not* just tell you to not drink nothin'?"

Dewayne rubbed his burning lips and said, "That fuckin' *hurt!* It sucks that dumb-shit cattle get to drink without paying for it, but us? No fuckin' way! And we live harder lives than them, Harlan! Am I right, Harlan?"

"You are right, Harlan," was the response of Barge, "but you still have to pay for dat shit."

This third interchange was completed at the moment Mandy threw her toothpick away, kept her eyebrows up, and silently, but gently, picked her seat.

"Show *you* who the boss is around here...," Barge muttered, then spotted his wife giving him a dirty look. He quickly gestured toward her in cowardice: "Gentlemen! My wife!"

The three 'customers' pulled on their knit caps and each nodded to Mandy, one at a time. "'s up, Mandy. We knew you was the *real* boss..."

She acknowledged the homage by saying, "Damn straight, losers! And don't you forget it!"

Then she gave them a hard look and glanced around the liquor store in a casual manner, leaning over the literature rack with apparent calmness and grabbing and slapping a copy of *Soap Opera Digest* down on the counter in front of her, quickly becoming absorbed in it.

"Gentlemen," said her husband, who had kept a fearful eye observantly upon her, "Good day. The car—furnished with plush interiors, power windows, stainless-steel chain steering wheel, neon under-glow, curb-feelers, and spinning rims—that you wished to see and were inquiring about the other day, is down at Foster's Garage. I'd tell you how to get there, but I know one of you has been there already. Gentlemen, adieu, mutha-fuckas."

DeWayne quickly cleaned up the shattered bottle—because Mandy shot him a look that needed no explanation—as they made for the door and left the place.

The eyes of Barge were studying his wife with her nose back in the *Digest*, when the middle-aged gentleman advanced from a back corner and begged the favor of a word.

"Of course," said Barge, and quietly stepped with him to the door so as not to disturb his wife's reading.

Their conference was very short, but very decided. Almost at the first word, Barge started and became deeply attentive. It had not lasted a minute, when he nodded and went out. The gentleman then beckoned to the young lady, and they, too, went out.

Mandy read with deep interest and steady eyebrows about Luke and Laura's opinion of BradJolina, and saw nothing. "Oh, no!" she yelled, having turned the page and suddenly sucking in all available air within the store, "They're canceling *Guiding Light*! Fuck!"

Travis Templeton and Bunnie Runyon, emerging from the liquor store, joined Barge in the parking lot. They walked to the backside of the store where a shabby wooden supply shed was located. The shed was in such bad disrepair that if one single termite had got it in his craw to exit the shed at any given moment, the entire structure would come down in an anti-climatic heap. It opened from the stinking little backyard, which was the general 'public' entrance for a great number of rats and raccoons.

In the gloomy brick-paved entry, Barge bent down on one knee as if of a child to his old master (but this being the New South for Chrissakes, he shall be refereed to instead as his old 'boss'...but, damnit, that doesn't sound much better...) and said, "You can kiss my ass if you think I'm going in *there*! I barely made the walk around the outside of the store without gettin' winded. You can't 'spect me to fight all them nasty rats and shit. Ya'all are goin' in there by your *own* damnselves. And don't pull nothin' while you're in there, missy, 'cause I'll cut a bitch!"

It was a gentle action, but not at all gently done; a very remarkable transformation had come over him in a few seconds. He had no good-humor in his face, nor any openness of aspect left, but had become a secret, angry, dangerous man.

"I gotta tell ya, the dude in there might be high, or a little difficult. Or *a lot* difficult. Better to go in slowly, so as not to startle his ol-ass."

This Barge said in a stern voice to Trip as he passed by and entered the shed.

"Is he alone?" the latter whispered.

"Alone? Ha! Not if you count his demons!" said Barge in a low voice.

"Is he always that way? Unmanageable, I mean?"

"Yep. I reckon so."

"Of his own desire?"

"Of his own necessity, at least according to him. Mean old bastard he is. Pro'ly chawin' the head off a rat as we speak!"

"I heard he came to Jesus in prison."

"*Jesus?*" The owner of the liquor store stopped

himself before nearly striking the wall with his hand and muttering a tremendous curse. If the place had come crashing down upon them all, no direct answer could have been half so forcible.

"As he was back when I worked for him," Barge said, "was as he was when I first saw him after they found me and demanded to know if I would take him. As he was then, so he is now."

"So then, why *did* you take him?"

"Felt sorry for the ol' bastard. He's had a rough go. Figured he could use a break."

Trip's spirits fell lower and lower as he and Bunnie stood just inside the shed. Barge stood, yanked a string, and a light came on revealing a door as if to a meat locker, with a huge handle and a padlock.

"He's locked in there, then?" said Trip, surprised.

"Oh, yeah," was the grim reply of Barge.

"You think it necessary to keep him locked up like that?"

"Shit yeah."

"Why?"

"Why? Because he's lived for eight years unjustly locked up, and would probably go nuts in a furious rampage through the streets tearing every man, woman, and child limb from limb! Pro'ly tear himself to pieces too, right on the courthouse steps! Who knows?—if this door were left open."

"But would it be possible?"

"Possible?" repeated Barge bitterly, "The motherfucker keeps shouting for hours on end, 'Long Live the Devil!' for Chrissakes! You think this town deserves a maniac like that let loose on its sorry ass? I don't *think* so."

Barge unlocked the locker and Trip and Bunnie further entered the uncontrollable and hopeless mass of decomposition.

The dirt floor spattered with rat droppings and poison was all they could view to guide their steps forward. Yielding to his own disturbance of mind, and to his young companion's agitation—which became greater every instant—they continued venturing forth at a slight decline, sniffing up languishing good airs that were somehow left uncorrupted among all the spoilt and sickly vapors that seemed to be crawling about on hands and knees.

Throughout the rusted locker, tastes rather than glimpses, were caught of the jumbled mass of stored items; and nothing within range, on shelves nearer or lower than the summits of the two great towers of Notre-Dame, had any promise on it of healthy life or wholesome aspirations.

By this time, the young lady trembled under such strong emotion, and her face expressed such deep anxiety—and above all, such dread and terror—that Trip felt it incumbent on him to speak a word or two of reassurance: "Pull your shit together, would ya? You're drivin' me fuckin' crazy!"

"I'm afraid of it," Bunnie answered, shuddering.

"I know," Trip shuddered too. "It's darker'n a nun's vagina in here!"

"Thanks for the visual, Dick-Lick, but that's not what I meant. I'm afraid of *it*."

"Of *it*? What?"

"I mean of *him*. Of my father."

She momentarily stopped, rendered in a manner desperate by her state. But by the beckoning of the strip club owner, hurried her forward.

Suddenly, from behind, footsteps approached and they both stood still, zombie-like. Not a breath was exchanged amongst them.

A light flicked on a face, which once was not there, and then seen!

"Thought you might need this," said Barge, handing over a flashlight.

They both exhaled in relief.

The back of the shed locker, built to be a depository for firewood sometime at the turn of the century, was dim and dark. Such a scanty portion of light was admitted through means of the flashlight that it was difficult, on first glance, to see anything.

But on the back wall, seated upon a standard issue army cot, a white-haired man sat, stooped forward, and very busily making shoes.

5

The Crazy Old Coot

"Hey, old man," said Barge, looking down at the white head that bent low over the shoemaking.

The head was raised for a moment, and a very faint voice responded to the salutation, as if it were at a distance: "Hey."

"You still hard at work, I see?"

After a long silence, the head was lifted for another moment, and the voice replied, "Yes, I'm working. Fuck off."

This time, a pair of haggard eyes had looked at the questioner, before the face had dropped again.

The faintness of his voice was pitiable and dreadful. It was not the faintness of physical weakness, though confinement and hard living no doubt had their part in it.

Its deplorable peculiarity was that it was the faintness of solitude combined with maniacal fits of screaming. It was like the last, and the first, feeble echo of a sound made long ago, and also just less than an hour ago. So entirely had it lost the life and resonance of the human voice, that it affected the senses like a once beautiful color faded away into a poor weak stain. So sunken and suppressed it was, that it was like a voice underground. So expressive it was, of a hopeless and lost creature, that a famished traveler, wearied out by lonely wandering in a wilderness, would have remembered home and friends in such a tone before lying down to die. But only if the home life had been good and worth remembering, which was far from the case here.

Some minutes of silent work passed, and the haggard eyes looked up again: not with any interest or curiosity, but with a dull mechanical perception, before-hand, that the spot where the only visitor they were aware of had stood, was not yet empty.

"I want," said Barge, who had not removed his gaze from the shoemaker, "to let in a little more light. You can bear a little more light, can't ya old man?"

The shoemaker stopped his work; looked with a vacant air of listening at the floor on one side of him; then similarly, at the floor on the other side of him; then, upward at the speaker.

"What did you say?"

"I said, I'm gonna turn on some lights!" said Barge with irritation, spoken loudly as if addressing a per-sonage with pronounced hearing aids.

"Well, if you must."

Barge took out a 50 cent lighter and lit a lantern nearby, looking as if it were last used by the Austrio-Hungarians in World War I.

A broad ray of light fell into the locker, and showed the workman with an unfinished shoe upon his lap, pausing in his labors. His common tools and various scraps of leather and plastic were at his feet and on the cot.

He had a white beard, raggedly cut, but not very long, a hollow face, and exceedingly bright eyes. He looked pretty much like Paul Newman's character in the HBO miniseries *Empire Falls*. The hollowness and thinness of his face would have caused his eyes to look large, under his yet dark eyebrows and his confused white hair—though they were naturally large, and looked unnaturally so.

His yellow rags of flannel shirt lay open at the throat, and showed his body to be withered and worn. He, and his old canvas frock, and his loose socks, and all his poor tatters of clothes, had, in a long seclusion from direct light and air, faded down to such a dull uniformity of parchment-yellow, that it would have been hard to say which was which.

He had put a hand between his eyes and the light,

and the very bones of it seemed transparent. Bunnie was grossed out, and said so. So the man put his hand down and sat, with a steadfastly vacant gaze, pausing in his work.

He never looked at the figure before him, without first looking down on this side of himself, then on that, as if he had lost the habit of associating place with sound.

He never spoke without first wandering in this manner, and forgetting to speak. It was clear drugs and alcohol had trashed him far beyond that of Keith Richards.

"You going to finish that pair of shoes today?" asked Barge, motioning to Trip to come forward.

"What did you say?" the old man croaked.

"I said, DO YOU MEAN TO FINISH THAT PAIR OF SHOES TO-DAY?"

"I can't say that I mean to, but I'm going to, if that's what you mean. I don't know."

The question reminded the man of his work, and he bent over it again.

Trip came silently forward, leaving the daughter in the middle of the room.

When Trip had stood, for a minute or two, by the side of Barge, the shoemaker looked up. He showed no surprise at seeing another figure, but the unsteady fingers of one of his hands strayed to his lips as he looked at it (his lips and nails were the same pale lead-color).

"My hand is not gross."

And then the hand dropped to his work, and he once more bent over the shoe. The look, the comment, and the action had occupied but an instant.

"You have a visitor," said Barge.

"What did you say?"

"HERE IS A VISITOR, YOU CRAZY OLD COOT!"

The shoemaker looked up as before, but without removing a hand from his work.

"Come!" said Barge in a lie. "Here is a man who

knows a well-made shoe when he sees one. Show him that shoe you're working on."

Trip gave Barge a confused look, and Barge shrugged his shoulders as if to say, *Well, I don't know. What do you want me to do?*

"Take the shoe, man," said the old man.

Trip took it in his hand.

"Tell the man what kind of shoe it is and why you made it," suggested Barge.

There was a longer pause than usual, before the shoemaker replied:

"I forget what it was you asked me. What did you say?"

"I said, TELL THE MUTHA-FUCKA ABOUT THE MUTHA-FUCKIN' SHOE! THE SHOE, MUTHA-FUCKA!"

"It's a basketball shoe, for the playing of basketball. I dreamed up the design on my own, in my head."

He glanced at the shoe with some little passing touch of pride.

"Does it have a name? Like 'Air Jordan,' or something like that?" asked Barge.

Now that he had no work to hold, the man laid the knuckles of the right hand in the hollow of the left, and then the knuckles of the left hand in the hollow of the right, and then passed a hand across his bearded chin, and so on in regular changes, without a moment's intermission.

The task of recalling him from the vacancy into which he always sank when he had spoken was like recalling some very sick person from a swoon, or endeavoring in the hope of some disclosure to stay the spirit of a fast-dying man.

"Did you ask me my name?"

"Yeah, Mutha-Fucka," Barge spat sarcastically, getting tired of this game. "I asked you your mutha-fuckin' name..."

"Recalled by Honda—12332325"

"Is that all?" Barge played along.

"Recalled by Honda—12332325"

With a weary sound that was not a sigh nor a groan, he bent to work again, until the silence was again broken.

"But you are not a shoemaker by trade," said Trip, looking steadfastly at him.

His haggard eyes turned to Barge as if he would have transferred the question to him: but as no help came from that quarter, they turned back on the questioner after they had looked at the ground.

Trip said, handing him back the shoe and still looking steadfastly in his face, "Mr. Runyon, do you remember nothing of me?"

Runyon dropped the shoe to the ground, and he sat looking fixedly at the questioner.

"Runyon," Trip laid a hand on Barge's arm; "do you remember nothing of *this* man? Look at him, he's huge! Hard to forget. Look at me. Is there no old strip club owner, no old 'business,' no free long-necks of Rolling Rock rising in your mind?"

As the captive of many years sat looking fixedly, by turns, at Trip and at Barge, some long obliterated marks of an actively intent intelligence in the middle of the forehead had fallen on him.

They were overclouded again, they were fainter, they were gone; but they had been there. And so exactly was the expression repeated on the fair young face of her who had crept along the wall to a point where she could see him, and where she now stood looking at him, with hands which at first had been only raised in frightened compassion, if not even to keep him off of her and shut out of sight of her, but which were now extending towards him, trembling with eagerness to slap the living shit out of him for touching her warm young breasts years ago—so exactly was the expression repeated (though in stronger character) on her fair young face, that it looked as though it had passed like a moving light, from him to her.

Darkness had fallen on him in its place. He looked at the two, less and less attentively, and his eyes in gloomy abstraction sought the ground and looked about him in the old way. Finally, with a deep long sigh, he took up the shoe, and resumed his work.

"Have you recognized him, yet?" asked Barge in a whisper.

The scraggly old man exhaled, as if in defeat, and came fully to life: "Yeah, I know who you two pissants are. I was just hoping if I played the role of the nutty old codger long enough you'd go away and leave me alone!"

Trip leaned forward. "So what's the deeli-o with all this shoemaking? The hell's going on here?"

"Well, you are correct in insinuating that I am not a shoemaker by trade. Of course I'm not! Nobody makes shoes by hand anymore! Jeezus! I simply taught myself to do this. This is one of the of the highest quality shoes you will ever see in the entire world! I call it: 'The Devil.' I made it to prove a point, but I'll get to that in a moment. I started out life in a worthy occupation—a veterinary doctor—then drink stole my soul, my wife, my daughter, and never returned them to me. I went to work at Chrysler at the plant over in Maple Falls and worked the brake-pad line for ten years, until my hands were nearly destroyed. Eventually, I had five workers under my charge, the fattest of them being a kid named Barge. You should've seen that poor sucker then. He could eat fifteen snickers bar in one sitting, then guzzle it down with three two-liters of Sprite! Incredible!"

"Just get on wit' your story, stupid old man!" Barge shot back. "Tell 'em about Dick Crack."

The old man nodded calmly. "I used to work directly under the plant manager, Richard Krak (pronounced 'crock'), which of course became 'crack' on the factory floor behind his back by all manner of rabble-rousing slackerdly human waste..."

"Easy..." Barge warned.

The old man looked slyly at Barge. "Anyway, Dick Crack was the meanest bastard ever to walk this earth."

Barge nodded in agreement.

"He worked us like slaves until we barely had nubs left for fingers. He turned us all mean, he did— by the time it was all said and done."

Barge again nodded in agreement.

"But the reason he worked us all like dogs, and I didn't realize until later, was because our car company was getting its ass kicked by the Japanese. However, the dick-heads in Detroit weren't willing to change their production style or modernize the designs of their cars to keep up with the Japanese competition. That's about the time we came up with the factory joke, which was that whenever Dick Crack would announce that our sales figures were up a quarter, we'd all slap each other on the back and say, 'Recalled By Honda!' meaning some line of Japanese line cars must've been recalled, and therefore took a bad publicity hit, there-fore, our sales numbers were up. Hee, hee, still cracks me up to this day. But old Dick Crack, he—he hated when we talked like that."

Barge nodded in agreement.

"Of course, over time, any progress made in our sales figures was like pissing in the ocean and hoping to drink ammonia. It wasn't long before the plant shut down and everyone lost their jobs."

Barge nodded sadly.

"Then I was sent to prison for eight years. But that's another story entirely."

"What about the shoe?" Trip asked, picking up 'The Devil' and turning it around in his grip. "You said you made it to prove a point?"

"That's correct, son. I made that shoe with my own bare hands. It took me exactly one month and twenty-nine days to do it..."

"That's amazing."

"...but at a cost of 500 dollars. However, if you factor in additional opportunity costs, it becomes more like 2,000 dollars."

"Opportunity costs?"

"Yes, opportuni...oh, forget it. The point is this: A child in Asia can make that exact same shoe in *fifteen* minutes for *ten* cents an hour at an opportunity cost of zero!"

"Dang!"

"That's right! That is what we're up against, gentlemen and little lady! We're up against it big time with that, that, that, *plan* those dick-heads on the Coon Spit town council—and that fucking panty-waste banker—are trying to push down our throats!"

Barge thought of all the mom and pop stores around town that were dying slow deaths from the mere rumor of such a plan. He knew it was choking the life out of his own business and would one day kill it altogether, just as it had done to Skeeter Rednougts' Photomat.

Then again, maybe the Photomat wasn't such a good example. That was taken care of cleanly by the advent of digital cameras, a separate matter altogether.

Still, things were bad in Coon Spit for small businesses, very bad. And only getting worse.

The old man pointed a finger in the air and solemnly said, "That is why it is of the utmost importance that we prevent this reign of terror from ruining our little slice of paradise here in the Kentucky hills."

He turned to Trip, and with sudden seeming recognition said, "And if you're not careful, young fellow, they'll take you down too..."

"Bullshit," was Trip's response, but he had to admit, with all that he had seen going on in Coon Spit lately, he was beginning to think the old man might be right. He had no idea how the 'monster' would do it, but you never knew these days.

It was taking over everything else, it seemed.

Bunnie moved from the far wall of the locker, very near to the cot on which the old man sat. There was something awful in the subconscious of the figure that could have put out its hand and touched him as he stooped over his cot.

He stared at her with a fearful look, and after awhile his lips began to form some words, though no sound proceeded from them. By degrees, in the pauses of his quick and labored breathing, he was heard to say: "So, who's the wench?"

With tears streaming down her face, Bunnie brought back an open palm and slapped him in the face with all the force of a mega-ton bomb, knocking one of his two remaining teeth to the ground, as the old man's head snapped to such a degree as to twist his body around and send him flailing to a crumpled heap upon the floor.

The old man rubbed his burning, most likely bleeding, cheek and said to Trip, "At first, I thought she was *your* daughter. Now I know she's mine."

He got back upon the cot, waving his hands as if in a truce, or simply to say, 'I surrender,' and looked at her with the golden hair, which was crimped this day in full 1980s fashion, complete with long bangs brushed straight up and back, taking on the appearance of a small loaf of bread balanced upon her head.

After doubtfully looking at her, two or three times, as if to be sure she were really there (as if the smack hadn't brought reality home faster than a swift kick in the nuts) he put his hand to his neck, and took off a scrap of blackened string with a folded rag attached to it.

He opened this, carefully, on his knee, and it contained a very little quantity of hair: not more than one or two long golden hairs, which he had, in some old day, wound off upon his finger.

He took some of Bunnie's hair into his hand and looked closely at it.

"It is the same!"

As the concentrating expression returned to his forehead, he seemed to become conscious that it had become hers too. He turned and looked at her in the dim light of the faltering lantern. "Your mother had laid her head upon my shoulder that night I was summoned out. She had a fear of my going, but I had none..."

"You mean the night you told us you were going out for a Slim Jim and a pack of Marlboro Reds, and you never came back?"

"The same."

He had formed the following speech with his lips many times before he could utter it. But when he did find spoken words for it, he spoke them coherently, though slowly: "When I confronted Coy Pepperton outside Tower Liquors over in Rabbit Grove that night, I found a picture in his back pocket of him and your mother, nekkid, lying on *our* bed—and this was well before the days of Photoshop, so you *know* it was true!

"Well, right then and there I knew I was gonna have to kick Coy's ass and right then and there in the parking lot we got down to it—a fightin' and a rollin' and a punchin' and a scratchin'—and when we was all done (cuz we was both dog tired), we called a truce and I said, 'That was some good fightin', Coy,' and he said, 'Yeah it was. Nice fightin' Runyon. Dang good fightin'.'

"And then he helped me up, and that was when he picked these two hairs off my sleeve your mother left on me when I hugged her 'fore leavin' the trailer. 'Give them to me, you fuckin' horn-dog!' I demanded of Coy..."

The old man paused as his eyes began to mist. He looked up at the ceiling. "Yep, those were the words I said, I remember 'em so well."

"So you're saying you saved her hair?" asked Bunnie, incredulous.

"Sure did."

"I don't believe it! I don't believe you have a romantic bone in your whole goddamned body, you old bastard, and you know it! You know what? I bet them hairs on Coy was pro'ly jus' dog hairs off some mangy Labrador 'triever somebody had in the parking lot that day! That's all they is..."

The old man looked sad. "I guess I never thought of that before..."

"Then you're a bigger idiot then ever I thought you were!" barked Bunnie. "And trying to convince me it was *her* fault you left—nigger, please!"

She shot Barge an apologetic look. "No offense, Barge."

Barge frowned. *Fuckin' crackers...*

The old man shook his head gloomily. "Bunnie, it's the truth. Your mom and I had something real special goin'. I met her at the rest stop over in Rabbit Grove ba'fore I started working on my vet'nary license. I had just been done takin' a leak and was exitin' the boys room—barely shook the dew from my lilly—"

"Dad."

"...when this vision of Heaven with this *strange* fuckin' accent came walkin' out the ladies room. I said, 'Hi!' and she said, 'Good day,' in this hot, sexy,..."

"Dad!"

"...accent. And that was all it took! We exchanged addresses and wrote letters back and forth, and soon she moved all the way from England just to be with me in Coon Spit!

"We worked hard to put together for ourselves a little strippin' act—she supplied the talent, and I played the pi'yaner—and we called ourselves 'Paul Runyon and Babe the Big Blue Box.'

"We toured all over the south, mostly in Nashville I reckon—God, they loved us in Nashville!—but 'ventually, we got tired of the travelin' life, and just like Elvis did in Vegas—God rest his soul—we 'ventually settled down in Grouse Gulch and made Tall Tales our home. Only it wasn't called Tall Tales at that time. At that time, the place belonged to an im'grant feller by the name of Flim Ho. He called the place Fire Ho's. But hell, me and my Babe were so pop'lar then, by the time Trip here took ownership, he changed the name to Tall Tales in our honor."

Trip nodded. "That's right."

The old man sighed. "But I guess I just wasn't enough man for your mamma. God knows how many more there were even 'fore Coy Pepperton got a hold of her..."

Bunnie exploded. "Are you outta your fuckin' mind? That's the craziest bunch of made-up horse-shit I've ever heard in my life!"

Trip tried to calm her. "It's true, Bunnie. What he's sayin's true."

Then Bunnie fell upon her knees, between the old man's legs, and with her appealing hands upon his waistline said, "Remember this?"

"Oh, good god, child!" the old man exclaimed.

"Yeah, *I* haven't forgot *that* little gem of a memory, Pa—how 'bout you? And do you remember this: "I pray to you to touch me! Kiss me! Kiss me! O my dear, my dear!"

Trip and Barge thought they would retch.

"I don't know if that's so," the old man rationalized, in deep denial, "but if you hear in my voice any resemblance to a voice that once said you were music to my ears—among other things—then weep for it, weep for it!

"And if I touched your hair and laid my head upon your breasts back when you were young and free (unlike today from what I hear)—then weep for it, weep for it!

"If it is true that I bring back the remembrance of a home long desolate, while your poor heart pined away for God only knows which one, if any, of the handful of them little toddler boyfriends you always had going on at any given point in time—and what were you then, nine-years-old? Christ!—then weep for it, weep for it!"

But instead of weeping for him, Bunnie smacked his other cheek with equal force to the first blow, knocking his final tooth from its solitary abode, twirling his head, his body following in grotesque fashion as he sprawled once again across the floor and into a heap in the far and dark back corner of the shed.

She ran over and grabbed him up by a fistful of his shirt, his head flopping like a rag-doll as she leaned in, putting her face so close she could bite off his nose—which Trip momentarily thought was her intention—and opened her mouth and snarled...quietly...slowly...savagely:

"Dearest 'dear' Pa, your agony has only just begun! I have come here to make sure you live every moment of that agony and to cause you to think of your pathetic life laid waste, and if you think for one second you're just going to go back to Grouse Gulch and be at peace and rest, then weep for it, weep for it!

"And if when I tell my dead mother someday in almighty Heaven that I used to have to kneel before my 'honored' father, and implore his pardon for thinking that I wasn't good enough (among other things), and having lain awake all night sobbing because of the 'love' of my so-called father and the torture he put me through, then weep for it, weep for it! Weep for her, then, weep for me!"

And she let go of him and he fell roughly into a barely conscious heap. He'd struck the floor so hard his face smashed against the pavement like so much a pumpkin be-splattered on an asphalt street: a sight so terrible set amongst the tremendous wrong and suffering which had just been described, that the two beholders of it felt the urge to cover their ears, and vomit violently.

But Bunnie turned suddenly to Barge and Trip, causing them to flinch reflexively. "Good gentlemen, thank God! I feel his scarred tears upon my face, and his sobs striking against my heart, same as his head just struck rightly against the concrete just now. O, see! Thank God for that, thank God!"

Barge leaned over to Trip, "I think she's losin' her fuckin' mind..."

Trip answered, "No, I think she's finally finding it."

"Would you two be so kind as to leave us here? You see how composed he has become, and you cannot be afraid to leave him with me now. Why should you be? If you lock the door to secure us from interruption, I do not doubt that you will find him, when you come back, as quiet as you leave him, if not quieter. In any case, I will take care of him until you return, and then we will remove him straight away."

"Removing him 'straight' is what we're afraid of," said Trip, as he and Barge were rather disinclined to this course of action, Barge adding, "I don't think we're leaving you alone with him anytime soon, Missy. Nuh uh. No way."

After the quiet of the locker had long been undisturbed for some time, and the old man's heaving chest and shaken form had long yielded to the calm that must follow all storms—emblematic of humanity, of the rest and silence into which the storm called Life must hush at last—Barge and Trip came forward to raise the old man from the ground.

"Don't touch him!" Bunnie commanded, raising her hand to Trip in preparation to knock his dumb-ass through the wall. "I want to leave Coon Spit at once and I'm taking him with me, back to our old place in Grouse Gulch."

"But consider. Is he fit for the journey?" asked Trip. "I mean look at him."

"Yeah, I guess you're right. He might be more fit than I thought. Maybe I should beat him a little longer?"

"No, no!" said Barge, kneeling to look into the man's eyes to see if there were any life left in him. There was, but barely. "I do agree with you on one thing, though," continued Barge, "Runyon is, for all reason, best out of Coon Spit, and definitely best out of this here locker. Trip, are you gonna take 'em or shall I give Donny Ray over at the Monkey Nut a call and have him give ya'all a ride to Grouse Gulch in his tow-truck?"

The Donny Ray from the Monkey Nut heretofore referred to was one Donny Ray Judge, the best mechanic in Grouse Gulch, and a damn honest one at that. The full title of the establishment of his employ was: 'Dirk Prouty's Monkey Wrench Nuts-N-Bolts Garage,' otherwise known simply to the good citizens of the surrounding territory as: The Monkey Nut, or even more simply, 'The Nut.'

"No, don't call him," answered Trip, "because that's business, and his cheap-ass would ask us to pay the entire cost of a tow that far, and that could come close to a thousand dollars pro'ly. And since she and I came here on Bunnie's motorcycle, if business is to be done, I had better do it. I'll call Hoss Cribbens, a bouncer at my club, and see if he'll come pick us up. He should be workin' over there today."

Trip went out to call Hoss on the pay phone out front the liquor store.

That being accomplished, he went inside and bought a six-pack of Bud Light and some Slim Jim's for the journey back to Grouse Gulch.

When he got back to the locker again, he found the daughter with her head laid down on the hard ground close to her father's side, watching him.

The darkness deepened and deepened as the lantern burned its dying flickers, and they both lay quiet; the father because he was knocking at death's door, feeling the hot tongues of Hades lapping at his whiskers; and she of her own volition.

Trip put down his beer and Slim Jim's and Barge shot him a look: "D'ju pay for dat shit?"

"Of course."

"Arite, arite, jus' checkin'," Barge said with two hands up.

Trip and Barge roused the captive, and assisted him to his feet. The tongues of Hades languished that they had to wait to lick the skin off his bones another day.

No human intelligence could have read the mysteries of the old man's mind, in the scarred blank wonder of his face and now toothless mouth.

Whether he knew what had happened, whether he recollected what she had said to him, whether he knew that he was 'free,' were questions which no sagacity could have solved.

They tried speaking to him; but he was so confused, beat-up, and so very slow to answer, that they took fright in his bewilderment, and agreed to let Bunnie tamper with him no more.

He had a wild, lost manner of occasionally clasping his head in his hands that had not been seen in him before; yet, he also held some perverse pleasure in the mere sound of his daughter's voice, and invariably turned to it when she spoke.

They began to ascend; Barge going first with the flashlight, Trip closing the procession.

They had not traversed many steps when the old man stopped, and stared at the roof and around at the walls.

"Do you think you're getting out of prison all over again, old man?" asked Barge. "That's pro'ly what dis feel like."

No crowd was about the door; no people were discernable at any of the windows at the back or sides of the liquor store as they came around; not even a chance passer-by was in the street. An unnatural silence and desertion reigned there. Only one soul was present, and that was Mandy Debarge—who leaned against the counter inside the store now reading the *National Enquirer*, and seeing nothing.

When the old man saw Hoss Cribbens waiting in the street, he clasped his head again. Then the 'prisoner' got help from Trip climbing up into the absurdly high truck with the big stupid tires, and his daughter mounted up to follow them on her motorcycle.

The miserable old man at once realized he'd forgotten his shoe he worked so hard and so long to make, and Mandy Debarge, having walked out to the parking lot to sit in the Lincoln and puff a fatty, passed her husband as he went in for a shift to mind the store, and called out to Trip that she would go get the shoe.

She got the flashlight from her husband and went, *National Enquirer*, fatty, and all, around back to the storage shed. She quickly brought out the shoe and handed it to them—and immediately afterwards she leaned against the door of the town car, faking reading the *Enquirer* as she waited for all to leave, and seeing nothing.

Hoss gunned the absurdly high truck with the big stupid tires and they exploded away down the street, Bunnie tearing after them on her muffler-challenged Harley.

The high-decibel procession set off car alarm after car alarm as they made their way through Coon Spit proper, passing very few shops with lighted signs; passing an antique store crowded with gays uncomfortably disguised in overalls and flannel shirts, with thin shafts (no pun intended) of wheat protruding from their lips and teeth: passing an illuminated coffeehouse barely still in business because of the Starbucks in nearby Slick Rock Hollow; and passing the Main Street Cinema barely still in business because of the Japanese owned Multiplex out by the highway—but they only stopped once, rolling into the 'golden arches' for a couple value meals to go.

"Do you have any coupons?" the pimply-faced teenager asked as they pulled up to the first window.

Trip handed him three.

"These are no good, see, looky here, the expiration date has expired."

Trip jumped out of the truck and vowed to take the boy apart. "Now you see here! These coupons are for that man inside the truck with the white head. He's so old! Can't you see he's old? Cut the man some slack, would ya? Christ!"

Trip dropped his voice, and there was a flutter

among the workers inside. The coupons were handed back through the window by the arm of a thirty-something manager in uniform, the eyes connected to the arm looked—not an every-day or an every-night look—at the man with the white head.

"It is well. Pull forward," said the manager in uniform.

At the next window they were handed their free-of-charge food by a cheerful older woman from Honduras, and sent on their way with Hoss Cribbens wondering, *wasn't that McDonald's manager an old line worker from the Chrysler plant...?*

They exited that most unmoved and eternal of fast-food chains, some so remote from this little patch of earth that the learned tell us they even have ones in Utah, and even Chiner as well!

All through the cold drive back across the holler, the shadows of the night were broad and black. They once more whispered in the ears of Trip Templeton—sitting next to the buried man who'd been dug out, and wondering what subtle powers were forever lost to him, and what were capable of restoration—the old inquiry:

I hope you care to go back home?
And the old answer:
I can't say.

THE END OF THE FIRST BOOK

- Book the Second -

The Golden Head

1

A Dive and the Doven

Tall Tales strip club with the Cock-N-Bull Tavern located in back was an old-fashioned place by the standards of gentlemen's clubs in the year one thousand nine-hundred and nintey-three. It was very small, very dark, very ugly, very incommodious, which some took to mean there were no bathrooms.

It was an old-fashioned place, moreover, in the moral attribute (*snicker*) that the patrons in the house were proud of its intimate feel, proud of its darkness, proud of its ugliness, proud of its icommodiousness, (which did not, in fact, mean there were no bathrooms).

The regular patrons were even boastful of its eminence in those particulars, and were fired by an express conviction that, if it were less objectionable, it would be less respectable (if that were at all possible).

This was no passive belief, but an active weapon which they flashed at more convenient places of 'business.'

Tall Tales (they said) wanted no elbow-room, Tall Tales wanted no light, Tall Tales wanted no embellishment.

The Gee String might; Noah's Stark might; but Tall Tales, Thank Heaven!—

Any one of these patrons would have dismembered his own son on the question of changing Tall Tales. In this respect, the club was much on par with the county; which did very often flog its sons for suggesting 'improvements' to laws concerning lewd and lascivious behavior that had long been not highly objectionable, making them all the more 'respectable' per se.

Thus it had come to pass, that Tall Tales was the triumphant perfection of objectionable respectableness. After bursting open a door and getting past the bouncer of idiotic obstinacy—since he was deathly afraid of getting caught by the 'thorities for allowing underage patrons—you fell into Tall Tales down two steps, something OSHA had been hassling about for years, and came to your senses in a miserable little shop with a stage and two poles, where the oldest of strippers could barely make your member shake even if the wind rustled it while they examined the signature on your government check by the dingiest of windows, which were always under a mud-bath shower from State Route 49, and which were made even dingier by the iron bars, a meager attempt to keep out teenaged vandals and other ne'er do-wells.

If your business necessitated your seeing what 'the House' had to offer, you were put into a species of Condemned Hold at the back of the room, where you meditated on a misspent life, until the house stripper—of equal to surpassing misspent life—came by in a g-string to perform on your personage a tango of the midsection.

Your money went into wormy old drawers (the g-strings), threads of which flew up your nose and down your throat when the dollar bill, or a denomination of higher value, was snapped into the string.

Your money had a musty odor, as if it was fast decomposing into a liquid pulp again. And if you were completely insane and decided to order food—God Forbid!—you could be rest assured your plate had been stored away among the neighboring cesspools in the dishwashing area.

Getting thrown out of the club, at that time, was a recipe much in vogue with the tradesmen and that rare professional that happened to wander in from time to time.

'Throw them out!' was Hoss Cribbens' remedy for all things. And why not? 'Got to keep the lawman happy!' he'd rationalize, 'You never know who might be undercover in here!'

Accordingly, a forger of government checks was thrown out; the utterer of obscene words toward the 'help' was thrown out; the unlawful opener of pants, or open exposurerer of man parts was thrown out; the purloiner of stripper's, waitress', or bartender's tips was also thrown out; the puller of loins before, after, or during a show—or at any moment while occupying space within the establishment (with the obvious exception of the commode) was definitely thrown out, and so on and so forth.

Not that any of this did the least bit of good in the way of prevention—it might almost have been worth remarking that the fact was exactly the reverse because some considered it a challenge—but it cleared off the trouble of each particular case, and left nothing else connected with it to be looked after by the 'thorities.

Thus Tall Tales, in its day, like lesser places of business (though I'm remiss to think of even one—and a legal one at that), had ruined so many lives and marriages, that, if the heads (no pun intended) laid low before it had been beaten (again, no pun intended) with a meat masher (*definitely* no pun intended) then the owners of such heads would have been, if you think about it, much better off in more ways than two.

Cramped in all kinds of dim back-booths and tables, the oldest of men carried the business gravely. When they took a young man with them into Tall Tales, which did happen occasionally, they hid him back in the Cock-N-Bull lest anyone on the main floor suspect anything.

They kept him in a dark place, like a cheese, until he had the full Cock-N-Bull flavor and blue-balls upon him. Then only was he permitted to be seen, spectacularly pouring large drinks, and casting his britches and hip-waiters into the general weight of the establishment.

Outside Tall Tales—never by any means *in* it, unless called in—was an odd jobs man (not exactly the rarest of things to find in these parts); an occasional house painter and messenger of occasional tidings—more oft than not of a less than legal (before the state as well as before God) nature, which he performed to and from the hill country on his trusty steed: a rusty old four-wheeler.

Jerry also served as the sign changer for the club, his above ground identity for purposes of the tax-man and other authorities who had such a mind as to inquire.

He was never absent during business hours, unless upon an errand, and then he was represented by his son: a grisly urchin of twelve, who was his express image.

People understood that Tall Tales, in a stately way, tolerated Jerry the odd-jobs-man. The club had always tolerated some person in that capacity, and time and tide had drifted this Jerry to the post.

His surname was Kracker, and on the youthful occasion of his renouncing by proxy the works of darkness, in the easterly parish of St. Pancreas, he had received the appellation of: Gerald.

The scene we take you to now is Mr. Kracker's private lodging in Grouse Gulch: the time, half-past seven of the clock on a windy March morning, anno domini one-thousand nine-hundred and ninety-three. (Mr. Kracker himself always spoke of the year of our Lord as Anna Dominoes, an homage to his favorite Tall Tales stripper bearing the same name.)

Mr. Kracker's trailer was not in a savory neighborhood—which I guess goes without saying—and was but one in number, even if a closet with a single pane of glass in it might be counted as one. But it was very decently kept.

Early as it was, on the windy March morning, the room in which he lay in a hide-a-bed was already scrubbed throughout; and between the cups and saucers arranged for breakfast, and the lumbering poker table, a very clean white cloth was spread.

Mr. Kracker reposed under his dead granny's patchwork quilt, far from a vision of a Harlequin Romance cover.

At first, he slept heavily, then awoke, and by degrees he began to roll and surge in bed, until he rose above the surface, with his spiky hair looking as if it must tear the sheets to ribbons. At which juncture, he exclaimed, in a voice of dire exasperation: "Goddamit, Reba McEntire, why do you still have to be so frickin' hot!"

Now spent, he tossed the TV Guide featuring the show 'Reba' in a corner, nearly hitting a woman of orderly and industrious appearance, who entered the room with all the haste and trepidation of Edith Bunker, and fell to her knees between his legs as he sat on the edge of the bed, rubbing his eyes.

"What?" said Mr. Kracker, barely cognizant enough to realize what was going on. "You're at it now, are you?" he said in a quiet and bored voice, though he was most certainly not complaining.

After all, he *was* a man.

He looked down. "What?—What are you up to, Agatha?"

She looked up, without a discontinument of her work. "I'm only sayin' my prayers," she gurgled.

"Saying your prayers? Is that what ye call it?" his eyes suddenly crossed and his mouth went agape.

After howling with his second salutation of the morning, Jerry drew back a boot and threw it at the woman as she retreated from the bedroom, in the most superlative display of ingratitude mankind has ever seen.

It was a very muddy boot, however, and it may introduce the odd circumstance connected with Mr. Kracker's domestic economy, that, whereas he often came home after club hours with clean boots, he often got up next morning to find the same boots covered with mud.

"What are you up to, Agatha?" he growled to himself, looking at the boot. "D'ja hear me, Agatha!" he called out. "What are you up to?"

"I was only saying my prayers..."

"Saying your prayers? You're a nice woman! What do you mean by flopping yourself down and 'prayin' against me—"

"I wasn't prayin' 'ginst you. I was prayin' *for* you, Gerald!"

"Bah!"

When his son came into his room without expectation, Mr. Kracker quickly threw granny's quilt over his shame and laid back on the bed, staring at the ceiling, completely spent from shooting his wad twice in a matter of minutes.

"She may be ugly as sin, my boy, but you've got a dutiful mother, you have," he breathily puffed out, nearly unconscious. "She may be dumber 'n a rock, but you've got a religious mother, you have, my boy," he yawned, "going and flopping herself down... and praying...with a mouthful of...."

"Gerald!" Agatha called sweetly from the kitchen, "Come eat your grits 'fore they git cold!"

"'Come eat yor grits, Ger-*rald*," he mocked from the bedroom in abject boredom. Master Kracker (dressed only in a wife-beater) next thought he'd have some fun at his wife's expense, of the teasing variety: "And what do you suppose, you conceited female, that the worth of your *prayers* may be? Name the price that you put your *prayers* at!"

"They only come from my heart, Gerald. They ain't worth no more than that."

"Worth no more than that?" repeated Mr. Kracker. *Christ! I know some scum down at Tall Tales that'd...hey...wait a minute...*

"They only come from my heart, dearest Gerald," his wife repeated.

"Then they ain't worth much, then!" the husband

barked, fleshing out his suspicions of dubidity. "Whether or no, *I* won't be 'prayed' again, I tell you! *I* can't afford it. And I'm not a going to be made unlucky by your refusal to contribute to the family coffer!"

"Suit yourself, then, dear..."

Mr. Kracker suddenly realized what he had said, and felt his cranial surface suddenly morphed into the likeness of a jack's ass.

Said he, thoroughly enraged: "Well, if you must go floppin' down, flop *in favor* of your husband and child, and not in *opposition* to 'em! You know we ain't got no money!" whined Jerry Kracker, slapping a fatalistic hand to his knee.

He got up and walked to the kitchen.

"If I had any but a unnat'ral wife, and this poor boy had any but an unnat'ral mother, I might have made some money last week instead of being counter-'prayed,' and 'religiously' circumvented into the worst of luck."

He said this as he paced around the kitchen tile in absolutely nothing save for a wife-beater.

"For the Lord's sake Gerald, put some pants on! There's chi'ren present, you know."

The husband took no never mind to this since he had already ramped up to a full whiny rant now, and made little sense as he addressed the ceiling: "...if I ain't been with that no good Petey and one blowed thing after another, been choused this last week into as bad luck as ever a poor devil of a honest tradesman met with...!"

"Please make sense, Gerald," the wife requested saccharinely, again in the Bunkerish manner of Edith, "It scares the child when you talk gibberish..."

Jerry stopped and looked around. With slooping shoulders he addressed his son: "Young Jerry, go dress yourself, my boy, and while I clean my boots for the *hundredth time this week*...keep an eye upon your mother now and then, and if you see any signs of more flopping, give me a call. For I tell you," here he addressed his wife once more, "I won't be 'gone' again when it happens. I know I'm as rickety as an old Amish coach, but damned if I'll be sleepy as a sloth on that there Vee-ay-gra, sportin' a four hour hoocher next few nights from now on; and my ass'll be strained to that degree that I shouldn't know (if it wasn't for the pain in it), which was not from me but which was from somebody else—but that's a whole other matter entirely, and I'm not 'zakly sure why I brought it up jus' now—but as far as what *yer* doin', Agatha, I'm none the better for it in the pocket; and it's my suspicion that you've been at it from night to mornin' to prevent me from being the better in the pocket for it, and I won't put up with it no more! Do you hear me? And I'll find where you been hidin' all the money all this time, I will! And what do you say now?"

Growling such phrases as "Ah! yes! And you're religious, too!" and throwing off other sarcastic sparks from the whiling grindstone of his indignation, Mr. Kracker betook himself to his boot-cleaning and his general preparation for business.

In the meantime, his son, whose head was garnished with a mohawk and an eye-brow ring or three, and whose young eyes stood too close to one another like his father's, kept the required watch on his mother, being not of age enough to realize his father had procured the remark in sarcasm.

For the next half hour, he greatly disturbed that poor woman at intervals every time she knelt down to scrub a stain from the tile, by darting out of chair with a suppressed cry of "You goin' to flop, mother?—Hey dad!" and, after raising this fictitious alarm, darted into his room again with a dutiful grin.

Mr. Kracker's temper was not at all improved when he came to his breakfast. He resented Mrs. Kracker saying grace with particular animosity.

"Now, Agatha! What are you up to? *More* prayers?"

His wife explained that she had merely 'asked a blessing'.

"Don't do it!" said Mr. Kracker, looking about as if he rather expected to see his toast disappear under the efficacy of his wife's petitions. "And you know what I'm talkin' 'bout! I ain't gonna be 'blessed' out of house and home..."

"I'm not sure I know what you're talkin' 'bout..."

"Bah!"

Exceedingly red-eyed and grim, as if he had been up all night at a party which had taken anything but a convivial turn, Jerry Kracker worried his breakfast rather than ate it, growling over it like any four-footed inmate of a menagerie.

Toward nine o'clock he smoothed his ruffled aspect, and, presenting as respectful and business-like an exterior as he possibly could overlay his natural self with, issued forth to the occupation of the day.

It could scarcely be called a trade, in spite of his favorite description of himself as an 'honest tradesman.'

His stock consisted of a wooden stool, made out of a broke-backed chair cut down, which stool, young Jerry, walking at his father's side, carried every morning to beneath the Tall Tales front window that was relatively far from the Cock-N-Bull in back: where, with the addition of the first handful of firewood that could be gleaned from the back of any number of spilled pick-up trucks on State Route 49 throughout the course of the day; to keep the cold and wet from the odd-jobs-man's feet, it formed the encampment for the day.

On this post of his, Mr. Kracker was as well known to State Route 49 and the Cock-N-Bull as to Tall Tales itself—and was almost as ill-looking.

Encamped at a quarter before nine, in good time to touch the brim of his John Deere high-rider to the oldest of men as they passed into Tall Tales, Jerry took up his station on this windy March morning, with young Jerry standing by him, when not engaged in making forays through the bar (always careful to skirt the 'thorities and the 'undercovers') to inflict bodily and mental injuries of an acute description upon any other boys who may be in there with their fathers, or grandfathers, but only those small enough for his amiable purpose.

Father and son, extremely like each other, looking silently on at the morning traffic on State Route 49, with their two heads as near to one another as the two eyes of each were, bore a considerable resemblance to a pair of hyenas. The resemblance was not lessened by the accidental circumstance, that the 'mature' Jerry bit and spat out chewing tobacco, while the twinkling eyes of the youthful Jerry were as restlessly watchful of him as of everything else on State Route 49.

The head of one of the regular bartenders attached to the Tall Tales establishment was put through the door (of his own volition), and the word was given.

"Jerry, you're wanted."

"Hooray, father! Here's an early job to begin with!"

Having thus given his parent God speed, young Jerry seated himself on the stool, entered into his reversionary interest in the chaw can his father had been chewing, partook, and immediately blended his upchucked breakfast with the mud infested terrafirma parking lot.

2

Kangaroo Court

"You know the Rebel well, no doubt?" said the oldest of bartenders—by age, not by time worked (it was morning shift after all)—to Jerry the messenger. "Over in the Coalmont County seat—over in Rabbit Grove?"

"Ye-es, sir," returned Jerry, in something of a dogged manner. "I *do* know the Rebel."

"Right. And you know Templeton."

"You know I know Trip, Ellsworth! I know Trip better than I know the Rebel, that's for sure. Much better...," said Jerry, not unlike a reluctant witness at the establishment in question, "...than I, as an honest tradesman wish to know the Rebel."

"I know, Jerry, I know. I'm jus' fuckin' wit' 'cha! Find the door where the Witnesses go in, and show the man at the door this note for Trip. He will let you in."

"Into the court, Ellsworth?"

"Into the court."

Mr. Kracker's eyes seemed to get a little closer to one another, and to interchange the inquiry, "What do you think of this?"

"Not sayin'."

"Am I to wait in the court, Ellsworth?" he asked, as the result of that conference.

"I am going to tell you. The man at the door will pass the note to Trip, and you do something that will attract Trip's attention, and show him where you stand. Then what you have to do is, to remain there until he wants you."

"Is that all, Ellsworth?"

"That's all. He wishes to have a messenger at hand. This is to tell him that you are there."

As the ancient bartender folded the note and

wrapped it in a 'benjamin,' Mr. Kracker, after surveying him until he handed over the note, remarked:

"I suppose they'll be trying forgeries this morning?"

"No, treason, smart-ass!"

"Could've fooled me..."

"Got that from a cus'mer last night."

"Who? That undercover cop who come in 'bout ten
o'clock?"

"That was the F.B.I., fool!"

"Yeah, my ass."

The ancient bartender looked both ways, "Speak
well of the law, boy! And take care your chest and
voice, my friend, and leave the law to take care of itself! I give you that advice."

"I think I got that there pig flu, Ellsworth, what's
in my chest and voice," said Jerry. "I leave you to judge
what a sick way of earning a living is mine too..."

"Well, well," said the old bartender; "we all have
our various ways of gaining a livelihood. Some of us
have sick ways, and some of us have less-sick ways.
Here is the note. Now git."

Jerry took the letter, and remarking to himself,
with less internal deference than he made an outward
show of, *You're a mean old one, too*, made his bow, informed his son, after tracking him down inside, of his
destination, and went his way.

They use lethal injection nowadays, not at all like
the old days of lynchings, firing squads and electric
chairs... er, uh... I mean *hangings* and firing squads
and electric chairs.

In the old days, such evil was done in a vast field
set off and aside from the old Rebel. Nowadays, that
field is still a vile place, in which most kinds of debauchery and villainy are practiced, and where dire
diseases are bred, that come spilling out across the
field, landing onto prisoners being led into the old Rebel courthouse (guilty 'til proven innocent, especially if
Nancy Grace gets a'hold of 'em) and sometimes rush-

ing straight at Judge Carmichael himself.

The old Rebel courthouse came by such a nickname in the year one-thousand nine-hundred and fifty when one of the last surviving confederate army veterans filed suit in a suit in the courthouse's hallowed halls seeking retribution and relief from medical bills, and to save a broken-down shack from foreclosure, citing time served in the confederate army and demanding payment for said service.

Sadly, the old gentleman chose the target of his lawsuit as not the federal government of the *U*-nited States of 'Merca, but, following the advice of his donkey's ass counsel (one honored barrister named Elmer T. Fogbenton) he lodged his complaint in a manner that became known statewide as: 'Horace K. Cooper. vs. the Confederate States of the United Confederacy, care of one Jefferson Davis, address: Atlanta, Georgia.'

Needless to speak, Horace did not get far.

In fact, Judge Wiggletoad at the time took the papers from the bench immediately, and with his understanding of his bound and honored duty under the law, leaned over and filed Horace's documents under the index classification system known as 'file the Numeral Thirteen.'

After news of that gully-ticklin' knee-slapper made its way like an apparition through the windows and doors of every outhouse and shotgun shack in southern Kentucky, the 'old Rebel' as Horace became known in the newspapers, transferred such nickname upon the courthouse itself (not without the people not having asked poor Horace's permission for such labeling, of course).

Such a nickname would likely have fallen by the wayside 'ventually; its humor having run its course not long after Horace's big blunder; but then came the comings of the first and second Kings.

The first King rose from very humble beginnings. The impact of such a birth was immediate, and apparent, and unquestioned. His coming disrupted the establishment, turned neighbor against neighbor, family against family, city against city, state against state. His coming managed to unite a country just as it surely as it divided it at the very same time. Sharp as the Mason Dixon line in its exactitude, the dividing spike he drove through the country staggers the mind in its unlimited aspects of future repercussions. Starting out in a mid-size southern town—and in small southern churches—this King worshipped and preached his message, and was worshipped alike, in all stately manner of cathedral life of bowing and kneeling, yet was especially worshipped in juke-joints and houses of perpetual pale body wiggling. Of course, we're speaking of none other than E. Aaron Presley, the King of rock-n-roll.

The coming of King Presley, however, holds no bearing whatsoever on the history of the naming— future, past, or present—of the old Rebel courthouse.

But it was a good story to tell.

The Coming of the Second King—now *that!*—that was a different story, which held maximum significance for the perpetuation of such a courthouse nickname.

For vastly different reasons and significance to his followers, the Second Coming of the King (M of the L to be exact) cemented the moniker 'old Rebel' for all time when an ironic twist of history accidentally on purpose fell upon it.

For you see, in the time of the reign of the Second M of the L King, said courthouse handled an amount of civil rights abuse filings, the extent of which caused the old Rebel to be lit for business for nigh span of ten plus zero trips of the earth 'round the life-provider; including three-hundred-six and five rotations 'round the Knight of darkness; including twenty-four and seven rotations of the big hand round what holds our days and nights safely and securely within its grasp.

At such a time that the civil rights lawsuits were occurring, the minority population took to using the

'Old Rebel' moniker upon the courthouse as their own, as it was finally their turn to rebel; their turn for revolution; their turn to turn the tables; their turn to yell from the rooftops what lesser men had whispered in quiet, and so on and so forth.

This courthouse was their Bunker Hill; their Bastille; their Che Guevera; and dare I say it? Their Nelson Mandela. It became their day in the sun; their time to set the record straight; they're time to punch the reckoning that much closer toward parity: And they whipped and flogged that new rebellion for all it was worth, not knowing that eventually the coming of a third King would rocket the hopes and dreams of the Second King a thousandfold—as every boy and girl in the land became a little less shackled in their journey of determining their individual footsteps along the footpaths by which their feet could now befall in a manner all that much more unhindered.

Upon his trusted and rusted four-wheeler, Jerry passed right by such a storehouse of history, gazing upon the 'old Rebel' as his steed wheeled past, for this was never his intended destination with which to begin; no, Jerry's intended destination was to alight himself in the service of Trip one building *past* the 'old Rebel', to a place that was once the old vile field of lore that produced such horrors, executions, lynchings and other vile goings-on as not to be mentioned amidst the more sensitive of women and children. But today such a field was not a field at all, but such vile histories of acts long ago intentionally played a part in the naming of the building built upon one such field in the year one-thousand nine-hundred seventy and five, a name which also carried an homage to the stately structure next of it, namely, this building in the old field was called, The Rebel Yell Bowling Alley, also known simply as: The Rebel Yell.

Now, one might think a decisively negatory reaction from the county's minority slice of life in calling such a place of pin-knocking entertainment The Rebel

Yell would have been in order; and a call would have come down immediately to prevent such a naming action, especially in the days of such a reigning judge known to all as Po'Litical Correctness; but, as it were, the Afric'n Mer'can folk didn't mind what would otherwise be construed as an offensive title prickling unfavorable memories toward a mangled and misappropriated heritage.

No, in another strange twist of historical irony, the owner of the Rebel Yell bowling alley, Copper T. Cladhopper, loved the Afric'n Mer'can folk dearly and let them yell their rebel yells at the ten pins each night for ten percent *less* than paler folk recompensed for the exact same action; thus was Cops humble way of equalfying the past economic inequitudes suffered in that community.

And as for the pale folk, hell, they never-they-minded. They loved Copper as much as he loved the Afric'm Mer'can folk, for no other reason than simply because he was an absolute stand-up guy, and wouldn't lift even so much as a grain of sugar off a roach.

People, of course (and I'm not sure why I'm even saying this) then paid to bowl at the Rebel Yell (just as they do now), just as in the really old days they sometimes paid to watch the 'show' at the old Rebel courthouse, depending on the degree of corruption any given sheriff was lended to—the latter show being much more entertaining in its gruesomeness, depending on your hue of skin, and the former on how bad a bowler one might be.

But in light of such seeming hand-holding across community racial lines, t'is such a shame that not-as-yet-described-in-this-story shenanigans went on about the place—in the Rebel Yell—by mi-norities and other-norities alike; things that went on, and still go on without Cops knowin' about them.

This being the reason why the 'Holy Bowler Witnesses' frequented the joint; to witness to the heathen community committing such debaucherous acts, and painfully witnessing the debauched drink ice-cold beverages such as Old Milwaukee—a.ka.: 'Old *Swill*-Waukee'— an act to cause consternation to even the most holy and devout for more reasons than one.

Copper couldn't keep out the Holy Bowler Witnesses, but he didn't want them loitering out front his 'stablishment neither, so he forced them, by agreement with the understatedly heathen sheriff, to come in the back side door, where they wouldn't be seen going in or out, and possibly scaring off other, more or less, 'respectable' clientele.

The Witnesses immediately filed a civil rights agreivement, which is still pending at the old Rebel courthouse, as they took it upon themselves—in a third, ironic twist of history—of joining together with one Mer'can Civil Liberties Union, a hitherto perceived historical enemy of the Witnesses.

Making his way through the tainted crowd in the bowling alley parking lot, dispersed up and down this hideous scene of action, with the skill of a man accustomed to making his way quietly, the messenger found the door he sought, and was extraordinarily cheerfully greeted by a Holy Bowler Witness:

"Glad you came bowling today, brother! Awesome to see you! Come right in! Jesus hopes you bowl a great game!"

Jerry obliged by stepping in with a tip of his John Deere high-rider. He made his way quickly, the Witness tagging along after him the whole way, unceasing of speech, until Jerry made it behind the café bar (employees only) and found two doors; one for the storage of drink and beer pretzels, the other for bodies to enter, legs to descend, and be-hinds to sit on stools round ten worn-out pool tables, the existence of which the public patrons above knew not.

This all took place under the auspices of the literal alley itself, an area known and reserved for only the best of Copper's closest acquaintances and confidants.

And for the secret combined meetings of county-wide Chambers of Commerce, all united under one goal—to be discussed at length later.

Jerry pushed his letter under the latter door and with knuckles to the fore of himself, struck thusly with one rap, then four quick raps, followed by a slight pause then two slow ones. After some delay and demur, the door grudgingly turned on its hinges a very little way, and allowed Mr. Kracker to squeeze himself through the door, and downstairs into 'court'. Round near fifty men and women sat, drinking beer, smoking pot, and *not* engaged in billiards.

"What's going on?" Jerry asked, in a whisper, of a man he found himself next to in the back of the room.

"Nothing yet."

"What's coming then?"

"The treason case."

"The one I heard about, huh?"

"Yep," returned the man, with a relish; "he'll be thrown over a hurdle on the high school running track, then half-hanged on the flagpole, then he'll be taken down and sliced in the face with Jimbo's huntin' knife, then his insides will be taken out and burned while he looks on, and then his head will be chopped off, and he'll be cut into burgers. That's the sentence."

"A bit extreme, don't ya think?"

The man gave him a sideways glance.

"...if he's found Guilty, you mean to say," added Jerry quickly, by way of proviso.

"Oh, they'll find him guilty all right. Don't you be 'fraid of that."

"That's not what I'm 'fraid of at the moment," blustered Jerry, spotting Jimbo's huge hunting knife dangling from said owner's hip waiters in front of him.

Mr. Kracker's attention was here diverted to the door-watcher, whom he saw making his way to Trip, with the note in his hand. Trip sat at a table, among men with fishing hats and bad combovers, and a smattering of horrendous toupees, not far from a toupee'd gentleman, the prisoner's counsel, who had a great bundle of chew before him: and nearly opposite a badly toupee'd combed-over gentleman with his hands in his pockets, whose whole attention, when Mr. Kracker looked at him then or afterwards, seemed to be concentrated on his own singular game of pocket billiards.

After some gruff coughing and rubbing of his chin and signing with his hand, Jerry attracted the notice of said billiards engager, who stood up to look at Jerry, then re-arranged himself and sat back down.

That was also about the time Trip noticed Jerry was in the room.

"What's *he* got to do with the case?" asked the man next to Jerry.

"Blast if I know," said Jerry.

"What have *you* got to do with it, then, if a person may inquire?"

Jerry shot a fearful glance towards Jimbo's knife again. "Blast if I know that, either."

The entrance of the 'judge,' and a consequent great stir and settling down in the 'court,' stopped the dialogue.

Presently, the 'judge' became the central point of interest. Two bowlers, who had been standing there, went out, and the prisoner was brought in, and put up on the bar.

Everyone present, except the one gentleman in the badly toupee'd combover who looked at the ceiling, stared at the 'prisoner'. All the human breath in the place, rolled at him like a sea, or a wind, or a fire. Eager faces strained round pillars and corners, to get a sight of him; spectators in back rows stood up, not to miss a fake hair of him; people in chairs on the basement floor laid their hands on the shoulders of the people before them, to help themselves, at anybody's cost, to get a view of him. Conspicuous among these latter, like an animated bit of a barbed-wire fence in Newark, NJ, Jerry stood: aiming at the prisoner the beer-y breath of a whet he had taken as he came along, and discharging a belch to mingle with the waves of other beer, and gin, and whiskey and bourbon and whatnot, that flowed at him, and already broke upon the cinder-block walls behind him in an impure mist and rain.

The object of all this staring and blaring was a young man of about five-and-twenty, well-liquored and three-sheets-past-the-wind, with a sunburnt neck and a black-eye.

His condition was far from that of a young 'gentleman.' He was plainly dressed in a black Hank Jr. T-shirt (or dark-gray now, after being washed a thousand cycles in cheap highly acidic powders), and his hair was long, scraggly and two-pints greasy, gathered not-at-all neatly about his shoulders.

As an emotion of the mind will express itself through any covering of the body, so the blackness which his situation engendered came through by the Hank Jr. T-shirt and a large brown mole on his cheek, showing the soul to be stronger than the sun. He was otherwise quite self-possessed, nodded to 'judge' Donny Ray Judge, and stood quiet.

The sort of interest with which this man was stared and breathed at, was not a sort that elevated humanity. Had he stood in peril of a less horrible sentence—had there been a chance of any one of its savage details being spared—by just so much would he have lost in his fascination.

The form that was to be doomed to be so shamefully mangled, was the sight; the immortal creature that was to be so butchered and torn asunder, yielded the sensation. Whatever gloss the various spectators put upon the interest, according to their several arts and powers of self-deceit, the interest was, at the root of it, ogre-ish.

Silence in the 'court!'

Charles Chuck "Bubba" Darnet had yesterday pleaded Not Guilty to an indictment denouncing him (with infinite jingle and jangle) as a traitor to our serene, illustrious, and excellent small-business way of life by reason of his having, supposedly been caught with a Sam Walton autobiography on his person, supposedly with the aim of passing it off to someone, possibly our illustrious mayor Bull Scythe, thus disturbing our said serene, illustrious, excellent, and so forth, small-business community in a wickedly, falsely, traitorously, and otherwise evil-adverbiously, way.

This much, Jerry, with his head becoming more and more spiky as the law terms bristled it, made out with huge satisfaction, and so arrived circuitously at the understanding that the aforesaid, and over and over again aforesaid, Charles Chuck 'Bubba' Darnet, stood before him upon his trial; that the jury were swearing at, and that Mr. Clint 'The General' Lee was making ready to speak.

The accused, who was (and who knew he was) being mentally hanged, beheaded, and quartered, by everybody there, neither flinched from the situation, nor assumed any theatrical air in it.

He was quiet and attentive; watched the opening proceedings with a grave interest; and stood with his hands resting on the slab of wood before him that made up the bar, so composedly, that they had not displaced an empty shot-glass with which it was strewn.

The court was all bestrewn with cigars, cigarettes and herbs (if you know what I mean) as a precaution against clean bowling alley air and possibly 'bowling fever,' which meant bowling with non-smoke tainted lungs, or worse, bowling while sober.

Over the prisoner's head there was a Coors Light mirror, throwing light down upon his bald-spot. Crowds of the wicked and the wretched had been reflected in it, and had passed from its surface and this earth's together. Haunted in a most ghastly manner that abominable place would have been, if the glass could ever have rendered back its reflections, as the ocean is one day to give up its dead. Some passing thought of the infamy and disgrace for which it had been reserved, may have struck the prisoner's mind. Be that as it may, a change in his position making him conscious of a beam of light across his face, he looked up; and when he saw the mirror, his face flushed, and his right hand pushed the herbs away.

It happened, that the action turned his face to that side of the court which was on his left. About on a level with his eyes, there sat, in that corner of Donny Ray's stool, two persons upon whom his look immediately rested; so immediately, and so much to the changing of his aspect, that all the eyes that were turned upon him, turned to them.

The spectators saw in the two figures, a young lady of little more than twenty, and a gentleman who was evidently her father, judging by the hatred splashed across her countenance. A man of a very remarkable appearance in respect of the absolute whiteness of his hair, and a certain indescribably insanity of face: not of an active kind, but pondering and self-communing, which was very unbecoming outside the privacy of one's own bedroom, or shower, or 'solitary' room in the basement of Tall Tales.

When this expression was upon him, he looked as if he were a nasty, dirty old man; but when it was stirred and broken up—as it was now, in a moment, on his speaking to his daughter—he became a moral and law-abiding man, not past the time when he was in and out of prison.

His daughter sat not close to him as if he smelled or had contracted and was contagious with some hideous disease. She left space between them, in her dread and pity for being his daughter. Her forehead had been strikingly expressive of an engrossing terror for her father and a compassion that saw nothing but the peril of the accused. This had been so very noticeable, so very powerfully and naturally shown, the starers who had no pity for him wished they could be touched by her, and touch her back; and the whisper went about, "Who are they?"

Jerry, the messenger, who had made his own observations, in his own manner, and who had been sucking the chew off his fingers in his absorption, stretched his neck to hear who they were. The crowd about him had pressed and passed the inquiry on to the nearest attendant, and from him it had been more slowly pressed and passed back; until at last it got to Jerry: "Pro'ly Witnesses."

"Her? She's too good lookin' for that."

"Well, pro'ly."

"But how'd they get down here?"

"Don' know."

"Maybe they're here 'cuz of the pris'ner."

"Pro'ly."

'Judge' Donny Ray Judge, whose eyes had gone in the general direction, recalled them, leaned back on his stool, and looked steadily at the man whose life was in his hand, as 'The General' rose to spin the rope, grind the ax, and hammer the nails into the scaffold.

3

On the Strength of Weak Witnesses

The 'General' had to inform the jury:

...*That* the prisoner before them, though young in years, was old in the treasonable practice which claimed the temporary forfeit of his freedom.

...*That* this correspondence with the public enemy was not a correspondence of to-day, or of yesterday, or even of last year, or of the year before.

...*That*, it was certain the prisoner had, for longer than that, been in the habit of passing and repassing between Coon Spit and Grouse Gulch, on secret business of which he could give no honest account.

...*That*, if it were in the nature of traitorous ways to thrive (which happily it never was), the real wickedness and guilt of his business might have remained undiscovered.

...*That* Providence, however, had put it into a heart of a person who was beyond fear and beyond reproach, to ferret out the nature of the prisoner's schemes, and, struck with horror, to disclose them to Donny Ray and a select few on the 'honorable' Coalmont County Chambers of Commerce and Small Businessman's Association 'council,' the entirety of which was assembled in the room today.

...*That* he had been the prisoner's friend, but, at once in an auspicious and evil hour detecting his infamy, had resolved to immolate the traitor he could no longer cherish in his bosom, on the sacred altar of his town.

...*That*, if statues were decreed in Coalmont County, as in ancient Greece and Rome, to public benefactors, this shining citizen would assuredly have had one.

...*That*, as they were not so decreed, he probably would not have one.

...*That*, Virtue, as had been observed on Jerry Springer (in many episodes he well knew the jury would have known word-for-word at the tip of the tongues; whereat the jury's countenances displayed a guilty consciousness that they did indeed know each such episode), was in a manner contagious; more especially the bright virtue known as frienditude, or loyalty to your friends, and a willingness to beat the living shit out of people on nationwide TV.

...*That*, he preferred the company of the two who's doing the accusin' to that of his own wife and kids, or even his own dead father and mother (which ain't sayin' much).

...*That* he called with confidence on the jury to come and do likewise (which again, was easily done and weren't sayin' much).

...*That* he, The General, had asked if them, the ones doin' the accusin', had gone through the prisoner's coat pockets earlier that day.

...*That* the evidence produced by the ones doin' the accusin', the document of their discoverment that would soon be produced, would show the prisoner to have been furnished on his person one autobiography of that notorious of all businessmen: Sam Walton himself; and would leave no doubt that the prisoner had habitually conveyed such information to a hostile power.

...*That*, for these reasons, the jury—being a loyal jury to the anti-Walmart movement made up of local small businessmen (and women) specifically formed to combat plans for a Walmart to be built in Coalmont County (specifically in Coon Spit town proper as per the latest rumor) and all assembled in this room at this very time—being a responsible jury (as he knew they were), must positively find the prisoner Guilty, and make an example of him by kicking him out of all Rebel Yell bowling leagues forever and all time, wheth-

er they liked it or not (since he was a pretty good bowler).

... *That* they could never lay their hands upon their
bowling balls; that they could never tolerate the idea of
their wives laying their hands upon their balls, or laying their hands upon someone else's balls; that they
could never endure the notion of their kids laying their
hands upon their own balls, or someone else's balls; in
short, that there never more could be, for them or
theirs, any laying of hands upon any balls at all, unless the prisoner's hands and balls were banished from
their midst forever. Those hands The General concluded by demanding of them, in the name of everything he
could think of with a round turn on it, and already
considered those hands as good as gone.

When The General ceased his speech, a buzz
arose in the court as a great cloud of horseflies
swarmed about the prisoner, pooping on him as if in
anticipation of what he was to become.

When the 'council' toned down again, one of the
two unimpeachable patriots of the anti-Walmart
movement described by The General appeared next
beside the bar.

Donny Ray, then, examined the patriot: John the
Bastard, gentleman by name only, which was odd. The
story of his pure soul was exactly what The General
had described it to be, despite the man's unfortunate
nickname. The Bastard concurred with everything The
General had said, and having released this noble Bastard of his burden, said illegitimatitati would have
modestly withdrawn himself, but the toupee'd gentleman with the cigarette papers before him, sitting not
far from Travis Templeton, begged to ask him a few
questions. The wigged-out gentleman sitting opposite,
still looked at the ceiling of the court with his hands in
his pockets.

Had he ever shopped at Walmart himself?

No, the Bastard witness scorned the base insinua-
tion.

Where did he live?

His property.

Where was his property?

He didn't precisely remember where it was.

What was it?

T'aint no business of nobody's.

Had he inherited it?

Yes, he had.

From whom?

Distant kin.

Very distant?

How distant could it be in the hills of southern Kentucky?

Ever gotten a DUI?

Certainly not.

Ever been to jail?

Didn't see what that had to do with it.

Never in federal prison?

—Come again?

Never in a federal prison?

Yes.

How many times?

Two or three times.

Not five or six?

Perhaps.

What do you do for a living?

Gentleman caller.

You know that's illegal, right?

Why you think I've been to prison so many times, Dickweed?

Ever been kicked?

—'Scuse me?

Ever been kicked?

Might have been.

Frequently?

—What's this got to do with...?

Just answer the question!

No.

Ever been kicked down the stairs?

—What? *These* stairs?

Sure, why not.

Decidedly not; but I once received a boot up th' ass at the top of them stairs, and fell all the way down 'cause I felt like it...

Kicked on that occasion? For cheating at bowling?

Something to that effect was said by the intoxicated bee-otch liar who committed the assault, but it t'was not true!

Swear it t'was not true?

Positively.

Ever live by cheating at bowling?

Never.

Ever live by betting on bowling?

No more 'n Pete Rose ever done...

Ever borrow money of the 'prisoner'?

Yes.

Ever pay him?

No.

Was not this intimacy with the prisoner, in reality a very slight one (we hope), forced upon the prisoner in cars, gas stations and bowling alleys?

—Jes' what t' hell you tryin' to say...?

Sure he saw the prisoner with the Sam Walton autobiography?

Certain.

Knew any more about it?

No.

Had not put it in the coat himself, for instance?

No.

Expect to get anything by this evidence?

No.

Not in regular government checks and employment, or to lay traps, or turn tricks?

Dear God, no!

Or to do anything?

Dear God, no.

Swear that?

Over and over again.

No motives but motives of sheer loyalty to the council?

None whatsoever.

The virtuous 'employee' of the prisoner, Wade Franklin, swore his way through his testimony at a great rate, so much so, that not too much of the paint was left on the walls at the conclusion. Even grown men had hands over their ears by the time he was done. He had taken employment with the prisoner, in good faith and simplicity, four years ago. He had asked the prisoner, one night upon a Greyhound, if he needed an oil change now and then, and the prisoner had engaged him. He had not asked the prisoner to take on the oil-changing man as an act of charity—never thought such a thing, after all, he was a 'good changer, a fast one, and didn't charge much.'

He began to have suspicions of the prisoner, and to keep an eye upon him, soon afterwards. In changing his oil, after traveling, he had seen similar books in the prisoner's car, over and over again. He had taken these books from the glove compartment, he had not put them there first. He had seen the prisoner show these identical books to gentlemen at Coon Spit, and at Rabbit Grove and at Grouse Gulch. He loved owners of small businesses, and couldn't bear it, and had given information. He had never been suspect of stealing a single CD from the car-stereo; he had been maligned for spilling mustard from a corn dog on the upholstery, but the seats turned out to be vinyl. He had known the last witness seven or eight years; that was merely a coincidence. He didn't call it a particularly curious coincidence; most coincidences were curious. Neither did he call it a curious coincidence that true loyalty was *his* only motive too. He was a true Coalmont Countian, and hoped there were many like him.

The horseflies buzzed again, and The General called up Mr. Travis Templeton.

"Travis, er, um, Trip, are you the owner of Tall Tales strip club?"

"I am."

"On a certain Friday night in November nineteen-hundred and eighty-eight, did business occasion you to travel between Grouse Gulch and Black Bear in a mail truck?"

"It did."

"Were there any other passengers in the mail truck?"

"Three."

"Did they get stuck in the road in the course of the night?"

"They did."

"Travis—I mean—Trip, look upon the prisoner. Was he one of those two passengers?"

"I cannot undertake to say that he was."

"You know, a simple yes or no will do. None of that hudduby-bubleby talk is needed."

"Sorry."

"Does the prisoner resemble either of the two passengers?"

"Both were so wrapped up, and the night was so dark, and we were all so stoned....er, uh, I mean, we kept to ourselves..."

"Thank you."

"...that I cannot undertake to say...er, uh, I can't really say."

"Trip, look again at the prisoner. Supposing him as wrapped up as those three passengers were, is there anything in his bulk and stature to render it unlikely that he was one of them?"

"Now look who's talkin' all hudduby-bubleby..."

"Just answer the question."

"No."

"You will not swear, Trip Templeton, that he was not one of them?"

"No."

"So at least you say he *may* have been one of them?"

"Yes. Except that I remember them all to have been—like myself—timorous of highway bandits, and the prisoner has not a timorous air."

"Trip, could you please talk so that even dumb ole' Cletus Clemmons there can understand it?"

"We were all afraid of highway bandits, and though the 'prisoner' looks like a puss, he didn't seem to be actin' like one at the time."

The crowd gasped.

"Have you ever seen someone faking like they t'weren't a puss, Trip?"

"I certainly have seen that."

"Trip, look once more at the prisoner. Have you seen him, to your certain knowledge, before?"

"I have."

"When?"

"I was returning from Coon Spit a few days afterward, and, at Rabbit Grove, the prisoner came on board Hoss's absurdly humongous truck with the big stupid tires, and went the rest of the way to Grouse Gulch with us."

"At what hour did he get up in the truck?"

"At a little after 8pm."

"In the dead of early evening, then. Was he the only passenger to climb aboard at that untimely hour?"

"Well, I wouldn't 'xactly say it was an untimely hour..."

"Just answer the question, Trip!"

"Ok! Yes! Yes, he happened to be the only one. Sheesh."

"Never mind about 'happening,' Trip. He was the only passenger who came on board in the dead of 8pm."

"Er, uh, yep. Yep he was."

"Were you travelling alone, Trip, or with any companion?"

"With two companions. A gentleman and a lady. They are here."

Several scoffs from the audience at the 'gentleman

and lady' label were heard.

"They are here!" mocked The General. "Had you any conversations with the prisoner?"

"Hardly any. The weather was stormy, it was colder 'n a witch's balls, and the road was long and rough..."

Beau Johnston called out, "Just the way your mama like's it, Trip!"

Several in the audience guffawed.

Trip was not amused.

"Bunnie Runyon! Aka, Bunnie Mancrizie!"

The young lady, to whom all eyes had been turned before, and were now turned again, stood up where she had sat. Her father rose with her, and she smacked him back down, pissed at his trying to share, or possibly steal, her limelight.

"Miss Mancrizie, look upon the prisoner."

"Is that *all* you want me to do?"

"Just look at him. That's *all* I'm asking you to do. Sheesh."

Bunnie frowned.

To be confronted with such pity, and such earnest youth and beauty, was far more trying to the accused than to be confronted with all the crowd. Standing, as it were, apart with her on the edge of his grave, not all the staring curiosity that looked on, could, for the moment, nerve him to remain quite still. His hurried right hand in his pocket was taken out momentarily, not from embarrassment, but so he could parcel out some of the herb in front of him: he rolled one and lit it, and his efforts to control his steady breathing shook her lips from which the color rushed from her heart. The buzz of the horseflies was loud again.

"Miss Mancrizie, your father is Paul Runyon, is that correct?"

"Unfortunately, yes."

"And your mother—your step-mother, that is—is Emelda Mancrizie-Priss, is that correct?"

"My foster mother more like it. She and my father

were never legally married."

"Who's ever were?" the crowd chuckled at this. "But whatever. Have you ever seen the prisoner before?"

"Yes, sir."

"Where?"

"On board Hoss's big stupid truck with the big stupid tires Trip just referred to. At the same occasion as him."

"You are the young 'lady'..."

Scoffs from the crowd.

"...just now referred to?"

"Oh! Most unhappily I am."

"I should say so," The General said under his breath.

"*What*?" Bunnie asked.

"Nothing.

"Bastard!"

"What?" John the Bastard inquired.

"Not you, Shithead! Go back to your daydreamin'!"

The plaintive tone of her uncompassion merged into the less colorful voice of 'judge' Donny Ray Judge, as he said something fiercely: "Answer the questions put to you, and make no other remarks, Bee-otch."

Thusly chastised, Bunnie shrunk slightly in stature.

Smiling, The General continued: "Miss Mancrizie, had you any conversation with the prisoner on that passage from Rabbit Grove to Grouse Gulch having to do possibly with the Discovery Channel?"

"Yes, sir."

"Tell us."

"When we stopped for gas he said he liked the Discovery Channel. I said I thought it was boring and only dick-heads would watch something like that. He said he guessed that made him a dick-head then, and I said, yeah, I guess so."

In the midst of this profound silliness, The General asked, "Can you describe what happened when you all first picked him up?"

"Who?"

"The prisoner. That *is* who we were talking about, isn't it?"

"Yeah, but 'prisoner'? Isn't that a bit harsh?"

"Just tell us, Bunnie."

"Well, when the *'prisoner'* first came on board, he noticed that my father," she turned her knifing eyes of hatred toward him as he lovingly stood beside her, "was much fatigued and in a weak state of health. I thought if he so much as farted he might break in two..." Several chuckles from the crowd. "...I was afraid he might croak just taking him out of the truck once we got to Grouse Gulch, so I rolled him onto the floor of the truck so as not to mess up the upholstery if he did. The *'prisoner'* was so good as to beg my permission to advise me how I could make the ride more comfortable for my father on the floor, maybe a pillow, or maybe a nasty old oily blanket Hoss might 'a had in back, or something better than I had done. Apparently, I had not known how to make him very comfortable, nor did I give a shit in all honesty—so the prisoner did it for me (only he wasn't 'the prisoner' at that time). He expressed great gentleness and kindness for my father's state, and I'm sure my father is alive today because of it. As I said, I could not have given a shit. That was the manner of my beginning to speak with the so-called *'prisoner.'*

"Let me interrupt you for a moment. Had he come on board alone?"

"No."

"How many were with him?"

"Two other dick-heads from Coon Spit."

"Had any books been handed about among them, similar to this Sam Walton autobiography?"

"Some papers had been handed about among them, but I am quite sure they weren't from books!"

Many chuckles from the crowd.

The General held up some rolling papers. "Like

these?"

"Possibly, but indeed I don't know, although they stood whispering very near to me: because they stood at the top rung of the ladder to get up in the big stupid truck with the big stupid tires, and they spoke very low, and I did not hear what they said, and saw only that they looked at the papers."

"Now to the prisoner's conversation, Miss Mancrizie."

"The 'prisoner' was as open in his confidence with me—which arose out of my fake helplessness with my father—as he was kind, and good, and useful to my father. I hope," bursting into tears, "I may not repay him by doing him harm to-day."

"Quit it with the water-works, Bunnie. You ain't foolin' no one," barked Donny Ray.

She immediately stopped.

Buzzing from the horseflies.

"Miss Mancrizie," The General continued, "if the prisoner does not perfectly understand that you give the evidence which it is your duty to give—which you must give—and which you cannot escape from giving—with great unwillingness, he is the only person present in that condition. So please, go on. And without the theatrics this time."

"He told me that he was traveling on 'business' of a delicate and difficult nature, which might get people into trouble, and that he was therefore travelling under the assumed name, 'Jack the Rubber.' He said that this 'business' had, within a few days, taken him to Coon Spit, and might, at intervals, take him backwards and forwards between Coon Spit and Grouse Gulch for a long time to come."

"Did he say anything about the war in Iraq, Miss Mancrizie? Be particular."

"He tried to explain to me how that 'quarrel' had arisen, and he said that, so far as he could judge, it was a wrong and foolish one on America's part. He added, in a jesting way, that perhaps George W. might gain almost as great a name in history as George the First, which of course ain't sayin' much, since he was kind of a wimp from what I understand. But there was no harm in his way of saying this: it was said laughingly, and to beguile the time..."

"Ahp! So Cletus can understand..."

She shot a look at Cletus. "It means to pass the time, *ray*-tard! Get an education!"

Cletus, and many others, were taken aback at the virulence of her tone. Any strongly marked expression of face on the part of a chief actor in a scene of great interest to whom many eyes are directed, will be unconsciously imitated by the spectators. Her highly cleavaged bosom was painfully anxious and intent as she gave this evidence, and, in the pauses when she stopped for Donny Ray to spit chew into his cup and put more in his mouth, watched its effect upon the counsel for and against. Among the lookers-on there was the same expression in all quarters of the court; mouths agape, tiny spittle of drool on lips, unable and unwilling to peel eyes away, when 'judge' Donny Ray Judge looked up from his chaw to glare at her for that tremendous heresy about George W.

The General scratched his ass and signified to Donny Ray that he deemed it necessary as a matter of precaution and form, to call the young 'lady's' father, Doctor Runyon—who approached the bar accordingly.

"Dr. Runyon, look at the prisoner. Have you ever seen him before?"

"Once, when he was called to my house in Grouse Gulch. Some three years or three-years-and-a-half ago."

"Three-and-a-half years ago would've been sufficient thank you, Doctor."

"Whatever. Kids today have no respect for the langua..."

"Can you identity him as your fellow passenger on board Hoss's absurdly humoungous truck with the big stupid tires, or speak to his conversation with your daughter?"

"Sir, I can do neither."

"Is there any particular and special reason for you being unable to do either?"

Donny Ray looked up and spat. "A simple 'Why not?' would have been good enough Lee."

Cletus nodded.

The General shot Donny Ray a dirty look.

Doctor Runyon answered, in a low voice, "Because..."

"Has it been your misfortune to undergo a long imprisonment, without trial, or even accusation, in your native county, Dr. Runyon?"

He answered, in a tone that went to every heart, "A long imprisonment."

"Were you newly released on the occasion in question?"

"They tell me so."

"Have you no remembrance of the occasion?"

"None. My mind has been a blank from some time—I cannot even say how long. I had my 'burlesque' act with my wife at the same time I was earning my degree in the veterinary arts, then I worked at the car parts plant, then I was put in prison, then I found myself living in Grouse Gulch with my dear daughter here. It also seemed she had become familiar to me at one point long ago..."

"Yeah," Bunnie said quietly, "in the biblical sense..."

No one in the crowd even flinched.

"...and now, when a gracious God restored my faculties, I am quite unable even to say how she had become so familiar..."

"It's called 'denial'," barked Bunnie.

"...I have no remembrance of the process."

"Wish I didn't neither, shit-head!" she barked a little louder.

The General sat down, and father and daughter sat back down together, though icily.

A singular circumstance then arose in the case. The object in hand being to show that the prisoner hitched a ride in Hoss' big stupid truck with the big stupid tires that night in November five years ago, and got out of the truck at some point, and traveled back some dozen miles or so, to Mrs. Garrison's Bookbarn, and there he bought the Sam Walton autobiography. A witness was called to identify him as having been at the precise time required, pouring nasty day-old coffee at a 7-11 in that same town as Mrs. Garrison's Bookbarn, waiting for another person with perhaps a similarly iron-clad stomach.

The 'prisoner's council,' one effete Mr. Stryker (apply whichever definition you want, since all apply) was cross-examining this witness with no result, except that he had never seen the prisoner on any other occasion, when the wigged gentleman who had all this time had his hands in his pockets looking at the ceiling, wrote a word or two on a napkin, crumbled it up, and tossed it to him. Opening this napkin in the next pause, the counsel looked with great attention and curiosity at the prisoner.

"You say again you are quite sure it *was* the prisoner?"

The witness was quite sure.

"Did you ever see anybody else that looked just like him?"

Not so like (the witness said) as that he could be mistaken.

"Take a good look at that man, my drunken friend over there—"

"Who? Cletus?"

"No, you idiot, my partner there, with his hands in his pockets," pointing to him who had tossed the paper over, "and then look at the prisoner. What do you say 'bout that?"

"*What?*"

"What do you say about that? Are they very like each other?"

"You mean, do they like each other?"

"Are they alike, you idiot! Alike!"

Allowing for my 'drunken friend's' appearance being careless and slovenly if not debauched, which he most certainly was, they were sufficiently like each other to surprise, not only the witness, but everybody present, when they were thus brought into comparison.

Donny Ray asked the man to lay aside his wig, and he gave no gracious consent. However, the likeness was remarkable anyway. Donny Ray inquired of Roscoe Stryker (the 'prisoner's' 'counsel'), whether they were next going to try Sydney 'Bubba' Cotton (the name of his drunken friend) for disloyalty? But, Mr. Stryker replied to Donny Ray, no; but he would ask the witness to tell him whether what happened once, might happen twice; whether he would have been so confident if he had seen this illustration of his rashness sooner, whether he would be so confident, having seen it; and more. The upshot of which was, to smash this witness like a tub of Country Crock margarine, and shiver his part of the case to wet useless firewood.

Mr. Kracker had by this time taken quite a lunch of chew in his following of the evidence. He had now to attend while Mr. Stryker fitted the 'prisoner's' case on the jury like a compact pair of hip-waiters; showing them how the loyalist—Bastard—was a hired spy and traitor, and unblushing trafficker of drugs and fornication, and one of the greatest scoundrels upon earth since accursed Judas—which he certainly did look rather like. How the virtuous oil-changer, Wade Franklin, was his friend and maybe his 'partner', and was worthy to be; how the watchful eyes of those forgers and counterfeiters who swore like sailors had rested on the 'prisoner' as a victim, because of some family affairs in Coon Spit, he being of a village near Rabbit Grove extraction, did require his making those passages between Coon Spit and Grouse Gulch by way of the Buckskin Trail—though what those affairs were, a consideration for others who were near and dear to him, forbad him, even for his life, to disclose. How the evidence that came from the warped and wretched young 'lady,' whose anguished cleavage shown while giving it they had most certainly witnessed, came to nothing, involving the mere little innocent gallantries and politeness likely to pass between any two young gentlemen and young 'lady' so thrown together—with the exception of that reference to George W., which was altogether too extravagant and impossible to be regarded in any other light than as a monstrous joke. How it would be a weakness in the combined Chambers of Commerce and Small Businessman's (and women's) Associations to break down in this attempt to practice for popularity on the lowest antipathies and fears, and therefore The General had made the most of it; how, nevertheless, it rested upon nothing, save that vile and infamous character of evidence too often disfiguring such cases, and of which the State of Kentucky courtrooms were full. But, there Donny Ray interposed (with as grave a face as if it had not been true), saying that he could not sit upon that bar and suffer those allusions.

Roscoe Stryker, counsel for the defense, then called his few witnesses, and Mr. Kracker sat by while The General turned the whole pair of 'hip-waiters' Stryker had fitted for the 'jury' inside out; showing how Bastard and Franklin were even a hundred times worse than he had thought them, and the prisoner a hundred times better. Lastly, came Donny Ray himself, turning the 'hip-waiters,' now inside out, now outside in, but on the whole decidedly trimming and shaping them into grave-clothes for the prisoner.

And now, the 'jury' turned to consider, and the horseflies swarmed again.

Sydney 'Bubba' Cotton, who had so long sat with hands in pockets looking at the ceiling, changed neither his place nor his attitude, even in this excitement. While his drunken friend, Mr. Stryker, massing his smoking papers before him, whispered with those who sat near, and from time to time glanced anxiously at the 'jury'; while all the spectators moved more or less, and grouped themselves anew; while even Donny Ray himself arose from his seat, and slowly paced up and down the bar, not unattended by a suspicion in the minds of the audience that his state was feverish; this one man sat leaning back, with a stain-filled wife-beater half-torn off him, strange wig untidy on his head, his hands in his pockets, and his eyes on the ceiling as they had been all day. Something especially reckless in his demeanor, not only gave him a disreputable look (which mattered not one shit in this crowd), but so diminished the strong resemblance he undoubtedly bore to the prisoner (which his momentary earnestness, when they were compared together, had strengthened), that many of the lookers-on, taking note of him now, said to one another they would have thought the two were twins. Mr. Kracker made the observation to his next neighbor, and added, "I'd hold down a fifth of Jack that he don't get no law-work to do. Don't look like the sort of one to get any, do he?"

Yet, this Bubba Cotton took in more of the details of the scene than he appeared to take in; for now, when Miss Mancrizie's fist dropped sharply upon her father's crotch, he was the first to see it, as everyone else was also first to hear his howl of agony, and to say audibly: "Hector! Look at that young 'lady'! Take her out and throw her into the parking lot! And see to it that she falls!"

There was much commiseration as her breasts, as well as the rest of her, were removed; and much sympathy for her father, who was now icing his marbles with an icepack Flo had grabbed from the bar. It had evidently been a great distress to him, to have his bag tagged like that. He had shown strong internal agitation when he was questioned, and that pondering or brooding look which made him old, had been upon him, like a heavy cloud, ever since. As he passed out, the 'jury', who had turned their backs and paused a moment, spoke through Jim-Bob Jones, a factory foreman.

They were all agreed that they wished to retire from their jobs, but if the new Walmart went up, they'd probably all lose their jobs and never be able to. Donny Ray (perhaps with George W. on his mind) showed no surprise that they were all agreed, but signified his pleasure that they should retire with watches of gold and bottles of Wild Turkey, and wished he could retire himself with them. Then the 'jury' formed a tight circle in the front of the room to decide the fate of the 'prisoner.'

The trial had lasted all day because of the heavy drinking and pot smoking, and the lamps above the pool tables were now being turned on. It was rumored that the 'jury' would be out for a long while—deliberatin' that is. The spectators continued to smoke, chew and stuff beer pretzels down their gullets, and the prisoner withdrew to the back of the room and sat down.

Trip Templeton, who had gone out when the young 'lady' had been thrown out, now reappeared, and beckoned to Jerry: who, in the slackened interest, could easily get near him.

"Jerry, if you wish to take something to eat, you can, just don't let anyone catch you. And don't drink so much that you pass out before the jury decides, because I want you to take the verdict back to the club. You have the quickest four-wheeler I know, and will get to Tall Tales long before I do."

Jerry had just enough forehead to knuckle, and he knuckled it in acknowledgement of this communication and a ten-spot from Trip. Bubba Cotton came up at the moment, and touched Trip on the arm.

"How is the young 'lady'?"

"She is greatly distressed."

"You mean she's bummed out?"

"Precisely. But her father is comforting himself

with an ice-pack on his ancient rocks, and she feels better for being out of the bowling alley."

"I'll tell the prisoner that. He'll get a kick out of it. But it won't do for a 'respectable' strip club owner like you to be seen speaking to him publicly, you know."

"I know. I suck. But we all cain't be 'respectable' lawyers like you now, can we Bubba?" Trip reddened as if he were conscious of having debated the point in his mind, and Mr. Cotton made his way to the bar. The way out of the basement lay in that direction, and Jerry followed him, all eyes, ears, and mouth dripping with chew.

"Bubba Darnet!"

The prisoner came forward directly.

Bubba Cotton addressed him: "You will naturally be anxious to hear of the witness with the bodacious ta-ta's, Bunnie Mancrizie. She is doing well, and is probably picking herself up off the blacktop as we speak. You have seen the worst of her agitation."

"I am deeply sorry she had to come here today. Could you tell her so for me, with my fervent acknowledgments?"

"I have no idea what you just say'd, ya big woman—but if it's some strange code about how you're going to get into her pants later, then more power to ya." Mr. Cotton's manner was so careless as to be almost insolent. He stood, half-turned from the prisoner, lounging with his elbow against the bar. "Anyway, if I do pass that on," said Bubba Cotton, still only half-turned towards him, "what do you expect will happen, Darnet?"

"The worst."

"It's the wisest thing to expect, you big puss, and the likeliest." Then he turned toward the huddled 'jury'. "What do you expect of that?"

"The worst."

"Ah, that is the wisest thing, and the likeliest," he repeated. "And that there jury takin' so long is pro'ly in your favor."

Loitering of non-members after 'court' not being allowed, Jerry heard no more: but left them and slinked off to the bar upstairs—as he walked away, he thought the two Bubbas so like each other in feature, so unlike each other in manner—standing side by side, both reflected in the Coors Light mirror above them.

An hour and a half limped heavily away in the thief-and-rascal crowded passages below, even though assisted off with many mutton-chops downing gallons of Sam Adams and Pete's Wicked Ale. A commotion near the 'jury' was not enough to wake the messenger from his bourbon induced coma, especially since his dumb ass was upstairs in the bowling alley bar.

"Jerry! Jerry!" Trip was already calling up the stairs.

"I'm here! I had to fight my way back down again. But here I am."

Trip handed him a paper through the throng leaving the basement. "Quick! Have you got it?"

"Yes, sir!"

Hastily written on a cocktail napkin was the word, 'Acquitted.'

"Wuz' 'at mean?"

"Not guilty, you boob!"

"Oh. By the way, if you had sent the message, 'Recalled by Honda,' again," muttered Jerry, as he turned, "I should have known what you meant this time."

He had no opportunity of saying, or so much as thinking, anything else, until he was clear of the Rebel Yell and the old Rebel; for, the crowd came pouring out with a vehemence that nearly took him off his legs, and a loud buzz swept into the street as twenty-five Harley Davidson's dispersed in search of other no-good rousings for the rabblement.

4

I'll Drink to That!

From the dimly lighted basement of the bowling alley, the last sediment of the human stew that had been boiling there all day was straining off when Doctor Runyon, his daughter Bunnie Runyon-Mancrizie, Travis 'Trip' Templeton, Sydney 'Bubba' Cotton and Roscoe Stryker, stood around Mr. Chuck 'Bubba' Darnet—just released—congratulating him in the parking lot on his escape from banishment from the bowling leagues forever.

It would have been difficult by a far brighter light, in fact even the sun probably wouldn't have begun to put a dent in it, to recognize in Doctor Runyon, 'the shoemaker of LaGrange Federal Penitentiary in Bluff City,' an intellectual face and an upright of bearing. Yet, no one could have looked at him twice, without looking again: even though the opportunity of observation had not extended to the mournful cadence of his low gravely whiskey-smoked voice, and to the abstraction that overclouded him fitfully, without any apparent reason. While one external cause, and that a reference to his long lingering agony—as his daughter had so inflicted upon him at the 'trial'—it was also in 'its' nature to arise without prompting, at the most inopportune of times and places, and without the aid of modern *Vee*-ay-gra or *Cee*-ay-lice tableture. Not so strangely, this drew a gloom over him, incomprehensible to those half his age, finding themselves plunging headlong (no pun intended) into the depths of the blue and yellow pill; those unacquainted with his story and his massive virility were as dark to him as the shadow of the actual Bay Steel Bank thrown upon him by a summer sun, when the substance actually was thirty-three miles away.

Only his daughter had the power of charming this black brooding from his mind, and that is what made him such a sick, twisted old man. She was the golden thread that tied him to a Past of misery, and to a Present of misery, as evidenced by her actions toward the end of that 'trial.' And the sound of her voice, the light of her face, the touch of her hand, had a strong beneficial influence with him almost always (in the most sick and twisted of ways, of what origin he truly knew not, though he began to have a sneaking suspicion). But not *absolutely* always, for she could recall some occasions on which her powers had failed and he had become enraged; but they were few and slight, and she believed the whole sick affair to be long over. *It goddamned better well be over!* she cursed in her mind. While, *I wonder if I ever acted in an inappropriate manner toward my daughter...?* lingered in his.

Bubba Darnet had kissed her hand fervently and gratefully, which she thought was weird and kinda gay-like. Then he turned to Mr. Stryker, whom he also warmly thanked. *Gay again*, she thought.

Mr. Stryker, a man of little more than thirty, but looking twenty years older than he was; stout, loud, red-faced from drink, buff and free from any drawback of delicacy (meaning he was proud of his gayness), had a pushy way of shouldering himself (morally and physically) into companies and conversations. That argued well for his shouldering his way up in life. In other words, he was a first-class ass-kisser.

He still had his toupee on, and he said, squaring himself at Bubba Darnet to that degree that he squeezed Trip Templeton clean out of the group: "I am glad to have brought you off with honor, Bubba....er, uh, I mean, I am glad to have gotten you out of trouble, son."

"I have an obligation to lay you for life," Bubba answered. "Er, um, I mean, you have laid me under an obligation to you for life...Dammit! That doesn't sound much better... Let me see—I am in your debt for life—that's better!—in two senses," he said, taking Stryker's hand.

Roscoe shook it immediately. "I have done my best for you, Bubba Darnet; and my best is as good as another man's, I believe....God, this conversation sounds ga..."

"You two sound fruitier than a stick of Fruit Stripe gum." Trip had said it; perhaps not quite disinterestedly, but with the interested object of squeezing himself back into the conversation again, which doesn't sound too good either.

"You think so?" said Mr. Stryker. "Well, you ought to know. You are a man of 'business' too."

"What's that supposed to mean?" quoth Templeton, who Stryker had now shouldered back into the group, just as he had previously shouldered him out of it—"Anyway, as such I will appeal to Dr. Runyon..."

"Oh, no! You three fairies leave me out of this." said Runyon, backing away from the group with his front facing forward.

Trip continued: "I hate to break up this little 'conference' and suggest we all go home, but Miss Bunnie looks ill, and Bubba Darnet here has had a terrible day, and the rest of us are worn out."

"Speak for yourself, Templeton," said Stryker. "I have a night's work to do yet."

"Jeezus Stryker!" Runyon let out. "Did we all *really* need to hear that?"

Stryker shot him 'fuck you' glance.

"I *will* speak for myself, ya jackass!" Trip answered Stryker. "And for Bubba and for Bunnie, and—oh, Bunnie, do you think I can speak for us all?" He asked her the question pointedly, and with a glance at her father. Her father's face had become frozen, as it were, in a bi-curious look at Darnet: an intent look, deepening into a frown of dislike and distrust, not even unmixed with fear. With this strange expression on him his thoughts had wandered away.

"*My* father," said Bunnie with a smirk, recognizing his gaze toward Darnet, and what it meant. She had softly put a hand on his shoulder. He immediately shook it off.

"Oh, bugger it all!" spouted Runyon. "I'm going home and leaving you poofs to yourselves!"

The friends of the acquitted prisoner had dispersed shortly after, under the impression—which he himself had originated—that he would not be 'released' that night. Which was of course the case, since everyone but Trip had left and Trip sure as hell wasn't going to hook up with him.

The lights were nearly extinguished in the bowling alley, the iron bars were being closed over the windows with a jar and a rattle, and the dismal place was being deserted until to-morrow morning's *Early-Bird Senior's Bowl* re-peopled it.

Bunnie and her father had called a cab, Mr. Stryker had left to shoulder his way back to the robbing-room, er, uh, the basement of the Rebel Yell, to find his companions and head over to the Cock-N-Bull. Another person, who had not joined the group, or interchanged a word with any one of them, but who had been leaning against a burned-out parking lot lightpost where the lot was darkest, had silently strolled over and looked on until the cab had drove away. He now stepped up to where Trip and Darnet stood upon the pavement.

"So, Trip! Men of 'business.' May I speak to Bubba Darnet now?"

"Cut that shit out for chrissakes," chirped Darnet, in a less than menacing tone, since he was quite incapable of producing one.

Nobody had made any acknowledgement of Mr. Sydney 'Bubba' Cotton's part in the day's proceedings; nobody had known of it. Now, stepping out of the shadows, he was disrobed save for a G-String and a grease-stained wife-beater, and was none the better for it in appearance.

"For chrissakes!" Trip intoned, turning away. "Put some fuckin' clothes on, Cotton! Whatever frickin' joke your pullin's been over for awhile now!"

"Don't get so testy-s on me now," replied Cotton, his canoe-shaped banana-hammock flapping his circus-freakishly large man-junk freely in the wind. "If you knew what a conflict goes on in the 'business' mind, when the 'business' mind is divided between good-natured impulse and 'business' appearances, you would be amused Mr. Darnet."

"I said the joke's over, Cotton. Now put some goddamned britches on!" barked Trip, reddening with fury.

"I know, I know," rejoined Cotton carelessly. "Don't be nettled, Trip. You are as good as another, I have no doubt: better I day say."

"Well, if I am, which I'm not, *you're* never going to find out," thrice-barked Trip.

"Indeed, sir." Cotton turned and pursued Darnet. "How about you?"

"That's not funny, Cotton," Darnet responded. "I ain't gay neither, and you know it."

"I ain't either," responded Cotton.

"Excuse me!" said Trip, a fatherly instinct for the boy coming over him. "As very much your elder, Cotton, I really don't see that you have any so-called 'business' being here with us just now. So why don't you just go home? Or go drink, or go find somebody else to mess with. We're tired of your shit."

"'Business'! Unlike you, Trip, *I* have no 'business'."

"Well, it's a pity you don't."

"I think so too," said Cotton, finally pulling on some britches.

"If you had," pursued Trip, "perhaps you would attend to it."

"Oh! Lord Jesus, no!—I shouldn't," said Cotton.

"Then whose fault is it if 'business' is bad for you? Nobody's but your own. What's the matter, Cotton? The legal profession dragging you down? You used to be such a hot-shit lawyer in this county. What happened?—You know what? Don't tell me. I don't want to know, nor do I care. You were an idiot and a loser in high school with my son, and now—well, apparently nothing's changed." Trip turned to Darnet, "Bubba, good-night and God bless. I hope you have been this day preserved for a prosperous and happy life. Peace be with you." Trip made the vulcan 'V' in front of Darnet, then made the sign of the cross in front of Cotton, and flipped him off. "And to you, whatever..."

Perhaps a little angry with himself, as well as with the lawyer, Trip bustled himself into his piece of shit car and was carried off to Tall Tales. Cotton, who smelled of box wine, and did not appear to be quite sober, laughed and turned to Darnet.

"This is a strange chance that throws you and me together! This must be a strange night for you, standing alone with your look-alike in a bowling alley parking lot?"

"I kinda feel like I'm still down there being bullied for something I didn't do."

"That's understandable. It's not so long since you were pretty much thrown out of the bowling leagues for good."

"I'm not feeling so good, neither."

"That's because you haven't eaten for hours, boy! Why didn't you at least eat some beer pretzels or something while those dunderheads deliberated your fate? I did. Most everybody did."

"I had other things on my mind."

"Then let's go eat. I know a great dive near here. Great grill food and cheap beer. Is there nothing better?"

"Ok, as long as you ain't gonna strip naked and talk queer again."

"I promise." Cotton held up two fingers. "Scouts honor."

They went down Main Street and crossed to Walnut and Vine and entered the Skinned Hare Tavern.

Here, they were shown to a smoky dank back booth, while a moldy Patsy Cline tune warbled forth from an ancient box of juke. Bubba Darnet was soon recruiting his strength with a good plain dinner of meatloaf hash—the house special—and a bottle of Wild Turkey: while Bubba Cotton sat opposite him in the same booth, with his separate bottle of Jack Daniels before him, and his full half-insolent manner upon him.

"Do you feel, yet, that you are fully acquitted, Bubba?"

"I am confused as to where we are right now..." Darnet slurred his words heavily from drink. "You could kick me in the nuts and I pro'ly wouldn't feel a thing."

"That must be an immense satisfaction!" Cotton said bitterly, and filled up each of their glasses again: which were large ones. "As to me, the greatest desire I have is to forget that I belong to this world. It has no good in it for me—except whiskey like this. We are not much alike in that particular. Indeed, I begin to think we are not much alike in any particular, you and I."

Darnet was at a loss at how to answer, mostly because he hadn't understood a word Cotton was saying; with his face wobbling three inches above the table, and of the four Bubba Cotton's across from him; he wasn't sure which one to address. Finally, he answered none of them at all, but decided to puke on his own shoes instead.

"Now that your dinner has come full circle," said Cotton presently, "why don't I buy you some toast?" Which of course, brought on another fit of gagging, since the mere thought of such a soggily buttered and jellied fare made Darnet's stomach recoil with violence.

"Toast?" Darnet warbled, mopping his lips with his shirtsleeve. "What a disgusting thought right now!"

"What are you thinking about, Darnet?"

"What are you—my girlfriend?"

"It's on the tip of your tongue. I'll swear it's there."

"Fuck you, Cotton."

"Say it!"

"Fuck you!"

"Say it!"

"Ok! Bunnie Mancrizie! There! Are you happy?"

"Ah, Bunnie Mancrizie. I knew it!"

Looking his companion full in the face while he drank his Wild Turkey, Cotton flung his own shot glass over his shoulder against the wall, where it shattered in pieces. Then he stopped an old waitress with saggy boobs and ordered another.

"Yer gonna hafta pay for the one you broke, asshole!" she barked, and slammed a new one on the table. "Try an' keep this one in one piece, ya jackass!"

Cotton continued, unfazed, and ignoring the sagging horse: "Bunnie was mightily pleased to get your message when I gave it to her. Not that she showed she was pleased, but I supposed she was."

The allusion served as a timely reminder to Darnet that this disagreeable companion had, of his own free will, assisted him in his strait of the day. He turned the dialogue to that point, and thanked him for it.

"I neither want thanks nor merit for doing it," was the careless rejoiner. "In the first place, it was nothing; in the second place, I don't know why I did it. Darnet, let me ask you a question."

"Shoot."

"Do you think I particularly like you?"

"Goddamit Cotton!" returned the other, understandably disconcerted, "I told you e'nuff with the queer talk!"

"But ask yourself the question now. I mean do you think I like you in a friendshiply way—man to man—as if we were cohorts at work, or in a war together."

"Well, you *have* acted as if you do, but I don't think you do."

"*I* don't think *I* do!" exclaimed Cotton. "And that is why I called you a sis and a puss back there at the bowling alley."

"Check please!" Darnet called out, then turned to

his 'companion.' "I'm going to pay the check, and hope there's no ill-will 'tween us, even though you are a fuckin' asshole."

"Are you going to pay the whole bill?"

Darnet answered in the affirmative.

"Well, then: Stewardess!" Cotton called out to the melting wax-figure with the unfortunate droopy bosom and the even more unfortunate duty of waiting upon him, "Bring me another Fifth! And don't wake me 'til morning."

"Closing time's at two, Shitweed!" barked the monstrosity as she slammed down another bottle. "You can sleep it off in the parking lot if you want, ass-wipe, see if I care."

The bill being paid, and the tip being next to non-existent, Darnet rose, stumbled, and wished Cotton a good-night.

Without returning the wish, Cotton rose too, with something of a threat of defiance in his manner, and said, "A last word, Bubba Darnet: Do you think I am drunk?" Cotton wobbled so hard he nearly crashed through the table.

"I do think you have been drinking, Bubba Cotton."

"Think? You *know* I have been drinking."

"Since for some reason you're making me state the obvious, then yes, I know it." Darnet also heavily slurred his words and wobbled nearly just as hard, almost crashing foreheads with the man found opposite him.

"Then you shall likewise know why. I am a disappointment to my mother and father and my friends! I care for no man on earth, and no man on earth cares for me!"

"Then it sucks to be you!" said Darnet, poking a middle finger slurredly into the opposite man's chest, "you should have used your talents better."

"Maybe so, Bubba Darnet; maybe not. But don't turn your back on me if you find us walking down the same street. You don't know what it might come to."

"Are you threatening me?"

"Absolutely, puss!"

"Then fuck you and good night!"

"Pussy!" Cotton called after Darnet, for good measure. But when he was left alone, this strange being struck up his lighter, walked over to the Bud Light mirror on the wall, and surveyed himself minutely in it.

"Do you particularly like the man?" he muttered at his own image in a creepy *Silence of the Lambs* way. "Why should you particularly like a man who resembles you? There is nothing in you to like; you know that. Oh, you fuckin' shithead! What a change you have made in yourself! A good reason for taking to a man, that he shows you what you have fallen away from, and what you might have been. Change places with him, and would you have been looked at with those blue eyes and those huge knockers as he was, and commiserated by that agitated face and huge knockers as he was? Come on! Have it out in plain words! You hate the fellow!"

He resorted to his Fifth for consolation, drank it all in a few minutes, threw up on the floor next to Darnet's greasy pile, then fell asleep on his folded arms, his hair nastily straggling unsanitarily all over the table.

5

The Jackass

Those were drinking days and most men drank hard. So very miniscule is the improvement Time has brought about in the southern hills of Kentucky in such habits, that a moderate statement about the quantity of bourbon and moonshine which one man would swallow in the course of a night (without detriment to his reputation since everyone else drank just as much, or more), would seem, in those days, a ridiculous understatement.

The learned profession of being a lawyer was certainly not behind any blue-collar profession in its back-breaking propensities; neither was Mr. Stryker—already fast shouldering his way to a large and lucrative practice—behind his compeers in this particular, any more than those of the drier side of the legal drinking age were any drier than those above it.

A favorite at the old Rebel Courthouse, Mr. Stryker had begun cautiously to hew away the lower staves of the ladder on which he mounted. The florid countenance of Mr. Stryker might be daily seen, bursting from the bed of bad combovers, like a great withering sunflower pushing its way at the sun from among a rank gardenfull of horrid companions.

It had once been noted at the Cock-N-Bull that while Mr. Stryker was a glib man, and unscrupulous, and a Helen Reddy fan, and a bold admirer of Cher; he had not the faculty of extracting the essence from a heap of statements, which is among the most striking and necessary of an everyday advocate's accomplishments. But a remarkable improvement came upon him as to this. The more business he got, the greater his power seemed to grow of getting at its pith and marrow; and however late at night he sat carousing with Sydney 'Bubba' Cotton, he always had his points at his fingers' ends in the morning, as well as having those points painted and carefully manicured.

Bubba Cotton, idlest and most unpromising of men, was Stryker's great ally. The two drank together, and between all the Jim Beam and the Captain Morgan, they might have safely floated the Titanic all the way to New York. Stryker never had a case anywhere where Cotton wasn't right there, hands in pockets and staring at the ceiling, as he downed eleven or twelve cans of Miller Genuine Draft before Stryker could even grab hold of one. They went to the same clubs, and there they prolonged their usual orgies late into the night, and Cotton was rumored to be seen with broads during the day, going home stealthily and unsteadily to his lodgings, like a cat that'd been pissed on. At last, it began to get about, among such as were interested in the matter, that although Bubba Cotton would never be an all-out gigilo, he was an amazingly good bitch, and he rendered suit and service to Stryker in that humble capacity on occasion.

Cotton suddenly awoke out back of the Skinned Hare to the sounds of desperate scratches and eager searching.

"*Wha...?*"

Cotton rolled over, a blazing hangover tearing through his skull, the full brightness of the sun nearly killing him. A few dull attempts to get back to sleep were dexterously combated by the stirring of refuse continually for five minutes by a vagrant in search of aluminum cans; for Cotton himself was not *next* to the dumpster out back the Skinned Hare, but was, in fact, *inside* it.

Cotton looked at the vagrant. "What time is it?"

"About ten, I guess," the toothless scrounger informed him.

Cotton got up, tossed a greasy ball-cap on his head that had not previously been in his possession, and crawled out of the dumpster. He walked an un-steady line (having no idea where he, nor his car, were) all the way down to the old Rebel, where he found Stryker in his quaint house across the street, which doubled as his office (for tax purposes).

Stryker's receptionist, who never assisted at these conferences but functioned more in the capacity of 'lookout,' had gone home, and Stryker himself opened the door. Stryker was wearing pink bunny-rabbit slip-pers and a lose-fitting gown, a feather boa wrapped about his neck (which, most of the time, he dared not wear in public).

Stryker had that rather wild, strained, seared marking about the eyes, which might be observed in all sirrosified livers of his class, all the way from the portrait of Jefferson Davis on his wall downward; and which can be traced—under various disguises of art on the walls of others with whom the spectre of fermentated beverages haunts on a regular basis—through the portraits of every Drinking Age.

"You are a little late, mammory," chided Stryker, adding quickly, "and what is that god-awful *smell*."

"I'm here about the usual time, I'd say; it may be a quarter of an hour later. And none of your goddamned business."

They went into a dingy room in the back lined with books and littered with papers, where a fire also blazed beneath a small working still. A kettle steamed upon a nearby wood-burning stove for the humidifica-tion of the room—and the careful preservation of the beautification of Stryker's skin—, and in the midst of the wreck of papers, a table shone, with plenty of whiskey bottles upon it—and brandy— and rum—and cigars—and even a few tightly rolled fattys.

"You have had your bottle, or two, or nine, by now I perceive, Bubba Cotton?"

"You have no idea...but I too have no idea. I had been dining last night with the day's client; or seeing him dine, or puking, or whatever...it's all running together through my splitting head..."

"That was a rare point, Bubba, you made yester-day about the identification and the look-alikes. How did you come up with it? When did it strike you?"

"Well, I thought Bubba Darnet was a rather hand-some fellow, and thought you should have the same sort of fellow, if you had any luck..."

Mr. Stryker laughed till he shook his precocious paunch. "You and your luck, Bubba! Get to work, get to work! And for chrissakes, why are you wearing a dress? Do you want to get yourself killed?"

Sullenly enough, the jackass loosened his dress to the floor (which he had found in the dumpster and drawn up upon himself accidentally), and went into an adjoining room, slipped on some slippers, got a wash-rag, ran it under cold water, folded it on his head in a manner hideous to behold, came back into the room, and sat down at the table. "Now I am ready."

"Not much boiling to be done to-night," said Stryker gaily, stirring the contents of the still.

"How much?"

"Only two sets of documents."

"Give me the worst first."

"Here they are Bubba. Fire away!"

The fat man, Stryker, then composed himself on his back on the sofa to one side of the drinking-table, while the jackass, Cotton, sat at his roll-paper be-strewn table proper, on the other side of it at least, with the bottles and mason jars ready at his hand. Both resorted to the drinking-table without stint, but each in a different way; the fat man for the most part reclining with his hands in his waistband, looking at the fire beneath the still, or occasionally flirting with some lighter port; the jackass, with knitted brows and intent face, so deep in his task that his eyes did not even follow the hand he reached out for his glass—which often groped about, for a minute or more, before it found the glass for his lips—worked away on the documents before him. Two or three times, the matter of drinking so heavily while working became so knotty, that the jackass found it imperative to throw the contents of his stomach forth, finding it then equally as imperative to get up, and steep some towels in the spew. From these pilgrimages to the jug and then the bathroom, he returned such expressions of wince and wallow as no words can describe; which were made all the more ludicrous when with a gravel of voice, and mason jar of 'shine in his hand, he cocked his head back and declared, "Smoooooooooth!"

At length the jackass had got together a Hungry Man TV dinner for the fat man, and proceeded to offer it to him. The fat man took it with care and caution, made his selections on it, and his remarks upon it, namely, "I can't believe I'm going to eat this shit after watching you blow all over my floor!" and then the jackass began to make himself a TV dinner as well. After the day's legal documents and distillations were fully discussed, the fat man put his hand in his waistband again, and lay down on the couch to 'meditate,' to which the jackass slapped the fat man's hands away from his waistband and remarked, "Not in my presence your not, you fat freak!"

The jackass then invigorated himself with a bumper for his throttle—in other words, a fresh application of 'shine down his gullet—and applied himself to micro-waving more Hungry Man TV dinners for the each of them; which was administered to the fat man in the same manner, and was not disposed of—neither in the trash can under the sink, nor in the toilet—until the clocks struck three in the afternoon.

"Now that we're done, Bubba, fill a tumbler full of 'punch'."

The jackass removed the towels from the floor—which had begun to steam with reek; shook himself, yawned, shivered, and complied.

"You were very sound, Bubba, in the matter of those witnesses yesterday. Every question told."

"I always am sound; am I not?" ordered Cotton

slurredly, in the manner of Yoda.

"I don't gainsay it. What has roughened your temper? Put some 'punch' down your gullet and smooth it again!"

With a deprecatory grunt, and being pissed that Stryker was making fun of his slurred and ridiculous speech, the jackass again complied.

"The old Bubba of the shrew Agnes Mader-Cotton," chided Stryker, nodding his head as he reviewed Cotton aloud in the present and the past, "The old seesaw Bubba! Up one minute and down the next; now in spirits and then totally sober!"

"Ah!" returned the other, sighing: "Yes! The same Bubba, with the same luck. Even then, back then in school when I still lived with my mother, I did exercises for the other boys, and seldom did my own."

"And why not? Hell, I do that even today!"

"And God knows why. But that is your way, I suppose. Not mine."

Bubba sat with his hands in his pockets and his legs stretched out before him, looking at the fire.

"Cotton," said his friend, squaring himself at him with a bullying air, as if the fire-grate beneath the still had been the furnace in which sustained endeavor was forged, and the one delicate thing to be done for the old Bubba Cotton of the shrew Agnes Mader-Cotton was to shoulder him into it, "your way is, and always was, a lame way. You summon no energy or purpose. Look at me, for example..."

"Oh, bother'tarnation!" returned Bubba, hawking a huge lugee upon the floor with a lighter and more good-humored laugh, "you're such a stinkin' fairy! It's a wonder you survived this long in these parts."

"How do you think I've I survived as long as I have?" asked Stryker; "how I have lived as long as I've lived?"

"Partly through paying people, and paying others to help you, I suppose. But its not worth your while to proselytize to me, or the air, about it. What you want to do, you do. You were always in the front ranks at school, *for example*, and I was always in the behind..."

"Don't you mean it the other way around?" asked Stryker slyly.

"I'm talking about when we were in school together at Bell Buckle High, you idiot! What are *you* talking about? Jeezus!" He spat again. "You know, you always got good grades and was on the honor roll, and I was always a no-trying putz!"

"And whose fault was that?"

"Yours, you jackass! That's what I think! You were always drinkin' and drivin' and revving your car engine and showin' off and doin' nothin' 'bout your education. It's a wonder you graduated high school at all from the effort you put in! But you *still* did better 'n me." Cotton drunkenly got up to leave. "Fuck. I don't gotta take this! Especially since it's gloomy outside and the day is breakin' and it's about time to drink again. Some *real* drinkin', that is! Not this rat piss you call 'shine! Shit should be illegal! Should be illegal for you to sell this slop!"

"It *is*, my boy. Why do you think it's hidden back here in the back room?"

Cotton headed for the door.

"Well, aren't you finally turned in a pleasant direction," smirked Stryker.

"Cut it out, Stryker! I'm not in the mood for your shenanigans right now!"

"Well, then, before you go, a toast to the pretty witness!"

"Pretty witness..." Cotton mumbled slurredly near the door, looking into his glass of 'shine and thinking of Bunnie, though he was sure that wasn't who Stryker was referring to. "I've had enough of 'witnesses' for to-day and to-night. But just out of morbid curiosity, who's your pretty witness?"

"The prisoner, of course..."

"Jeeee-zus..."

"Who were you thinking of? That picturesque doctor's daughter?"

"You never stop, do you?"

"She *is* pretty, is she not?"

"No."

"Why, man alive! She was the admiration of the whole court! Are you blind, or do you just have your nuts hitched high to a combine? How could you have missed that bodacious rack? Even *I* noticed *those* beamers!"

"Fuck the admiration of the 'court'! Who made the Rebel Yell the judge of beauty? She was a goddamned big-haired blow-up doll!"

"Do you know, Bubba," said Stryker, looking at him with sharp eyes, and slowly drawing a hand across the floral pattern of his muumuu: "Do you know, I rather thought at the time that you sympathized with the big-haired blow-up doll, and were quick to see what happened with that big-haired blow-up doll?"

"Quick to see what happened! If a girl, doll or no doll, swoons within a yard or two of a man's nose with *that* rack, he can see the writing on the wall without even the aid of beer goggles! You are my friend and all, but I deny the beauty. Too much makeup and the boobs are probably fake. And now I'm going out to get more to drink, then pass-out in bed. Or *hopefully* in bed this time..."

When his host followed him out of the 'distillery' with a candle, wishing he had some stairs to throw Cotton down, the day was coldly looking in through his grimy windows.

When Cotton got out of the house, the air was cold and sad, the dull sky overcast. In other words, normal Kentucky weather.

The river was dark and dim, the whole scene like a lifeless desert. Wreaths of dust were spinning round before the morning blast of foot traffic, as if the desert-sand had risen far away, and the first spray of it in advance had begun to overwhelm the city.

Waste forces within him—especially in his bowels and bladder—and a desert all around with no Port-O-John in sight, this man stood still on his way across a silent street, and fell for a moment face-down on the pavement before him. He lay in a drunken haze, imagining himself being pulled into a mirage of being an honorable man with honorable ambition, self-denial, and perseverance.

In the fair city of this vision, there were airy abandoned gas stations from which past lovers looked upon each other from backseats of their cars, pretty young things from which the be-nippled fruits of young life hung ripening; waters of Hope that sparkled even before they were spat upon the floormats.

And in a moment, the vision was gone.

Climbing high up the back iron staircase of his apartment, he went in and threw himself down, still in his nasty clothes, on a neglected bed; or maybe not so neglected since the pillow was wet with wasted semen—and not his own—causing him to toss it disgustedly aside with the speed of the Human Torch.

Sadly, sadly, the sun went down; it sank upon no sadder a sight than the man of good abilities and good emotions, incapable of their directed exercise, incapable of his own help and his own happiness, sensible of the blight upon him, and resigning himself to let it eat him away.

6

Delusions of a Grander Time

The quiet lodgings of Doctor Runyon—which was turned into a backwoods brothel of sorts when he went away to prison and was forced to leave Bunnie behind—was a quiet shotgun shack behind Grouse Gulch's solitary 7-11 near the *Squire Arms* apartment projects.

On the afternoon of a certain fine Sunday when the waves of four months had rolled over the trial for 'treason,' and carried it, as to the public interest and memory, far out to sea, Mr. Travis Templeton walked along the sunny lane of Chickenwell Street, on his way to dine with the Doctor. After several relapses into 'business' absorption, Trip had become the Doctor's friend, and the quiet street was the sunny part of his life at that time.

On this certain fine Sunday, Trip walked down Chickenwell Street and past the *Squire Arms* apartment projects, early in the afternoon, out of three reasons of habit:

Firstly, because, on fine Sundays, he often walked out before dinner with the doctor and Bunnie; secondly, because, on unfavorable Sundays, when the Bengals were doing bad (which was most Sundays), he was accustomed to be with them as their family friend, talking, drinking, looking out the window, and generally getting through the day; thirdly, because he happened to have his own little shrewd doubts to solve, and knew how the ways of the Doctor's household pointed to that time as a likely time for solving them.

A more horrendous corner than the corner where the Doctor lived, was not to be found in all of Grouse Gulch. There was no way around this fact, and the front window of the Doctor's shotgun shack contained the corpses of little pheasants who tried to make their way through, but failed, and which now had the air of genital rot and excrement upon them. There were no other buildings back there, and except for a few choking flowers and some gagging forest-trees, there was an old ox and several emaciated goats in a now barren field. As a consequence, 'country airs' circulated often toward the *Squire Arms* with vigorous freedom; and in addition, languishing teenaged paupers often threw unripe peaches at the south wall of the building. When the summer light struck this wall brilliantly in the earlier part of the day, it didn't help the smell one damn bit. But when the field grew hot, the wall was shadowed and the excrement soup in which the livestock walked all day in the barren field came nearly to a boil.

There ought to have been a bark from a transient dog in such an anchorage, and there was—emitted from a miserable mangy mutt tied to a fence post near the back of the shack.

The Doctor occupied one upstairs room, and Bunnie the other, so there was room enough for the still in the big room below, where several callings purported to be pursued by day, but whereof little was heeded any day, and which was shunned entirely by the family at night. Occasionally, a stray dog traversed the field, or a strange animal peered about here and there, and distant sparrows could be heard in the plain tree out back.

Doctor Runyon often received 'patients' here as his old reputation, and its revival in the floating whispers of his story, brought him. His paltry knowledge of the veterinary arts, and his vigilance and skill in conducting extreme and bizarre experiments, brought him into moderate question, and he only earned as much money as any rational person would think he would, which of course wasn't much.

These things were within Travis Templeton's knowledge, thoughts, and notice, when he wrapped his knuckles on the rusty-hinged door of the tranquilized house, on that fine Sunday afternoon.

"Runyon at home?"

Expected home.

"Bunnie at home?"

Expected home.

"Priss at home?"

Possibly at home, but of a certainty impossible for the drunk, still-tappin', 'shine stealin' ne'er do well he was speaking with to determine.

"And just who are you?" asked Trip.

"Just a friend. Runyon wanted me to check on his 'shine."

"Sure he did," sarcasticated Trip. "Well, as I practically call this place home myself, you need to git the hell outta here before my boot goes all the way up your ass and out your nostrils. I'm going upstairs, and you better be gone 'fore I come back down. Understood?"

The stranger immediately abandoned the premises under the threat of the severe boot-assing.

In other matters, although the Doctor's daughter had known nothing of the county of her birth, she appeared to have innately derived from it that ability to hoard things of little use, which was one of her most useless and disagreeable characteristics. Simple and crappy as the furniture of that shack was, it was set off by so many little trinkets and knick-knacks—of no value whatsoever, excepting for what you could get by melting them down—that its effect was disarming. The dispositions of everything in the rooms, from the largest object to the least; the arrangements of colors (or the lack thereof), the horrid variety and contrast obtained by what they could get at thrift stores and flea markets by callused hands and blood-shot eyes, and their lack of common sense; were at once so unpleasant in themselves, and so expressive of their owner, that, as Trip stood looking about him, the very chairs and tables seemed to laugh at him and ask— with something of the peculiar expression of the signing fish on his own office wall—Whether he approved?

Indeed, he did not, as any rational person would agree. The place looked like the gift shop at Cracker Barrel threw up.

There were three rooms in the whole place, separated by hanging sheets such that anything communicated was loud, and the wind passed freely through the walls and sheets as if none existed at all. Trip, frowningly observant of the fly-strips hanging all around him, walked from one room to another.

The first was upstairs and the best room in the place, and in it were Bunnie's stuffed birds, wilted flowers, and books...of matches, that is—and a desk that had never seen a minute of work, and the canvas of a paint-by-numbers she got for Christmas when she was eight-years-old by the good-heated folks at Project Angel Tree.

The second was the Doctor's room, which he used as a 'consulting' room, which he also used as a dining room, which he also used for a bedroom; and downstairs, taking up the whole room, was the still, over-used and looking much the same as it did when it was sitting in Jenkin Dillingham's basement over in Coon Spit, before Dillingham died from a terrible hunting accident, which meant he was caught fooling around with Hubbard McFarland's wife, and Hubbard hunted him down and killed him with the blunt end of a dull and rusty Philip's head.

"I wonder," asked Trip of himself out loud, pausing in his looking about to focus on a pair of prison britches slung over a dusty brown recliner, "why he keeps a reminder of his sufferings about?"

"And why wonder at that?" was the abrupt inquiry that made him start.

It proceeded from Miss Priss, the red-haired wild woman strong of smell, whose acquaintance he first made at the Royal George Motor Inn in Black Bear many, many years ago, and again not too long ago when she barged into the hotel room to supposedly save Bunnie from himself—the same day the young teen planted her knee firmly into the resting place of his man-junk.

"I should have thought—" began Trip.

"Pooh! You'd have thought!" retorted Miss Priss.

Trip shrank back.

"How do you do?" inquired the old lady then—sharply, and yet as if to express that she bore him no malice.

"I'm pretty well, thank you," answered Trip, in his meekness; "how are you?"

"Nothing to boast of," said Miss Priss.

"Indeed?"

"Ah! Indeed!" said Miss Priss. "I am very put out about all these ladybugs!"

"Excuse me?"

"For gracious sake, say something else besides 'huh?' you dullard, or you'll fidget me to death!" said Miss Priss: whose conduct, and disassociation of mind, revealed her to be crazier than a bat.

"Really?" said Trip, as an amendment.

"'*Really?*' is bad too, ya shmuck," returned Miss Priss, "but better. And yes, I very much put out..."

"Oh, I know that! Or it's what I hear, anyway..." smirked Trip, "I guess some things never change, huh, old girl?"

"I don't want dozens of people who are not at all worthy to come looking for ladybugs!" expulsed Miss Priss.

Trip decided to play along. "Do *dozens* come for that purpose?

"*Hundreds!*" countered Miss Priss.

"Holy shit!" said Trip, as the safest remark he could think of, "but Priss, I'm not so sure it's ladybugs they're after..."

It was characteristic of this lady (as of some other people before her time and since) that whenever her original propositions were questioned, she exaggerated them.

"I have lived with the 'darling'—or the 'darling' has lived with me—and even paid me for it—which she certainly *should* have done—since she was ten years old. And it's really very hard..." began Miss Priss, but she ended abruptly without finishing her point.

Not seeing with precision what was very hard, especially since they we're talking about two women, Trip shook his head, using that important part of himself to think with instead of his brain.

But before he could say anything, Priss continued: "All sorts of people who are not in the least degree worthy of my pet are always turning up. And *you* began it—"

"*I* began it, Priss?"

"Didn't you? Who brought her here when her father 'died,' and who brought her father back to life?"

"Oh! If *that* was beginning it—"

"It was ending it, do you suppose?" barked the battered old Madame sarcastically, "I say, when *you* began it. It was hard enough; not that I have any fault to find with Doctor Runyon, except that he is not worthy of such a daughter, which is no imputation on him, for it was not to be expected that anybody should be, under any circumstances. But it really is doubly and triply hard to have crowds and multitudes of people turning up when he went away (I could have forgiven him for that), and even now after he came back, to take Ladybug's affections away from me..."

Trip knew Miss Priss to be very jealous, but he also knew her by this time, beneath the surface of her eccentricity and fancy-talk mumbo-jumbo, to be one of those selfish creatures—found mostly among old Madames and aging lesbians, Trip supposed—who will, for pure love and admiration, bind themselves as willing slaves to youth when they have lost it, to beauty they never had, to accomplishments they were never fortunate enough to gain, to bright hopes that never shone upon their own sombre lives. Trip knew enough of the world to know that there was nothing in it better than the faithful service of the heart; so rendered and so free from any mercenary taint, he had such exalted respect for it, that in the retributive arrangements made by his own mind—and we all make such arrangements, more or less—he stationed Miss Priss much nearer to the lower demons than many of the older lesbian whores that were immeasurably better off who had once worked for Trip in their brighter days.

"There never was, nor will there be, but one man worthy of Ladybug," said Miss Priss; 'and that was me! Er, um, I mean, my brother Solomon! If he hadn't made that mistake in life..."

Here again: Trip's inquiries into Miss Priss's personal history had established the fact that her brother Solomon was a heartless scoundrel who had stripped her of everything she possessed, losing it after investing it all in Beta Max players, abandoning her to her poverty forevermore, with no touch of compunction. Miss Priss's belief in Solomon (deducing his losing all of her money as a 'slight mistake') was quite a serious matter with Trip, and made him think maybe she had 'shmaked' around with her brother possibly in younger years.

He shivered at the thought.

"As we happen to be alone for the moment, and are both people of 'business'," he said when they had gone round the still in the middle of the room and found a couple rickety old chairs to set their asses upon, "let me ask you—does the Doctor, in talking with Bunnie, ever refer to being in prison, or his shoemaking?"

"Never."

"And yet he always keeps a bunch of leather and rubber on hand?"

"Ah!" returned Miss Priss, shaking her head. "But I don't say he doesn't refer to it when talking to himself."

"Do you believe that he thinks of it much?"

"I do," said Miss Priss.

"Do you imagine—" Trip had begun, when Miss Priss took him up short with:

"I never imagine anything! I have no imagination at all."

"I stand corrected; do you suppose—you go as far as to suppose sometimes, right?"

"Now and then," said Miss Priss.

"Do you suppose," Trip went on, with a laughing twinkle in his bright eyes, as they looked harshly upon her, "that Doctor Runyon has any theory of his own, preserved through all those years, relative to the cause of his being so oppressed; perhaps, even to the name of the one who framed him?"

"I don't *suppose* anything about it except what Ladybug tells me."

"And that is—?"

"That she thinks he has."

"Now don't be angry at my asking all these questions; because I am a mere dull man of 'business,' and you are a woman of 'business'..."

"Dull?" Miss Priss inquired, with placidity.

Rather wishing his modest adjective away, Trip replied, "It is not remarkable that Doctor Runyon, unquestionably innocent of any crime as we are all well assured he is, should never ask that question? He won't talk about it with me, though he had relations with me many years ago, and we were intimate—and I can*not believe* I just admitted that out loud...but, oh, well, no turning back now...but as to his being framed and sent to prison, Priss, does he talk about it with the 'fair' daughter whom barely speaks to him? And who is so disgusted with him right now? Because believe me, Miss Priss, I don't approach the topic with you because I ain't got nothin' better to do, but because of great interest."

"Well! To the best of my understanding," said Miss Priss—softened by the vulnerability of his comment at having once been 'intimate' with the Doctor, which she could easily use to destroy his reputation, and his business as well— "he is afraid of the whole subject."

"Afraid?"

"It's plain enough, I should think, why he might be. It's a dreadful remembrance. Besides that, his loss of himself and his coming to Jesus grew out of it. Not knowing how he lost himself, or how he came to Jesus, he may never again feel certain of not losing himself and having to come back to Jesus again. That alone would make the subject unpleasant, I should think."

If it weren't for the fact that her comment surely made no sense to a rational person, and being fairly sure himself that the old bag had now completely and for all time lost it, it might have been a profounder remark than Trip had looked for.

"True," he said, having no idea what he was agreeing to, "and fearful to reflect upon." He knew his comment made no sense whatsoever as well, but hoped the old bat wouldn't catch on. "Yet, a doubt lurks in my mind, Miss Priss, whether it is good for Doctor Runyon to have that suppression always shut up within him. Indeed, it is this doubt and the uneasiness it sometimes causes in me that has led me to having this conversation at all, and my admission of once having slept with the old man..."

"Then your uneasiness obviously comes from somewhere else, my lad!" Priss spat out. "That much I'm absolutely sure of!"

Trip cocked his head in a quizzical fashion.

"It can't be helped, my boy, take it from me," said Miss Priss, patting his knee. "Touch his thing, and he instantly changes for the worse. Better to leave it alone. In short, you *must* leave it alone, likey or no likey."

Trip continued to gaze at her with the same quizzical look.

Priss felt bad for him, so she sighed and then switched back to the original point of his inquiry:

"Sometimes he gets up in the dead of the night, and will be heard, by us in the other room, walking up and down the stairs, up and down the stairs, and walking in circles in his room. In his mind, he's back in prison. Bunnie hurries to him and tries to knock him down the stairs and put him out of his—and our—misery forever, but he never says a word about the true reason for his restlessness to her, and she finds it best not to hint at it to him. In silence she goes on trying to knock him down the stairs as he walks, til 'ventually her punching and kicking brings him back to himself."

The tread of coming feet interrupted her.

"Here they are!" said Miss Priss, rising to break up the conference; "and now we shall have hundreds of people here pretty soon."

Trip realized the old Madame was merely pining away for her past days of 'glory.' Or did she really have some hallucinatory notion that all those people were coming back? Trip could hardly think so. Not at her age, and seeing as how horrible she looked now. Or maybe she was just referring to the hundreds that would be coming after Bunnie now that she was legal? And the jealously of that thought might be what was driving her mad.

The four had an amicable dinner of take-home KFC, and then by request of Bunnie, they went out back and sat in rusted patio chairs beneath the plain tree. Bunnie carried out a jug of 'shine for the special benefit of Mr. Templeton, and had installed herself on Trip's lap to function as his cup filler-upper. And the whole time they sat under the plain tree, talking, she kept his cup replenished.

Now three sheets beyond the wind, Trip hallucinatingly thought he saw mysterious back-ends peeping at him from the top balconies of the *Squire Arms* apartments as they talked, and the plain tree whispered to him the lyrics of Bob Marley songs in its own way above his head.

Still, the hundreds of people Priss predicted would come never presented themselves, although Bubba

Darnet did soon present himself while they were sitting under the plain tree—however, he was the only one.

Doctor Runyon received Bubba Darnet kindly, as did Bunnie. But, Miss Priss suddenly became afflicted with a twitching in the head and body as she struggled and squirmed to fight off the imaginary flesh-eating spiders that attempted to devour her body and soul. She dumped the rest of her 'shine into the ground and retired into the house. Besides, when the men got to talking whilst slushing themselves with 'shine,' the talk often reduced itself to asininity of the highest order. And Priss was not unfrequently the victim of this disorder, as she called it in familiar conversation, 'a fit of the jerks.'

Being three sheets past the wind himself, the Doctor was in his best condition (or so *he* thought anyway), and looked especially ancient. The resemblance between him and Bunnie was very strong at such times (sadly), and as Bunnie and her father sat side by side (Trip had kicked her off his lap by now), she leaning away from him, and he creepily resting his arm on the back of her chair reminiscent of bygone days, it was very agreeable to trace the likeness. The Doctor had been talking all day, on many subjects, with manic vivacity, and making sense not one bit.

"Doctor Runyon," slurred Darnet, as they sat under the plain tree—and he said it in the natural pursuit of sucking up to the father of a hot young snatch—"have you been to Tower Liquors much since you been outta the joint?"

"Bunnie and I have been there, 'cause she wanted to see where Coy and I scrapped that one day. But we have seen enough of it to know that it teems with business in this bad economy, and little more."

"*I* have been there, as you remember," slurred Darnet, with a smile, though reddening and a little angrily, "in another disguise, so that I could buy pornography straight from the rack without being recognized...but that is another matter...the last time I was there, though, they told me a curious thing."

"What was that?" asked Bunnie.

"In making some additions to the back of the store, the workmen came upon an old mason jar buried out back, presumably by a prisoner on a chain-gang once laboring to clear littler from the field behind the store. Above the buried jar they found a short thick stick, which one prisoner seemed to have placed at an angle above the jar and into which had also been cut three letters. It was done with some very poor instrument, and hurriedly, and with an unsteady hand."

"How could you tell?" inquired Trip.

"'Cause I watch CSI like all the rest of 'merica, dumbshit! Duh!" retorted Darnet harshly.

Runyon implored Bubba Darnet, with great interest, to go on.

"Well," continued Darnet, "at first, the letters were read as D.I.C.; but, on being more carefully examined, and brushing some mud away, the last letter was found to be K. There was no record of any prisoner on the chain-gang with those initials, and many fruitless guesses were made what the name could have meant. At length, it was suggested that the letters were not initials, but the complete word, DICK. The field was examined very carefully under the inscripted stick, and, as I said before, a mason jar was found, and inside the jar were found ashes of paper, mingled with ashes of a small leather case or bag. What the unknown prisoner had written will never be read, but he had written something, and hidden it away to keep it from the chain-gang boss."

"Father," exclaimed Bunnie, "you are ill!"

While Darnet had still been speaking, Runyon had suddenly stood up, with his hand to his head, and threw up his cookies, splashing his feet and everyone else's in the circle. Then he wobbled a bit, as if to fall face-first into the mess, which everyone was content to let him do, since his manner and his look made them all want to puke as well.

"No, my dear, I'm not ill! It's just that there are large drops of purple rain falling, and they surprised me. We had better go inside."

Once inside, the Doctor recovered himself almost instantly. "Did I say it was raining purple rain out there?" he questioned. He held up the back of his hand, which was wet, proving that rain had really fallen in large drops. But of course, it was far from purple. Be that as it may, he said not a single word in reference to the mason jar discovery that had been told of, and, as they went into the house, the 'business' eye of Trip either detected, or fancied that it detected, on his face, as it turned toward Bubba Darnet, the same singular look that had been upon it when it turned towards him in the passages of the bowling alley basement.

Runyon recovered himself so quickly, however, that Trip had doubts of his 'business' eye. Then the arm of a large giant made of solid gold hallucinatorily steadied Trip as he stepped in through the back door, and he stooped to remark to the golden giant that he was not immune to slight surprises (if he ever would be), and that the purple rain had not startled him one bit.

Miss Priss, in the kitchen making tea, was pissed that the 'fit of the jerks' had moved inside and was bothering her again. Still, no hundreds of people had come, and yet, Bubba Cotton had wandered in, but he then made only two.

The night was so very sultry, that although they sat with the doors and windows open, the group was overpowered by the heat. When the supply of 'shine had run out, they all moved to one of the windows, and looked out into the heavy twilight. Bunnie sat by her father; Bubba Darnet sat next to her; Bubba Cotton leaned hard against the window, feeling sick to his stomach. The curtains were worn and thin, and some of the thunder-gusts that whirled in the corner caught the curtains up to the ceiling, and waved them like spectral wings, scaring the living shit out of all who were hallucinating on the bad 'shine.

"The purple rain-drops are falling, large, heavy, and many!" said Doctor Runyon. "They come slowly..."

"It comes surely...," added Cotton, having caught up to them in their drinking while bullshitting with Priss as she made tea in the kitchen.

They spoke in low tones, as people watching and waiting to be attacked by imaginary trolls often do; as people who sit in a dark room, watching and waiting for Superman to come save them often do.

There was a great hurry in the street, of people speeding in their cars to get to shelter before the storm—before they'd have to get wet walking from their cars to their apartments—while the wonderful echoes of footsteps coming and going were heard throughout the house, and yet not an actual footstep was there.

"A multitude of people, and yet a solitude!" cried Bubba Darnet, when they had listened for awhile.

"Is it not impressive, Darnet," asked Bunnie slurredly. "Sometimes, I have sat here in the evening, until I have made myself orgasm—but then again, the thought of an orgasm makes me shudder tonight, when all is so black and solemn—"

"Let us shudder then!" the men said excitedly (with the exception of her father), led most loudly by Bubba Darnet— "That we may know what it is!"

"It will seem like nothing to you," she answered. "Such whims are only impressive as we fantasize about them I think; they are not as good in real life."

"Oh, no, try it! Try it!"

"I have sometimes sat alone here in the evening, listening, until I have made the echoes out to be the echoes of all the footsteps that are coming by-and-by into our lives."

The men drooped their heads, sure now that she wasn't going to do it. But the footsteps were incessant, and the hurry of them became more and more rapid to all as the bad 'shine did its dirty work. The room echoed and re-echoed with the tread of feet; some it seemed under the windows; some it seemed in the room; some coming, some cuming, and some going; some pulling out, some having not started altogether as a result of E.D., and as an indirect result of Congress' refusal to cover *Vee*-ay-gra under Medicaid. But all such were in the distant past, and not currently within sight.

"Are all those footsteps destined to come to all of us, Bunnie, or are we to divide them among us?"

"I don't know, *Mister* Darnet; you're talking foolishly..."

"Not *too* foolishly," Priss piped in with a wink.

Trip winced.

"...but you asked for it," exclaimed Bunnie. "When I have yielded myself to it, and I have been alone..."

"Yield to it now!" pleaded the men (with the exception of her father), led most loudly by Bubba Darnet, "For godssakes, yield to it now!"

"... and then I have imagined thems to be the footsteps of the people who are to come into my life, and my father's..."

"But we are here now!" begged Darnet, "Please? For the love of God, please!"

Bubba Cotton suddenly stood, wobbled, and with the full hallucinatory effect, and with bad 'shine coursing through his brain, shouted, "*I* take those people into *my* life! I ask no questions and make no stipulations! There is a great crowd bearing down on us, Miss Bunnie Mancrizie, and I see them—coming along with Superman to save us from the trolls!"

His last words were added after there had been a vivid flash of lightning outlining his body as he stood in the window.

"And I hear them!" he added again, after a peal of thunder—Trip wondering if Cotton had actually been *struck* by lightning—"Here they come, fast, fierce, and furious!"

It was the rush and roar of rain that he had heard

in actuality, and it stopped them all, for no voice could be heard above it. A memorable storm of thunder and lightning broke with that sweep of water, and there was not a moment's interval in crash, and fire, and rain, until after the moon rose at midnight.

The great bell of St. Pancreas Church on the other side of town was striking One in the cleared air, when Trip, who had just called Jerry to come help get his drunk-ass home, set forth after a time upon Jerry's four-wheeler.

Trip always retained Jerry late into the evenings for just this purpose, though it was usually performed two hours earlier since Trip was such a lightweight when it came to alcohol.

"What a night it's been! Almost a night, Jerry," said Trip, "to bring the dead out of their graves!"

"*What?*" Jerry shot back, over the roar of the mufflerless engine. "I'm sorry, you're not making sense..."

"*What?*" asked Trip.

"I never go into graveyards at night myself, dude— nor do I expect to anytime soon. No, I wouldn't do that," answered Jerry.

Twenty minutes earlier, the night of revelous 'shine and hallucinatory revelry had ended in this such way:

"Good-night, Bubba Cotton," said the man of 'business.' "Good night, Bubba Darnet. Shall we ever see such a night again together?"

Perhaps.

And perhaps Bunnie would also take them up one day on their pleadings to see her parlor trick, since for the duration of the rest of the evening she had flatly denied their requests to have it performed.

And perhaps Priss, too, would one day see her great crowd of people with its rush and roar, bearing down upon her once thriving brothel; but somehow, Trip doubted it. By the looks of her now, he seriously doubted it.

7

Father Mesphistopheles and Incubus Boy

Father Mossenger, one of the great lords in power at St. Jude's Catholic Church in Coon Spit, held his forthrightly 'reception' in a flea-bag hotel room at the Grand Motor-Lodge out by the highway.

Mossenger was in his sanctuary of sanctuaries, his Holiest of Holiests, sitting before a small crowd of 'worshipers' in his room. He was about to take his treat, his 'candy,' which is to say several slightly underage (but as yet not unwilling) altar boys. Mossenger even returned their favor (being able to swallow a great many things with ease) but, this morning's 'candy' could no more get into the throat of Father Mossenger without the aid of a little Vaseline, and not a few wrestles and shoves, as could he personally assist any given parishioner with questions about the life, death, and meaning of the Christ.

Father Mossenger had been out at a little supper last night, where first Wacky Willy's comedy club and later Noah's Stark strip club were charmingly represented.

Mossenger was out at a little supper most nights, with frighteningly unfascinating company. So polite and so impressionable was Mossenger, that the comedy club and the strip club had far more influence with him than the wants of the church or the needs of his parishioners.

Mossenger had only one truly noble idea for his church, which was, to let everything go on in its own way; for his private affairs, he had the equally truly noble idea that it must all go on *his* way—and he tended to his own power, pocketbook and sexual perversions. Of his pleasures, public and private, Mossenger had the only other truly ignoble idea that the world was made for *him*. The biblical proof-text of this notion (altered from the original by as much as a single pronoun) ran: 'The earth, and the fullness thereof, are *mine*, saith Father Mossenger.'

Yes, Mossenger had slowly found that vulgar embarrassments crept into his affairs, both private and public; so he had, as to both classes of affairs, to ally himself with a respected farmer-rancher in town of utmost upstanding repute and impeccability of character. This was mostly because after generations of squandering public church finances on his own private pleasures, and the farmer-rancher being relatively rich—having one of the only remaining farm/ranches in southern Kentucky to turn a profit—Mossenger was growing poor.

Hence the Father had taken his sister from a faraway convent in North Carolina, while there was as yet time to ward off his impending homelessness, and had bestowed her as a prize upon the well-off farmer-rancher. Which such farmer-rancher, carrying an appropriate cane with a golden calf atop of it, was now in an adjoining room, acting as a watchdog/bodyguard for the corrupted Catholic official. He did so always expecting superior treatment and appreciation from Mossenger, but, like his once virginal, and horrifyingly homely ex-nun wife, they both looked down upon him with the loftiest of contempt.

A sumptuous man was the farmer-rancher. Three horses stood in his stable, four dogs ran through his halls, and no one, not even he, waited on his nearly-unbearable-to-gaze-upon wife. But as one who did nothing but plunder and forage where he could (read: many, many extra-marital affairs), the farmer-rancher—howsoever his matrimonial relations conduced to the social immorality of both families—was at least the greatest ally the Father had among the personages who attended his Motor Lodge disgraces this day.

He looked around the musty, dank and smelly adjoining room adorned with bad art and worse furniture, and leaned back against the bed's headboard and lit a cigarette. He turned a pre-season Notre Dame game onto the television and wondered how his life of fortune thus far could have taken such an overpoweringly sour turn for the worse.

Mossenger having eased his four men of their burdens, and taken his own 'candy,' caused the adjoining door of the Holiest of Holiests to be thrown open, and issued the farmer-rancher forth. Then, what submission, what cringing and fawning, what servility, what abject humiliation he felt in front of those boys getting ready to leave.

Bestowing a word of promise here and a smile there, a whisper to one happy 'slave,' and another hand on another, Mossenger affably passed through the room to the remote region containing the Circumference of Truth—otherwise known as the toilet.

There was soon but one person left in all the room besides the farmer-rancher, and he, with hat tucked under his arm and his chaw-box in his hand, slowly passed among the minors on his way out.

"I devote you," said this person, stopping at the bathroom door on his way out and turning toward Mossenger's 'sanctuary,' "...to the devil!"

And with that, the man shook the chaw from his fingers as if he had shaken the dust from his feet, and quietly walked down the stairs to the parking lot.

He was a man of about sixty, handsomely dressed, haughty in manner, and with a face like a fine mask. A face of transparent paleness; every feature of it clearly defined; one set expression on it. The nose, beautifully formed otherwise, was very slightly pinched at the top of each nostril. In those two compressions, or dints, the only little change that the face ever showed, resided. They persisted in changing color sometimes, and they would be occasionally dilated and contracted by something like a faint pulsation; then, they gave a look of treachery, and cruelty, to the whole countenance.

Examined with attention, its capacity of helping such a look was to be found in the line of the mouth, and the lines of the orbits of the eyes, and the lines he snorted up his nose, being much too vertical and thin; still, in the effect the face made, it was a handsome face, and a remarkable one.

Its owner went down stairs into the parking lot, got into his BMW 528i, and drove away. Not many of the childish altar boys had talked to him at Father Mossenger's 'reception' (probably because he was as old as Mossenger himself, and because of that, creepy to them). He had also stood a little space apart, and it probably wouldn't have killed Mossenger to have been a little warmer to him in his manner.

It appeared rather agreeable to him to see the common people's piece-of-shit cars and trucks dispersed on the roads among his BMW, and they often barely escaped from being run down, or run into, by him. The man drove as if he were charging the enemy, and his furious recklessness brought no check into his face, or to his lips.

The complaint against his driving had sometimes made itself audible at city council meetings, even in that deaf and dumb city of Coon Spit, that, on the narrow back-streets and four-way stops, his fierce patrician custom of hard-driving endangered and maimed the vulgar in a barbarous manner. But, few on the city council cared enough to think of it twice, and, in this matter, as in all others, the common wretches were left to get out of their difficulties, and get out of the way of the crazed BMW, as best they could.

With a wild rattle and clatter, and an inhuman abandonment of consideration easily understood *these* days, the Beamer dashed through the streets and swept around corners with men screaming before it, and women clutching each other and clutching their children out of its way.

At last, swooping at a street corner by an old Rexall Drug Store with a soda fountain still in operation (thanks to the constant patronage of a nearby high school), one of the BMW's wheels came to a sickening little jolt, and there was a loud cry from a number of voices, and the BMW grinded a hard downshift and squealed to a stop.

But for the latter inconvenience, the BMW probably would not have stopped; Beamers and Porsches were often known to drive on, and leave their wounded behind, and why not? They were driven by rich dicks.

But the frightened high schoolers had come upon this BMW straight away, and twenty hands were suddenly on his car.

"What has gone wrong?" asked the asshole, stepping from the car.

A tall boy in a hoodie had gathered up a bundle of smashed plastic from under the wheels of the Beamer near the steps of the drug store (with the soda fountain), and was down in the mud and wet, howling over it like a wild animal.

"Pardon me, asshole!" the boy's buddy, a ragged and submissive lad told him, "That was his GameBoy."

"Why does he make that abominable noise? It's just a GameBoy."

"Excuse me, asshole," said a girl nearby, also in a hoodie, "the kid's a fucking nerd, you dick, and that's a pity yes—but he still didn't deserve for you to crush his fuckin' GameBoy."

As the tall lad suddenly got up from the ground and came running at the Beamer, the asshole clasped his hand for an instant on his Gloch, which he carried in his belt.

"Killed!" shrieked the impoverished nerd in wild desperation, extending both arms at their length above his head and staring at the asshole. "Dead!"

The high schoolers closed round, and looked at the asshole banker. There was nothing revealed by their many eyes that looked at him but simple watchfulness and eagerness; there was no visible menacing or anger.

Neither did the kids say anything after the first cry; they had been silent, and they remained so. The voice of the not-so-submissive boy who had first spoken, was flat and tame in its extreme submission now. The asshole banker ran his eyes over them all, as if they had been mere rats come out of their holes.

The banker took out his purse from his car, and they all laughed and jeered.

"Look, he's got a fuckin' purse!"

"It's a man-bag, thank you very much!" the banker defended.

"Yeah, right!"

"It's extraordinary to me," said the banker, "that your parents cannot take care of their own children. One or the other of you is always in the way. How do I know what injury you have done to my Beamer? See! Give him that."

And he threw out a Susan B. Anthony dollar for the crushed boy to pick up, and all heads craned forward that all the eyes might look down at it as it fell. The tall lad called out again with a most unearthly cry, "Dead!"

The boy momentarily stopped his whining by the quick arrival of another man, for whom the rest made way. On seeing him, the miserable creature fell upon the parted man's shoulder, sobbing and crying, and pointing to the steps of the drug store and soda fountain where some nerds were stooping over the motionless bundle, and poking it gently with a stick. They were as silent, however, as the cool kids.

"I know, I know," said the last comer, "but be a brave man, Grady. It is better for that outdated scum-incrusted piece-of-shit GameBoy of yours to have died than to have lived. It has died in a moment without pain. Could you seriously have lived happily another hour with it?"

"You must be a philosopher," the asshole banker said to the boy's consoler. "You there, who are you?"

"They call me Barge."

"Where do you work?"

"I own the liquor store out on 25, Dick-Sandwich. What's it to you?"

"Pick that up, philosopher and dispenser of escapism to the wretched masses," said the banker, throwing another Susan B. Anthony dollar coin to the ground, "and spend it as you will. By the way, does my front tire look all right?"

Without feigning to look at the tire a second time, the asshole banker folded himself into the Beamer, turned up the air-conditioner, and was just about to drive away with the look of a man who had accidentally broken a common thing, and had paid for it, and could afford to pay for it, and even buy as many as he wanted to; when his ease was suddenly disturbed by a coin flying into his carriage and hitting him in the face.

"Hold it!" said the asshole banker. "Just hold your horses! Who threw that?"

He looked to the spot Barge, the dispenser of escapism, had stood a moment before; but the wretched tall lad was groveling on his face in the mud in that spot, trying to find a lens that had fallen from his glasses, and the figure that stood beside him was the figure of a dark stout woman, reading a *Soap Opera Digest.*

"You dogs!" said the banker, but smoothly, and with now visible flecks of white powder shining under his nose from an upper lip beaded with sweat. "I would ride over any of you very willingly, and exterminate you from the earth, if I knew which rascal threw that at my Beamer. And if that butt-hole were sufficiently near it, he should be crushed under my wheels!"

So cowed was their condition, and so long and hard their experience of what such a man could do to them—within the law and beyond it—that not a voice, or a hand, or even an eye was raised. Among the men and boys, not one.

But the woman who stood reading looked up

steadily from her magazine, and looked the asshole banker in the face. It was not for his dignity to notice it; his contemptuous eyes passed over her, and over all the other rats; and he leaned back in his seat again, and slammed the accelerator. "See ya! Wouldn't want to be ya!"

8

A Fool Opens His Mouth...And Proves It

A beautiful landscape, with the corn bright in it, but not abundant. Patches of poor rye where corn should have been, patches of poor peas and beans, patches of most coarse vegetable substitutes for wheat. On such inanimate nature—as on the men and women who cultivated it—a prevalent tendency towards an appearance of vegetating willingly, and a dejected disposition to give up and whither away, was sadly to be found.

The asshole banker, otherwise known as Clay D. Markee, in his Beamer, fagged up a steep hill, though that word has a slightly different meaning today than when Dickens first wrote this. A blush on the countenance of Clay D. Markee was an impeachment of his high breeding; it was not from within; it was occasioned by an external circumstance beyond his control—the setting sun.

The sunset struck so brilliantly into the traveling BMW's windshield as it gained the hill-top, that its occupant was steeped in crimson. "It will die out," said Clay Markee, glancing at his hands on the steering wheel, "soon."

In effect, the sun was so low that it dipped at the moment. When the heavy drag had been adjusted to the car, and the Beamer slid down hill (with a smell of burning brake-pads) in a cloud of dust, the red glow departed quickly, and the sun and Clay Markee were going down together, and there was no glow left when the car reached the bottom of the backside of the hill.

But there remained a broken countryside, bold and open, a little village at the bottom of the hill, a broad sweep and rise beyond it, a church-tower, a windmill, a forest for hunters chasing deer. Round upon all these darkening objects as the night drew on, Markee looked, with an air of one who was coming near home.

The village had its one poor street, with its one poor traffic light, and it's poor tavern— The Fountain— and poor stable-yards for horses. It had its poor people too. All its people were poor, and many of them were sitting at their doors, shredding spare onions and the like for supper, while many were at The Fountain, washing down Sam Adams' and Blue Moons, with such small yieldings of buffalo wings, which could hardly be considered digestable food. Expressive signs of what made them poor were not wanting; the tax for the state, local tax and federal income tax, sales tax and a tithe to the church, were to be paid here and to be paid there, according to solemn inscription in the little village, until wonder was that there was any village left unswallowed.

Few children were to be seen, but there were about a million dogs. As to the men and women, their choice of earth was stated in the prospect: Life on the lowest terms that could sustain it, down in the little village under the mill; or captivity and Death in the federal penitentiary.

Clay D. Markee pulled up to the post office (where people also paid utilities, and some of their taxes), which was right next to The Fountain. The peasants suspended their operations of walking in and out of the bar to look at him. He looked at them back, and saw in them, without knowing it, the slow but sure filing down of misery-worn face and figures, that was to make the meagerness of southern Kentuckians an American stereotype which has survived the best part of a couple hundred years.

Clay D. Markee cast his eyes over the submissive faces that drooped before him, as his had drooped before the hard-bargaining representative from Walmart he had met with earlier that day—only difference was that these faces drooped merely to suffer, and not to propitiate—when a grizzled road construction worker joined the group.

"You! Come here!" called out Markee to the fellow.

The fellow came over, blue hard-hat in hand, and the other fellows closed round to look and listen, in the manner of the high schoolers outside the drug store (with the sweet soda fountain).

"I passed you on the road, didn't I?"

"Yes, I had the honor of seeing your BMW pass by me on the road. It's a sweet ride you got here."

"Coming up the hill?"

"Yes."

"What were you looking at so intently?"

"I was looking at the man."

"Well, I appreciate the compliment, but I'm not that *type* of man. So stop staring and leave me in peace!"

The worker was miffed. "Don't flatter yourself, Donald Rump! I was looking at the man in the woods. That's what I meant. The tall dude on the motorcycle."

"What tall dude on a motorcycle?"

"A Honda 250 Enduro. The guy was huntin' something, or someone."

"I don't believe you. You have misinformed me on purpose for some reason I haven't quite been able to distinguish."

"Well ain't we a hoity-toity la-dee-da? But no, I ain't lyin'. So don't you go accusin' me of no lyin, 'cuz I'll cut a bitch!"

"You are most certainly lying! Why did you come over here just now to tell me lies?"

"You're the one who called *me* over, asshole! So fuck you!"

"Gabriel, knock him in the jaw for me, would ya?"

Mr. Gabriel, as we met in an earlier chapter, was the Postmaster here in Reams—an over-the-years bastardized version of the French city of *Rheims* (to which the town founder, Franscois DeCracsmelle, tried with incredible—if flawed—pretension to honor his birthplace). Postmaster Gabriel was also the tax and utility collector for the region, as well as the local Department of Motor Vehicles. He was also a very good and longstanding friend of one Clay D. Markee, asshole extraordinaire.

"Bah! He's not worth it," barked the Postmaster.

"If you see this man in your village tonight, be sure that his business is honest," said Markee. He said this because Gabriel also had limited powers of enforcing the law in the Reams region, since the police department was horribly understaffed, underpaid, and over-worked.

Markee did the business he had stopped in for—paying his bills—then he got back in his car. The burst with which the BMW 528i started out of the village and up the rise beyond was soon checked by the steepness of the hill.

At the steepest point of the hill, there was a little burial ground, with a cross and a large new figure of Our Savior on it; it was a poor figure in wood, done by some inexperienced redneck carver, but he had studied the figure from the life—the carver's own life, maybe—for the carving of Christ upon the cross was dreadfully spare and thin, with a spitting wad of chew coming forth from its lips.

To this distressful emblem of a great distress that had long been growing worse—whatever that means—a woman was kneeling. She turned her head as the Beamer came upon her, rose quickly, and presented herself in the way of it in the road.

"It is you, Markee! Markee, wait!"

With an expletive of impatience, but with his unchangeable face, Markee rolled down the window.

"What is it?"

"Markee. For the love of God! My husband, the lumberjack…"

"And what of your husband, the lumberjack? Always the same with you people! He cannot pay for something?"

"He has paid all, Markee. He is dead."

"Well, then, he is quiet, as you should be! Do you think I can bring him back from the dead?"

"Hell, no, Markee, but he lies yonder, under a little heap of poor grass."

"And...?"

"Markee, there are so many little heaps of poor grass."

"Again—and...?"

She looked an old woman, but she was actually young. Her manner was one of passionate grief; by turns she clasped her veinous and knotted hands together with wild energy, and laid one of them on the Beamer door—tenderly, caressingly, as if it had been a human breast and could be expected to feel the appealing touch. Markee thought he heard the Beamer purr.

"Markee, hear me! Markee, listen to my request! My husband died of bad 'shine, and so many die of bad 'shine, so many more will die of bad 'shine..."

"Again! And...? Can I help that?"

"Markee, the good God knows; but I don't ask it. My request is that a morsel of stone or wood, with my husband's name be placed over him to show where he lies. Otherwise, the place will quickly be forgotten. It will never be found when I am dead of the same malady, I shall be laid under some other heap of poor grass..."

"Well, then stop drinking, Bee-otch! It's not rocket science!"

"Markee, they are so many, they increase so fast, there is so much bad 'shine. Markee! Markee!"

Clay put her away by opening his door and slamming it into her, knocking her sillier than she already was, her falling in a heap near her husband's heap. The only difference was, she was still breathing. At least, for the moment. The Beamer then broke into a brisk trot, and she was left far behind. Markee was rapidly diminishing the mile or two of distance that remained between him and his 'chateau.'

The sweet scents of the summer night rose all around him, and rose, as the rain falls, impartially, on the dusty, ragged, and toil-worn group at The Fountain not far away; to whom the road construction worker, with the aid of his blue hard-hat (without which he was nothing) was still engorged in drinking heavily with his buddies, until they could no longer bear it and puked in cycles inside the bar, and out.

By degrees, as they could bear even this no more, they dropped one by one, and lights twinkled behind closed eyelids as they slumped against an alley dumpster. These lights, and the stars coming out to join them, seemed to have shot up into the sky behind eyelids instead of having been come into the sky, which was probably a good thing, since that assured the men that they were at least still alive.

The shadow of a large high-roofed house, and of many overhanging trees, was upon Clay D. Markee by that time; and the shadow was exchanged for the lights of the driveway leading up to the old plantation home of past glory—or infamy, depending on how you looked at it and the color of your skin— and with a push of a button, the garage door was opened to him.

He flipped his cell-phone and pushed one button.

"Has Charles arrived yet?"

"No sir," replied the butler. "Not yet."

9

The Kracken is Released

It was a heavy mass of building, 'The Chateau,' as Clay D. Markee so named it, with a large stone courtyard before it, and two stone sweeps of staircases meeting in a stone terrace before the principal door. A stony business altogether, with stone urns, stone flowers, and stone faces of men, the stone heads of lions; in all directions, as if Medusa's head had surveyed it, when it was finished, around about double centuries ago.

Up the broad flight of shallow steps Markee proceeded from his detached garage, sufficiently disturbing the darkness as to elicit loud remonstrance from an owl on the roof of the stable away among the trees. All else was so quiet that other than the sound of the owl's voice there was none, save the falling of a fountain into its stone basin; for it was one of those dark nights that hold their breath by the hour together, and then heave a long low sigh, then hold their breath again.

The great door clanged behind him, and Clay D. Markee crossed a hall hung grim with certain old harpoons, swords, and knives of the chase; grimmer still with heavy fishing-rods and shotguns—of which many a trout and a pheasant had gone to his benefactor 'Death,' and had felt the weight of his Lord when he was angry.

Avoiding the larger rooms, which were dark and made fast for the night, Clay D. Markee went up the staircase to a door in a corridor. This thrown open, he admitted himself to his own private suite of three rooms adjoined after a recent re-model: his bedchamber and two others. They were all high vaulted rooms with crown molding and hard-wood floors, two dogs lying before a hearth for the burning of logs in wintertime. All the luxuries befitting a high–powered banker in such a luxurious age and country.

A supper table was laid for two in the dinning room downstairs; a round room, with one of the mansion's four fire-extinguishers close at hand. A small lofty room, with its windows wide open, and the cheap pull-blinds he'd just bought from Target closed, the dark night only showed in slight vertical lines of black.

"My nephew," said Markee, glancing at the supper preparation; "you said he has not yet arrived?"

"He hasn't. That's right sir, he's not here."

"Ah! It is probable he will arrive to-night, Baldwin?" spat Clay Markee sarcastically. "Nevertheless, leave the table as it is. I shall be ready to eat after I take my shower."

"Could you please talk a little less gay, sir? You're kinda freakin' me out."

"Piss off, Baldwin!"

"Of course, sir. But you know, your nephew will definitely be here tonight, sir. He's a redneck and good-for-nothing moocher, so sure as shit, he'll be here."

"That will be all, Baldwin! When I want your opinion, I'll ask for it, thank you very much!"

"*Ahem!* Yes, sir. *Ahem!*—gay."

"What was that?"

"Nothing, sir. Just a little cough..."

In a quarter of an hour, Markee was ready, and sat down to his sumptuous and choice supper—now look who's talking gay—his chair was opposite to the window, and he had taken his soup and was raising his glass of Bordeaux to his lips, when he suddenly put it down.

"What is that?" he calmly asked, looking with attention at the vertical black lines of the cheap Target blinds.

"What?"

"Outside the blinds. Open the blinds, Baldwin."

It was done.

"Well?"

"It's nothing, sir. The trees and the night are all right there as they should be."

"Thanks, smart ass."

The servant who spoke had thrown the blinds wide, and looked out into the vacant darkness, and stood, with that blank behind him and a blank look on his face, looking round for more instructions.

"Good," said the imperturbable master. "You can close them again."

That deed was done too, and Markee went on with his supper. He was halfway through it when he again stopped with his glass in his hand, hearing the screech of wheels. It came on briskly, and came up the front drive of 'The Chateau.'

"See who's arrived."

It was the nephew of Markee. He had been some miles behind Markee earlier, and diminished the distance rapidly, but not so rapidly as to overtake Markee upon the road. After all, his 1985 Pontiac Fiero was no match for the BMW 528i. He had also heard Markee had been at the post office right before him.

He was to be told (ordered Markee) that supper awaited him then and there, and he better get his scraggly ass in and eat it. The nephew loitered a few minutes in the courtyard, finishing a smoke, then came in to eat. He had been known in Grouse Gulch as Charles (Chuck) 'Bubba' Darnet.

Markee received him in a courtly manner, but they did not shake hands.

"You left Coon Spit an hour ago, uncle?" he said to Markee, as he took his seat at the table.

"Yes. And you?"

"I came direct."

"From Grouse Gulch?"

"Si."

"You have been a long time in coming," said

Markee with a smile.

"On the contrary, I drove fast. But not all of us can afford Beamers, you know."

"Oh, pardon me. I meant not taking a long time to get here; a long time intending to come visit."

"Well, you see, I have been detained by"—the nephew stopped a moment in his answer—"various 'business'."

"No doubt," said the polished and possibly gay uncle.

So long as Baldwin was present, no other words were passed between them. When coffee had been served and they were alone together, the nephew, looking at the uncle and meeting the eyes of the face that was like a fine mask, opened a conversation.

"Unc, I gotta ask you. Are you gay?"

"What?"

"Just wonderin'. You ain't gotta answer, I was jus' wonderin'..."

"You know my wife died long ago."

"Right. Anyway, I have come here, uncle, finally, to confront you about an ordeal I was just involved in. One that might have caused my death."

"Not your death," said the uncle; "it is not necessary to say your *death.*"

"I doubt," returned the nephew, "that even if I *had* been carried to the brink of death you would have cared to rescue me there."

The deepened marks in the nose, and the lengthening of the fine straight lines in the cruel feminine face, looked ominous because of that; the uncle made a graceful gesture of protest, which was so clearly a slight form of bullshit that it was not reassuring.

"For all I know," pursued the nephew, "you might have worked to give me a more 'spicious appearance to thems already 'spicious circumstances that surrounded me by planting that autobiography of that Sam Walton dude on me your own damn self, and then paying those two chuckle-heads to testify against me at the chamber meetin'."

"No, no, no," said the uncle, pleasantly.

"Well, if you say it *wasn't* you," resumed the nephew, glancing at him with deep distrust, "I'm sure you would've gone to great lengths to help me out in my time of need if I had needed it?"

"Yes, my friend," said the uncle, with a fine pulsation in the two marks, "I do believe that is what I've always told you. Do me the favor of telling me that you do remember me telling you that often."

"I remember."

"Thank you," said Markee—very sweetly indeed.

His tone lingered in the air, almost like the tone of a musical instrument.

"So," pursued the nephew, "Are you gay or what?"

Markee slammed a palm face-down on the table. "Do not ask me that again!"

"Sorry, fancy pants, it's just that…"

"The matter is closed!"

"All right," said Bubba Darnet, holding two hands up in surrender and backing off. "All right. But as far as that shit you pulled, or at least as far as that shit I *think* you pulled, goes, I believe it was your bad luck, and my good luck, that kept me from being banned from the bowling leagues forever."

"I do not quite understand," returned the uncle, sipping his coffee with his pinky finger extended high in the air. "Dare I ask you to explain?"

"Sure I'll 'splain. Fuck you. How's that?"

"You should take the opportunity to consider that being kicked out of the bowling leagues might have been better for you in the long run. But it is useless to discuss the question. I have, as you say, bad luck. These little instruments of correction, these gentle helps to the power and honor of families, these slight favors that might so annoy you, are only to be obtained by interest and insistence. They are sought by so many, and they are granted (comparatively) to so few! It used not to be so, but Coalmont County in all such things has changed for the worse. Our not so remote ancestors held the right of life and death over the Negroes, you know..."

"That's African-Americans..."

"Whatever."

"They prefer to be called African-Americans..."

"I said, Whatever!" barked Clay D. Markee, getting annoyed. "From this very room, many such 'dogs' had been taken out to be hanged..."

"Oh, jeezus. Here we go..."

"... in the next room, my bedroom, one fellow, to my knowledge was impaled to death on the spot for professing his love to one of our ancestor's daughters—his *white* daughter."

Darnet stood up. "I don't have to listen to this shit, George Wallace."

"We have lost so many privileges, and a new philosophy—political correctness—has become the mode; and the assertion of our station, in these days, might (I do not go so far as to say would, but I might) cause us real inconvenience! All very bad! Very bad!"

"Nice George Bush Sr. imitation, Lester Maddux. Now if you'll excuse me, *you* have issues. I'm busy, and you're a *very* sick man, and I must be going. But I must say, I'll be back to kick your ass on Martin Luther King Day. See ya then!"

He began to leave.

Markee took a gentle little pinch of chew, then shook his head.

His nephew felt so sorry for the racist wretch, that he sat back down and said gloomily, "We have so 'asserted our station,' as you say, both in the old times and in the modern times also, that I believe our name is now more detested than any other name in Coalmont County, and especially in Coon Spit and Grouse Gulch."

"Let us hope so," said the uncle. "Detestation of the high is the involuntary homage of the low."

"*What*? Where'd you get that fuckin' tripe from?

Marie *fuckin'* Antoinette? And while your at it, Henry the VIII, why don't you just make them eat cake, you sick fuck. The hell's the matter with you? Jeezus, get with the modern times, would you. There's not a dark face I can look at in all the county here, which looks at me with any thought on its mind than fear and slavery, and how we fucked them people over for so long a time."

"A compliment," said Markee, "to the grandeur of the family! Merited by the manner in which the family has sustained its grandeur. Hah!" And he took another gently pinched morsel of chew, and lightly crossed his legs.

His nephew, leaning an elbow on the table, covered his eyes thoughtfully and dejectedly with his hand.

"Have you completely lost your fucking mind?" to which the fine mask looked at him sideways with a stronger concentration of keenness, closeness, and dislike, than was comfortable with its wearer's assumption of indifference.

Markee continued grim-faced: "Repression is the only lasting philosophy. Those of us who kept the darks under the fear of slavery for so long my friend," observed Markee, "will also keep the dogs of this county obedient to the whip, as long as this roof," looking up to it, "shuts out the sky."

That might not be for long, thought the nephew. Because if only his uncle could have seen this 'Chateau,' and hundreds others like it, during General Sherman's devastating March the Sea—prior to a hundred years spent—he might have been at a loss to pluck it from the ghastly fire charred plunder-wrecked ruins of Atlanta. And as for the roof he vaunted, he might have found shutting out the sky to have a new use—to shield himself from the eyes and bodies from which lead was fired out of the barrels of a few thousand muskets, and not a few hundred cannons.

"Meanwhile," said Markee, "I will preserve the

honor and repose of the family, if you will not. But you must be tired. Shall we terminate our conference for the night?"

"The conference isn't exactly what I was thinkin' of terminatin'," said the nephew, by this time so appalled and enraged he was shaking like a leaf. "You...y-y-you got issues, man! Serious issues! You need help!"

"I just thought of something else. A moment more if you please..."

"No, I won't give you a minute more, James Earl Ray! Our family has done wrong, uncle, and are reaping the fruits of that wrong."

"*We* have done wrong?" repeated Markee, with an inquiring smile, and delicately pointing, first to his nephew, then to himself.

Bubba nodded. "That's right. Our family has. Our 'honorable' family has. Even in my father's time we did a world of wrong, injuring every human creature who came between us and our pleasure, whatever it was. And why should I speak of my father's time when it's equally yours? Can I separate you—my father's twin brother and joint inheritor—from him?"

"Death has done that!" said Markee.

"And has left me," answered the nephew, "to an uncle that is frightfully fucked in the head! I'm only tryin' to do the last request of my mother, to obey the last look in her eye, which was to make past wrongs right, and do the right thing from here on, but it seems I cannot do them without having to seek assistance and favors from the corrupt powers that be, and it seems I'm seeking them in vain anyway..."

"Seek them from me, my nephew," said Markee, grinning slyly like the Grinch with his heart ten sizes too small, "and you will *forever* seek them in vain, be assured. So stick that in your pipe and smoke it, James Earl Jones!"

Every fine straight line in the clear whiteness of his face was cruelly, craftily, and closely compressed, while he stood looking quietly at his nephew who was snickering at him for his absurd misquote, his chew-pouch in his hand.

"My snickering friend," said Markee, with death in his eyes, "I assure you of this: That I will die perpetuating the system under which I have lived, and under which our family has lived for centuries before us."

When he said this, he took a culminating pinch of chew, putting it between his cheek and gum, and stuck the pouch back in his pocket.

"Better to be a rational creature," added Markee, after ringing a small bell on the table, "and accept your natural destiny. But you are lost I see, Mr. Chuck...or Bubba...or whatever the hell people call you nowadays."

"This property and my inheritance are lost to me," said the nephew, looking around sadly; "You can have 'em. You can even fuck yourself with them for all I care..."

"Is this house yours to renounce?"

"I have no intention of claiming it. If it passed from you to me to-morrow—"

"Which I have the good sense to hope is not probable..."

"...or twenty years from now..."

"You do me too much honor," said Markee. "Still, I prefer that supposition."

"...I would abandon it, and live otherwise and elsewhere. It is not much to give up, this shit-hole. Look at it! It's nothing but a wilderness of misery and ruin. A whitewashed tomb!"

"Hah! How poetic of you, John Boy!" said Markee, glancing around the luxurious room.

"Yeah, some things in here are pretty fuckin' cool, I admit—like them harpoons and shit hangin' in the hallway—but seen in the light of day, under the clear blue sky, it is a crumbling tower of waste, misman-agement, extortion, debt, oppression, racism, hunger, nakedness and suffering."

"Hah! Keep it up, dear boy! I didn't know you had

it in you, Walt Whitman," said Markee in a well-satisfied manner.

"If it ever becomes mine, I'll give it to better qualified hands that might free it slowly (if that is possible) from the weight that drags it down, so that the miserable fucks who cannot leave it, and have overstayed their welcome long ago..."

The butler had just walked into the room.

"...including you, Baldwin."

The butler flipped him off.

"No," continued Bubba. "I don't want this piece of shit. It's not for me. There's a curse on it, and on all this land."

"And you?" said the uncle, "Forgive my curiosity; but under your new philosophy, what work do you intend to do to live on?"

"To live, I'll do what others in this county do to survive. I'll go on Welfare."

"And live in Grouse Gulch?"

"Yeah, since no one there knows me or my family name, I think that's safe."

"Grouse Gulch is very attractive to you, seeing how you have prospered there while being indifferent to work," his uncle observed, turning his calm face to his nephew with a smile.

"Fuck you, Clay! You're a steaming pile of refuse..."

"Refuse? Speaking of refuse, have you seen that doctor of the veterinary arts that has newly moved here?"

"Yeah."

"And he's with his daughter?"

"Yeah. What of it?"

"You lying sack of shit. Good night." As Markee bent his head in a most courtly manner, there was a secrecy in his smiling face, and he conveyed an air of mystery to those words, which struck the eyes and ears of his nephew forcibly. At the same time, the thin straight lines Markee had snorted earlier in the evening made his nose curve with a sarcasm that looked handsomely diabolic. "Yes," repeated Markee, "a doctor with a daughter. So commences the new philosophy! But still, you're a lying sack of shit. Good night."

It would have been to as much avail to interrogate any stone face outside The Chateau as to interrogate that face of his. The nephew looked at him in vain, and with pity, and passed on to the door.

"Good night," said the uncle again, "I look to the pleasure of seeing you again in the morning. Sleep well! Baldwin, show my nephew to his room—and burn my nephew in his bed if you will."

"Fuck you, Clay!" responded Bubba. "You're a fucking idiot!"

The nephew left, slamming the door on his way out.

Markee, still hopped up on coke, walked to and fro in his bed chamber to come down enough for sleep that hot still night. Rustling about the room, he moved like a refined tiger; looking like some enchanted marquis of the impenitently wicked sort, in story, whose periodical change into tiger form was either just going off, or just coming on.

He moved from end to end in his voluptuous bedroom, looking again at the scraps of the day's journey that came unbidden into his mind; the slow toil up the hill at sunset, the setting sun, the descent, the little village of Reams down in the hollow, the 'peasants' at The Fountain, the road worker with his blue hardhat—The Fountain suggesting the soda fountain at the Rexall in Coon Spit, the little bundle lying on the step, the girls bending over it, and the tall boy with his arms up shouting, "Dead!"

"I am cool now," said Clay D. Markee finally, at 2 a.m, "and may go to bed."

And so the president of the Bay Steel Bank of Coon Spit, Kentucky—with corporate offices in Pittsburgh and Tampa—leaving one ember burning on the large hearth, let his thick comforter fall over him and heard the night break its silence with a long sigh as he masturbated himself to sleep.

The stone faces, on the outer walls stared blindly at the black night for three heavy hours; for three heavy hours the horses in the stable rattled at their racks, the dogs (who had been put outside) barked, and the owl made a noise with very little resemblance in it to the noise conventionally assigned to the owl by men-poets, whatever the hell that means.

For three heavy hours, the stone faces of The Chateau, lion and human, stared blindly at the night. Dead darkness lay on all the landscape; dead darkness added its own hush to the hushing dust on all the roads. The burial-place had got to the point where its little heaps of poor grass were undistinguishable from one another; and the figure on the Cross might have come down and danced a jig for all anyone knew. In the hamlet of Reams, taxers and the taxed were fast asleep, dreaming, perhaps of large pizzas, as the starved usually do, and good 'shine instead of shit 'shine, and of ease and rest, as the overworked and the yoked ox may, its lean inhabitants slept soundly, and were fed and beat their bosses asses in their sleep.

The Fountain in the village flowed unseen and unheard to the outside world with Old Milwaukee and other cheap drafts flowing for a dollar ninety-nine on special.

The fountain at The Chateau dropped unseen and unheard—melting away, like the minutes that were falling from the spring of Time—through three dark hours. Then, the gray water of the fountain and the grey tap water of The Fountain both began to be ghostly in the light, and the eyes of the stone faces of The Chateau were opened.

Lighter and lighter, until at last the sun touched the tops of the still trees, and poured its radiance over the hill. In the glow, the water of The Chateau fountain and the gray tap water at The Fountain seemed to turn to blood (much to the horror of the barmaid until she realized she had accidentally poured the Bloody Mary mix into the tap water spigot. Then *everybody* wanted water), and the stone faces of The Chateau and the chiseled faces of The Fountain turned crimson. The carol of the birds was loud and high, and, on the weather-beaten sill of the great window of the bed-chamber of Clay D. Markee, one little bird sang its sweetest song with all its might. At this, the nearest stone face seemed to stare amazed, and, with opened mouth and slacked jaw, looked awe-stricken.

Now the sun was full up and movement began in the village of Reams. Casement windows opened, crazy doors were unbarred, and people came forth shivering—chilled, as yet, by the new sweet air. Then began the rarely lightened toil of the day among the village population. Some, to The Fountain; some, to the fields; men and women here, to dig and delve; men and women there, to see to the poor livestock, and lead the bony cows out, to such a pasture as could be found by the roadside. In the church and at the Cross, a kneeling figure or two; attendant on the latter prayers, the led a cow, trying for a breakfast among the weeds at its foot.

The Chateau awoke later, as became its quality, but awoke gradually and surely. Doors and windows were thrown open by Baldwin, horses in the stable looked round over their shoulders at the light and the freshness pouring in at doorways, leaves sparkled and rustled at iron-grated windows, dogs pulled hard at their chains, and sniffed each other's rears.

All these trivial incidents belonged to the routine of life, and the return of morning. Surely, not so the running up and down of the stairs; nor the hurried uniformed figures on the terrace; nor the booting and tramping here and there and everywhere, nor the quick rushing of cars and riding away?

What winds conveyed this hurry to the grizzled road worker, already at work on the hill-top beyond the village, leaving his day's coffee thermos behind ly-

ing in a bundle—not worth a crow's while to peck at—
on a heap of stones? Had the birds, had they been able
to carrying a coffee bean of it to a distance, dropped
one over him as they sow chance seeds? Whether or
no, the road worker ran, on the sultry morning, as if
for his life, down the hill, knee-high in dust, and never
stopped til he got to The Fountain.

All the people of Reams were at The Fountain,
standing about in their depressed and early morning
drunken and hung-over manner, whispering low (at
the request of the hung-over), but showing no other
emotions than grim curiosity and surprise. The led
cows, hastily brought in and tethered to anything that
would hold them, were looking stupidly on, or lying
down chewing their cud of nothing particularly repay-
ing their trouble, which they had picked up in their
uninterrupted saunters.

Some of the people at The Chateau, and one man
(at least) at the post-office, were armed more or less.
Already, the road worker had penetrated into the midst
of a group of twenty particular friends, and was hitting
himself in the chest with his blue hard-hat. What did
all that portend, and what portended the swift hustling
of Postmaster Gabriel into the back of a black and
white, and the conveying away of said Gabriel at high
speed, like an episode of these people's favorite TV
show *Cops*?

It portended that there were one stone face too
many up at The Chateau.

Medusa had surveyed the building again in the
night, and had added the one stone face wanting; the
stone face for which she had waited through about one
hundred and seventy-five years.

The stone face lay back on Clay D. Markee's pillow. It was like a fine mask, suddenly startled, made
angry, and petrified. Driven home into the heart of the
stone figure attached to it, was a knife. Round the hilt
was a post-it note on which was scrawled:

'*Dear Satan: Drive him fast to Hell in that fucking*

BMW of his. This, from Harlan.'

10

A Snowball's Chance

More months, to the number of twelve, had come and gone, and Mr. Bubba Darnet was established in Grouse Gulch as a maker of French Fries at the local McDonalds who was also able to load the milkshake machine with fake ice-cream mix. At his age, he should have been a manager, but alas, he was a just a lowly fry guy.

He worked with young men, and women, a few middle-aged Mexicans and the odd elderly, and not a few mentally challenged persons, who found interest in working with that universal of languages, spoken all over the world: 'Would you like fries with that?'

Bubba Darnet quickly cultivated a taste for stores of hamburgers and high cholesterol. He could even take orders from the drive-thru in basic Spanish, and render change in basic Spanish. Such masters were not at that time easily found. So, with great persever- ance and untiring industry, he prospered.

In Grouse Gulch, he expected neither to walk on pavements of gold, nor to lie on beds of roses; if he had any such exalted expectation, he would not have pros- pered. He had expected labor, and he had found it, and did it, and made the best of it. In this, his pros- perity consisted.

Ironically, a certain portion of his time was passed at Burger King, where he sat with 'undergraduate burger flippers' as a sort of tolerated double-agent, who drove a contraband trade in ways of making French fries taste better ('A dash of A-1 sauce in the boiling fryer is the first step...'). The rest of his time he passed at KFC scarfing popcorn chicken.

Now, from the days when it was mostly summer in

Eden, to these days when it was mostly winter in fallen latitudes, the world of a man has invariably gone one way—Bubba Darnet's way—the way of the love of a woman.

He had loved Bunnie Runyon-Mancrizie from the hour of his danger of being kicked out of the county bowling leagues forever. He had never heard a sound so sweet or dear as the sound of her whiskey-smoked voice; he had never seen a face so harshly beautiful as hers when it was confronted with his on the edge of the grave that had been dug for him.

But, he had not yet spoken to her on the subject; the assassination at The Chateau far away beyond the next hill over and the long, dusty Buckskin Trail—the solid wood 'chateau' which itself had become the mere mist of a dream—had been done a year ago, and he had never yet, by so much as a single spoken word, disclosed to her the state of his heart.

That he had his reasons for this, he knew full well. It was again a summer day when, having completed a double shift in the drive-thru, he turned onto the quiet street of Chickenwell bent on seeking an opportunity to speak his mind with Doctor Runyon. It was the close of the summer day, and he knew Bunnie to be out with Miss Priss.

He found the Doctor tinkering with the still, trying to find the right balance to make the effect of the 'shine more alcoholic-haze drunk-like, and less hallucinogenic drunk-like. The fake-insanity routine that had once supported him under his old sufferings and aggravated his sharpness, had been gradually laid aside as no longer being of any use.

He was now a very energetic man indeed, with great firmness of purpose, strength of resolution, and vigor of action. In his recovered energy, he was a little prone to fits of sudden violence, just as he had been back in the day; but this had not been of late frequently observable, and had thankfully grown more and more rare.

He studied the still much, slept little, and sustained a great deal of fatigue with ease (contrary to what I'd just stated in the above paragraph) and was equably cheerful. To him, now entered Chuck 'Bubba' Darnet, at sight of whom he put aside messing with the still and held out his hand.

"Bubba Darnet! I'm glad to see you. We have been counting on your return these past three or four days, although I have to say, Bunnie was just a little creeped out the last time you were here. Stryker and Bubba Cotton were both here yesterday, and both made you out to be a pretty big perv."

"Well, I'm glad they seem to be overly interested in my business," he answered coldly. "But, Miss Bunnie—"

"Is well," the doctor said, cutting him short, "and your return will delight us all. She has gone out to buy some makeup and some more of that confounded Miss Clairol crap—makes the whole house smell like horse shit, you know—but she will be home soon."

"Doctor Runyon, I knew she wasn't home. I took the opportunity of her not being here so I could speak to you alone."

There was a blank silence.

"Ok," said the Doctor with evident restraint, "Bring a stool in here, sit your ass down and talk to me."

Bubba complied as to the stool, but found the speaking part a little less easy.

"I've been so happy to hang out wit' ya'all, and I've felt so comfortable here in Grouse Gulch for the past year and a half," so he at length began, "but I'm a little afraid to bring up what I've come to say..."

He was swayed to stop by the Doctor putting up a palm in a 'speak to the hand' sort of way. After leaving it up for several seconds, he withdrew it and said, "Is Bunnie what you've come to talk about?"

"Yep. She is."

"It's hard for me to speak of her at any time. It is

very hard for me to hear you speak of her in that tone of yours, Bubba Darnet."

"What tone?"

"That tone where it's clear to me you want to jump her bones! But right now you're being all polite and old fashioned and shit, wanting to talk to her *father* first, and all that kind of shit..."

"It is the tone of fervent admiration, true homage, and deep love, Doctor Runyon!"

"See! There you go again, letting loose with all that gay sounding romantical nonsense! What the fuck, Darnet? You been watching *The Notebook* on that Lifetime Channel again? Is that what you're gonna tell me?"

There was another blank silence before her father rejoined:

"Ok, you like my daughter. I believe it. I didn't do you justice."

The old man's total 180 on the subject so confused Bubba Darnet, he hesitated.

"Shall I go on, sir?"

Another blank. "Only if you'll never use the word 'shall' in my presence again, ya fuckin' fruit loop! What's the matter with you, boy?"

The old man calmed down. "Ok, go on."

"You anticipate what I would say, though you cannot know how earnestly I say it, how earnestly I feel it, without knowing my secret heart, and the hopes and fears and anxieties with which it has long been laden..."

"Apparently, that's not all that's been latent," the father remarked.

"I said 'laden'."

"Yeah, whatever. Go on."

"*Laden.* I said *laden.*"

"Sure ya did, Will and Grace."

"Dear Doctor Runyon, I love your daughter fondly, dearly, disinterestedly, devotedly. If ever there were love in this world, I love her..."

"Boy, you're makin' me puke! And did you just call me *dear*?"

"...and you have 'loved' her yourself. So let your old 'love' speak for me!"

The Doctor turned his face away, his eyes focused on the ground. At the last words, he put his head in his hands and cried, "No, not that! Let that be! I beg you, do not bring that up! Now, or ever again!"

His cry was so like a cry of actual pain that it rang in Bubba Darnet's ears long after he had ceased. Runyon motioned with a palm extended, once again seeming to signal 'speak to the hand,' appealing for Bubba Darnet to stop. Bubba got the message and stopped.

"I beg your pardon," said the Doctor, in a subdued tone after some time. "I do not doubt your love for Bunnie. Rest assured."

Runyon turned toward him on his stool, but did not look at him, or raise his eyes. His chin dropped upon his hand, and his white hair overshadowed his face.

"Have you spoken to Bunnie about this?"

"No."

"Nor written?"

"Never."

"Not so much as an email?"

"Nope."

"A text?"

"Nada."

"Well, boy, seems for all that pansy-ass *Notebook* watchin' you been doin', you ain't learnt a fuckin' thing."

Darnet stared at him with a blank expression.

Runyon waved off the comment. "Ok, I'm fixin' to give you the benefit of the doubt, Peter Pan, 'cause I guess it seems to me that all your silence has been due to wanting to check with the father first, to try and get his 'blessing' or some other old-fashioned sort of bullshit such as that. But, be that as it may, her father thanks you anyway."

"But *you're* her father..."

"Yes, I know."

Runyon offered his hand, but his eyes did not go with it.

"I know," said Darnet respectfully, "—how can I *not* know Doctor Runyon, since everybody else knows it too, and I have seen you and Bunnie together day to day—that between you there is an affection so unusual, so grotesque, and so belonging to the circumstances in which it was nurtured, that it can have few parallels, even in the most graphic of pornographic novels and films coming out of Albania..."

"*What?*"

"Nevermind."

"Ok. Go on."

"I know, Doctor Runyon—how can I *not* know?— that mingled with the affection and duty of a daughter who has become a woman, there is in her heart, towards you, a vile hatred that would make even Satan himself cringe. I know that for most of her childhood she had no parent, and that for the times in which you were there, she is now so devoted to revenge against you that I can't even begin to imagine how you're able to sleep at night without one eye kept open. I know perfectly well that if you had been restored to her from the world beyond this life (most likely from Hell), you could hardly be seen by her in a more demonic light than she sees you now. I know that when she has her hands around your throat, and is trying to choke the living shit out of you, her hands are the clinging grips of Charles Manson, Jeffrey Dahmer and Ted Bundy all rolled into one. I know that in choking you she sees her mother, and her lost childhood; she sees and hates you at my age, sees her mother broken-hearted (and we all know you lied to her with that bullshit story about fightin' Coy in the parking lot of Tower Liquors)— I have known all this night and day since I have come into your home."

Her father sat silent, with his face bent down. His

breathing was slowed, and he repressed any other signs of agitation, much to Bubba's relief.

"Dear Doctor Runyon, always knowing this, always seeing you and her at each other's throats, literally—though mostly her at yours—I have been patient, and been patient, as long as it was in the nature of a man to do so. I have felt, and do now even feel, that to bring my love—even mine! as shitty as it is—between you at this time, might very well save your life and keep her out of prison. I lover her. Heaven is my witness, I love her!"

"I believe you, buns-up," Doctor Runyon conceded, "I really do. I'm not sure why...but for now, I do."

"But do not believe that if I may be so happy as to one day make her my wife, I would not do everything in my power to help restore the relationship of a father to a daughter, and vice-versa. I believe it can be done. And since I've heard tell a rumor that maybe you'd come to Jesus in that prison cell of yours, I believe that could only help matters."

"You speak so emotional and feminine-like, Bubba Darnet, but, as I said before, I'm willing to give you the benefit of the doubt. By the way, have you any reason to believe that Bunnie loves you?"

"None, sir. None at all."

"Well, there's one big strike against ya, don'tcha think?"

Silence.

Runyon continued: "So why you comin' to me then, boy? You tryin' to find out if the poor girl likes you? Why didn't you just open the door when you first got here and hand me a note like some pre-pubescent middle-school jackoff—'Check here if Bunnie likes me, Yes or No.'?"

"I admit, sir, I haven't had the balls to ask her out yet, and I might not have the balls to do so for weeks—but then again, maybe I'll do it tomorrow."

"You might want to check and see if you've got any balls at all, son. I've gotta say, I'm worried for ya.

When you go pee, have you ever felt a little sack 'a marbles dangling there under your stick? Them's would be your balls."

"Anyway..."

"By the way, do you seek any guidance from me?"

"About what?"

"Relationships, you nitwit, what do you think?"

Darnet stifled a laugh. "No, no, that won't be necessary. But I'll let ya know if I ever need some."

"Do you seek any promise from me?"

"Uh...strangely enough, I do. Funny that you should know to ask that..."

"Well, out wit' it then! What is it?"

"Well, I understand that, with you around, and even the memory of you—as things stand between you now—that I should have no chance in Hell with Bunnie, since you seem to inflame a hatred of men in her beyond all reason."

"Sadly, 'tis true."

"I well understand that even if Miss Bunnie held me at this moment in her innocent heart..."

Runyon nearly choked on his wad of chew.

"Her *innocent* heart?"

"Do you not think I have the presumption to assume as much?"

"Not unless you've been livin' in a frickin' cave the last ten years! What's wrong with you boy? Everyone knows she been ridden more than a New York subway..."

"But the problem I have is that I can retain no place in her heart next to the all-consuming hatred she has for you, her father."

"If that be so, what you want me to do about it?"

"Wait, I'm not finished..."

"Ok, then go on, Jughead. Nobody's stoppin' ya."

"I also understand equally well that a word from her father in favor of a particular man, me, would most likely make her hate that man with equal vengeance as she hates you at this time."

"I must admit, that'd be a fair enough assumption..."

"For which reason, I'm asking...well, sir, all's I'm trying to get at is... well, what I'm trying to say here is...

"Spit it out, boy! You're making me sick!"

"I'm asking that when it comes to me and Bunnie—and especially between the two of you when I'm not around—that you'd just keep your big yap shut."

"Done! Now Bubba Darnet, let me tell you something I learned long ago..."

"Oh, Jeezus..."

"Mysteries arise out of close love..."

"Now who's quotin' from *The Notebook*?"

Runyon held up a hand. "Just, just hear me out, ya sis. Now, mysteries arise out of close love, as well as out of long division; in the latter's case, well, I simply fucked up in math long ago. But that's neither here nor there. In the former's case, the mysteries of love are subtle and delicate, and difficult to penetrate..."

"I know Bunnie's not a virgin, if that's what your gettin' at..."

"Boy! Shut up and let me finish!" Runyon took a deep breath and looked at the ceiling, trying to quell his rage. He calmed himself, then continued, softly: "My daughter Bunnie is to me, in many respects, a mystery. And I can make no guess as to the state of her heart. And for godssakes, everyone knows she ain't a virgin, you cock and balls!"

The Doctor got up and poured himself a cup of 'shine. To Bubba Darnet, he offered none.

Deep in thought, Darnet said, "May I ask sir, if you think she is—" he hesitated.

"A virgin? I thought we already covered that, Tinker Bell."

"No! What I was going to say before you so rudely interrupted me was, do you think she's being pursued by any other tools at the moment?"

"Any *other* tools? Does that mean you're calling *yourself* a tool, boy?"

"No, I meant the others. Not me. The others. Others besides me. Not including me. I'm no tool, no siree."

Runyon enjoyed seeing the young man squirm. Such was one of the finer points of having a hot young daughter. *This boy is clearly a tool...*

The old man paused a moment to consider how to answer Darnet's question.

"You have seen Bubba Cotton here yourself. Stryker is here too, occasionally. If there be one at all, it's one of those, far as I cain tell."

"Or both."

Runyon laughed. "I had not thought of that. Both? Ha! Most likely not, seeing as how old Stryker is clearly a fairy of the highest order..."

"You think so?"

The Doctor gave him a sideways glance. "That tain't even worth answerin', boy..."

"Sorry, I guess I was just overly excited about the prospect of at least one elimination..."

"Is there anything else you want, boy?"

"There is. And that would be that if she should ask you about me when I am not around, or even if I am around, that you would only speak good things of me, even if you do secretly think I'm a tool and a piece of shit."

"I don't think you're a piece of shit, boy. I *do* have my concerns, but that don't mean I think you're a piece of shit. In fact, I give you this promise. I believe your objective to be pure and truthful as you have stated it here today. I believe your intention is to perpetuate, and not to make worse—if that were at all possible—the ties between myself and that little street whore I calls my daughter. If she should ever tell me that you are essential to her perfect happiness, I will speak well of you, or a least, if I cain't do that, I will, as you say, keep my big yap shut."

At the sound of these words, Bubba Darnet struggled hard to choke back tears, since this was the nicest thing anyone had ever said to him. And also because if he did let the tears go, he was sure Doctor Runyon would stuff him into the still and drink him with his dinner.

"Bubba Darnet, if there were any reasons, any apprehensions, anything whatsoever, new or old, against any man who has ever really loved Bunnie— and especially if the direct responsibility for any such debacle, such as beatins and whatnot, lie upon *his* head—I swear to you that I would obliterate that cock-sucker in one punch without so much as spillin' a drop of my 'shine from my mason jar! It may not seem so now, especially not to her anyway, but she is everything to me; more to me than suffering, more to me than the wrong I did to her—hell, this is idle talk anyway..."

So strange was the way in which he faded into silence, and so strange his fixed look when he had ceased to speak, that Bubba Darnet felt his own hands turn cold, though he stood so near the still's burning fire.

The Doctor momentarily snapped out of his reverie. "You said something to me jus' now," the old man said, breaking into a smile, "What was it you said?"

"I didn't say nuthin'."

"Yes you did. Jus' a bit earlier."

"I said I loved your daughter. And let's see...I said that she powerful hates you, with all the hate of Nazi Germany...."

"No, not that. After that. Later on."

"Oh, I said I hoped you wouldn't say anything bad about me in front of her, and that I'd like to try and help you two sort out your differences, if that be possible..."

"No, no..."

"Well, then fuck it! I cain't remember! But I got somethin' else to tell your old ass before I ski-dattle outta here. My present name, though but slightly changed from my mother's, is not my own. I wish to tell you what that is, and why I'm here in Grouse Gulch."

"Stop!" said the Doctor in a haze.

"But I got's to tell ya, that I may better deserve your confidence, and keep no secrets from ya."

"Stop!"

For an instant, the Doctor held his hands over his ears; in another instant, he had his two hands on Darnet's chest, ready to bash him in the face.

"Tell me when I ask you," the Doctor requested, "but not now. If your shit should prosper, and if Bunnie should love you, tell me on your wedding night, promise?"

"How 'bout the morning *of* the wedding, 'stead?"

"Ok, done. Now let's shake hands on it and you get your ass outta here. Bunnie'll be home directly, and it's better she not see us together to-night. So go, and God bless you!"

He shoved Darnet to the door and out of it, but before closing it, Darnet turned to him and said, "God *bless* me? Does that mean...?"

Slam.

It was dark when Chuck 'Bubba' Darnet left him, and it was an hour later and darker when Bunnie came home; she hurried into the room alone—for Miss Priss had gone straight upstairs—and was surprised to find her father's maggot infested Laz-Y-Boy empty.

"Pa! Pa dear!" she called to him. "Hey shithead! Where the fuck are you?"

Nothing was said in answer, but she heard a low patting and squeaking sound in his bedroom. Passing lightly across his closed door, she came running back downstairs, frightened, crying to herself with her blood chilled. *What shall I do? What shall I do?*

Her uncertainty lasted but a moment; then she hurried back up and tapped at his door, and softly called to him. The noise ceased at the sound of her voice, and he presently came out to her.

"What were you doing in there, father?"

"Bunnie, I've got good news! The gov'ment finally agreed to pay for Vee-*ay*-gra!"

11

Partners in Dysfunction

"Bubba," said Mr. Stryker, on that same night—or the next morning, who knows—to his jackass; "mix another round of Appletini's. I have something to say to you. But finish your work here first."

Bubba Cotton had been working a double shift that night, and the night before, and the night before that, and a good many nights in succession at the Rebel Yell Bowling Alley, desperately working down an inflated and insatiable bar tab. Now, he set about catching up on a gaggle of Stryker's extraneous law documents having gone wanting while Cotton cleansed ten-pin shoes of fungi; and when he was done, he planned to take a good long time off between both occupations, and go on vacation.

Bubba Cotton was none the livelier, and especially none the soberer, for such application. It had taken an extra deal of wet-toweling to pull him through the night, to which each time Stryker emerged from the bathroom dressed *seulement* in wet-towel, Cotton would exclaim, "Jesus Christ, Stryker! Put something on!" To which Stryker would always reply, "Just making sure you're awake, my boy, and getting those documents finito'ed."

A correspondingly extra quantity of wine proceeded each toweling—in an attempt for Cotton to crowbar the image of Stryker in a wet towel from his squishy gray matter; and eventually Cotton was in a very damaged condition, on account of all three acts. But it being late into the night, and almost morning, Stryker needing him to get caught up before daybreak, the deadline for the lawsuits to be filed.

Soon Stryker took to walking around wearing

nothing excepting a wet-towel as a turban, to which Cotton repeatedly puked his guts into a companionable bucket each time he saw the fat man's wrinkly crinkly and pimply physique, or the image of such reflected in a mirror.

Now Stryker had pulled off the turban and threw it in the bathtub, where he had steeped it for the last four hours, and walked back into the living room.

"Are you mixing that batch of Appletini's?" asked the portly Stryker, stark raving nude and glancing around from the sofa where he lay on his back.

"I am," said Cotton from the kitchen.

"I had to have that mix imported from Indianapolis, you know."

"Really?"

"By the way, are the documents done?"

"They are."

The papers were indeed caught up at last, meaning the Stryker arrears were handsomely caught up (though Cotton would have objected to that choice of words, and probably puked his guts out as well when he heard them); everything was got rid of until November should come with its fogs atmospheric and its fogs legal; the time when they would have started firing people again down at the mill for preferences sexual and disputes over skin pigmentation.

"Now look here," shouted Stryker from the other room, "I'm going to tell you something that will rather surprise you, and it perhaps will make you think me not quite as shrewd as you usually think me..."

"What's that?"

"I intend to marry."

"You *do*?"

"Yes. And not for the money. What do you say now?"

"What's his name?"

"What?"

"Are you going to Vermont?"

"*What?*"

"I said, what's—*ahem!*—name?"

"Guess."

"Do I know...*ahem!*-her-*ahem*?"

"What's the matter with you?"

"Just a little something stuck in my throat..."

"Well, get going on those Appletini's then! God, you'd think you were mixing it one molecule at a time in there. Ok, so...Guess!"

"I'm not going to guess at four o'clock in the morning, with my brains frying and my guts splattered all over that bucket. If you want me to guess, you must ask me to dinner first."

"That can be arranged!"

"I meant *buy* me dinner, *ya fuckin' fruit cake*," finished Cotton under his breath.

"*What?*"

"Nothing."

"Well, I'll tell you then," said Stryker, coming slowly into a sitting posture on the couch, then changed his mind to a different course, and lay back again. "Bubba, I rather despair of making myself intelligible to you..."

"*Not a stretch to believe that one...*"

"...but it is because you are such an insensible dog."

"*Well isn't that the pot calling the stick a faggot...*"

"You say something?"

"No. Go on."

"You know," rejoined Stryker, laughing boastfully, "I don't make any claim to being the Soul of Romance—for I'd hope I know better! Still, I am a tenderer sort of fellow than *you.*"

"*Not arguing that...*But you are luckier, if you mean that."

"I don't mean that. I mean I am a man of more—more—"

"Flamboyancy?"

"Well, I'll say 'gallantry'," said Stryker, inflating himself toward his friend as his friend made the

Appletini's, standing in a backward and partially out of sight position to Stryker. "My meaning is that I am a man..."

"*That's questionable...*"

"...who *cares* to be more agreeable, and who takes more *pains* to be more agreeable, who knows *how* to be more agreeable, in a woman's society than you do."

"*Not arguing that one either...*Go on."

"Before I 'get on,' I'll have this out with you..." said Stryker, whipping his head back... and "*Oh God!*" panting heavily.

"What are you doing in there?"

"Nothing! Not a thing!"

"Ok, this is almost ready."

"Good, good!" The fat man huffed, then slouched like a soft tub of Gell-o on the couch after finishing his business.

"Are you ok in there?" called Bubba from the kitchen.

"Never better!"

"You sure? Because I could stop what I'm doing and come in there..."

"NO! Don't come in here! Don't stop stirring! You're doing fine! The drink needs to be continually stirred! I'm all right, I'm ok! Just a bit winded at the moment...whew!...and fatigued..."

"Ok, then, but if you need help..."

"Bubba, allow me to change the subject for a moment."

"Ok."

"You've been at Doctor Runyon's place as much as I have, or more than I have..."

"True."

"...and I have been ashamed of your moroseness there..."

"My what?"

"Your moroseness— moroseness!"

"*What the f...?*"

"Your manners there have been of that silent and

sullen and hang-dog kind, so that, upon my life and soul, I have been ashamed of you, Bubba Cotton!"

"You should be ashamed to be a man of your practice hanging out at the Cock-N-Bull Tavern, if there's anything to be ashamed of around here," replied Cotton.

"You shall not get off in that way," rejoined Stryker.

"Don't worry, wasn't planning to, Mr. McWeirdy..."

"What?"

"Nothing."

"No, Bubba, it's my duty to tell you—and if you were in here I'd tell you to your face, but DON'T COME IN HERE!—that you are a *dee*-vile-ish and ill-conditioned fellow among those in that family. In other words, you are a disagreeable fellow."

"...look who's calling the kettle black again..." Bubba drank a tumbler-full of 'punch' he had made, and laughed aloud as he continued to get drunker than snot.

"Ok, you can come in here now," Stryker said, having fetched a robe.

Cotton obliged.

"Look at me!" the big man said, adjusting himself inside his closed robe—to which Cotton first thanked God it was closed, then second blanched hard, not needing to see what he did see—"I have less need to make myself agreeable than you have."

"Are you sure 'bout that?"

"Fuck you and your smart mouth, Cotton! I have more money than God'll ever have, and it's not like I really *need* you for anything around here anyway. Jeezus, why do I do it?"

"Well, I've never seen you do *it* yet... *at least not with the opposite sex...*"

"What was that last part?"

"Nothing... Look, just get on with telling me about your matrimonial intentions. I'd *love* to hear about that."

"From the way you're acting, you have no business to know anything about my so-called 'matrimonial intentions'."

"I have no business to *be* at all, that I know of," said Bubba Cotton, "so let's just get on with it...Who's the broad?"

Stryker brightened. "Now, don't let my announcement of the name make you uncomfortable, Bubba," said Stryker, preparing him with ostentatious friendliness for the disclosure he was about to make, "because I know that you don't mean half of what you say; and if you meant it at all, it would be of no importance anyway..."

"Same to you, Bubble-Butt..."

"I make this little preface because you once mentioned this particular young lady in negative terms..."

"Young?...I mean, I did?...When?"

"Certainly, and in this house."

Bubba Cotton looked at his Appletini then looked at his flamboyant friend; he took a sip of Appletini then looked at his flamboyant friend.

Stryker told him, "You said she was a golden-haired Barbie-doll, the young woman being Bunnie Mancrizie."

Cotton spewed Appletini all over the living room, soaking the furniture adequately, including the fixture in front of him that was Mr. Stryker.

"Quite." Stryker said, reaching for a towel and patting his face. "If you had been a fellow of any sensitiveness or delicacy of feeling, Cotton, I might have been a little resentful of your employing such a designation as 'Barbie' to her; but you are not. You'd rather be a smart-ass, as usual; therefore I am no more annoyed when I think of that expression you used than I should be annoyed by a man's negative opinion when he sees a photo of me, someone who had no eye for a robustly exquisite man."

Bubba Cotton drank the 'punch' in his cup to finality and went back into the kitchen for a refill. He came back out and downed it at a great rate whilst looking at his friend.

"Now that you know all about it, Bubba," said Mr. Stryker, "I don't care about what is right, or what *should* be: she's a charming creature, and I have made up my mind to please myself: on the whole, I think I can afford to please myself..."

"Looks like that's been done already," said Cotton, pointing to the Lewinsky stain on the front of his robe.

Stryker ignored the comment and continued: "She will have in me a pretty man who is well off, and a man who can rise rapidly..."

"Huh?"

"...and a man of distinction."

"Don't kid yourself, F. Lee Redneck..."

"This is a piece of good fortune for her..."

"It's a piece of something..."

"But she is worthy of good fortune. So then, tell me...are you astonished?"

"You have no idea." Cotton quickly threw down another cup of 'punch', and winced. "But just for the sake of argument, *should* I be astonished?"

"Does that mean you approve?"

Cotton, walking again into the kitchen and back, poured more 'punch,' and said, "Why should I not approve?"

"Well!" said his friend Stryker, in all manner of Rip Taylor-ness, the only thing lacking being the confetti. "You take it more easily than I fancied you would and are less mercenary on my behalf than I thought you would be; though, to be sure, you know well enough by this time that your pretty, but ancient, chum is a man of strong will. Yes, Cotton, I have had enough of this style of life..."

"That style being...?"

"With all its same old boring routines. I feel that it is a pleasant thing for a man to have a home where he feels inclined to go, and when he doesn't, he can stay away. And I feel that Miss Mancrizie will always look good on my arm, and will always do me credit. So I have made up my mind. And now, Bubba, my boy, I want to say a word to *you* about *your* prospects: You are in a bad way, you know."

"You have no idea..."

"You really are in a bad way. And you don't know the value of money..."

"I have a pretty good idea..."

"You live hard. And one of these days, you'll knock someone up, and end up ill and poor. Maybe even catch The AIDS. So here is my advice: You really ought to think about shacking up with a nurse."

The preposterously patronizing tone with which he said it made Stryker look, to Cotton, like he was twice as big as he really was—like a Santa Claus on crack—and four times more offensive.

"Now, let me recommend you look it in the face," pursued Stryker, "I have looked it in the face, in my different way..."

"A *very* different way..."

"And you must look it in the face also, in your different way..."

"What way is that, pray tell...?"

"Marry! Marry someone for godssakes, you idiot! Find someone to take care of you! Nevermind your having no enjoyment of 'women's society' nor understanding of it, nor tact for it..."

"Understandably so..."

"Find a woman, Cotton! Find someone! Anybody! Whatever! Hell, find someone with a little property—or someone who rents to others so you can make some easy money—and marry her! Even if it's on a rainy day! That's the kind of thing for *you*, Bubba. So think about it."

"I'll think about it," said Cotton.

12

Asininity Acted Upon

The very next morning, Mr. Stryker, having made up his mind to that magnanimous bestowal of good fortune on the Doctor's daughter, resolved to make her happiness known to her before he left town for a long vacation himself. After some mental debating of the point, he came to the conclusion that it would be as well to get all the preliminaries done with, and they could then arrange at their leisure whether he should give her his hand a week or two before Hanukah, or during her Christmas break from school, if she were even still *in* school. He did not know.

As to the strength of his case, he had not a doubt about it. This would be easier than 'If the glove don't fit, you must acquit,' he decided.

Accordingly, Mr. Stryker decided to inaugurate his long vacation with a formal proposal to take Miss Mancrizie four-wheeling in the hills of Tennessee, to which he would hang back while she went, since nothing sounded more dreadful to the old barrister than gallivanting across heavily forested acreage and sailing through muddy creek-beds at high rates of speed. But he knew Bunnie would simply love it. And if this failed to grab her interest, he'd take her skydiving in Knoxville; that failing, they'd go para-sailing in Virginia Beach; failing that, they'd swim with the dolphins in the Caymans. One of those options ought to get, and hold, her attention, he figured.

Toward Chickenwell Street, therefore, Mr. Stryker shouldered his way from Temple Hillel, the only Jewish outpost in all of southern Kentucky. His way taking him past Tall Tales, and he both frequenting Tall Tales (more specifically, the Cock-N-Bull Tavern in the back), and knowing Travis 'Trip' Templeton to be an intimate friend of Runyon and Bunnie's, it entered Mr. Stryker's mind to enter the strip club, and reveal to Trip the brightness of the Chickenwell Street horizon.

So, Stryker pushed past the bouncer in his high chair, who gave no resistance, stumbled down the two steps, walked past Ellsworth the ancient bartender, and shouldered himself into the musty back office with parallel iron bars in the window where Mr. Templeton sat at a computer staring at Quick Books, in an attempt to do some simple accounting.

"Hola!" said Mr. Stryker to Trip. "How do you do? I hope you are well!" It was Stryker's grand peculiarity that he always seemed too big for any place, or space. He was so much too big for Tall Tales (with its low ceilings), that the old dicks in distant corners looked up with looks of remonstrance, as though he squeezed them against the wall. The hos themselves, magnificently shedding their garments onstage, were also displeased, as if Stryker's large form was somehow covering up their nakedness from clear across the club, thus diminishing their tips.

The discreet Trip Templeton said, in a sample tone of the voice he would recommend under the circumstances, "What's up, Stryker? What brings you here so early?" and shook his hand. There was a peculiarity in his manner of shaking hands, always to be seen in any bartender or waitress who shook hands with a customer while the hos pervaded the air. He shook in a self-abnegating way, as one who shook on behalf of the entire staff and ownership of Tall Tales.

"Can I get you a drink, Stryker?" asked Trip, in his business character.

"Why, no, thank you; this is a private visit to yourself, Mr. Templeton."

"Well, you know I don't do that sort of thing personally, at least not when I'm on the clock, but if you give me a minute, I'll look around and see if..."

"No, Mr. Templeton, that's not what I mean. I'm

here for a private *word* with you."

"Oh! Oh, Jeezus...I'm sorry. Yes, of course. You just want to talk," said Trip Templeton, his face turning several shades of red, while his eyes strayed to the stripping ho afar off.

"I am going," said Mr. Stryker, leaning his arms confidentially on the desk: whereupon, although it was a large double one, there appeared to be not half desk enough for him: "I am going to make an offer of myself in marriage to your agreeable little friend, Bunnie Mancrizie."

Trip choked. "*Ass-sphincter* says what?"

"What?"

"Um, I mean, what'd you say? I'm not sure I heard you right," said Trip, rubbing his chin and looking at his visitor dubiously.

"Azz Fincter says what?" repeated Stryker, drawing back. "What did you mean by that?"

"My meaning," answered the man of business, "is, of course, friendly and appreciative, and that it does you the greatest credit, and—in short, my meaning is to wish upon you all good things. But really, you know, Stryker—" Trip paused, and shook his head at the big man in the oddest manner, as if he was compelled against his will to add aloud, 'You do realize, Stryker, that you're old, and fat as hell, and there ain't a fucking snowball's chance in Costa Rica that....'

Stryker slapped the desk, hard. "Well!"

"...Whoops. Did I say all that out loud?"

"If I understand you correctly, Mr. Templeton, then I'll be god-damned!"

"If you wish."

"Damn you, Trip!" cried Stryker, staring at him, "Am I not eligible?"

Trip nearly coughed up a lung trying not to laugh. "Oh, dear me yes! Yes. Oh yes, you are eligible. If you say you are eligible, then you are eligible." His eyes bulged, and he released a short snort.

"Do I not have more money than God?"

"Well, if it's about that, then sure, you have some dough. No question there."

"And advancing toward partnership in my firm?"

"Yes, yes, I suppose so."

"Then what on earth is your meaning, Mr. Templeton?"demanded Stryker, perceptibly crestfallen.

"Well, I—Oh, you want go there, then? Is that it? Are you *sure* you want to go there? Because..."

"Straight!" said Stryker with a plump of his fist on the desk.

"I think I wouldn't, if I were you..."

"Why?" asked Stryker. "If we don't 'go there,' as you say, then I'll knock you into that corner straightaway! And don't think I won't!"

Trip leveled his eyes at him. "Nobody puts Trip in a corner."

Stryker shook a sausage-like forefinger at him. "You are a man of 'business,' and are bound to have your reasons why you think I'd be rejected. So let's hear it then! Why shouldn't we 'go there'?"

"You sure you want to do this?"

"Absolutely!"

Trip glanced at the distant ho, then looked back at the angry Stryker. "Well, for one thing you're, what?— old as my dead grandma's buckskin panties? And what?—bald as a fuckin' marble bowling ball shaved with a Gillette Triple-Threat action-blade with built-in Sensor Shaver and shoved up a cow's ass lined with sandpaper? There's two strikes against ya, right there, Bobo Brazil..."

"But I wear a toupee! And it's a good one, too!"

"Yeah, if your lookin' to make out with an eight-hundred pound squirrel, Bullwinkle! Come on, get a frickin' clue!"

Stryker winced and patted his crown.

"For another thing, you're wearing a fuckin' feather boa. A fucking *feather boa*! Which begs the question, how the *fuck* d'ju get in here with that thing, and what were you thinkin' about gettin' yourself back out?

'Cause you sure as hell ain't gonna get outta here alive! Jeezus, man! Where the *hell* do you think you are? San Fran? These are the hills of southern Kentucky! *Kentucky* for chrissakes! You'd be lucky not to get your balls sheared off and handed to you shoved inside a fifth of Jack!"

"But I wear this into the Cock-N-Bull all the time, and no one's ever said anything..."

"Yeah, well, that freak show doesn't open for another six hours, so I'd just watch myself in here if I were you."

Stryker now sat quietly in a slump, as if he were a steaming pile of melted cow dung.

"Look," said Trip, in a last-ditch effort at compassion, "all I'm sayin' is that no hot young snatch like Bunny Mancrizie is going to go for an old...uh...um...whatever you are....like you. It jus' ain't gonna happen."

"But..."

"Ain't...Gonna....Happen!"

"So what you mean to tell me, Mr. Templeton," said Stryker, squaring his elbows, "Is that your opinion of Bunnie Mancrizie is that she's a dick-teasing bubble-headed bleach-blonde Barbie doll?"

"Uh, no. Not exactly. What I *do* mean to tell you, Stryker," said Trip, his face reddening, "is that if I ever hear you disrespecting that young lady again, then I will personally rip those fat lips of yours off your chubby little cheeks and pickle them in four-month-old horseshit so I can shove them so far down your throat you'll be able to feel 'em in your ass-crack as you walk! Am I bein' clear?"

"Perfectly."

"Good."

"You know, I'm sorry, Mr. Templeton, but this is all very new to me. I'm not exactly the sharpest tool in the shed, or at least, that's what I've been told. But do I understand you correctly in that you are advising me *not* to go to Chickenwell Street and offer myself—

myself, Stryker, of the Law firm of Beauregard and Shittim, to that beautiful young lady?"

"You got it, Tubby. Hit the nail right on the head."

Stryker sat dejected again, and again, Trip felt a tinge of compassion. "Do you want my advice, Stryker?"

"Yes I do."

"Now understand me," pursued Trip, "As a man of 'business,' I am not justified in saying anything about this matter, for, as a man of 'business,' I know nothing of it. But, as a middle-aged feller, who has carried Bunnie Mancrizie in his arms, who is a trusted friend of Bunnie and her father, and who has a great affection for them both, I have spoken. Now again, am I being clear?"

"Crystal. But I think I still have a chance. And if it's all the same to you, Templeton, I'm still going over there when we're done here and give it a shot."

Trip leaned back in his chair and paused for a moment, slowly letting out a long, deep exhale.

"Ok, look. I was just thinking, Stryker, that you're one of my most valued customers at the Cock-N-Bull. And that as your friend, I've got to tell you that it might be a tad painful for you to go over there and find out that you're mistaken. It might be painful for you to have Doctor Runyon tell you 'Fuck you, Fatty!' to your face. It might be painful for you to have that hot twenty-two year-old piece of snatch tell you 'Fuck you!' to your face. So tell ya what I'm gonna do for you. I'll go over there and act totally ignorant of everything we've talked about this morning 'tween the two of us, and scout out the territory for you. I'll find some way to bring it up in a manner that will answer your question, and hopefully not embarrass the living shit out of the both of us. Then I'll come by your place and tell ya what I found out. What you say? Fair enough?"

"How long will I have to wait?"

"Oh, well, only about a few hours I suppose. I could go over to Chickenwell Street this afternoon and have an answer to you by early evening. How's that?"

"Ok, I say yes," said Stryker: "I won't go over there now, but I'll go on home and wait for you to come by tonight. You have yourself a good morning, Mr. Templeton."

"Same to you. And thanks for coming in. And I'll have Hoss walk you out so you don't get your ass kicked by one of them truckers in there."

"'preciate it. You're a good man, Trip."

Then, just before Stryker burst forth from the club, his butt-cheeks burst forth such a concussion of air on his passage through the stage area that to stand up against it required the utmost remaining strength of Ellsworth the ancient bartender.

On his way to the car, the attorney, unprepared as he was when he arrived at the club to take down such a large pill as he now had to swallow, now clearly had no choice, and got the pill down nonetheless.

"And now," said Stryker, in the parking lot shaking an extended middle finger at Tall Tales, "I consider it her loss." It was an old trick of the 'old Rebel' tactician, one in which he found great relief. "You shall not reject me, young lady," said Stryker, "I reject you first!"

Accordingly, when Trip Templeton came around that night as late as ten o'clock, Stryker—among a quantity of 'shine and bottles littered about for the purpose of transport to the nether regions—seem to have cared less about the subject of the morning. He even showed surprise when he saw Trip, and was altogether in a absent-minded drunkerdly state.

"Welll!" said the good natured, chuckle-faced tubster after a full gallon of J.D.'s finest, and about a gallon of homemade 'shine. "La Dee Daaaaaa...!"

"Stryker, I've been to Chickenwell."

"To Chickenwell?" repeated Stryker, again, in all manner of Rip Taylor-ishness. "Oh, to be sure! What was I thinking?"

"And I have no doubt," said Trip, "that I was right in the conversation we had. My opinion is confirmed and I stand by my advice."

"I assure you," returned Stryker, in the friendliest way—maybe even overly-friendly, "That I am sorry for it on your account, and sorry for it on that wretched father of hers' account. I know this will go down as a horrible loss for that poor family; let us say no more about it."

"Uh, I don't think I understand..." said Trip.

"I should say not," rejoined Stryker, in that grumpy-drunk way. "But it doesn't matter anyway."

"But it does matter," Trip urged.

"No it doesn't. I assure you it doesn't," said Stryker slurredly. "I am well done with her mistake, so there is no sense to keep harping on it. Young women have committed similar follies often before, and have repented for them in poverty and obscurity often before. In an unselfish way, I am sorry that the matter is behind us. For Bunnie's sake, of course. But in a selfish way, I am sorry that the matter didn't turn out well for her, too, because now I realize she is a flaming *bee*-otch of the highest order. And I realize now I could have gained nothing by being with her, so there is no harm done. I have not proposed to the young bee-otch, and, between you and I, I am certain that on reflection I should never have committed myself to that extent. Templeton, you cannot control the vanities and giddiness of ditsy little girls; you must not expect to, or you will always be disappointed. Now, let's not say another fucking word about it. I tell you, I regret it on so many levels, 'cause after she came so close to having *this*," he grabbed his paunch and shook it, "how could she possibly ever settle for anything else? Everything else is just chump-change for her from here on out, if you ask me. But Templeton, dear Templeton, I really do appreciate you being a sounding board for my drunken tirade tonight. I am most sure I won't remember a goddamn thing of this conversation in the morning. Oh, and by the way, speaking of things I won't remember—FUCK YOU AND THAT PIECE OF SHIT RUST-

BUCKET YOU RODE IN ON!"

Trip was so taken aback that he looked quite stupidly at Mr. Stryker, now shouldering him toward the door. Stryker actually had the balls to kick Templeton in the ass before slamming the door and firing off an acidic, "Good *night!*" from safely on the other side of the now locked door.

Trip Templeton was out in the night before he knew what the hell had just happened.

And soon Stryker was lying back on his sofa, stark raving naked, with his wireless web-connected laptop fired up and ready to go.

13

A Cacophonous Conversation

If Bubba Cotton ever shone anyway, he certainly never shone in the shack of Doctor Runyon. He had been there often, during a whole year, and had always been the same moody and morose dipshit. When he cared to talk, he talked well; but, the cloud of caring for nothing, which overshadowed him with such a fatal darkness, was very rarely pierced by the light within him.

And yet he did care something for the streets that environed that shack, and for the senseless dirt that made their pavements. Many a night he drunken-hazily and unhappily wandered there, when 'shine had brought no transitory gladness to him; many a dreary daybreak revealed his solitary figure lingering there, and still lingering there when the first beams of the sun brought into strong relief removed beauties of architecture such as hog-barns and hay-lofts—and the occasional rare 'Mail Pouch Tobacco' relief—as perhaps the quiet time brought some sense of better things, else forgotten and unattainable, into his mind. Of late, his neglected bed over near the Temple Hilel had known him more scantily than ever; and often when he had thrown himself upon it no longer than a few minutes, he had got up again, and haunted that old neighborhood.

On a day in August, when Mr. Stryker (after notifying his jackass that 'he had thought better of that marrying matter') had carried His Delicacy to work for a time in Clarksville, Tennessee to get away from the embarrassment of it all, Cotton's feet still tread these dusty streets, and going from irresolute and purposeless, to his feet becoming animated—if not solely from the effects of a raging case of athlete's foot—by an intention, they took him to the Doctor's door.

He went upstairs, and found Bunnie at her work, to which the startled bastard in bed with her immediately grabbed up his clothes, threw down a Hamilton on the bed, and jumped stark-naked from the second-story window, thinking Cotton might be one of the 'thorities.'

Bunnie, for herself, had never quite been at ease with Cotton, and grabbed up the ten spot and received him with little (maybe too little) embarrassment as he seated himself on the edge of the bed. But, looking up at his face during the interchange of their first few pleasantries, she observed a change in it.

"You look like shit, Cotton."

"The life I lead, Bunnie, is not conducive to health. Not like yours, anyway," he remarked in all sarcasm.

She stuck her tongue out at him.

"I meant that you were in good health," he rejoined.

"Yeah, right. So what you doin' here anyway, Cotton?"

He looked up at the ceiling and heaved a heavily melancholy sigh. "But what should I expect of such wanton vices?" he said.

"Huh?"

"The way I live my life. In such debauchery."

"Yeah, it's a shame you don't live a better life. And if you're going to keep talkin' like that, you'll have to excuse me while I get my dictionary..."

"I know it's a shame!" he said, ignoring her last directive, "Even God knows it's a shame!"

"Then why don't you change it?"

Looking gently at him for the first time ever, Bunnie was surprised and saddened to see that there were tears in his eyes. There were tears in his voice too, as he answered:

"It is too late for that. I shall never be better than I am now. I shall sink lower, and be worse. Probably end up on that stupid celebrity rehab show on cable."

"Don't you have to be a *celebrity* first?"

He shot her a dirty look, at the moment feeling too sorry for himself to ejaculate even the weakest of fuck you's.

He leaned an elbow on her in-table, and nearly knocked her birth control pills whither and nigh across the wooden floorboards. He covered his eyes at such a close call, knowing she would have sliced his balls off for having done that, having somewhat of an idea the expense she paid each month to obtain them.

But she had never seen him more softened, and was very distressed. She also couldn't help but wonder if she was about to be the victim of a horrifying mur-der-suicide.

He knew what she was thinking, so without look-ing at her, he said, "Please forgive me, Bunnie. I falter amidst the words I want to say to you."

"*What*? Did you just say 'falter amidst the words I want to say to you'? Are you fuckin' out of your mind or did you just watch *The Notebook* or something? Cause I hear that that movie is pretty gay..."

"Bunnie! Would you shut your friggin' crank for the tiniest of instances and hear me out?"

"Ok, it's your nickel..."

"I'm not paying for this!"

"It's an expression, dumbshit! Jeezus!"

"Oh. So are you ready to hear me out?"

On the bed, Bunnie sighed a sighed of heavy sar-casm. "If it will do you some good, Cotton; if it will make you happier, then it will make me happy too."

"Well, God bless you for such soothing words. 'Preciate it," he struck back with equal sarcasm.

Then, for some ungodly reason, he stuck a lampshade on his head just to be goofy and try and make her laugh (it didn't). Then he spoke steadily, "Don't be afraid of me, Bunnie. Don't shrink away from anything I say. I am like one who died young—all of my life I have been like that."

She was suddenly pale and trembling. "I hope

your just quotin' Hendrix or Jim Morrison or something, cause this ain't where you're gonna pull out a knife and kill me is it? I've heard of that kinda thing happenin', and I ain't gonna lie, it scares the shit outta me. God, I knew this was gonna happen some day! I jus' knew it! This is where I pay for my sins...!"

"Bunnie, calm down. I'm not gonna do that."

"Good, cause you had me goin' for a second. With all that 'don't be afraid of me' bullshit, and 'I died young' crap..."

"You know, this isn't working out so well. Maybe I should go..."

"No, wait! I'm sorry if I offended you, Cotton, I really am. But you're talkin' real creepy-like and..."

"You think I'm a first rate jack-ass, don't you, Bunnie?"

"Well, no. No. Not really. Not totally, anyway. Well. Yeah. Kind of. But you know, it's kinda weird how you always come 'round our place and just sit and mope all day. That cain't be healthy on anyone. But other than that, you're a real stand-up guy, Cotton. I'd screw ya if I had to."

"Thanks," he said flatly. "But do you really mean that?"

"Sure!"

"You know, if I didn't know better, I'd think you just paid me a compliment."

"Consider it yours."

"I'll never forget it, Bunnie. Truly."

"That's fine, honey," she said, rubbing his arm as if he were a little boy. "You just take that and you hang onto it. You enjoy it."

He suddenly got real serious:

"All joking aside Bunnie, if it had been possible that you could have returned the love of the man you see before you—self-flagellated, wasted, drunken, poor creature of misuse—he would have been conscious this day that he would only be capable of bringing you misery, bringing you sorrow, and bringing you blight.

That he would only disgrace you, pull you down with him..."

"Your scarin' me again, asswipe...Maybe you better leave."

"...I know very well that you could have no tenderness for me..."

"Are you quotin' from *The* fuckin' *Notebook* again? Does anybody get killed in that?"

"... but I ask for none! I am even thankful that we cannot be together..."

"Help! Police! Dad! Somebody!"

"Bunnie, for chrissakes, I'm not gonna hurt you! I'm just tryin' to tell ya something here. I'm tryin' to tell you in confidence something what's in my heart."

"Well, ok. If that's all it is, then I jus' gotta tell you right now—I cain't save you, Cotton. I have this really bad history with dating losers, you know, and thinkin' I can change them an' all. But isn't that what all us hot women do? And isn't that shit just soooo fucked up? Cause the men, you know, they don't never change. And the nice normal guys out there? They don't never get to hook-up with hot pieces of snatch like me, cause, you know, I'm jus' always lookin' for the bad boy; the fucked up dude; the guy who'd sell his own mother for a friggin' ferret then smack me 'cross the jaw with a Louisville slugger..."

"Ok, Ok! Time-out! Jeez, I get your point. But you do realize that all that's just because you were born with an affliction commonly known in psychiatric circles as *bum-magnetisis*?"

"What?"

"That you shop exclusively with a platinum card from the Bank of Losertonia accepted only at the Mall of Shitheadsia?"

"*What*?"

"Nevermind. But I gotta tell you, Bunnie, I'm not looking for you to save me. Now will you just sit back and hear me out a little bit more?"

"Oh, all right."

"All you can do for me, Bunnie, is done. I wish you to know that you have been the last dream of my soul. In my degradation I have not been so degraded but that the sight of you with your father, and of your home, has stirred old shadows that I thought had died out of me long ago. Since I've known you, I've been troubled by a remorse that I thought would never reproach me again, and have heard whispers from old voices impelling me upward, ones I thought were silent forever. I have had unformed ideas of starving for flesh, being born anew, shaking off sloth and embracing sensuality, fighting out long abandoned fights. A dream, all a dream, that ends in nothing, and leaves the sleeper where she lay down. But I wish you to know that you have inspired it all."

She stared at him. "Is that from *A Nightmare on Elm Street*? Cause I love that movie! God, Cotton, maybe you should be an actor! You'd be real good at it..."

"I'm not acting...Nor am I quotin' from no movie! As I said before, all's I'm tellin' you is what's in my heart."

"Ok, that's what I thought, because if that is the case—HELP! POLICE! DADDY! PRISS! SOMEBODY! HELP!"

"Bunnie, I, I..."

"Fuck you, Dahmer! You gotta *go*! And now! HELP! POLICE! I'M BEIN' MURDERED IN HERE! HELP ME!"

Cotton immediately jumped up and held his arms in the air.

"Look! I have nothin'...!"

"HELP! HELP ME!"

He turned out all his pockets. "No knives, no guns, nothin'!"

"I'M BEING KILT IN HERE!"

Cotton didn't know what else to do, so he whipped off all his clothes and held up his arms, wearing nothing but a wife-beater and his BVDs. The look of distress on his harried face was so extremely pitiful, and so humiliatingly *painful*, that Bunnie had to laugh.

"Ha, ha, Cotton! Look at you, standin' there with your junk all floppin' around in your tighty-whities in front of me! Ok, I believe you that you're not gonna kill me."

"Thank you. But I can see that I've distressed you, so I will draw this to an end. Will you at least let me believe, that when I think of this day in the future, that the last confidence of my life was given to you, and that it lies there alone, and will be shared by no one?"

"Bubba Cotton, you ain't plannin' on killin' yourself are you? Cause if you are, then by all means, your secret's safe with me. I didn't understand a goddamned word of what you just say'd, and it majorly creeped me out, but if it will help you to consider continuin' on livin', then of course your secret's safe with me."

"Thank you. And again, God bless you."

"God bless you...too...?"

He reached over and put her hand to his lips, then he moved towards the door.

"Don't worry, Bunnie, I'll never mention this conversation to anyone and will never mention it to you again. In the hour of my death, I shall hold sacred the one good remembrance—and shall thank and bless you for it—that my last avowal of myself was made to you, and that my name, and faults, and miseries, are gently being carried in your heart. May it otherwise be light and happy."

He was so unlike what he had ever shown himself to be, and it was so sad to think how much he had thrown away, and how much he every day kept down and subdued, that Bunnie Mancrizie wept mournfully for him as he stood looking at her from the middle of the room.

"Be comforted!" he said suddenly, in the manner of Ace Ventura—but in total seriousness. "I am not worth such feeling, Bunnie! An hour or two from now, all the low habits that I scorn I will but yield to once again, rendering me worth even less for those tears of yours now running down your cheeks; worth less than any dog who creeps along in the streets. Be comforted! But within myself, I shall always be towards you what I am now, though outwardly I shall be what you have heretofore seen me to be..."

He stopped, suddenly realizing she was not shedding tears of sadness, but tears of....laughter?

He stared at her. "What's the deal?"

"Ha ha ha ha ha ha! I'm sorry! But it's so hard for me to take you all serious like sayin' all that junk while you're standin' there in the middle of my room with your willy all floppin' around in your undies! But really, Cotton. You need to go to Hollywood. I'm tellin' ya, you'd be great in one of them movies out there."

Cotton sighed and began gathering up his clothes, not bothering to put them on.

"Just know, Bunnie, that there is someone in this world who loves you so much that he would make the ultimate sacrifice to see to it that the one you truly love remains beside you."

Then he turned, and exited the door.

Bunnie waited a beat, and then: "Ha ha ha ha ha ha ha ha!"

14

Things No One Should Ever Have To See

To the eyes of Jeremiah Kracker, sitting on his stool outside Tall Tales with his grisly urchin beside him, a vast number and variety of objects were thrown at them from vehicles passing on State Route 49. Who could sit upon anything outside Tall Tales during the busy hours of the day and not be hit with a french fry, or the last half-gallon of a Big Gulp, a cigarette butt or two—or five—and even the occasional Whopper Jr. in its entirety with pickles and extra mayo (hold the onions).

Who could also sit outside Tall Tales and not be dazed and deafened by the booming stupid-loud car stereos, booming forth from insanely large pick-up trucks with big stupid tires, and booming loud Harley-Davidsons driven stupidly without mufflers?

One lane of Route 49 tended westward with the sun, the other tending eastward from the sun, both tending to send drivers and their vehicles smashing into each other at high rates of speed and out over the fields when the red and yellow glare of the sun going down, or coming up, hits the windshields of either lane just so.

With the straw from a Burger King Coca-Cola Slushie in his mouth, Mr. Kracker sat watching the two streams of vehicles, like the heathen rustic who has for several centuries been on duty watching one stream—saving that Jerry had no expectation of their ever running dry. Nor would it have been unrealistic to assume there might have been an expectation of a hopeful kind, that a car or truck or bus would accidentally run off the road and mercifully blast his wretched form into the world beyond.

It should be pointed out that another small part of Mr. Kracker's income was earned by piloting widowed women around on their daily and simplest of errands. Brief as such companionship was in every separate instance, Mr. Kracker still never failed to become so interested in the old bag as to express a strong desire to have the honor of drinking to her very good health. Which normally resulted in a scream from the widow, and a slight scratching out of his eyeballs, when he pulled out his flask and the old girl realized he was probably driving drunk already.

Usually this resulted in him losing his tip, and more than that, the resulting swerve to get the old bag off his face usually resulted in him being pulled over and slapped with an open container violation, having to walk a straight line, and touching his finger to his nose more than once, and then, the finale: The dreaded breathalyzer.

There used to be a time and place when a poet sat upon a stool in a public place, and mused at the sight of men (most likely in ancient Greece if I had to guess, or in modern day San Francisco), but Mr. Kracker, sitting on a stool in a public place, but not being a poet, and most goddamned assuredly *not* being interested in looking at men, mused as little as possible as he looked about him.

It fell out that he was thusly engaged upon said stool in a season when crowds were few, and widows needing driven fewer, and when his affairs in general were so unprosperous as to awaken a strong suspicion in his chest that Mrs. Kracker must have been 'flopping' a lot just to help make the rent, when an unusual concourse pouring westward down State Route 49 attracted his attention. Looking that way, Mr. Kracker made out that some kind of funeral was coming along, and that there was popular objection to this funeral, which engendered uproar in the form of incessantly honking horns, birds flipped from rolled-down windows, and not the slightest shortage of expletives shouted from the tops of lungs.

"Little Jerry," said Mr. Kracker, turning to his off-spring, "it's a buryin'."

"Hooray, father!" cried Little Jerry.

The young redneck uttered this exultant sound with mysterious significance. The elder redneck took the cry so ill, that he watched for his opportunity, and smote the young redneck on the ear.

"What d'ye mean? What are you *hoo*-rayin' at? What do you want to convey to your own father by sayin' such a thing?" *This boy is gettin' to be too much for me!* thought Kracker, surveying the lad, *Him and his hoo-rays!* "Don't let me hear no more of you, or you shall feel some more of me! D'ye hear?"

"I warn't doin' no harm," Little Jerry protested, rubbing his cheek.

"Drop it then," said Kracker; "I won't have none of your 'no harm, no foul's. Get atop that there seat, and look at the vehicles goin' by."

His son obeyed, and the vehicles approached; they were booming (from stereos) and hissing (from leaky radiators) behind a dingy hearse. Riding in the hearse, Mr. Kracker noticed a lone figure with a gray hoodie pulled up over the face, bowed in all manner of deep prayer, or deep mourning, or both.

Funerals had at all times a remarkable attraction for Mr. Kracker; he always pricked up his senses, and became excited when a funeral passed Tall Tales. Naturally, therefore, a funeral with this uncommon attendance excited him greatly, and he asked of the first man pulled over to fix a flat tire:

"What is it brother?"

"A fuckin' flat tire, genius. What's it look like?"

"No, what's this all about?"

"*I* don't know," said the man. "Nails in the road, you know, some kind of shit like that..."

"No goddammit! The funeral! Oh, fuck it..."

Jerry asked another man, pulled over with an over-heatin' radiator: "Who is it?"

'I don't know," returned the man, clapping his hands to his mouth and spitting on them, vociferating at the surprising heat when he took the radiator cap off too soon. "Pro'ly a spy. And a spic, if I had to guess."

At length, a person better informed on the merits of the case, tumbled out of his car to puke up some early morning 'shine, and from this person Jerry learned that the funeral was the funeral of one Manuel McCly.

"Was he a spic?" asked Mr. Kracker.

"We say 'hispanic' now, you fuckin' redneck!" Little Jerry chided, in a fit of courage. "Get with the times!"

"He was an 'old Rebel' sp...*Hispanic*," returned the informant.

"Why of course!" exclaimed Jerry, recalling hearing of trials and hearings due to the recent influx, or slow dribble more like it, of illegals up from the down south territories—*way* down south territories— though he really wasn't sure yet what it all meant. "Is he dead?"

"Now what do you think? Of course he's dead! Dead as the mutton chops on old General Lee's fuckin' jowls (God rest his soul)."

Then the redneck informant turned toward the temporarily stopped procession (because when farmer Jed Jenkins on his John Deere tried to cross the road ahead of the funeral, it too broke down) and shouted, "Let's pull 'em out! Spies! Mex-ee-cains! Pull 'em out!"

The idea was so acceptable in the prevalent absence of anyone with half a brain, that the crowd was caught up in the ensuing uproar reminiscent of an old-time Klan rally, and they loudly repeated the suggestion to 'have 'em out!', and to 'pull 'em out!'

The mob mobbed the hearse and on the crowd's opening of the door, the single mourner scuffled out and was in their hands in no time. But the young Latino lad was alert, and made such good use of his fists, that in another moment he was scurrying away up the cow pasture, after shedding his hoodie, ball-cap, bandana, a job application, a pack of cigarettes, a lighter, and other paraphernalia for the making of homemade tattoos.

These the people tore to pieces and scattered far and wide with great enjoyment, while farmer Jenkins hurriedly tried to crank his ancient tractor back to life, because he knew crowds like this in these hills stopped at nothing, and was a monster much dreaded, and they would probably next be turning on him and shredding his tractor all the way down to its last gear.

They had already got the asinine notion to open up the hearse and take the coffin out, when some bright genius decided it was better to let the coffin be and have everyone instead herd over to Tall Tales and raid the place for some early morning whiskey and some young female flesh.

Among the first, and only, somewhat level-headed person to know that you didn't want to be within a hundred miles of Tall Tales when that went down, Jerry Kracker hustled across the street and made his escape by jumping into the hearse alongside the newly put-back-in coffin.

The hearse driver made some protest against this change in the ceremonies, but the mob still being alarmingly near, and several voices remarking that maybe they'd rather continue the riot around the hearse than look at female skin (only God would know why), Jerry looked at the driver and said, "You better step on it, asshole, if you know what's good for you!" and the hearse darted away, spewing gravel toward the crowd as it whipped around the shoulder to avoid farmer Jenkins' still stalled-out tractor.

Thus with beer-drinking, pot-smoking, song-roaring, and racial slurs being thrown about like beach balls at a *Wham!* concert, the disorderly crowd debauched themselves into the late afternoon at Tall Tales, and Trip Templeton made a killing off it.

As to the funeral procession, or what was left of it, which is to say, only the single hearse, its destination was the old church of Saint Pancreas, far off in the fields. It got there in course of time; the driver insisted on dumping the load in the ground without delay; and finally, the internment of one deceased Manuel McCly began in this way.

The dead man disposed of, and it being early in the evening, and the crowd being under the influence of untold gallons of alcohol and immeasurable amounts of sexual frustration, finally decided to exit Tall Tales in search of providing itself with some other form of entertainment.

Another bright genius (or perhaps the same one) suggested they go and sack the downtown area of Grouse Gulch; on their way also harassing casual passers-by as if such innocents were old Rebel 'spies' themselves, and needed to have vengeance wreaked upon them. Chase was given to some scores of inoffensive persons (and several offensively smelling ones), who had never been near the old Rebel in their lives, and were roughly hustled and maltreated. The transition to the sport of window-breaking, and then, to the plundering of the VFW, was easy and natural.

At last, after several hours, when sundry store awnings had been pulled down, and some area railings had been torn up, to inflame the more belligerent spirits, a rumor was sent around that the National Guard was coming. Upon hearing this rumor, the crowd gradually melted away, and perhaps the Guard *did* come, or perhaps it didn't, but this was the usual progress of a southern Kentucky hills mob.

Mr. Kracker remained at the churchyard to assist in covering the coffin with earth, after the undertaker who had first duggen the hole had somehow heard tell there was a riot in town—he and the hearse driver having quickly jumped into the undertaker's '77 Gremlin to go join it. Jerry stayed and found the place to have a soothing influence on him. Then he drove the hearse to a neighborhood crack-house, procured a blunt and smoked it, leaning over a railing on the porch and staring at one spot on the ground for hours.

"Jerry," said Mr. Kracker, apostrophizing himself in his usual way when he was higher than the observation deck of the Burj Kalifa in Dubai, "you see that there McCly today, and you see with your own eyes that he was pro'ly the brother of the boy who ran, or his father, or maybe his grandfather, or maybe he was no relation at all, or maybe he was the boy's probation officer, or maybe..."

God, he needed to stop smoking weed.

But having smoked his blunt out, and ruminating uncontrollably about nothing in particular for another hour or so, he turned himself about and drove himself in the hearse back to Tall Tales an hour before its closing. Whether his meditations on nothing in particular had touched his liver, or whether he needed to take a piss like a Russian race-horse, or whether he simply desired to suppress the urge to show a little attention to an eminent congressman enjoying the last show of the night—whatever the reason—he made a quick call to his 'medical advisor,' a psychic named Rhonda, and asked if she'd read his tea leaves even at this late hour, to which she did agree. So he left once again in the hearse.

Little Jerry relieved his father at the stool with dutiful interest, and reported No Job in his absence. The club now closed, and Ellsworth the ancient bartender (working a rare late shift) came out, and Mr. Kracker and his son on the way home discussed what he'd learned from Rhonda's tea leaves.

"Now I tell you what," said Mr. Kracker to his wife on entering the trailer, "If as an honest tradesman, my dentures go wrong tonight, and I find out that you've been 'flopping' without me, I shall work you just the same as if I were payin' for it."

The dejected Mrs. Kracker shook her head.

"Why, you've been at it before my face!" said Mr.

Kracker, with signs of angry apprehension.

"I am saying nothing..."

"Well, then *don't* say nothin'. You don't have to! I cain see old Artie Klebald out that there window a runnin' down the trailer park with his britches all down around his ankles having come from only one possible *die*-rection. This one!"

"Yes, Jerry..."

"*Yes, Jerry,*" he mocked, flopping down at the kitchen table, too tired and too wasted to do anything about it. "You and your 'yes, Jerry'!"

"Are you going back out tonight?" asked his 'decent' wife.

"Yes I am!"

"May I go with you father?" inquired Little Jerry.

"No you mayn't. I'm a goin'—as your mother knows—a fishin'."

"Your fishing rod gets rather rusty even though you seem to use it a lot, don't it dad?"

"Never you mind about that, Squirt."

"Are you gonna bring us some fish home, father?"

"If I don't, we'll all be stuck eatin' your mama's crappy cookin' again!" returned the gentleman, shaking his head. "Now that's about enough questions out of you for one night. I ain't goin' out till you've been long in bed. So hop to it."

He devoted himself during the remainder of the evening to keeping a most vigilant watch on Mrs. Kracker, and sullenly holding her in conversation that she might be prevented from going out and 'flopping' to his financial, and marital, disadvantage.

"And mind you!" said Mr. Kracker to his wife, "no games to-morrow! If I, as an honest tradesman, succeed in providin' a slab of meat or two, then I'll cook it my own damn self! You and your Martha-Stewart's-evil-twin's fingers ain't a-gonna touch it!"

"I thought you said you was goin' fishin'?"

"Huntin'! Didn't I say huntin'?"

"No, you say'd fishin'."

"Well, whatever! And if I, an honest tradesman, feel like bringin' a little 'shine home to-morrow, then the two's of you is just gonna hafta be happy with water! Like they say—when you go to Rome, do as Rome does. Rome will be an ugly customer to you if you don't do as it says, and *I'm* your Rome!"

Then he began grumbling again: "I don't know how you feed any of us with your dog-awful cookin'! Look at your boy there—he is your boy, ain't he?—he's as thin as a waif! And you call yourself a mother? Don't you know that the first duty of a mother is to blow her son out?"

"*What?*"

"Uh, feed him! Feed him's what I said!...*Didn't* I?"

This touched Little Jerry on a tender place, in more ways than one, who'd begged his mother to perform her first duty, and above all, to lay especial stress on the discharge of that maternal function so delicately referred to by his other parent. (Food that is. Food is what we're talking about here. Feeding the boy.)

Thus the evening wore away with the Kracker family, until Little Jerry was ordered to bed, and his mother, laid under similar injuctions by her husband to soon be laid, turned in also.

Mr. Kracker did not start upon his excursion until nearly four o'clock in the a.m. Toward that early and ghostly hour, he rose up from his bed, took a key out of his pocket, opened a locked cupboard, and brought forth a sack, a crowbar of convenient size, a rope and chain, and a fishing pole with tackle-box. Packing these items on and about himself in a skillful manner, he made a stupid face at the sleeping Mrs. Kracker, extinguished the light, and went out.

Little Jerry, who had only made a feint of undressing when he went to bed, was not long after his father. Under cover of darkness, he followed him out of the room, out of the trailer, out of the trailer park and down the street.

Impelled by a laudable ambition to study the art

and mystery of his father's honest calling, Little Jerry, keeping as close to house-fronts, walls and doorways as his eyes were close to one another, held his honored parent in view. The honored parent steering northward had not gone far, when he was joined by another disciple of Captain Ahab, and the two trudged on together.

Within half an hour from starting, they were out beyond old man Winkleman's place and out upon a lonely road. Another fisherman was picked up there—and done so silently, that if Little Jerry had been superstitious, he might have supposed the second fisherman to have, all of a sudden, split himself in two.

The three went on, and Little Jerry went on, until the three stopped under a bank of weeping willow trees overhanging the road. Underneath the bank of trees was a low brick wall, surmounted by an iron railing. In the shadow the three turned off the road, and up a blind lane, of which the wall—there, risen to some eight or ten feet high—formed one side. Crouching down in a corner, peeping up the lane, the next object that Little Jerry saw was the form of his honored parent, pretty well defined against a watery and clouded moon, nimbly scaling an iron gate. He was soon over, and then the second fisherman got over, and then the third. They all dropped softly on the ground within the gate, and lay there a little—listening perhaps. Then, they moved away on their hands and knees.

It was now Little Jerry's turn to approach the gate: which he did, holding his breath. Crouching down again in a corner there, and looking in, he made out the three fisherman creeping through some rank grass, and all the gravestones in the churchyard—it was a large churchyard that they were in—looking on like ghosts in white, while the church tower itself looked on like the ghost of a monstrous giant. They did not creep far before they stopped and stood upright. And then they began to fish.

They fished with a spade at first. Presently the

honored parent appeared to be adjusting some instrument like a great corkscrew. Whatever tools they
worked with, they worked hard, until the awful striking of the church clock so terrified Little Jerry that he
made off, with his hair as stiff as his father's morning
wood.

But, his long-cherished desire to know more about
these matters, not only stopped him in his running
away, but lured him back again. They were still fishing
perseveringly, when Little Jerry peeped in at the gate
for the second time; but, now they seemed to have gotten a bite.

There was a screwing and complaining sound over
in the bushes, and two bent figures (not the honored
parent, thank God) had straining voices as if they were
being held by a weight.

"What the...?" the honored parent exclaimed, in a
low terse whisper, "What the hell are you two doin'
over there? Whatever it is, cut it out, and come help
me lift this thing out!"

By slow degrees, the 'thing' broke away the earth
upon it, and came to the surface. Little Jerry very well
knew what it was going to be; but, when he saw it, and
saw his honored parent about to wrench it open, he
was so frightened, being new to the sight, that he
made off again and never stopped until he had run a
mile or more.

He would not have stopped then for anything less
necessary than to relieve a bladder about to explode, it
being a spectral sort of race that he ran, and one highly desirable to get to the end of. He had a strong idea
that the coffin he had seen was running after him;
and, pictured it as hopping upright behind him, upon
its narrow end, always on the verge of overtaking him
then hopping at his side—perhaps taking his arm—
nonetheless, it was a purser to be shunned.

It was an inconsistent an ubiquitous friend too,
for, while it was making the whole night dreadful, he
darted out into the roadway to avoid dark alleys, fear-

ful of its coming hopping out of them like a Chinese box-kite without tail or wings.

It hid in doorways too, rubbing its horrible shoulders against doors, and drawing them up to its ears, as if it were laughing. It got into shadows on the road, and lay cunningly on its back to trip him up. All this time it was incessantly hopping on behind and gaining on him, so that when the boy got to the door of his trailer, he had reason for being half-dead.

And even then it would not leave him, but followed him into the trailer, bumping across the faux-tile floor, scrambling into bed with him, and bumping down, dead and heavy, on his chest when he fell asleep.

From his oppressed slumber, Little Jerry in his closet was awakened after daybreak and before sunrise, by the presence of his father in the parental bedroom, otherwise known as the living room. Something had gone wrong with him; at least, so Little Jerry inferred, from the circumstance of his holding Mrs. Kracker by the ears, and knocking the back of her head against the head-board of their hide-a-bed.

"Jerry...Jerry...Jerry!" his wife implored.

He smacked her lightly on the rump.

"I try to be a good wife, Jerry!"

"Bad wifey, bad wifey, bad wifey..." Jerry patted her rump some more.

The altercation was conducted in low tones of voice and heavy breathing, and terminated in the honest tradesman belting out at a moment of crisis, "Yeehaw, LeAnn Rimes! I'll love ya til the day I die!" then a slumping down over Mrs. Kraker, then a kicking off of his clay-soiled boots, then a kicking of him off the bed by Mrs. Kracker, then the former laying down in a heap, stretched out on the floor.

Mrs. Kracker leaned over: "Fuck you and your LeAnn Rimes! She's a fuckin' little tramp anyway..."

After taking a shockingly unforgettable and completely scarring peek at his honored parent lying on his back— with his rusty hands under his head for a pillow, and his man-pole saluting so near to the ceiling fan that Little Jerry figured he could run a flag up it (if it t'weren't going to be chopped off first by his angry mother flipping on the fan) his son lay down too, and fell asleep again.

There was no fish for breakfast, but mysteriously, there *was* meat. Mr. Kracker was out of spirits, including 'shine, and out of temper because of it all, and kept an iron pot by him in case he needed to projectile vomit from withdrawal of such life-sustaining liquidities.

He was brushed and washed at the usual hour, and set off with is son to pursue his ostensible calling.

Little Jerry, walking with the stool under his arm at his father's side across the sunny and crowded Tall Tales parking lot, was very different from the Little Jerry of the previous day, and wished like hell he could shoe-horn the image of his father's saluting man-junk from his highly impressionable memory.

"Pa," said Little Jerry, as they walked along: taking care to keep at arm's length and have the stool well between them, "What's an Erection-Man?"

Mr. Kracker came to stop on the pavement. "Er, uh...how should I know? Where'd you hear that anyway?"

"From Billy Patterson."

"Why don't you ask him?"

"I thought you knowed everything, father?" said the hapless, naïve boy.

"*Ahem!* Well," returned Mr. Kracker, starting to walk again and lifting his ball-cap on and off a few times with extreme agitation. "You mean like Homo-Erectus or Cro-Magnon Man; or Homo-Habilis—shit like 'at?"

"I guess so. What are his 'goods' father?"

"Er, um...*ahem!*...*ahem!* Let's see now. His 'goods,' as you say, are...*is*, um, a...a branch of 'scientific goods', I believe...er, um..."

"Ain't it his body, father?" asked the lively boy.

"I believe it is something of that sort," said Mr. Kraker, relieved.

"Oh father, I should so like to be an Erection-Man when I'm all growed up!"

Mr. Kracker was not shocked, but soothed by this hearing, knowing now his boy was a confirmed complete and total nitwit, also understanding that this was the best way to get through life, ignorance being bliss and all.

"It all depends on how you develop your talents, son. Be careful to develop your talents, and never to say no more than you are to a woman. But there's no tellin' at the present time what you might come to be fit for."

Little Jerry, thus encouraged—if not also confused as hell from what his father just said—went on a few yards in advance to plant the stool in the shadow of the club and plop himself down on it as if he'd been turned into a man at that very hour.

15

Digesting Soap Opera Digest

There had been earlier drinking than usual in the liquor store of Barge. As early as eight o'clock in the morning, sallow faces peeping through its barred windows had descried other faces within, bending over under the wine sample taps. Barge sold a very thin wine at the best of times, but it would seem to have been an unusually thin wine that he sold at this time. A sour wine, moreover, or a sour*ing*, for its influence on the mood of those who drank it.

This had been the third morning in succession, on which there had been early drinking at the liquor store of Barge. It had begun on Monday, and here was Wednesday come.

There had been more of early brooding than drinking; for, many men had listened and whispered and slunk about the place from the time of the opening of the door, who could not have laid a shekel of money on the counter to save their souls. These were to the full as interested in the place, however, as if they could have commanded whole barrels of wine; and they girded from corner to corner, swallowing talk in lieu of drink, with greedy looks.

Notwithstanding an unusual flow of company, the master of the liquor store was not visible. He was not missed; for nobody who crossed the threshold looked for him, nobody asked for him, nobody wondered why Mandy Debarge was the sole proprietor there, presiding over the distribution of wine from the wine sample taps, with a bowl of small coins before her, as much defaced and beaten as the chump-change of humanity from whose raggedy-ass'ed pockets they had come.

A suspended interest and a prevalent absence of

mind, perhaps observed by 'spies' who looking in at the liquor store, as they looked in at every place, high and low, from the *Taco Bell* to the soccer fields. Water cooler talk of last night's idiotic reality TV programming languished, the cardboard cutout of the old men playing dominoes and drinking ripple was amusingly defaced, and drinkers carved figures of naked women on the counter with knives of butterfly. Madame Debarge herself paid no mind, instead she herself picked at a loose thread on her sleeve with the emory board that doubled as a toothpick. Suddenly, she saw and heard something inaudible and invisible a long way off.

Possibly she heard the bells of St. Pancreas, many miles, and hills, away.

The bells signaled noonday, and two dusty men passed through the streets under swinging bags filled with Slim Jim's: of whom, one bag carrier was Barge: the other a road construction worker in a blue hard-hat. All a-dust and all a-thirst from eating too many Slim Jim's, the two entered the liquor store. Their arrival had lighted a kind of fire in the breast of St. Antwan, fast spreading as they came along, which stirred and flickered in the flames in the faces of those in the store lighting up with their cheap-ass Bic lighters.

Yet, no one had followed them, and no man spoke when they entered the liquor store, though the eyes of every man there were turned upon them.

"Wasssss-up, Niggas?" said Barge upon entering.

It may have been a signal for loosening the general tongue. It elicited an answering chorus of, "Wazzzzup? Wassssup? Whaaaaaaaaaa...!"

"Shitty weather out there," said Barge, shaking his head.

Upon which, every man looked at his neighbor, and then all cast down their eyes and sat silent. Except one man, who got up and went out.

"Wife of mine," said Barge aloud, addressing Mandy Debarge: "I've been out dickin' around with this here road construction dude. He's a good man. His name is Harlan. I met him—by accident—about twenty yards down the road on my way to the 7-11. He's a good man, this road construction dude named Harlan. Give him a drink, wifey!"

A second man got up and went out. Mandy Debarge set some cheap wine before the road construction dude named Harlan, who dipped his blue hat to the company, and drank. He reached in the bag he was carrying and passed a Slim Jim to all who wanted one; stood munching one himself at the counter near Mandy Debarge. A third man got up and went out.

Barge refreshed himself with a bottle of Wild Turkey, but he took less than he gave to the stranger—the stranger being a full-blown alcoholic who could drink the shit like water—and stood waiting until the man finished his Slim Jim. He looked at no one present, and no one now looked at him; not even Mandy Debarge, who had taken up the latest copy of *Soap Opera Digest* and devoured it with the same vivacity as the men who ate their Slim Jims.

"Have you finished that beef-stick yet?" asked Barge, in due season.

"Yep," and the man, belching a belch of Slim Jims, wine and Wild Turkey that smelled of opossum rectum.

"Come on, then. I'll show you the 'apartment' in the shed out back. It ain't much, but probably better'n bein' homeless."

Out of the liquor store and into the parking lot, out of the parking lot and into the side yard, out of the side yard and into the backyard, then into the shed and through the shed and into the locker—formerly the locker where a white-haired old man sat on a low cot, stooping forward and very busily making shoes.

No white-haired man was there now; but the three men who had gone out of the liquor store singly. And between them and the white-haired man afar off, was the one small link that they had once looked in at him (for some perverse reason) through cracks in the wall.

Barge closed the door carefully, so as not to engage the lock that only unlocked from the outside, and spoke in a subdued voice:

"Harlan One, Harlan Two, Harlan Three! This is the guy I told ya'all about. The guy I, Harlan Four, found the other day in the street. He will tell you everything. Go ahead, Harlan Five."

The road construction worker, blue hard-hat in hand, wiped his swarthy forehead, feeling as though he might pass out from the combination of Slim Jim's, wine and whiskey ripping at his intestines this very moment like the rustiest of garden rakes, and said, "Where should I start, big guy?"

"Start," was Barge's not unreasonable reply, "at the mother-fuckin' beginning. Where do you think?"

"I saw him then, guys," began the road construction dude, "a year ago this summer, tracking Clay D. Markee through the woods on a red and yellow Honda 250 Enduro, with a hunting rifle. This is how it went down: I was finishing up work on the road at the top of the hill near The Chateau, the sun nearly gone down, when Markee's BMW came up the hill, and the guy was tracking through the woods—like this," and he made a sputtering sound in the likeness of a motorcycle engine.

The road construction guy went through the whole performance again, since everyone present there was three sheets into the wind already, and besides that, the three who'd got there early had already partaken of a shared doobie.

Harlan One butted in, and asked if he had ever seen the man before?

"Never," answered the road construction dude, recovering from his stupid performance.

Harlan Three demanded, How then did he recognize him later?

"By his tall figure," said the road construction

dude, softly, and with his finger picking his nose. "I told that mother-fucker Clay D. Markee that night that he was probably being followed, and he asked me, 'What's he look like?' and I said, 'fuckin' tall as King Kong'."

"You should have said short as mother-fuckin' Mini-Me," returned Harlan Two.

"But what did I know? The deed was not done at that time, and neither did the tall mother-fucker tell me what he was doing. I thought he was just out huntin' for all I knew. Markee points his finger at me, standing near The Fountain, and says, 'Come here, scum!' Scouts honor, fellas, I told him nothing."

"He's right about that, Harlan," murmured Barge to the ass who'd interrupted, "Go on."

"Ok," said the road construction dude, with an air of mystery, "The tall man is missing, though they've been looking for him for how many months now—nine, ten, eleven?"

"Who gives a shit about the number," said Barge, "The fucker's gone, and most likely won't be found. Keep going!"

"I am again working up on the hill, and the sun is almost down. I am collecting my tools and shutting down the steam-roller to go home and have a beer and smoke a fatty with my old lady in town below where it is already dark, and when I look up, I see six cop cars coming over the hill, and in the backseat of one of them is a tall boy most likely handcuffed—like this!"

And he put down his hard-hat to demonstrate being handcuffed.

"We know what being handcuffed is, ya fuck-stick!" spat Barge. "Just get on with the mutha-*fuckin'* story already!"

"I step off the road and watch the cop cars with the prisoner go by, you know, since there's not much else to look at up there—usually we all stop and watch something go by, especially if it has to do with law enforcement..."

"Mother Fucker!" yelled Barge. "Get on wit' it!"

"Ok, Ok! As they approach, I see six cop cars with this tall boy in the back of one of 'em, and most all of them are white cops, as far as I could tell—except on the side where the sun was going down—that guy looked kind of yellowish-red..."

Barge rolled his eyes.

"...also, I noticed that the cop cars were covered with dirt, but it hadn't rained in awhile. But when they come up on me, I realized I recognize the tall boy, and he recognizes me. He gave me a look like he should have just minded his own business and stayed in the woods, just like on the night I first saw him."

The worker described it as if he were right back there again, and it was evident he saw it vividly. Perhaps he had not seen too much in his lifetime, or perhaps he did some 'x' whilst he was excusing himself to the bathroom just before coming out to the shed with Barge.

"I didn't let on to the cops that I recognized the tall boy; and he doesn't let on that he recognizes me either; we made kind of a pact, with our eyes, you see. Then the cops hit the gas hard and raced down toward Reams. I got in my car and followed. I can see them taking him out of the car and into the police station, you know, the one with the jail in back. I see his wrists are swollen because his handcuffs are so tight. Then they knocked him around, taking him inside," he imitated the action of a man being man-handled by the cops, "one pig smacks him in the back with his club and the boy winces and gasps for air—like this," he opened his mouth as wide as he could, not bothering to close it anytime soon.

Barge impatiently snapped, "Go on!"

"Everyone in town," pursued the road construction dude, on tiptoe and in a low voice, "ain't exactly shocked by the brutality of the police when I tell 'em about it. Soon everybody's discussin' it; at The Fountain, especially. Then it seems we all even dreamed about it that night, picturin' our own selves bein' beaten by the cops. But that is neither here nor there...

"In the morning, with my tool belt slung over my shoulder, eatin' a Slim Jim as I go, I make a stop by the jail on my way to work. There I see him, high up there, behind the bars of that iron cage, bloody and dusty as the night before, looking out the winder'. He has no hand free to wave to me, so I figure he must still be in cuffs. I dared not yell to him; he just looks at me like a zombie."

Barge and the three glanced darkly at one another. The looks of all them were dark, repressed, drunken, high and revengeful, as they listened to the hick's story; the manner of all of them, while it was secret, was authoritative too.

They had the air of a rough tribunal; Harlan One and Two sitting on the old nasty cot, each with his chin resting on his hand, and his eyes intent on the road construction dude; Harlan Three, equally intent, on one knee behind them, with his agitated hand always gliding over the network of deadened nerves about his mouth and nose; Barge standing between them and the narrator, whom he had stationed in the light of the lantern he brought in with him, by turns looking from him to them, and from them to him.

"Go on, Harlan," said Barge.

"He remains up there in the iron cage for a few days. Some teenagers went up to look at him and threw rocks and hard-candy at his window just to fuck with him. But at the end of the workday, when everyone was hangin' out at The Fountain, talk always turned to him. Used to be people only talked about what was goin' on at the post-office. Now they only seemed to care about him. They talked at The Fountain about folks in Coon Spit gettin' together a petition to have him released, since he was obviously enraged and made mad by that fucker Clay Markee runnin' over his GameBoy. They say the petition has been given to the sheriff himself. But what do I know? It's possible, right? Maybe, maybe not?"

"Listen, Harlan," Number One of that name stern-ly interposed, "Yes, a petition was presented to the sheriff. Everyone here saw him take it. It is Barge here who went over and gave it him himself, at risk for his life, since that sheriff is a no-good cock-sucking racist bastard."

"Tell us how you *really* feel," said Barge flatly.

"And again, listen, Harlan," said the kneeling Number Three: his fingers ever wandering over and over those deadened nerves, with a strikingly greedy air, as if he hungered for something that was neither food or drink (at least the non-alcoholic kind); "the sheriff, and his redneck deputy, surrounded Barge and beat him like Rodney King. You hear?"

"I hear."

"I got the brusies to prove it. Go on, then," said Barge.

"Again I heard it whispered at The Fountain," re-sumed the hick, "that he is to be transferred to the federal pen and held on charges of murder one."

"Listen again, Harlan," said the man with the rest-less leg syndrome and the craving air, like someone withdrawing from a five-year habit of crystal-meth. "How old are you, anyway?"

"Thirty-five," said the road construction dude, who looked not a day over seventy.

"You ever watch Sesame Street when you were growin' up?"

"Enough!" said Barge, with full knowledge that his mentally deficient and strung out colleague was a huge fan of Elmo. "Jesus Christ! Go on!"

"Well, some whisper this, some whisper that; they speak of nothing else down at The Fountain. Then, on Sunday night when everyone was asleep, some cops come down from the jail, all laughin' and shootin' their guns in the air, totin' the tall boy away in the backseat of one of their cars again."

The road construction dude looked *through* rather

than *at* the low ceiling, and pointed as if he saw that very same cop car floating through the sky. But it was probably just the effects of the 'X.'

"All work is stopped, everyone is gathered outside The Fountain, nobody leads the cows out, the cows are all there minglin' with us, nobody workin' on the roads...At midday, we hear a roll of drums. Then we realize its just the house band doin' a sound-check."

The jones'n Harlan gnawed on one of his fingers as he looked at the other three, and his finger quivered with the craving that was on him.

"That's all, fellers. I left The Fountain at sunset, and I walked on that night and half the next day, until I met this fine man here, Barge."

"Why didn't you just drive your car?" asked Number Two.

"My ca...? Shit! I didn't think of that! And it's back at The fuckin' Fountain with the windows down and all the doors unlocked. Fuck!"

"Well, it pro'ly ain't there no more, that's for sure," said Harlan number Two.

"Fuck! And I live in that car, too!"

After a gloomy silence, the first Harlan said, "Well, now you can jus' collect the insurance on that old piece of shit."

"Um..."

"It was a piece of shit, wasn't it?"

"Oh yeah, definitely! But no insurance..."

"You're fucked."

"Yeah."

"Ok, man," Barge finally interrupted, "would you mind waitin' outside the shed for a minute while we talked amongst ourselves a bit?"

"Yeah, no problem," said the road construction dude, whom Barge walked out, then closed the door and came back in.

The three had risen when Barge came back.

"What d'you say, Harlan? Certifiably insane?"

"Fuck yeah, but I think he's tellin' the truth."

"But shouldn't we tell that hillbilly to get on out of town soon? He's a fuckin' simpleton and doesn't that make him dangerous to be around us?"

"He knows nothing," said Barge; "at least nothing that'd put any of us in danger for that matter."

"And what about the register of 'spies'?"

"There is no physical register of 'spies'," returned Barge, drawing himself up. "That's just a myth. My wife Mandy's got the 'register' in her head, and she won't lose a word of it—not a syllable of it knowing *her* fuckin' memory."

He looked away, disparaged for half a second, as a man used to being beat down like the lowest of canines, then said, "It'd be easier for Oprah to reach a healthy body weight than to erase one incident from that woman's memory."

There was a murmur of agreement, and also of confidence in Mandy's strength of recall, then the man who was jones'n asked: "So we gonna take down The Chateau, and all those rich fuckers with it?"

Barged looked at him and smiled. "Doomed to destruction!"

"Hells yeah!" croaked the jones-er.

"Fuck yeah!" seconded Number One.

"Shit yeah!" joined Number Two.

And the jones-n' man threw in, in a rapturous croak, "Fuckin'-A Hells Shit yeah!"

"Harlan!" Barge shot to him. "Back it down a notch, arrright? Jus' chill."

Nothing more was said, and the road construction dude, being found outside the shed sleeping face down in a pile of dung was advised to get his stank-ass a change of clothes and a shower, then he was invited to use the cot in the shed to get some sleep before walking all the way back to Reams, or finding himself a ride back there. Or, as Barge suggested, he could live in the shed for as long as he liked.

No one needed to twist his arm. The man was soon cleaned-up and fast asleep in his new home.

Worse quarters than Barge's liquor store shed could be found in Coon Spit for a hill-jack of that degree. Saving for dreading the likes of Mandy Debarge—by which he was constantly hounded 'cause she thought he was a bum and a ne'er do-well, of which, as usual, she was exactly right—he found his new life very agreeable. But, Mandy sat at her counter all day and pretty much ignored him for the most part, and so particularly determined not to perceive that his being there had anything to do with anything going on 'underground', that he shook in his Timberlands whenever his eye lighted upon her. He made peace with the fact that he had no way of predicting what fantasies she might come up with in her head to believe to be true, and that being the case, knew that if she took it into her Tammy Faye Baker made-up head to pretend that she had seen him do a murder and afterwards flay the victim, she would unfailingly go through with it until the play was played out.

Therefore, when Sunday came, the road construction dude was not enchanted (though he said he was) to find that Mandy was to accompany Barge and himself to Mole Creek to do some fishing and relaxing. It was additionally disconcerting to have Mandy reading *Soap Opera Digest* the whole way there; it was additionally disconcerting yet, to have Mandy among a small crowd of fisherman on the dock, still with her *Digest* in her hand as the others waited for a tug on the line.

"You must really like that shit," said a man near her.

"Yes," answered Mandy Debarge, "I have a good deal to catch up on."

"Which show is your favorite? Personally, I like *The Bold and the Beautiful*. My wife makes me watch it."

"Yeah, right. Sure she does..."

"No really. She does, that's why I watch it. So what's your favorite soap? Tell me one of your favorites. For instance—"

"For instance," returned Mandy Debarge, composedly, "I mostly enjoy *The Murder of the Nosy Fucking Fisherman.*"

The man moved a little further away as soon as he could, and the road construction dude fanned himself with his blue hard-hat; feeling everyone mighty close and the heat oppressive. If he needed two people to restore him, he was fortunate in having his remedy in hand; for soon, the large faced Ken Kween, who took over the bank after Clay D. Markee's untimely demise, stepped from his golden Cadillac Century, along with the shiny-headed Ron 'Bull' Scythe, mayor of Coon Spit, here to do a little fishing of their own.

The road construction dude, so intoxicated with being in the presence of such power and local celebrity—the only 'famous' people he'd ever seen in real life—that he ran over and begged them shake his hand and then fumbled and found pen and paper with which to secure the autograph of each esteemed personage.

When he came back to gleefully show Barge and Mandy what prestigious signatures he had managed to secure, Barge said—in all absence of sarcasm or ridicule—"Bravo!" then slapped him on the back, adding, "Now that's a good boy!" as if he were a common kickable mutt.

The road construction worker, wary to Barge's motives, thought he might have just suffered a belittlement; but no.

"You are the fellow we want," said Barge, in his ear, "you make those fools believe they'll be able to do whatever they want in this county. Then, they become even more arrogant, and it is ended for them sooner."

"Hey," cried the road construction dude, "you're right!"

Mandy Debarge made a silly face at the simpleton road worker, nodding in agreement. "I'll bet you would completely crap your pants if a *real* famous person walked up just now, like a movie star, or one of them TV reality persons, wouldn't you?"

"Absolutely, Mandy! At least I think so, if I had the courage to stay in their presence..."

"If you were shown a great heap of chickens and asked to pluck the very last one of 'em down to the skin, you'd pick out the biggest and juiciest of 'em to keep it for your own damn-self, then cook up the rooster, wouldn't ya?"

"Absolutely, Mandy!"

"And if you were shown a flock of birds who couldn't fly, and asked to throw them into the sky so they could be free, even though you know'd they'd only plummet back to earth surely to their deaths, you'd pick out only the ones with the finest feathers and throw only them, wouldn't you?"

"Absolutely!"

She nodded toward Ken Kween and Bull Scythe. "You have seen both chickens and birds to-day, now let's git on home."

16

Still *Digest*ing

Mandy Debarge and her husband returned amicably from Mole Creek, having dropped off awhile ago a speck in a blue hard-hat who now toiled through the darkness, and through the dust, and down the weary miles of backwoods roads out in B.F.E, slowly tending toward that point of the compass where The Chateau of Clay D. Markee—now in his grave—listened to the whispering trees.

The Chateau and the BMW (still in the driveway), stone faces and red stains on the floor, nasty barely drinkable tap water still flowing at The Fountain—and thousands of acres of wooded hills—the cities of Coon Spit, Reams, Rabbit Grove and Grouse Gulch—and all of Coalmont County itself—lay under the night sky, concentrated into one gigantic hillbilly carnival, just as a whole world, with all its greatness and littleness, lie in a twinkling star.

And as mere human knowledge can split opposing charges of the atom, and look to and understand the manner of its composition, so, sublimer intelligences may analyze in the feeble shinning of this earth of ours every thought and act; every vice and virtue; every episode of *Cagney and Lacey*; every 'Shaz-bot!' from *Mork from Ork*; every 'Aayyyy!' from Fonzie; every 'Oh, my nose!' from Marsha; every 'Whatchu talkin' bout, Willis?' from Arnold; every "Hey, Mrs. G!' from Tootie; every 'Sit on it, Malph!' from Potsie; every 'Hello!' from Lenny and Squiggy; every 'Hi there!' from Washington, every 'Dyn-O-Mite!' from J.J; and pity every irresponsible creature who ever watched all of that crap in its first run in prime-time, now to further run in never ending rotation in syndication, and on YouTube and on TVLand on the cable.

All that business aside, the Debarges, husband and wife, came lumbering under the starlight in their mufflerless Lincoln Towncar, to a place in Coon Spit where their journey naturally tended; the usual stoppage at the police station, where Barge greased a few palms to get otherwise inquiring eyes to look another way from the less than admirable goings on at his liquor establishment.

Barge knew a few of the deputies in attendance, and was well acquainted with one highway patrolman who randomly happened to be there—someone he'd experimentally been intimate with once (though no one else knows that, and they were both teenagers anyway)—and the two affectionately embraced, though supposedly those feelings had long since melted away.

When Saint Antwan's Liquors and Beers had once again enfolded the Debarges in its musty wings, and they, having finally alighted their land-yacht in the parking lot of said merchandary establishment, they were picking their way on foot through the black-mud and potholes when Mandy Debarge spoke to her husband:

"Say, old buddy of mine, what did Harlan of the police tell you back there?"

"Who?"

"That strapping highway patrolman."

"There was a highway patrolman there?"

"Yeah, big dummy! And you gave him a great big hug! Don't you rememb...Say, what's the matter with you?"

"Um, ub...oh him! Him! Oh, I thought you was talkin' bout some *other* highway patrolman. Yeah, I know *him*, he's a good guy."

"So?"

"So? So! Jus' mind your own business, that's so! Ain't nothing inappropriate going on..."

"That's not what I was askin' you, dildo-brain! What's the matter with you, anyway? Your sweatin' like a whore in church! You sure you all right?"

"Yeah, I'm fine! Now what was the question?"

"I said...*what* did Harlan the *po*-liceman tell you?"

"Very little tonight. That's all he knows. There is another 'spy' assigned to our neighborhood. There may be more for all that he can say, but he know of at least one for sure."

"Ah, well," said Mandy Debarge, raising her eyebrows with a cool business air, "I'll need to 'register' him then. What's his name?"

"He's from North Carolina."

"So much the better. What's his name?"

"Bastard," said Barge, "pardon my French." Then he spelled it out for her. "B-A-S-T..."

"I can spell 'bastard', you bass-*tard*!"

Barge immediately clammed-up at the reproof.

"Bastard," repeated Mandy, Barge not sure who she was referring to, "good Christian name," she said sarcastically. "Does he have a last name? Or is that his first name...or what?"

"John."

"'John the Bastard'? Sounds biblical...How old's this fucker? Give me his specs."

"Age, about forty; height, about five foot nine; black hair; complexion dark; I've heard he has a handsome face; eyes dark, face thin, long, and sallow; nose aquiline but not straight, having a peculiar inclination toward the left cheek; expression, therefore, sinister..."

That is when he noticed Mandy was staring at him, still as a statue.

"What?" he asked.

"Really? Did you need to be *that* specific, Ryan Seacrest? What's the *matter* with you?"

They went into the liquor store, which was closed (for it was two-thirty in the morning) and Mandy immediately took her post at the counter, counting the small monies that had been taken in her absence; examined the stock, printed out the receipts, made other entries of her own in the computer, checked and rechecked the receipts again to see that Jerome (who minded the store that day) hadn't ripped them off, then made a bank statement for the morning and put all monies back in the safe.

All this while Barge walked up and down the aisles smokin' weed complacently (and now hungrily) admiring her work, but never interfering; in which condition he normally conducted his business and personal affairs in life.

The night was hot, and the shop—closed shut and surrounded by so foul a neighborhood—was ill-smelling. Barge's olfactory sense was by no means delicate, but the reek from the bathrooms was so strong that one could taste it, and so was the smell from the wine sample taps, and the rum and the brandy and the ripple (which was flat, so Barge put it on special that morning, selling the flat ripple as 'flapple', for half-price). He brushed the offending odors away, and tossed his roach out the front door.

"Smells like shit in here."

"You're stoned!" said Mandy, raising her glance over her *Soap Opera Digest*. "That's the way it always smells in here."

"Maybe you're right. I guess I'm just a little tired."

"And a little depressed, too, I'd say," said Mandy, whose quick eyes had never been so intent on the *Digest*. Then they got a spark. "Oh! The men, the men!"

"But my dear...!" began Barge.

"*But my dear*," mocked Mandy, nodding firmly, "*But my dear!* You were a bit too fluttery of heart, Clay Aiken, when I mentioned that *po*-liceman tonight. And that description of John the Bastard...what the hell was *that?*"

"Well, then," said Barge, as if a confession were being wrenched out of his breast, er...I mean, his chest, "that *was* a long time ago."

"*That* was *a long time ago*," mocked his wife, snarlily. "Not long enough, if you ask me."

"It didn't mean a thing. The chances of it happening again are like the chances of getting struck by lightning."

"Well, there's a huge thunderstorm heading our way tomorrow I've heard…"

Barge raised his head fearfully, as if there might be something to that. Then he shook it off. "Impossible."

"And what about the coming earthquake that's about to swallow Coalmont county? What do you think are the chances of an earthquake hitting southern Kentucky?"

"Not too good, I suppose."

"But when it's ready, it'll happen, and grind to pieces everything with it. In the meantime, it is always preparing, though it is not yet seen or heard…"

"Are you sayin' you're wantin' to divorce me, or are you jus' speakin' allegra-gorically about that Walmart shit? Damn, I wish I wouldn't've smoked so much weed."

She wanted to tie him in a knot with her flashin' eyes; she wanted to throttle him as if he were a foe. "As far as divorce is concerned, you poke some man-ass on your own damn time! I don't care about that shit. Damn, Barge, how long we been together? And you don't think I don't know you by now? I love you whether your Brad *fucking* Pitt or fucking Officer Barbrady. It don't make no matter to me! What I'm talkin' about is Walmart. Wal-*fucking*-mart! It's been a long time in the works, and now it's on the road and coming. It never retreats and never stops; it's always advancing. And I'm telling you, we ain't ready for it, Baby! Look around us, and consider all our friends, consider the rage and discontent on the faces of all the Harlans. And what about that In'jun who lost his pho-to-mat and goes around pissin' on everyone's houses 'cuz he's half out of his fuckin' mind since he can't feed his family? You want to end up like that? I sure as hell don't! Honey, Walmart is gonna *destroy* us! And you know it will."

"My wife," said Barge, standing before her with his head a little bent, and his hands clasped at his back, like a docile and attentive pupil before his catechist, "Be brave. And if you can't be brave, then at least join me in doing a little more weed. It'll take the edge off, believe me."

"*What?*" demanded Mandy, still wanting to tie him in a knot and strangle him.

"Well?" said Barge, with a half-complaining, half-apologetic shrug. "We're goin' down anyways; might as well enjoy the ride."

"We could have helped it!" returned Mandy, with an extended hand in strong action, like President Kennedy when he said, 'ask *not* what your country can do for you'; "But we've also done what we could to prevent that Walmart from coming to Coon Spit, and I believe it were not done for nothin'. I believe with all my soul that we can still triumph. But even if we don't, give me a knife and show me the neck of that banker Ken Kween, or that mayor, Bull *fucking* Scythe, and I'll...!"

"Hold it!" cried Barge, reddening a little as if he felt charged with cowardice (and deservedly so), "I too, my dear, will stop at nothing!"

"Yes, but sometimes it is your weakness that you sometimes need to see your victim and your opportunity—and apparently that gnarly-ass patrolman—to sustain you."

"That was a *long* time ago I'm telling you!"

"Whatever...But sustain yourself without those things! When the time comes, let loose the tiger and the devil! And I'm not talkin' about with that patrolman..."

"Would you *let it go* already!"

Mandy Debarge enforced the conclusion of this little piece of advice by slamming the *Soap Opera Digest* down on the counter, figuratively and symbolically knocking the brains out of the air-brushed tools and bitches contained therein. Then she observed that it was time to go to bed.

Next noontime saw the admirable (?) woman at her usual place in the liquor store, reading away assiduously. A rose lay beside her, and if she now and then glanced at the flower, it was with no infraction of her usually preoccupied air. There were a few customers—some drinking from the sample taps and some standing, some drinking and some talking, some talking and some not drinking, some not talking and some not drinking—sprinkled about.

The day was very hot, and heaps of flies, who were extending their inquisitive and adventurous perquisitions out of the bathroom and into all the glutinous little plastic glasses used for wine samples, fell dead in the bottoms of them. Their decease made no impression on the other flies (or sample wine drinkers) out promenading, who looked at them in the coolest manner as if they were elephants, or something far removed, until they met the same fate (the flies, that is. Some of the wine drinkers actually made it several more hours before being rushed to the hospital in the middle of the night to have their stomachs pumped).

Curious to consider how heedless flies and alcoholics are! Perhaps they both thought how nice death would be—if it came to them that sunny summer day—compared with living on amongst the smelly and gnarled liquor store with its equally smelly and gnarled patrons.

A figure entering at the door threw a shadow on Mandy Debarge which she felt to be a new one. She laid down her *Digest*, and began to pin the rose to her Little Steven head-scarf before she looked at the figure.

It was curious. The moment Mandy Debarge took up the rose, the customers (read: loiterers) ceased talking, and began gradually to drop out of the liquor store.

"Good morning," said the newcomer.

"Good morning. Name's Mandy."

She said it aloud, but added to herself, as she resumed her *Digest*: *Good morning, age about forty, height about five feet nine, black hair, generally hand-some, complexion dark, eyes dark, thin long and sallow face, aquiline nose but not straight, having a peculiar inclination towards the left cheek which imparts a sinister expression! Good morning, one and all!*

"Would you be so kind as to give me a double-shot of ripple, Mandy? And a mouthful of cool fresh water."

Hallo, tall cool drink of water! thought Mandy, *you can give me a mouthful of* some*thing any time you want...*

She poured the man his shot with a flirtatious flair.

He took a drink. "Marvelous ripple, this!"

It was the first time the ripple had been so complimented. "Well, it is a little *flat*, unlike myself," giggled Mandy as if she were at a middle-school dance speaking to a boy for the very first time in post-pubescence, "We call it 'flapple.' It's half-price."

She bashfully took up her reading once more and the visitor studied the tool on the front cover for several moments, then took the opportunity of observing the place in general.

He looked back at her. "You read that pretty intently."

"I'm accustomed to it."

"And such a pretty boy on the cover, too!"

Damn! There goes the neighborhood... "You think so?" said Mandy, looking at him with a frown.

"Absolutely. May I ask who it is?"

"Bart Bender," said Mandy, still looking at him with a frown. "He used to be on *The Young and the Restless.*"

"Is that his real name or his stage name?"

"Both."

It was remarkable: but the taste of the liquor store seemed to be decidedly opposed to a rose in that Little Steven head-scarf of Mandy Debarge. Two men had entered separately, and had been about to steal some Mad Dog, when, catching sight of that novelty, they faltered, made a pretence of looking about as if for some friend who was not there, and went away. Nor, of those who had been there when this visitor entered, was there one left. They had all dropped off. The 'spy' had kept his eyes open, but had been able to detect no sign. They had lounged away in a poverty-stricken, purposeless, accidental manner, quite natural and unimpeachable.

John, thought Mandy, memorizing the features of the man before her, *stay long enough, you bastard, and I'll have you batting for the other side...*

"You have a husband, Mandy?"

Why you *askin'?* "I have."

"Children."

"A million. Want one?"

"No. Is business bad?"

"Business is very bad; the people are so poor."

"Ah, the unfortunate, miserable people! So oppressed, too—as you say."

You elitist fuck... "As *you* say," Mandy retorted, correcting him, and deftly calling him other names in her head that boded him no good.

"Pardon me; certainly it was I who said so, but you naturally think so, of course."

"You're tellin' me what *I* think?" returned Mandy in a high voice, in the manner of Wanda Sykes, "I and my husband have enough to do keepin' this here liquor store open, without some elitist *fuck* like you comin' 'round spoutin' off like he *knows* somethin' 'bout miserable oppressed people! All *we* think, here, my friend, is how to survive! That's all *we* think about! And that gives us, morning, noon, and night, enough to think about, I assure you, without worrying our little heads about other people. *Me* think about what other people are doin'? Oh, no, no, no!"

The 'spy', who was only there to pick up any crumbs of information he could, did not allow his baffled state to express itself in his sinister face; but, stood with an air of elitist gallantry, leaning an elbow on Mandy Debarge's counter and occasionally sipping at his double-shot of 'flapple':

"A bad business this, Miss Mandy, of Grady's impending trial and imprisonment," he said with a sigh of great compassion.

"Jee-*zus* Christ!" returned Mandy, coolly and heavily. "Boo hoo for him! If people are going to use knives for such purposes, then they gotta know they gonna pay for it. He knew beforehand what the price of that luxury was; now he's payin' for it."

"Between you and me," said the 'spy', dropping his soft voice to a tone that invited confidence, and expressing an injured revolutionary susceptibility in every muscle of his wicked face, "I believe there is much compassion and anger on this side of town."

"No shit, Sherlock," said Mandy, vacantly.

"So you would agree?"

"—Ah, here comes my husband," said Mandy Debarge with a sarcastic flourish of her hand.

As the keeper of the liquor store entered at the door, the 'spy' saluted him by touching his hunting cap, and saying, with an engaging smile, "Good morning, Harlan!"

Barge stopped short, and stared at him, saying nothing.

"Good morning, Harlan," the 'spy' repeated; with not quite so much confidence, or quite so easy a smile under his stare.

"You must be out'chour damn mind!" returned the keeper of the liquor store to him, "I ain't Harlan. My name's Michael Jackson Debarge."

"Sure. Whatever," said the 'spy' haughtily, but discomforted, too.

"I was saying to Mandy here, with whom I have had the pleasure of chatting before you got here, that they tell me there is—and no wonder!—much fear and anger in these neighborhoods of Coon Spit, most likely because of what's happened with that young boy Grady."

"Don't know nothin' 'bout it," said Barge, shaking his head. "Don't nobody told me a thing."

Having said it, he passed behind the counter and put his hand on his wife's back, looking over that barrier at the person to whom they were both opposed, of whom either of them would have shot dead with the greatest satisfaction.

The 'spy', well used to his business, did not change his unconscious attitude, but threw back the remainder his 'flapple,' took a sip of the grungy tap-water, and asked for another double-shot of his chosen alcohol. Mandy Debarge poured it out for him, took up her *Digest* again, and hummed a little song over it. *"You take the good, you take the bad, you take it all, and there you have, the facts of life—hmmm-hmmm— the facts of life..."*

"Dude, seems like you're tryin' to say you know this neighborhood better'n I do? Am I correct in that assumption?" observed Barge.

"Not at all, but I hope to know it better. I am so profoundly interested in its miserable inhabitants."

"Then you better get yo' ass a gun if you gonna take that attitude, Slappy!"

"You know, it's occurred to me while talking to you, Mr. Debarge," pursued the 'spy', "that I have known some interesting associations tied to your name."

"Really, fuck-stick? And what would those be?"

"When Dr. Runyon was released from prison, I know he was delivered to you— and later also to that loser who owns that dungeon of a strip club out on 49. You see, you aren't the only one who knows his 'shit' around here."

"That's right, mutha-fucka," said Barge, who had had it conveyed to him that he should answer in the affirmative with an 'accidental' touch of his wife's elbow to his ribs as she seemingly indifferently read along her *Digest* and warbled god-awful sit-com themes.

"...Sunday, Monday, Happy days..."

"It was to you," said the 'spy,' "that his daughter came; and it was from your care that his daughter took him, accompanied by that—how shall we say?—cracker Travis Templeton of Tall Tales over in Grouse Gulch?"

"S'rigth," said Barge.

"Interesting memory!" said the 'spy'. "I have also known Dr. Runyon and his daughter over in Grouse Gulch."

"Known them, or *known* them—in the biblical sense?" asked Barge slyly.

"I'm *acquainted* with them, you idiot!" charged the rankled elitist 'spy,' "But you don't hear much about them anymore, do you?"

"Nope," said Barge.

"Actually," Mandy struck in, looking up from her magazine and her little songs, "we never hear about 'em at all. We got the news of their safe arrival, and perhaps an email or a text or two, but since then, they've pretty much kept to themselves—and we to ourselves—and have never heard nothin' more from 'em. They could be finalists on *American Idol* for all we know."

"Yeah, not likely," replied the 'spy,' "because she's going to be married, you know."

"Going to be?" echoed Mandy. "Why, I'd a thought she'd have been married long ago! But then again, who'd want a clam that's been wore out more than Phil Michelson's sand-wedge? Not to mention it got to be cold in there by now I'd have to reckon."

"I'm sure it is," said the 'spy,' taken slightly aback and unsure how to respond.

"I bet your heart is, too!" returned Mandy. "For what the man is, I 'spect the heart is too."

He did not take this as a compliment; but he made the best of it, and shrugged it off with a laugh. After sipping his 'flapple' to the end, he added:

"Yes, Bunnie Mancrizie is going to be married, but

not to a Grouse Gulchian. No, to one who is, like her, a Coon Spitter by birth. Or maybe he was from Reams? I'm not sure. But speaking of Grady (ah, poor Grady! It was cruel, cruel what happened with his GameBoy!) it's a curious thing that she's going to marry the nephew of one Clay D. Markee, for who Grady was taken away in those tight—oh, so tight!—handcuffs. But this man lives unknown in Grouse Gulch, and he is no 'Markee' there; he is Mr. Bubba Darnet. Dunnay is the name of his mother's family. His mother being Bonnie and his father being Ronnie. They had some cousins, too—Cheetah, Greeda and Ethel. And some nieces and nephews on his father's side, Wanda and Virgil..."

"Enough!" bellowed Barge, slamming his fist on the counter, nearly scaring Mandy out of her penciled-on eyebrows. Then in the ensuing silence, Barge tried to light up a cigarette, and his hand trembled oh, so slightly from the information he had just digested. The 'spy' would have had to be a complete and total jackass not to have noticed it (and record it in his mind)—though he was most decidedly the hugest of jackasses anyway.

Having made, as least this one hit, whatever it might prove to be worth, and no customers coming in to help him to any other, Mr. Bastard paid for what he had drunk, and took his leave: taking occasion to say, in a genteel manner before he departed, that he looked forward to the pleasure of seeing Mandy and Barge Debarge again. But especially Mandy. For some minutes after he had emerged into the parking lot of Saint Antwan's Liquors and Beers, the husband and wife remained exactly as he had left them, lest he should come back.

"Can it be true," said Barge, in a low voice, looking down at his wife as he stood smoking with his hand on her back, "what he said of Bunnie?"

"Judging that *he* said it," returned Mandy lifting her drawn eyebrows a little, "it's probably false. But...it could be true."

"If it is—" Barge began, then stopped.

"If it is?" repeated his wife.

"—And if it does happen that we beat this Walmart thing, I hope for her sake her muther-fuckin' husband stays out of Coon Spit."

"Don't worry, her husband's dick will probably take him wherever he wants to go, and that will probably be the death of him. That much I know."

"How you know dat?"

"'Cuz he's a man, ig'nurnt!"

"But isn't it strange that after all we did for Doctor Runyon and Bunnie, that we gots to count her husband as a 'spy,' right along with that jack-a-lope that just went outta here?"

"Stranger things than that will happen when victory is indeed ours," answered Mandy. "You can bet on that."

She rolled up her *Soap Opera Digest* when she had said those words, and presently took the rose out of her Little Steven head-scarf. Either Saint Antwan had the instinctive sense that the objectionable decoration was gone, or Saint Antwan was on the watch for its disappearance; either way, the Saint took courage to lounge in, very shortly afterwards, and the liquor store recovered its habitual loiterers.

In the evening, this being summer, Saint Antwan turned himself inside out doing a relatively booming business, which wasn't saying much at this time, and 'he' sat in the hands of folks drinking outdoors on door-steps and window-ledges, and up and down vile streets and courts. For a breath of fresh air, Mandy Debarge, with her *Soap Opera Digest* in hand, passed from place to place and from group to group: a sort of Missionary of Spirits, if you will, a missionary hopefully the world will never breed again. With her push-cart stocked with the Saint's finest, she walked and sold whilst men drank—and some women—but most of the women read the gossip rags and talked of other worthless things spewed from the noxious hole of Nancy

Grace the night before.

But all the drinking and chatter was merely a substitute to quell the bodily cravings for a more substantial substance; that being: food. With the food stamps having been used up for the month, if the alcohol and worthless chatter had stopped flowing, the stomachs would be even more famine-pinched.

But as the alcohol poured, so the eyes went, then the thoughts, then the minds, then the bowels, then one by one, folks completely passed out in pools of their own excrement and vomit—some right there in the street. And as Mandy Debarge moved on from group to group pushing along her Chariot of Blessed (but ultimately empty) Escapism, she somehow managed to stay blissfully oblivious to the destruction she left behind.

Her husband smoked a 'j' at the door to their empty store, picturing her on her rounds with great admiration.

A great business woman, thought he, *a strong bitch, an awesome bitch, a frightfully strong and awesome bitch!*

17

The Good, The Bad, and the Ugly

Never did the sun go down with such a brighter glory in a quiet part of Chickenwell Street than one memorable evening when the Doctor and his daughter sat under the plain tree together. Never did the moonshine flow with a milder smoked-wood flavor all across Grouse Gulch, than on the night that found them still seated under the tree, three sheets to the wind and mumbling incoherently to the other, each at the same time.

Bunnie was to be married to-morrow. She had disturbingly reserved this last night for her father, which is why she made sure they stayed outside the shack, and in full view of the folks at the *Squire Arms* apartments all day and all night, in case the old man should get a hankerin' for his old squirrelly and incestuous ways.

"Are you happy, pa?" Bunnie asked in a more lucid moment, when the two had stopped mumbling incoherently to each other in a duel drunken stupor.

"Very much so, my child."

"Then fuck you old man for making my life so miserable!"

"Oh, Jeezus...here we go again..."

"Don't 'oh Jeezus' me, you pervert! Good God! What were you thinking back when I was a little girl?"

"Bunnie,...I...uh..."

"Bunnie, I, uh, nothing! There's no excuse for what you did! You're just a wretched old piece of horeshit is what you are!"

In the sad moonlight, she leaped forward and clasped him by the neck, choking him until he was darn near the shade of the Velvet Elvis proudly displayed above the commode.

"I'm so fucking miserable tonight, Pa, and it's all because of you! I'm unhappy with the unhappiness of Hell, and can't begin to imagine how horrible it will be for Bubba to be with me, even if he does actually love me, which I seriously doubt he does. And once we're married, I'm sure I'll be even more unhappy and self-reproachful than I can tell you!"

"Dearest dear," squeaked Runyon, amidst her choking of him, "For the last time (cough, cough), can you tell me (cough) you will never listen to my pleadings (hack) for forgiveness for the heinous wrongs (cough, cough) I have done to you? In your own heart (hack, hack), do you think you'll ever be able to forgive me? (cough?)"

It was the first time of her ever hearing him refer to that period of her horrible suffering. It gave her a strange and new sensation—not necessarily a good one—but a strange and new one, and she slightly loosened her grip.

Slightly.

"Are you sure you're being straight up with me, old man?"

"S..t..r..a..i..g..h..t u..p," wheezed her father, with his final breath of air.

She let him go and he fell in a heap to the ground, nearly breaking a hip. She was considering what he presently had said, and besides that, she didn't think she had the energy to try and beat a murder rap on the eve of her wedding.

"(cough, gag) More than that, I believe I have a brighter future, Bunnie, living vicariously through your marriage, because I was such a pig's ass in my own. I just want you to know that I will do everything I can to help you two kids to succeed. Whatever I can do."

"If I could only believe that, pa..."

"Believe it, Bunnie! It's the truth. I know I've put you through some horrible suffering, but now that I've come to Jesus..."

"So the rumor is true?"

"You cannot fully appreciate the anxiety I have felt that your life should be the waste that mine's been."

She moved toward him, still keeping a fist cocked in case the old man was just playing games.

"—wasted, my child!—and your's should not be wasted because of me and what I've done to you! I'm wondering even now how I can ever be happy knowing I've made you so miserable for so long."

"I can see this is truly tearing you up, pa, so I gotta tell ya, that if you wasn't my pa, I would definitely have hooked up with you instead of that sex-addicted *ray*-tard Bubba Darnet."

Her father smiled at her conscious admission that she would have been happier with him (if he wasn't her father) instead of Bubba Darnet.

Then...he made things worse, if that were at all possible...

"Well, I know that if it weren't me, or Chuck, then it would have been another. And another. And possibly another..."

As opposed to any negative reaction a normal self-respecting female would have had in this situation, surprisingly, Bunnie took this comment very well, and nodded as if to say, *'Yeah, you're probably right. I do loves me my menfolk...'*

"Ok, pa. I forgive you."

She wasn't sure whether it was these such tender words that were spoken that caused the bizarre reaction that follows, or whether it was just a new wave of 'shine he'd drunk splashing its way across his cranial cortex, but either way:

"See that?" he said, raising his hand toward the moon, "I have looked at her from my prison window when I could not bear her light. I have looked at her when it has been such torture to me to think of her shinning upon what I had lost, that I have beaten my head against my prison walls. I have looked at her, in a state so dull and lethargic, that I have thought of nothing but the number of horizontal lines I could draw across her at the full, and the number of perpendicular lines with which I could intersect them. It was twenty either way, I remember, and the twentieth was difficult to squeeze in."

The strange thrill it gave her to think that he had finally and completely lost his fucking marbles was almost more joy than she could bear. But then she remembered that she had just forgiven the old coot, so the thrill turned to a long forgotten emotion toward the geezer: that of compassion.

Suddenly, he continued: "I have looked at the moon, speculatin' thousands of times whether my daughter would some day seek revenge against her pa."

Bunnie was now stricken. "Well, you don't have to worry about that now, pa. When I say'ed I'd forgaven you, I meant it."

He ignored her, lost in another world. "I have pictured my daughter, to myself, as perfectly forgetful of me, rather ignorant of me and unconscious of me..."

"But I'm here, pa! I'm right here!"

"...I have tried to imagine the stages of her life, year after year. I have seen her married to a man who had nothing of my bad luck. I have been blotted from the memories of the living, and the next generation of my kinfolk would have no 'membrance of my livin'..."

"Pa! It's hard to for me to hear this! 'Cuz I think you's either hallucinatin' somethin' powerful off that nasty 'shine, or you's talkin' 'bout another daughter somewheres. An ili'gitmit one maybe?"

"What did I say just now?" he pa asked in a haze with a far away gaze.

"That you had, or have, a daughter somewheres that knows nothing of you? That cares nothing for ya...?"

"Yes. On other moonlit nights, when the sadness and the silence had touched me in a different way—as did my cellmate, Benny 'The Thug' Tripowski—and afflicted me with something like a powerful sorrowful sense of peace anyway, I have imagined her coming into my cell and leading me out to the freedom beyond the fortress, and there, in a clear, abandoned farmer's field, she kicks the living shit out me and leaves me there for dead..."

"Oh, pa! The figure was not...was not...the image of your cousin Nancy?"

"No, that was another thing altogether. She def'nitly stood before my sight on more'n one occasion and disturbed me—mostly 'cuz the image of her was like that of an old buzzard being sliced open with an exact-o knife...Naw, in my fucked up visions, old Nancy never moved. The phantom I'm talkin' 'bout was another and more real person, a child. She had a likeness similar to you, but was not the same. You followin' me, Bunnie? Not really, I 'spect. You probably have to have been a prisoner like me to understand such distinctions in visions."

His collected and calm manner could not prevent her blood from boiling again, as again he tried to anesthetize his condition.

"No, pa, I understand you," she lied, hoping to get the old bastard to shut up and quit confusin' her. Beside, at this point she was also sick of his rambling.

"In that more peaceful state, I have imagined her..."

"You didn't kill her, did you, Pa?"

"No, no no! Don't speak of such ridiculous horseshit! I imagined her in the moonlight, and she took me to her married home and showed me the horrible life I had caused her. There were pictures of me everywhere, with darts throw'd at 'em. My poor history pervaded the place."

"I was that child father! You must be thinking of me!"

"No, I'm sure I wasn't, cuz she showed me her chil'ren, and there were thousands of 'em—maybe millions!—and they had all heard of me, and were taught that I was the Devil. She never let me go free, but always took me back to prison after showing me such things as where't she lived and her chil'ren and all.

"Bunnie, first off, I believe these old troubles is the reason I came to Jesus, and number two, it's the reason that tonight I can love you as a pa should, better'n I ever have in the past. My thoughts, when they was wild—wilder than they are now, if you cain believe that—never rose me to the planes of happiness I have now with you, and what we's may have in the future if we's keep a-workin' at it."

He embraced her, and she let him—though still wary—and he solemnly commended her to Heaven, and humbly thanked Heaven for having bestowed her on him. Soon after that, they went into the house, Bunnie now being fairly confident he wasn't going to pull any of his old horse shit.

There was no one invited to the wedding but Trip Templeton; there was even to be no bridesmaid but the ghoulish Miss Priss. The marriage was to make no change in their place of residence; they would just have to make do with the cramped conditions, as they had been doing all along.

Doctor Runyon was very cheerful at the rehearsal dinner, mostly because Father Mossenger had brought with him some 'kick-ass quality 'shine,' according to the now drunk Doctor. There were only four at the dinner, and Miss Priss made the fourth. The Doctor regretted that Chuck 'Bubba' Darnet was not there; and was half disposed to track him down and kick his ass after learning of his plot to lie in loving arms across town instead; but the effects of the high quality 'shine would not let him carry out such an act, so instead, he sat back and decided to drink to Bubba affectionately.

So, when the drunk-ass *pree*-verted Father

Mossenger had finally been kicked out the front door, the time came for the Doctor to bid Bunnie good night and they retired to their separate rooms. But, in the stillness of the third hour of the morning, Bunnie crept across the way and stole into his room; not free from unshaped fears, of course. But hell, *she* was the one goin' to *him* this time.

All things, however, were in the their places; all was quiet; and he lay asleep, his white hair picturesque on the nasty slobber-stained pillow, one of his hands lying on the quilt, the other around the old lesbian Miss Priss, who needed some lovin' now and then any way she could get it, just like all the rest of us.

Bunnie crept up to his bed, put her lips to his; then leaned over him to imagine being married to him instead of Bubba Darnet. Through the lines of his face, she imagined the bitter waters of her captivity flowed. But she covered up such tracks in her mind and nearly forgot about it again, his mastery over her being so strong even as he lay unconscious. A more remarkable face in its quiet, resolute, and guarded struggle with her as her assailant was not to be beheld in all the wide dominions of sleep that night.

Then she timidly put one hand on his upturned shoulder, and raised an open palm above his face as a wave of nausea overtook her when she realized the sickness and depravity of what she was thinking, and the sorrows she had not deserved. She brought the open palm down as quick as lightning, and with the force of a thousand cannons, upon the lips she had just so tenderly just kissed, smashing his head damn near in half, and knocking Miss Priss clear out of the bed.

"What in tar'nation...!"

Bunnie withdrew her hand and quickly went away.

So when the sunrise came, Miss Priss was still on the floor, and the shadows of the leaves of the plain tree out back moved upon the red outline of her palm across his lips, as a reminder of just how hard his daughter had hit him in the mouth.

18

Crack'd

The marriage day was overcast and rainy, and they—the beautiful bride, Trip Templeton, and Miss Priss—were ready outside the closed door of the Doctor's room, where he was speaking with Bubba Darnet.

Inside the room: "And you better stop yer gamblin' and yer womenizin', or I'll crack yer skull inside out with my friend Smith and his drinkin' buddy Wesson! Is that understood?"

Outside: They were ready to go to the church, and were banging furiously on the door. Miss Priss, who stood silently looking on, would have looked forward to the event with absolute bliss, save for her jumbled relationship to Doctor Runyon, her continued pining for the young Bunnie, and her wish that her deadbeat brother Solomon could have been the bridegroom in place of that heap of excrement known as Charles 'Bubba' Darnet.

"And so," said Trip Templeton, who could not sufficiently admire the bride without being deeply embroiled in a cataclysm of roiling lust, especially a few minutes ago when he moved around her dress to take in every excruciatingly perfect curve of her whore-ingly low-cut dress. "And so it was for this that I brought you here to this shack in Grouse Gulch when you were a baby, Bunnie. Jeezus! If I had only known then that you were going to turn out like this...God bless Mother Mary, Baby Jesus and the Holy Ghost too—mmm, mmm, *mmm!*—what a service I was doing to mankind apparently! And how lucky is that shit eatin', *Vee*-ay-gra needin', Chuck Darnet? Good God in heaven!"

"Stick that slimy tongue of yours back into your manhole *if-you-please,* Sewage McPhereson!" barked

Miss Priss, engulfed at once in a jealous fit of rage and repulsion that a *man* should look upon her precious china doll with such lustfully tes-tosteric abandon.

"Really?" asked Trip. "That's how you want to play it, ya old bat? Well, now, don't cry Miss Priss, there's a lot more young rug out there for you to mow, if you can just convince it to let you."

"I'm not cryin'!" rejoined Miss Priss, "you are!"

"Am I, Miss Prissy?"

"You were, just now; I saw you do it, and I don't wonder at all. You men are all alike, you see a strong, capable woman like me in front of you, and all you can do is cry over a sweet young box like her."

"Priss, that's because your face went on *The Apprentice* last season and Trump told it, 'You're fired!'...Or was it *fifty* seasons ago? I can't remember."

"There's not a fork or spoon in this house that I wouldn't love to use at this very moment to dispossess you of your vital organs...!"

"All right, all right! That's enough!" intervened the bride. "I love you both, and was hoping you could get along, at least just for today. Is that too much too ask? For me?"

And she batted her irresistible, naturally long and lush young eyelashes at the two of them, stirring up in each of their respective loins such excess that each damn near had to ask to use the bathroom for a spell.

"Absolutely, Sugar," said Trip, giving her an innocent peck on the forehead. "For you, anything...And to think all these years there could have been a Mrs. Templeton, or at least, one bangin' hot stripper down at my club!"

"Oh poo-poo!" said Priss.

"What? You poo-pooin' that I could have married someone, or you don't think she would've made one bangin' hot stripper?"

"What were you going to do, *Trash*? Marry her in the cradle? Oh, the sickness...!"

"Well, why not? Anything's possible..."

"Dis-*gustin'*!" roared Priss.

"Ok! Ok!" said Bunnie, stepping between them, "Once again, need I remind you it's *my* wedding day, here? Hell-oo! Me? My? Mine? What part of that are we *not* understandin'...?"

"Bunnie's right," agreed Trip. "Enough of this." He turned to her. "Now Bunnie, my dear," he said as he slipped an arm around her waist, "I hear them two moving in there, which means they've moved from the 'father-in-law to son-in-law talk,' to some nasty 'son-in-law father-in-law bonding.' I know Miss Priss and I, as two folks of 'business,' are anxious not to lose this final opportunity to spring the door open and embarrass them possibly beyond recoverable measure. So what you say, Priss?"

"Absolutely! Let's skewer the old geezer and that little sack-a-parakeet balls that's in there with him!"

But, for a moment, Trip regarded Bunnie's face and the well-remembered expression on that forehead, and brushed a curl of golden Clairol damage from her shoulder with a genuine tenderness and delicacy, which, if such things be old-fashioned, and are as old as Adam, then so be it.

Trip said: "Yes, well. I guess you don't want to be seein' that on your wedding day, do you?"

Bunnie looked at him blankly.

"Yeah, I guess not," he sighed.

The door to the Doctor's room finally opened, from the *inside*, and the Doctor came out with Bubba Darnet. The Doctor's face was so deadly pale—which had not been the case when they went in together—that no vestige of color was to be seen in his face. But, in his composure of manner he was unaltered, except that to the shrewd glance of Trip Templeton it disclosed some shadowy indication that the old air of pre-Jesus findin' behavior was back like a cold wind.

Darnet, for his part, was rather red-faced and sweaty, with a kind of flushed relief detectable upon his countenance and in his eyes. He was also shaking slightly as if he were too loose to stand himself up at the moment.

Runyon gave his arm to his daughter, and he took her downstairs to their 'chariot'—a 1976 drag-ass Vega—which Trip had rented for them in honor of the day. The rest followed in their assortment of rust-buckets and big trucks with big stupid tires, and soon, at the church of St. Pancreas—in front of Father Mossenger—Charles 'Bubba' Darnet and Bunnie Mancrizie were (somewhat) happily married. Besides Bubba's quick but perceptible wink in Doctor Runyon's direction just before the ceremony was concluded, one rather small cubit-zirconium diamond was placed on the finger of the bride's hand.

The entire wedding party then headed to the Waffle House for breakfast, and remarked about how all had gone well. Afterward in the parking lot, it was a hard parting, but her father cheered Bunnie on, and said at last, gently disengaging the raptor-like grip of her hand on his arm, "Take her, Bubba! Jeezus, take her! She's *yours* now!" And her agitated hand waved to them from the Vega window, as it dragged-ass away, and she was gone.

In due course, the golden hair that had once mingled with so many other men—including the whitened locks of a doctor of the veterinary arts—was mingled with Bubba's thinning ranks on the threshold of a gas-station bathroom, three blocks from the Waffle House. The Coalmont County comptroller, having found himself trapped in a back stall, waited out the bit of theater all the way to its dramatic conclusion before washing his hands and resuming to his vehicle.

The preparations for the wedding having been very few, Trip, the Doctor, and Miss Priss found themselves back in the cool shade of the shack, underneath the plain tree, and quite alone. It was then that Trip observed a great change to have come over the Doctor; as if the hand attached to the arm attached to the golden hair had struck him another blow.

Doctor Runyon had much repressed, naturally, and some revulsion might have been expected as a result of his shenanigans with his daughter's husband right before her wedding, but Trip recognized this as not that, but probably just the old troubled lost look that was so often known to hang from Runyon's withered face; and through his absent manner of clasping his head and drearily wandering away into his own room upstairs, Trip was reminded of the Doctor's captivity under Barge the liquor store owner, and the starlight ride.

"I think," Trip whispered to Miss Priss, after thinking an anxious moment, "I think we had best not speak to him just now, or disturb him at all..."

"I agree, so why don't you saw off your ugly face, then? I think that would help."

"Very funny. Now I gotta go check-in at Tall Tales, so I'll go there and come back later."

"Don't rush."

"When I get back, let's take him to the Cracker Barrel out by the highway, 'cause all will be well by then I 'spect."

It was easier for Trip to check-in at Tall Tales than it was for him to check-out of Tall Tales. He was detained two hours. When he came back, he ascended the old staircase alone, and going thus into the Doctor's room, he was stopped by a low sound of knocking.

"Good God!" he said with a start, "What's that?"

Miss Priss, with her terrifying face, was immediately at his ear. He nearly jumped so high as to get a knot on his head from hitting the ceiling beams.

"Dear me!" the old bag crowed, "Dear me! All is lost!"

"What'd you do? Did you finally kill the old man?" asked Trip when he had regained his wits.

"What are we going to tell Ladybug? He doesn't know me! And has started making shoes again!"

"Well, first off, I wouldn't admit to knowin' you either. You look like Carol Channing's butt-uglier half-sister (if that be possible), and second, who cares if he's making shoes again?"

Trip raised a hand to smack her, then thought better of an assault charge. He went instead into the doctor's room and found him bent over, as before in Barge's shed, and very busy.

"Doctor Runyon? Doc?"

The Doctor looked at him for a moment—half inquiringly, half as if he were angry at being spoken to—and bent over his work again.

His shirt was open at the throat, as it always was when he did that work; and even the old haggard color of the surface of his faded face had come back to him. He worked hard—impatiently—as if in some sense of having been interrupted.

Trip glanced at the work in his hand, and observed it to be a shoe of odd size and shape. He took up another that was lying by him, and asked what it was.

"A young lady's walking shoe," the Doctor said, without looking up. "It ought to have been finished long ago. Let it be."

"Doctor Runyon, look at me!"

Runyon obeyed, in the old mechanically submissive manner, without pausing in his work.

"Do you recognize me, Runyon? Hey! This is a waste of time what you are doing here! You can't sell these."

Nothing would induce the doctor to speak more. He looked up for an instant at a time, when he was requested to do so; but no persuasion would extract a word from him. He worked, and worked, and worked, in silence, and words fell on him like they would an echoless wall, or on the air, the only ray of hope that Trip could discover, was, that sometimes he furtively looked up without being asked. In that, there seemed to be a faint expression of curiosity or perplexity—as though he were trying to reconcile some doubts in his mind.

Two things at once impressed themselves on Mr. Templeton, as important above all others; the first, that this must be kept secret from Bunnie; the second, that it must be kept secret from all who knew him.

In conjunction with Miss Priss, he took immediate steps toward the latter precaution by telling her that he thought the Doctor had caught The Aids, and required a few days of complete rest. In the aid of the deception to be practiced on his daughter, Miss Priss was to text Bunnie on her honeymoon and tell her the Doctor had been called away professionally, and refer to an imaginary email sent to the Doctor that a Hollywood movie was being filmed over the border in Tennessee, and he needed to take care of a bunch of horses who'd also caught The Aids.

With these measures, Trip hoped he'd bought enough time for the Doctor to come to his frickin' senses. If that should happen soon, he kept another course in reserve; which was, that he'd fake like *he* was actually the one who'd caught The Aids, and that he went insane, and then he'd go around kickin' everyone else's asses like a crazy man.

In the hope of Runyon's recovery, and thereby making it a strong possibility Trip'd have to resort to that latter course, Trip resolved to watch him attentively, with as little appearance as possible of doing so. He therefore made arrangements to absent himself from Tall Tales for the first time ever in his life since taking ownership—charging Hoss and Ellsworth with keeping an eye on things for him—and took a post by the window in the same room.

Trip was not long in discovering that it was useless to talk to Runyon, since, on being pressed, he became very worried. He abandoned that attempt on the first day, and resolved merely to keep himself always before him, as a silent protest against the delusion into which he had fallen, or was falling. He remained, therefore, in his seat near the window, reading and writing, and expressing to his old friend in as many pleasant and natural ways as he could think of, that he was no longer in prison.

Doctor Runyon took what was given him to eat and drink, and worked on that first day until it was time for the Jay Leno show. Then he put his tools aside as useless until the next morning, Trip rose, turned off the TV and said to him:

"Leno's a rerun. Will you go out?"

"Out?"

"Yeah; go for a walk with me. Why not old timer?"

Runyon made no effort to say why not, and said not a word more. But, Trip thought he saw, as the Doctor leaned forward on his bed with his elbows on his knees and his head in his hands, that he was asking himself in some mystical way, 'Why not?' The sagacity of the man of 'business' perceived an advantage here, and determined to hold it.

Miss Priss and he divided the night into two watches, though she stayed in Bunnie's room so as not to catch The Aids. Runyon paced up and down for a long time before he lay down; but, when he finally did lay himself down, he fell asleep. In the morning, he was up with the sun, and immediately went back to work.

On the second day, Trip saluted the Doctor cheerfully by his name, and spoke to him of topics that had been on late night TV, then remembered that they had gone for a walk, so Runyon hadn't seen the reruns being referred to. The Doctor returned no reply, of course, but it was evident that he had heard what was said, and had thought about it, however confusedly since he likened his affection for the escapades of the Kardashians to be in the same league with finding the discarded toenail of a monkey shoved up his ass. This encouraged Trip enough to figure the Doctor could be left alone without harm, and for periods of time he went down and talked with Miss Priss about Bunnie and Bubba, and things of that sort, as if nothing were amiss. This was done without insult or injury, and it helped that he didn't stay downstairs long enough for her to harass him, either verbally or with her putrid looks.

When it fell dark again, Trip asked the old man as before:

"Doc, will you go out?"

As before he repeated, "Out?"

"Yes; go for a walk with me. Why not? Leno sucks again tonight. Seen it."

This time, Trip feigned to go out when he could extract no answer from him, and, after remaining absent for an hour, returned. In the meanwhile, the Doctor had removed to the seat by the window, and had sat there looking down at the plain tree; but, on Trip's return, he slipped away to his bed.

The time went very slowly on, and Trip's hope darkened, and his heart grew heavier again, and grew yet heavier and heavier every day. The third day came and went, then the fourth, and the fifth. Six days, seven days, eight days, nine days, ten days.

With a hope ever darkening, and with a heart always growing heavier and heavier, Dickens kept on writing the exact same thing over and over again at this point in order to fill his allotted quota of story length for his editor that the publisher demanded for that particular week's installment of this story when it was first published in serial form in England in 1859. (Most likely this was because he'd waited until the eleventh hour Sunday night to start writing said week's installment, because he was probably out having fun with his friends and family all weekend, and was in all likelihood a nasty procrastinator like most writers—both aspiring and successful—are want to be.)

So, though this chapter should have ended by now, Dickens wants me to mention *again* that Trip passed through this anxious time with a heavy heart, growing ever heavier, and that the secret was well kept from Bunnie, and that Bunnie was definitely kept in the dark about this whole thing; and by God, she was happy on her honeymoon at that moment, though there was no particular reason at this point to need to point *that* out (except for Dickens to fill space, of course).

But before this chapter mercifully comes to a close, and the wasting of your valuable time is finally quitted, we must also unnecessarily mention that Trip could not fail to observe that the Doctor, whose hand had been a little shaky when he had first taken up making the shoes, was growing dreadfully skillful and that Runyon had never been so intent on his work, and that his hands had never been so nimble and expert, as in the dusk of the tenth evening, blah, blah, blah.*

(*) Whew! Thank God that's done. Now I can get some sleep while everyone else heads off to work...!

Signed,

C.D.

In the early hours of a random Monday morning, circa 1858-1859.

19

That's All I Can Stands, I Can't Stands No More

Worn out by anxious watching, Trip fell asleep at his post. On the eleventh morning of his suspense, he was startled by the shining of the sun into the room where a heavy slumber had overtaken him when it was dark night, which is a long way to go to say he had awoken at dawn.

He rubbed his eyes then roused himself, and he doubted during the progression of the rousing whether he was still asleep, since Pamela Anderson still seemed to be dancing naked right beside him.

Afterwards, he went to the Doctor's door and looked in, he saw that the old man was not working, but had put everything aside and was sitting at the window reading the label on a whiskey bottle. He was in his usual morning dress, which Trip was getting used to seeing him in (Priss more than willing to lend him one), his face, which Trip could distinctly see, should have been embarrassed red for such an unmanly act in the hills of southern Kentucky, but instead was very pale, and calmly studious and attentive.

Even after he had satisfied himself after waking, Trip felt giddy and light-headed for some moments (naturally), and uncertain whether the man making shoes might not be in a dream of his own; possibly as Klinger from M*A*S*H.

Trip was confused and astonished, then wondered why in the hell he was even there to begin with, much less having been there for so long, his place of business was at this moment most likely floundering like the axle-crushed skull of an opossum lying dead by the side of the road. How came he to taking light night walks with the mean old scraggly man, falling asleep in his clothes only to see that man again first thing in the morning wearing a dress and staring at a bottle?

In short, what the *fuck?*

Within a few minutes, Miss Priss...*And don't even get me started on her!*...stood whispering at his side.

If he had had one atom of sanity left, her talk would of necessity shred it to protons. He advised that they should let the time go by until the regular grit-n-gravy hour, and then should meet the Doctor as if nothing unusual had occurred. If he appeared to be in his customary state of mind, Trip would then cautiously proceed to seek direction and guidance from the opinion he had been, in his anxiety, so anxious to obtain.

Miss Priss submitted herself to his judgement for the first time in both their lives, and the scheme was working out with care. The Doctor was soon summoned in the usual way—by Priss' God-awful high-pitched squelching voice—to come down to breakfast.

At first the old coot said something about his daughter's marriage having taken place only yesterday, in all other respects however, he was so composedly himself that Trip determined to have the conversation he'd been thinking of having for sometime now.

A digging, perhaps.

A digging of a different sort than when he dug to recall the man to life.

When the breakfast was over, and Trip and the Doctor were left together, Trip said:

"Runyon, I'm anxious to have your opinion, in confidence, on something I'm very interested in..."

"Is it about 'shine?"

"No."

"Cause I don't know 'bout nothin' else but 'shine."

"It's not about 'shine! Please! Please, just listen to

me. It's something that is very curious to me. But maybe when you tell me what you know, it will be just nothing at all."

"Ok, but if your lookin' to git my secret recipe for 'shine, I cain'ts gives it to you."

"Doctor, it's about something else..."

Glancing at his hands, which were discolored by his late work, the Doctor looked troubled, and listened intentively. He had already glanced at his hands more than once.

"Runyon, if you're in there somewhere" said Trip, as if the shell of the man had been possessed by a space alien, "what I need to know concerns a friend of mine. So please consider carefully helping me out, since it also concerns his daughter. His daughter being Bunnie Mancri....well, now Bunnie Darnet, I suppose."

"If I understands you," said the Doctor, in a subdued tone, "this has something to do with a mental shock?"

"Yes, but it's not about your daughter gettin' married."

"Yeah, that *would* be a shock."

"But it happened."

"What happened?"

"You daughter. She got married."

"Tar'nation! The bitch went and got hitched without tellin' me? And without invitin' me to the weddin'?"

"Yes, she did. But she did tell you, and you were at the weddin'."

"I was?"

"Yeah."

"Oh. I s'pose I was..."

"Doctor Runyon, in the case of this 'shock,' it seems the sufferer has been weighed down by it, no telling for how long, because I believe you don't even know yourself, but I've heard you refer to this 'shock' before, even in public. But whatever it was, you seemed to have recovered from it for awhile, but then it seems to have come back."

The Doctor, in a low voice, asked, "How long's it been that this person you're referring to has been under this 'shock'?"

"Ten days and nights."

"Ten days and nights! What the hell's he been doing all that time? Somethin' he's good at, I hope? Like makin' shoes?"

"Yes, exactly."

"Now, did you ever see him," asked the Doctor, distinctly and collectedly, though in the same low voice, "engaged in that pursuit before?"

"Only once before."

"And when this 'shock' relapsed him, was he in most respects—or in all respects—as good as he was then?"

"I think in all respects, far as I can tell."

"You spoke of his daughter," said the Doctor.

"She's *your* daughter."

"Does his daughter know of the relapse?"

Trip sighed and played along. "No, It has been kept from her, and I hope it will always be kept from her, cause somethin' here ain't quite right. That's what I'm tryin' to figure out."

The Doctor grasped his hand, and murmured, "That was very kind. That was very thoughtful."

"Now Runyon," said Trip, in his most considerate way, "I am a mere man of 'business,' and unfit to cope with such tomfoolery and difficult matters as these. I do not have the kind of information necessary; I'm not a very smart man, I admit—I need help sometimes. But right now, there is no one in the whole world on whom I can rely. So tell me, how does this relapse come about? Is there danger of it happening again? Can it be prevented? How should it be treated? How does it come on? What can I do for my friend? Teach me how I can be a little more useful."

"Jeezus boy, get a hold of yourself! You're as manic as a drippin' faucet! Can't we talk about 'shine or somethin'? *That* I can teach you. You sound like a lun'tic talkin' about all that other stuff!"

"No, we gotta have this out right here and now, I'm afraid. I haven't been to my club in two weeks. The place could be all burned down for all I know..."

"Ok, ok. Keep your shirt on. Yeah, I knew the relapse was comin' on."

"Were you dreading it?"

The Doctor shuddered. "Hells yeah!"

"I can see that. You have no idea how much whatever is bothering you weighs you down. You can't even speak when you're like that. Don't you think he'd be relieved to tell someone what it was that bothers him when it comes on him?"

"Yeah, I 'spect so. But it seems next to impossible. In fact, I know it's impossible."

"So," said Trip, as carefully as possible, "tell me now while you're somewhat coherent—what's in your mind in those times that bothers you so much?"

"I believe," returned Doctor Runyon, "that there be some intense associations of a most distressing nature vividly recalled—say, under certain circumstance—say, on a particular occasion. 'He' tried to prepare himself, but nothin' doin'. Perhaps the strain of tryin' to prepare himself is what does him in."

"So what is it? What's taking place in the relapse?"

The Doctor looked desolately round the room, shook his head, and answered, in a low voice, "I don't know."

Trip sighed. "Ok, now as to the future..."

"As to the future," said the Doctor, recovering firmness, "I should have great hope. Cause I make a great 'shine! And because it pleases Heaven in its mercy to restore 'him' so soon. I hope that the worst should be over. In fact, let's drink some 'shine to that!" And he got up to pour two glasses of 'shine.

"Well, well," said Trip, happily receiving the glass, "that's good comfort, that is, and I am thankful!"

"I am thankful, too," parroted Runyon, raising his

glass.

"But may I go on with my questioning?"

"Jeezus, boy, cain't you just shut your yap and enjoy the 'shine?"

"No. We need to resolve this."

"*Jee*-zus Christ..."

"Maybe you're just under too much stress. You don't need a job since you're collectin' government aid, and yet you work harder than anyone I know, doing weird experiments and scientific stuff and stuff like that. Don't you think it's all too much?"

"Not at all."

"You're sure?"

"Quite sure."

"But if 'he' were overworked at this moment..."

"I'm tellin' you, boy, I really doubt it. There has been a violent stress in one direction, yes, but it needs a counterweight in 'nother direction."

"And that's the work?"

"Yes. Now you're gettin' it!"

"So being overworked will not trigger it again?"

"No," said the Doctor with the firmness of self-conviction, "nothin' but the one train of association will trigger it. And even then, far as the future is concerned, nothin' but an extraordinary jarring of that chord could trigger it. I think the ship that causes those episodes has sailed."

Then Trip spoke something with the diffidence of a man who knew how slight a thing would overset the delicate chemical balance of the mind, and yet with the confidence of a man who had slowly won his assurance out of personal endurance and distress. But he also knew, now was the time to face those inner-demons once and for all:

"Let's say, for the sake of arg'ment, that this guy's been doing crystal meth while in this state..."

"Meth? Oh, that shit's awesome!"

"Ok, bad example....something not addictive...Ah! Let's say the man loves to bake cookies..."

"*What?*"

"Ok, not good either...Let's say the man has taken a likin' to fixin' cars."

"Ok, I don't care 'bout that shit. I *know'd* he ain't been doin' that..."

"But just for the sake of arg'ment, let's say he has been."

"Whatever..."

"So if in this 'crazied' state, all the man's been doin' is fixin' cars—don't you think it's time for him to put down his tools and walk away from the cars?"

The Doctor shaded his forehead with his hand, took a sip of 'shine, and shook his leg up and down nervously.

Trip continued: "He's always had his cars and his tools with him," he said with an anxious look at his friend, "now, would it not be better that he should let them go?"

Still, the Doctor, with shaded forehead, shook his leg up and down nervously.

"I hear they got somethin' for this now," said the Doctor of his shaking leg.

"Something for what?" asked Trip.

"'Restless Leg Syndrome' they call it. Bet I could get some gov'ment money for that..."

"Whatever. You know, Doctor, let's just stick to what we was talkin' about, ok?"

"Suit yourself, but my leg's not gonna stop til I git some pills and gov'ment money..."

"I don't care 'bout that. Just answer my question."

"What was the question?"

"Don't you think the man should put away his cars and tools?"

"Oh. That crazy talk of yours. Ok, I'll play along," said the Doctor. "No, I don't think the man should put them away. Because it's hard to explain the way the poor man's mind works. Doin' that, fixin' cars as you say, relieves his pain so much when it comes on him. I don't know if he'll be able to bear not having it within reach. Even now, when he is hopeful and more confident that it won't happen again, the idea that he might possibly need it again, and won't find it there, gives him a sudden terror shake, know what I mean? Kinda like that 'separation anxiety' kids get I saw Oprah tell 'bout one day."

Trip thought Runyon looked like the scared child on Oprah himself. He addressed the Doctor: "For chrissakes, I'm just a simple man of 'business' here. I don't know nothin'. I ain't claiming to be no guru of this sort of shit. I'm jus' suggestin' that maybe the work itself is what brings on the spells. What about that?"

There was another silence.

"It's like this here 'shine here," said the Doctor. "It's like an old companion. Like an old shoe, or boot..."

The old man started violently, dropped his glass, and it shattered into a thousand pieces.

Trip shook his head. "You see? I would not keep at it. For 'his' daughter's sake, if nothing else."

The mention of his daughter moved something in the Doctor. "In that case, let's do it. But don't take it away while the man is around. Remove it when he's not around."

Trip readily agree to that, and the conversation was ended. They passed the rest of the day in a drunken haze under the plain tree out back, and it seemed that the Doctor was completely restored to his old self. On the three following days he stayed stupid-drunk and happy, and on the fourth went to join Bunnie and her husband on their honeymoon, camping somewhere near Lake Cumberland.

On the night of the day he left the house, Trip went into Runyon's room with a hacksaw, attended by Miss Priss carrying a flashlight. Why they didn't think to just turn on a light is without being able to be understood. There with closed doors, and in a mysterious and guilty manner, Trip and Priss made out for a short while, then Trip came to his senses and hacked the shoes to pieces, while Miss Priss stood there contemplating murdering Trip for getting her all hot and heavy and not finishing the job—for which, indeed, in her grimness, she was no unsuitable figure.

The burning of the shoes—which included the pair so-called 'The Devil', the pair of women's shoes he made right after the wedding, and several pairs of knee-high boots he'd been making ever since—was commenced without delay in the fire under the still; the shoes, boots, tools, and leather were all burned to ashes and then buried out back for good measure. So commonplace do destruction and secrecy appear to dishonest minds, that Trip Templeton and Miss Priss—while engaged in the commission of their deed and in the removal of the shoes and tools—felt almost, and looked, like accomplices in a crime either one of them would commit at any day, at any hour.

And that's a pretty disgustin' thought indeed.

20

A Waste-of-Space Reconsidered

When the newly married pair came home, the first person who appeared, to offer his congratulations, was Bubba Cotton. They had not been at home many hours when he presented himself. He was not improved in habits, or in looks, or in manner; but there was a certain rugged air of fidelity about him, which was new to the observation of Bubba Darnet.

Cotton watched his opportunity for coaxing Darnet into his piece of shit Vega, which Cotton bought from the rental car establishment after the wedding, having been unable to find his piece of shit Chevette the night he got drunk with Darnet at the Skinned Hare and woke the next morning in the dumpster. He coaxed him with the promise of sharing a fatty where no one would think to look for them, and because he had no other to share.

"Darnet," said Cotton, "I wish we could be friends."

"We're friends already, I thought," replied Darnet, exhaling a larger than needed toke on the fatty, filling the car with smoke.

Cotton coughed. "You are nice to say so, in a manner of speaking; but, I don't mean to be speaking in a manner of speaking, if you mind my manners..."

"*What?*" asked Bubba. "Maybe you should ease back on the grass a bit..."

"Indeed, when I say I wish we might be friends, I scarcely mean to say that friends of ours won't be friends much longer than you and I are friends..."

"*What?*"

Bubba Darnet was starting to get worried.

But Cotton continued, smiling: "God-dog'nation! I

find this easier to understand in my own mind that trying to 'splain it to you!"

"I should say so."

"However, let me try."

"Oh, Jeezus..."

"You remember a certain famous occasion when I was more drunk than usual?"

"Yeah, right. When would that be? I remember a 'famous' occasion when you told me to my face you didn't like me, after you was all talkin' queer all night and shit."

"I remember that too. The curse of those occasions is heavy upon me, for I always remember them..."

"Dude, you are *way* too fucked-up..."

"Stop interrupting me! I'm just tellin' you what the old toothless prospector in my brain is tellin' me to tell you! Now hush a moment so I cain continue."

"Whatever, dude, it's your weed..."

"So—as I was saying, I hope it may be taken into account one day, when all things are at an end, and the Lord Jeezus Almighty is sittin' up there on his throne, lookin' down on us ants, gittin' ready to squash some, and fixin' to eat others for breakfast..."

"*What?*"

"Oh, don't worry. I ain't gonna preach to you."

"I ain't worried 'bout that. I'm worried that your brain is gonna open up and some demon is gonna come out and eat me. You're talking so much shit, Cotton."

"Oh, I see," said Cotton, with a careless wave of his roach, nearly burning Darnet in his left eyeball. "That night I was drunk and you thought I was talkin' all gay; about liking you and shit, and then not liking you. All I'm trying to say is why don't we just forget about all that?"

"I forgot it long ago. It's in the past, my friend."

"You lyin' box of animal crackers! You know it still bothers you, you know it does! I haven't forgotten it, so you haven't it forgotten it neither! I know this."

"Look, I'm just tryin' to enjoy this here weed you've givin' me, so if it will help you to tell you I haven't forgotten it, then fine, I haven't forgotten it. But I have forgotten it a long time ago. Jeezus Christ, man! You think all's I got to do all day is sit around and think about that? Well, I don't ok? But I do want to thank you for what you did for me earlier that day, re-establsihin' me in the bowling leagues and all."

"I was jus' doin' my job, nothing more."

"But no one got paid..."

"I know. But still. I did it as a professional courtesy."

"To whom? 'Cause 'fore that day, I didn't even know you."

"And I'm not really sure that I gave one shit about what would become of you, until I saw how you looked so damned pitiful up there, and scared, and all shriveled up and pussy-like..."

"All right now, just take it easy...I know I'm higher than Shaquille O'Neal's balls right now, but I could still give you a good ass whoopin' if I wanted to!"

"You and what army, Sniglet? You couldn't fight your way out of a box with a paper bag stuck inside that box made of paper on the outside..."

"Aw, shit, here we go again..."

"Now look, muther-fuckin' Darnet!—I been tryin' to speak here 'bout us bein' friends! Now that you know me, you know I'm capable of talkin' shit while bein' higher than a fuckin' 747 on steroids. If you doubt it, you can ask Stryker!"

"No, that's all right. I prefer to form my own opinion without the benefit of *that* pansy's. Besides, I can pretty much see it for myself right here..."

"Well, at any rate, you'll know me as a disgustin' dog who ain't never done no good, and never will."

"I don't know that you *never* will."

"But *I* do! And you must take my word for it. Now, to change the subject, let's talk about matters in the future. Do you think in the future you could have such a worthless fellow hangin' around your house, permitted to come and go as he pleases—and not worthy of much more attention than a ten day old jar of 'shine; and maybe only three or four times a year? And you won't even notice that I'm there. I'll make myself invisible. I'll use a Klingon cloaking device. I'll be like Wonder Woman's airplane. I'll..."

"Jeezus! Would you shut the fuck up? Ok! You can come over from time to time, Jeezus! I don't 'spect Bunnie'd mind too much, I guess."

"Oh, thank you, Darnet! Thank you! And do you think I can use your name when I'm runnin' up the bar tab in..."

"Don't fuckin' push it, Cotton! I 'preciate the weed and all, but don't fuckin' push it!"

They both shook hands, and Darnet got out of the car. Cotton drove away. Within a minute afterwards, he was, to all outward appearances, completely and beyond fucked-up.

When he was gone, and in the course of an evening passed with Miss Priss, the Doctor, and Trip Templeton; Bubba Darnet made some mention of this conversation in general terms, and spoke of Bubba Cotton as a problem and a careless and reckless piece of baboon shit. He spoke of him, not bitterly or meaning to trash his character or nothin', but as anybody might who endured such a rod of human fecal matter talking out his ass the way Bubba Cotton did earlier that day sitting in his piece of shit drag-ass Vega.

Darnet had no idea that such a vivid description could dwell in the thoughts of his young foul wife for days, but then, after they had joined themselves together in their own room, and staring at the ceiling smoking cigarrettes, he found her scrinching her heavily peirced forehead in deep consternation.

"We are thoughtful 'bout somethin' tonight, are we?" asked Darnet, drawing his arm about her, and nearly burning her Aqua-Net saturated hair with his cigarrette.

"Yes, *dearest* Bubba," she barked, removing his hands from her breasts, her eyes boring holes through his stupid numbskull. "*We* are rather thoughtful tonight, cause *we* have something on *our* mind!"

"Oh, Jeezus. Here it comes..."

"If I tell you something, will you promise not to ask me a certain question in return, and if you do, I'll rip your nut sack over your head and nail it to the wall next to the velvet Elvis?"

"What is it I'm promisin' to?" he said with one hand caressing her golden Clairol hair, while the other tried again to cop a breast.

"I think, Bubba, that Bubba Cotton deserves better consid'ration and respect than you been givin' him lately."

"And why is that, my lovely?"

"That's the fuckin' question I was warnin' you about, you no-balls piece of shit! Get ready Elvis...!"

"No! Wait! I didn't understand the question. I mean, I didn't understand the answer! I mean...!"

His wife suddenly calmed. "Well, I think he does deserve better consid'ration. In fact, I *know* he does."

"What the fuck? Have you been messin' around with...?"

"No, putrified ball-hair, I haven't! All's I'm sayin' is that I'm askin' that you'd treat him a little nicer, and not talk bad 'bout him when he ain't around s'all. I'm askin' for you to believe me when I say he's got a heart under all them layers of shit somewheres, and I think it's been wounded..."

"Are you sure you ain't been...?"

"Look, testes-taster! I'm trying to tell you somethin' all tender like here, and all's you can think of is I'm screwin' the bastard! Take your head out my crotch for five fuckin' minutes and give me a break, would ya?"

"Ok, hun. I 'pologize."

"'Pology accepted."

"I guess I just never thought that there could be

anything good underneath all that shit."

"There is. But I am also quite certain that he will pro'ly always have bad luck, and never be able to fully get his shit together, but that bein' said, I also think him capable of good and gentle things. Maybe even great things..."

"Are you *sure* you haven't been...?"

She grabbed his ball-sack in a vice-like grip.

"Arrrgghhh...! Ok! Ok! My dearest! My dearest love! Please! Let...go...!"

She clung even harder and moved closer to him on the bed, her breasts grazing his shoulder as she raised her eyes to his. "Remember how strong we are in our happiness, and how weak he is in his misery!"

Darnet huffed and puffed, gasping for air. "I'll remember! I'll remember! I'll remember it for as long as I live! Now, would you please let me go? I think I'm fixin' to taste my own man-marbles any a second here, you're squeezin' 'em so tight-like. And I'd really rather not do that if it's all the same to you."

She let go and at once he collapsed with a heavy exhale into the fetal position with continued shortness of breath.

"Woo-wee, woman! You got some grip on you!"

Bunnie rolled her golden hair away from his pain, and looked at the wall.

If one forlorn wanderer then pacing the dark streets, could have heard her disclosure and could have seen the drops of pity in those soft-blue eyes of hers pissed away by her husband, and heard him cry out in the night because of it, his lips might have said for the first time ever, 'God bless her for her sweet compassion!'

21

Plottings and Subplottings

A wonderful corner for illegally dumping trash, it has been remarked, was that corner where the Doctor lived. Some came to dump, some came to dig. Ever dumping and ever digging, people came and went, digging and dumping, dumping and digging. Bunnie sat alone in the still house, ever digging herself out of marital disharmony, listening to the echoing footsteps of the years.

For, there was something coming in the echoes, something light, afar off, and scarcely audible yet, that stirred her heart too much. Fluttering hopes and doubts—hope, of a love as yet unknown to her: doubts, of her remaining upon earth to enjoy that new delight—dividing her like that straight line cruising down her heavily cleavaged breasts. Among the echoes then, there would arise the sound of footsteps at her own early grave; and thoughts of the husband that would be left so desolate, and who would mourn for her so much (she hoped) swelled to her eyes, and broke like waves.

That time passed, and her little Brittany lay on her bosom. Then, among the advancing echoes, there was the tread of her tiny feet and the sound of her prattling words. Let greater echoes resound as they would, the young mother at the cradle-side could always hear those coming. They came, and the shade-starved house was sunny with a child's laugh. Her husband's step was slovenly and lazy; her father's drunk and hazy. And Lo, Miss Priss, now barely able to walk—and crazier than a hyena undergoing shock-therapy—was hung from a sling in a harness, awakening the echoes as an unruly charger as she snorted and pawed at the earth beneath the plain tree.

Even when there were sounds of sorrow (which were many) and words that were harsh and cruel (which were many), and even when a halo of golden-hair much like her own (for she dyed the baby's as well) laid on a pillow with the round face of a little boy and said with a frown and a hack of a newborn exposed to smoking—among other things—"Paw! Maw! I'm sorry to leave ya, and my sister too, but the fightin' in heaven's gotta be a whole lot cleaner and calmer than the fightin' that's goin' on here. All righty then, take care now, bye-bye then!"

Those were not tears all of agony that whetted his young mother's cheek, as the spirit departed from her embrace that had been (for some ungodly reason) entrusted to it.

The echoes rarely answered to the tread of Bubba Cotton. Some half-dozen times a year, at most, he claimed his privilege of coming in uninvited, and would sit among them through the evening, as he had once done often. He never came there drunk as a skunk, and one other thing regarding him was whispered in the echoes, which has been whispered by all true echoes for ages and ages:

No man ever really loved a woman, lost her, and knew her with a un-pornographic charged mind (except when she became his wife and a mother), but her children had a strange sympathy with him—an instinctive delicacy of pity for him. What fine hidden sensibilities are touched in such a case (and hopefully there were no children involved in the touching), no echoes tell; but it is so, and it was so here. Cotton was the first stranger to whom little Brittany held out her chubby little arms, and he kept his place with her as she grew (but not *too* close). The little boy had spoken of him, just before leaving this world: "Poor Cotton! Kiss him for me!" because apparently they *had* been too close.

Mr. Stryker shouldered himself through the law,

like some great engine forcing itself through turbid water, and dragged his useless friend in his wake, like a boat towed astern. As the boat so favored is usually in a rough plight, and mostly under water, so, Cotton had a swamped life of it.

Stryker was rich; had married a widow in the advanced stages of alzheimer's with property and three boys, who were immediately remanded to the care of the state by their own recognizance after receiving an anonymous letter of warning sent by one 'Siddhartha Coxsin.'

These were among the echoes to which Bunnie—sometimes pensive, sometimes higher than a rabbit at a dog party—listened in the echoing Chickenwell Street until her little daughter was six years old.

But, there were other echoes, from a distance, that rumbled menacingly down Chickenwell Street all through this space of time. And it was now, about little Brittany's sixth birthday, that they began to have an awful sound, as of a great storm in Coon Spit, or as of a coal mine explosion.

On a night in mid-July in the year two-thousand exactly, Trip came in late from Tall Tales and sat himself with Bunnie and her husband around the old still. It was a hot, wild night, and they were all three reminded of the old Sunday night when they had hallucinated and looked at the purple rain and lightning from the same vantage.

"I think," said Trip, "that I'll have to spend the night at Tall Tales. We've been packed to the gills all day with business so that the girls have not known who to do first...er, I mean, what to do first, or which way to turn! There is such an uneasiness in Coon Spit, that we have actually had a run of pervs upon us. There seems to be such a mania in the clubs over there, that all the business is coming over here."

"That looks bad," said Darnet.

"A bad look, you say, Darnet?"

"Well...for the clubs over there, I mean. It's good

for you, of course."

"Of course. But we don't know what the reason for it is yet. Some of us at Tall Tales are gettin' old, and can't handle all the new traffic no matter how much money we're making off it. I simply can't do accounting and addin' up receipts until five-thirty in the morning each night. I'm not gettin' no sleep!"

"Still," said Darnet cryptically, "you know how gloomy and threatening the 'sky' is."

"I know that, to be sure," assented Trip, "But I'm determined to get fucked-up higher than Broom Hilda's girdle tonight. Where the hell is Runyon with that weed, anyway? And by the way, how's the 'shine lookin' tonight?"

"Here he is!" said the Doctor, entering the dark room at that moment.

"I'm quite glad you're home. All those skeezes and pervs I've been around all day make your dumb-ass look like Mother fuckin' Tare-*ay*-sa. But you're makin' me nervous, you being all skittish and shit. What you doin'? You fixin' to go out?"

"No, I'm goin' to play backgammon with you if you like," said the Doctor.

"Hell no! I ain't playin' no pussy backgammon! You should know better'n 'at! You still got some 'x' over there for me, Bunnie? I cain't see..."

"Of course. We've kept some for you."

"Awesome! Thank you, my dear. The precious child is safe in bed?"

"Only because Father Weezer here is in sight of us," remarked Darnet.

Runyon scowled at him. "I ain't done nothin' to that..."

"I know, dad, I know!" calmed Darnet. "I's jus' fuckin' wit'cha..."

"All right, that's enough of that. Just hand me over some of that 'X' and we'll get this party started. We should be hearing the echoes soon enough, eh Bunnie? Heh, heh. Let's all sit in a circle now and listen to Bunnie's fucked-up theories about what's happenin' in this God-forsaken county of ours."

"Oh, they're not theories. They's reality."

"Whatever you say, my wise old Bun-Bun," said Runyon. "They are very numerous and getting loud, that's all I know! Hear 'em! Hear 'em!"

"Jeezus, jus' got here and the old man's fucked-up already..." Darnet complained.

But that had been Clay D. Markee's evil plan all along. Not to have Runyon fucked-up so quickly, but matters much more important, and affecting the wider community. For you see, Clay had known if it were first suggested and planned to have the Walmart put in Coon Spit proper, then the Harlan's would spend all their time and resources battling the zoning laws and whatever else at their disposal until they had depleted their resources, but declared a temporary victory. Then Clay and the Bay Steel Bank would take the deal over to Rabbit Grove, where it would be accepted without batting an eye, and the Harlan's would no longer have any resources to fight it. Such a vile plan was completed under the watch of Ken Kween, now the bank president after the death of Clay D. Markee.

Thus the Harlan's, and the combined chambers of commerce of Coalmont County, were forced to sit back and watch the Walmart be built right in the shadow of The Rebel Yell Bowling Alley itself, and there was not a goddamn thing they could do about it.

Once Clay's (and now Ken's) Rabbit Grove Walmart deal was in motion, the evil bankers (one dead, one very much alive) had frozen all retirement, savings, and mortgage accounts for everyone in Coalmont County inside such a powerful county institution that was the Bay Steel Bank.

It also came to light—after the automatic doors of the Walmart slid open and skivvies were begun to be sold at the unheard of price of two dollars a three-pack—that Markee had indeed framed Doctor Runyon on outlandish charges that he stole money from the union treasury at the auto-parts plant. An upstart investigative reporter looking to fast-track himself to the Chicago Tribune uncovered the fact that Runyon had applied for a job at the Bay Steel Bank (around the time of Markee initially hatching his evil Walmart plan) wanting to better his situation in life, and his impending hiring was assured at the uppermost levels, but levels just below Clay Markee. Knowing the old man would most certainly give him trouble when the time came to freeze the citizenry assets, Markee had the framing fast-tracked through the courts at the 'old Rebel' and there wasn't a goddamned thing Runyon, or anyone else, could do about it at the time.

So presently, Coon Spit was in twice a bind. Business was being flushed away from them by the new Walmart (as the Harlan's had feared all along), drying up the town's economy to near dust-bowl proportions, and yet now they didn't even have the benefit of the jobs and tax revenue the Walmart could have afforded them had it been built in their district to begin with.

But Rabbit Grove, where Postmaster Gabriel lived and worked, and where The Chateau was located (though of course Markee was no longer around to enjoy the fruits of his labor) thrived so much with the new Walmart that the town was able in just one year to lower the tax burden on its townsfolk to a mere trickle. And even that trickle was promised to be obliterated within the next two years.

Now, as to the group well along in getting plastered and huddled around the Doctor's still out on Chickenwell Street, Bunnie's espoused theory was that her husband was working at the Rabbit Grove Walmart as a greeter (in disguise, of course) as evidenced by a fake beard, mustache, toupee, and name tag, which read:

Hello! My name is Bubba Darnet!

If you are not completely satisfied with my service to you, please feel free to turn me into my manager so he or she can fire me right away.

Thank you and have a pleasant visit with us!,

which she found in the glove compartment of his rusted-out Fiero. Of course, Bubba Darnet remained in the room with them, fucked-up and flatly denying it to his dying days, and yet Bunnie knew a sudden influx in the family income had appeared as soon as the last parking slot had been hap-hazzardly painted on the Rabbit Grove Walmart asphalt.

The group, of course, was left without means of confirming or denying it (Darnet's word being against hers), since self-respecting Coalmont Countians (and luckily for Human Resources at Walmart, there were thousands who *weren't* self-respecting) swore they'd never step foot in such a den of the Devil; Trip Templeton, Doctor Runyon, Bunnie, Bubba Cotton, and Miss Priss (back when she was still in her right mind) included among them. For them to shop at that Walmart would be like throwing their babies over Lake Cumberland Falls, or quittin' chew. It just wasn't going to happen.

And so they were left to their speculations. It was all they had. And just like everything else in their lives at this point (with the noted exception of Trip's now thriving strip club), it wasn't much.

The Harlan's had nothing left either, excepting their rage.

The Walmart had done the evil they fully well expected it would, and those who didn't bow to it—by selling off their small businesses and taking jobs as cashiers, stockers, or greeters—simply wouldn't be seeing food nor shelter in the foreseeable future. And since the Bay Steel Bank still controlled all their assets, selling off was the only thing they were allowed to do at this point. No further loans or bail-outs would be issued. The county was closed for business to all but one: The Bastion of affordable Wonder-Bras; the harbinger of low-cost household appliances and patio furniture; the Gigantor of Chinese venture capitalism— the Almighty Walmart.

Headlong, mad, and dangerous footsteps forced their way into everybody's lives, footsteps not easily made clean again without tough-actin' Tenactin. The footsteps raged at Saint Antwan's Liquors and Beers, just as they did in the little circle that sat around the still on Chickenwell Street.

Saint Antwan's had been, that morning, a vast dusky mass of scarecrows heaving to and fro, with frequent gleams of light above billowy afros, where DVD's of *Blade* and *Gladiator* 'interrupted' from their shipment to Walmart sat stacked on the counter next to Mandy Debarge. A tremendous roar rose from the throat of Saint Antwan, and a forest of arms struggled in the forest in the open air like shriveled branches of trees in a winter wind: all the fingers convulsively clutching at every sporting good and kitchen supply thrown off the back loading dock at Walmart to wild-eyed stalks of grabbing arms below. It was the hillbilly equivalent of The Boston Tea Party, and oh, yes, they took the tea too.

But who gave it out? And from whence did it come? Through what agency crookedly quivered and jerked and tossed goods from the trucks of the loading dock? As if it were Zorro, the Lone Ranger or the Incredible Hulk, no eye in the throng could have told exactly who it was; but, clothes for toddlers were being distributed—as were Men's Wear: Casual and Big and Tall; cheap dinette sets, camping lanterns, bathroom fixtures, bouncy balls, fun packs of Snickers, a TV or two, axes, nutrition bars and everything else you could think of under the sun, was being pilfered as if from the pockets of Sam Walton himself, to hopefully be felt as far away as the headquarters in Arkansas, and maybe even in Shanghai.

People who could lay hold of nothing else, took to taking bricks and railings from the loading dock itself, with the goal of crippling the next shipments as best they could. Every pulse and heart at Saint Antwan's was on high-fever strain and at high-fever heat. Every living creature there held discount pricing as of no account, and was demented with a passionate readiness to sacrifice it.

As a whirlpool of boiling waters has a center point, so, all this raging circled around one Mandy and Barge Debarge, and every human drop in the caldron of Coon Spit had a tendency to be sucked toward the vortex of Barge himself (already begrimed with cheap Walmart wines and cocktail sauces) who issued orders, thrust a man back, dragged this one forward, and labored and strove in the thickest of the uproar to decide where they would hide and store all the goods they were 'confiscating' from Walmart.

"Keep near to me, Harlan Three!' cried Debarge; "And you, Harlan One and Two! Separate yourselves and put yourselves at the head of as many of these 'patriots' as you can! Where's my fuckin' wife?"

"Here I am, Dick-Lick!" said Mandy, as composed as ever, but not reading her *Digest* today. Apparently, the Walmart had much more and much greater a variety of gossip rags and women's magazines, and she was feverishly intent on flipping through each and every one of them.

"Come on, Mandy! We ain't takin' this shit so's you can read it! That ain't what we're tryin' to do! Now what you gonna do that's *useful?*"

"I'll go with you on the next run then, Balls-for-Brains. But I'll head up the women."

"Come then!" cried Debarge in a resounding voice. "Patriots and friends, we are ready! To the Bay Steel!"

This elicited a gasp like static electricity through the crowd, and with a roar that sounded as if all the breath of Coon Spit had been shaped into the detested title, the living sea rose, wave on wave, depth on depth, and overflowed the streets on the way toward downtown. Car alarms ringing, boom-boxes booming, the sea raging and thundering on its new beach, the attack had begun.

Double-glass doors, cheap furniture, the smell of bad 1970s wood paneling, and jars of lollipops were scattered at locations throughout; monies were grabbed from daily deposits shoved lazily into drawers by careless tellers—Barge of the liquor store and his horde looted the bank for ten solid minutes, and by all accounts he could've been considered a type of hillbilly Robin Hood.

"Work, Harlans work! Work Harlan One, Harlan Two, Harlan Ten, Harlan Twenty-Five; in the name of all the Angles and Devils—whichever you prefer—work!"

"Come with me, women!" cried Mandy. "We'll take all the toilet paper from the shitters and the cleaning supplies from the closets!"

And with a shrill thirsty cry, trooping women went for the bathrooms, all alike in their hunger for revenge.

Out front, Barge cried to the men, who at this point were tired and jones-in' for alcoholic input: "Get the records! The receipts of everyone's accounts! Let's get proof of the secret plan to put the Walmart in Rabbit Grove from the beginning! It must be on someone's computer somewhere! Find it! Find it!"

Of all the cries and incoherent barkings of the rednecks, this was heard over all: "The savings account records! Get the savings accounts records!"

"Show me Ken Kween's computer!" cried Barge to Harlan One. "Quick!"

There was a back office with a heavily-grated stained-glass window, with a screen-saver of Mel Tillis dancing across a computer screen. There was a small jar of lollipops on the desk, and a Picachu-head stress-ball filled with jell.

"Get into his computer so that I can see what's in there. You might need to bust the passwords."

But no password busting was needed, as bank president Ken Kween was far too lazy for that, and lulled into thinking nothing would happen in such a backwoods Kentucky town, so that all files were open and ready for access.

Harlan One moved the mouse around, deciding which to open first.

"Stop!—Look there, Harlan!"

"P. R.?" croaked Harlan One, as he read greedily.

"Paul Runyon," said Barge in his ear, following the letters with his bloodshot eyes, his fingers now filled with paper-cuts from grabbing receipts and account numbers out front.

Harlan One announced: "The file is called 'A Poor Doctor of the Veterinary Arts'

"Open it up, and print it off!" ordered Barge. "Then let's get the hell outta here!"

Out in the bank proper, they tossed all blank withdraw and deposit forms into the middle of the lobby where they were burned along with the cheap furniture and bad wood paneling pulled from the walls. And after all Harlans, and women, had escaped, eventually the entire Bay Steel Bank building was aflame.

An hour was come before the police and firefighters could comb the ashes for clues as to who perpetrated such a crime, when Saint Antwan executed his brilliant statement of protest by hanging all merchandise confiscated of late from the Walmart from telephone poles, streetlights, cell-phone towers, and just about anywhere else in town anything could be hung, including a massive display of sporting goods arrayed at the high school athletic fields; and most notably, from the goal-posts.

And not a single drop of evidence of theft or maldoing was left in or on the hands of any one single Harlan.

Saint Antwan's blood was up, and the blood of

tyranny and domination by the 'Iron Hand of Arkansas' was down. The sea of black and threatening waters, and of destructive upheaving of wave upon wave, whose depths were yet unfathomed and whose forces were yet unknown, had been set loose in motion. The remorseless sea of turbulently swaying shapes, voices of vengeance, and faces hardened in the furnaces of suffering until the touch of pity could make no mark on them, were burst forth upon Coon Spit, the effects of which were soon to create a shock-wave throughout greater Coalmont County.

Now Heaven keep the theories of Bunnie Darnet, and keep these footsteps far out of her life! For they are headlong, mad, and dangerous; and in the years so long after Delbert's spilling of that shipment in Barge's liquor store parking lot, souls are not so easily purified when once stained with bad 'shine.

22

Lunch, Interrupted

Haggard Saint Antwan had had only one exultant week, in which to soften his modicum of hard and bitter liquors and beers and sell it to such an extent as he could. With the relish of fraternal embraces and congratulations, Mandy Debarge sat at her counter, as usual, lording herself over the customers. Mandy Debarge wore no rose in her head, for the great brotherhood of illegals, er, um, I mean, 'spies' had become, even in one short week, extremely wary of trusting themselves to the Saint's mercies.

Mandy Debarge, with her arms folded, sat in the morning light and heat, contemplating the liquor store and the street. In both, there were several knots of loiterers, squalid and miserable, but now with a manifest sense of power enthroned on their distress. The most raggedy-assed redneck had this crooked significance in them: that 'I know how hard my life has been. How hard I have worked or suckled at the Welfare teat, or justly or unjustly bilked the government and the working taxpayers out of tens of thousands of dollars just so's I could live and survive e'ry day, e'ry year; but now, do you see how easy it's become for me to shoplift that Walmart? And I don't even have to go *in* to shoplift it, since there's some fool out back throwing shit off the trucks to people whenever he sees a crowd a-gather'n in.'

Every lean redneck and hillbilly that had been out of work before had this work at the ready for him, or her, now, to loot the Walmart by way of the back loading docks, and the benevolent shit thrower, whenever a strike was organized.

And never was the police force of any one town,

especially in Rabbit Grove, the wiser. For no one tattled on the mysterious thrower, and the store manager was simply at as loss as he was forced to report over and over again to the home offices in Arkansas massive, and quite inexplicable, losses, since the store's video surveillance system was in no way disengaged or strapped by malfunction, but yet it showed no perpetrator in the act of perpetrating any sort of crime.

Mandy Debarge sat observing the masses who held these thoughts of lootenment with such suppressed approval as was to be desired the leader of the Saint Antwan women. One of her sisterhood gossiped on beside her, the short, rather plump wife of a starved mom and pop grocer, and the mother of two—this 'lieutenant' had earned the complimentary name of 'The Vengeance.'

"Hey!" said The Vengeance. "Listen, Mandy! Look who's comin' in!"

As if a free line of white coke powder had been sniffed-up from the outermost bound of Coon Spit proper straight to the door of Saint Antwan's is how fast a murmur came rushing along, into and through the store.

"It's just Barge," said Mandy. "But shut the hell up anyway, ya'all. I'm sick of your yappin'."

Barge came in breathless, pulled off an oversized cowboy hat he wore (and got from you know where, and you know how—) and looked around him.

"Hey, everyone!" Mandy Debarge suggested. "Looks like he wants to tell us somethin'. Let's listen to the old dunder-britches!"

Barge stood, panting, against a background of eager eyes and open mouths formed inside the door; all those within the liquor store having sprung to their feet.

"Come on, numb-nuts! Out with it!"

"News from the other world!" exclaimed Barge.

"Oh, jeezus...," countered Mandy, "Sorry everyone, he's just jacked on meth again. Go back to whatever you was doin'..."

Barge continued: "Does everybody here recall Councilman Fallon, the first man to suggest a Walmart be built here, and who told the famished small business owner's association that when the Walmart came, they would be better off, and even if they weren't, then they could just eat grass and kiss his ass? And when he heard the first tiniest bit of opposition from us, he told us we could all go to hell?"

"No, but I'm pretty sure I recall a shithead right in front of me now who's *smoked* too much grass today," answered Mandy on behalf of the crowd.

Then it suddenly occurred to her, and the others, what her husband was saying.

-"Is he *here*?"

-"In Kentucky again?"

-"In the *county*?"

-"In Coon Spit?"

"Patriots!" said Barge, in a determined voice, "Are we ready?"

Instantly, Mandy slipped a butterfly knife into her bra and everyone took to the streets as if a drummer had summoned them for battle from the parking lot. The Vengeance, uttering terrifying shrieks, and flinging her arms about her head like all the fury of Hell, was tearing down the street past house after house, empty closed-up store after empty closed-up store, rousing the women.

The men were terrible, in the blood-minded anger with which they looked from windows—caught up what drugs, smokes and chew they had— and came pouring down into the streets; but, the women were a sight to chill the boldest. From such household occupants as their bare poverty yielded; from their children; from their aged and their sick and crouching on the bare ground famished and naked; they ran out with bleached-out hair, urging one another, and themselves, to madness with the wildest cries and actions. Villain Fallon is here, my sister! Old Fallon is here, my mother! Miscreant Fallon is here, my daughter! Then, a score of others ran into the midst of these, beating their chests, tearing their hair, and screaming. Fallon is here again! Fallon who told the starving shop owners that they could kiss his ass! Fallon who told my father he could kiss his ass from one pew behind him in church! Fallon who told my baby to suck it, not referring to my milk starved breasts, but to his nasty ol' shriveled up wee-wee! O mother of God, this Fallon! O Heaven's above, our suffering! Hear me, my powdered-milk starved baby and my withered father: I swear on my knees, on this pavement beneath me, to avenge you on Fallon! Husbands, and brothers, and young men, Give us Fallon, Give us his heart, his soul, his balls! Rend Fallon to pieces, and dig him into the ground, that grass may grow over *him*!

With these cries, numbers of the women, lashed into a blind frenzy, whirled about, striking and tearing at their own friends until they dropped into a passionate swoon, and were only saved by the men belonging to them and those who simply took the opportunity to cop a feel.

Nevertheless, not a moment was lost; not a moment! This Fallon was at the Horse Chaw and Vittles restaurant in downtown Coon Spit, reportedly having lunch and minding his own business after having moved away from the county shortly after being thrown from office, literally, after having told all his constituents to kiss his ass.

The mob was soon gathered where this old man, ugly and wicked, was, the rest of them overflowing into the adjacent dinning areas and out into the streets. The Debarges, husband and wife, The Vengeance, and Harlan Three, were packed nearest around the booth where he sat, at no great distance, in front of him.

"See this!" cried Mandy Debarge, pointing with her knife to a patch of grass she had cut from a field on the way over. She threw it down on his table and some dirt, and possibly a few pill-bugs, flew into his soup.

"Ha Ha!" someone yelled. "That was well done! Let him eat it now!"

Mandy put her knife under her arm and satisfactorily clapped her hands as if she were a kindergarten teacher coaxing a young imbecilic child to act.

"Yes, eat it! Come on now, you can do it!"

The people immediately behind Mandy explained her actions to those behind them, and those again explained to others, and those to others, the neighboring streets soon resounded with the clapping of hands.

Soon, a cry seemed to go up all over the city: "Bring him out! Bring him out!"

Down, and up, and head foremost on the floor of the restaurant, now on his knees, now on his feet; now on his back—the man had cerebral palsy, so it took quite awhile for him to get his ass out of the restaurant.

Once again, the police too short handed and too late in acting, were not seen nor heard from. Out in the street two men held Fallon while several others, including shrieking women, put grass in his pockets and pants, and smeared mud on his suit jacket to which more grass gathered by some small children was splattered, the children having thought seeing adults having a grass and mud fight was the most awesomest thing they'd ever saw in their whole lives.

Then the town's people left Fallon there, dazed and dirty and as confused as ever, and swearing by God Almighty in Jesus' Sweet name to Heaven to never, *ever*, step a palsied foot in Coalmont County again.

Ever.

Now this was not the end of a day's bad work for the mob, for Saint Antwan so shouted and danced his angry blood up, that it boiled again. It was so decided that the humiliation of Fallon was not enough, but that his own son-in-law deserved some retribution as well, for he was also one of the small business owner's enemies and insulters, yet he lived just a few blocks away and was a mere substitute teacher.

But be that at it may, he was hated enough for his words in defense of Fallon at subsequent council meetings on the issue of the impending Walmart, that he garnered a reaction of the mob this day to hang risque and embarrassing women's lingerie—direct from the women's department at Walmart, of course, and of course, all unpaid for—from all manner of tree, porch and bushes of the unsuspecting substitute teacher's house.

He also had the added embarrassment of having been taken down to the sheriff's office and interrogated as if he had something to do with the Walmart merchandise that continued to show up missing from the stores shelves where for all intents and purposes, it should have resided for retail purchase.

Not before dark night did the men and women come back to the children, wailing, breadless, and mostly milkless. Then, the miserable baker's shops were beset by long files of them, patiently waiting to buy bread; and while they waited with stomachs faint and empty, the very store (Walmart) in which they had swore an oath the they would not buy from, had shelves stocked to the full with bread, milk and other necessities, and for less than half the cost of the mom and pop bakeries (though not as good).

But those in line beguiled the time by embracing one and another and laughing about their triumphs of the day, and achieving them again in gossip. Gradually, these strings of ragged rednecks shortened and frayed away; and then poor light began to shine in high windows, and slender fires were made in oil drums outside Saint Antwan's.

It was almost morning when Barge's liquor store parted with its last knot of customers, and Barge said to Mandy his wife, in husky tones, while fastening the door:

"At last it is here, my dear!"

"Well," returned Mandy. "Almost."

Saint Antwan, whomever and wherever he was,

slept: even The Vengeance slept with her starved grocer.

23

More Dirty Dealings

There was a change in Reams where people still stumbled out of The Fountain at all times of the day, and where the road construction dude went forth daily to hammer out the pavement out on the highway where he ate such scant lunches of morsels of bread that they doubled not only as patches to hold his poor reduced body together, but also his poor ignorant soul.

Far and wide lay a ruined county, yielding nothing but desolation. Every forest, cave, coal shaft, and hollow was as shriveled and poor as the miserable people. Everything was bowed down, dejected, oppressed and broken. Habitations, fences, domesticated animals, men, women, children, and the soil that bore them—all worn out.

The only thing currently thriving was the new Walmart, and this despite the back-dock looting that continued to confound the sheriff.

As the road construction dude worked, solitarily—as his boss and co-workers were assigned to a different duty that day—he worked to patch some of the more troublesome potholes in the highway by himself, and in the dust, not often troubling himself to reflect that dust he was and to dust he must return, being for the most part too much occupied in thinking how little he had for supper (and working in clear sight of a Cracker Barrel off the next exit in front of him didn't help matters in the least) and how much of a pounding he would put on that frickin' salad bar if only he had a few Washington's to do so. But, right now, as he raised his eyes from his lonely labor, he viewed the road in front of him and saw a rough figure approaching him on foot, apparently from out of the nearby woods. As it advanced, the road construction dude would discern without surprise that it was a shaggy-haired old man of an almost barbarian aspect, like Grizzly Adams, a member of ZZ Top, or that guy from the Oak Ridge Boys. The old man was carrying nothing but an ax, and was covered from head to toe, including in his beard, with mud and dust and thorns and leaves and moss from trekking through the woods for only God knows how long.

Such a man came upon him, like a ghost— and a nasty one at that— at noon in the July weather, so you know it was hotter'n a bitch's balls out there on that highway. He said in a dialect barley intelligible to the craziest of gold-rush prospectors:

"How goes it, Harlan?"

"It goes well, Harlan."

"Shake my hand, then."

"I wouldn't touch your hand with my dead grand-daddy's ass hairs! Get that thing away from me."

"Haven't eaten today?"

"Fuck no!" said the road construction dude with a hungry face.

"If you want, you can take a chaw on this." And the man held up in his hand, heretofore camouflaged against his dirty gnarly body, a dead opossum hanging upside down by its tail.

"Good Jeezus!" the construction worker yelped, "Get that thing away from me!"

"Ok, but it's good meat," remarked Grizzly Adams, and tossed the animal aside. "I'll leave it there for some passing motorist."

"You do that."

Grizzly then took out his pipe which he stuffed full of the foulest smelling tobacco this side of India, and lit it with a bright glow from what looked to be a homemade match constructed of toothpicks and gun-powder.

"Tonight?" asked the road construction worker.

"Tonight," said the man, putting the pipe in his

mouth and nearly lighting his nasty beard on fire.

"Where?"

"Here."

"We talkin' about the same thing, right?"

"You talkin' 'bout that toe tappin' thing that Senator did in the commode in that airport there...in Minneapolis? What was his name? Larry Craig...?"

"No, you idiot! I'm talkin' 'bout the other thing!"

"Oh! Oh, yes! The other thing. *That* thing. Yeah, it's on. It's *so* on."

"Good."

"Now how do I get there?"

"You don't know how to get there?"

"Nope."

"Jeezus! Ok, you go about five miles beyond the summit of that hill, and then down into Reams and then five more miles out, and up and over another hill."

"Damn, that's a long way! But I don't go through no town. I's sticks to the woods!"

"Ok, suit yourself. Then just skirt around the town by way of the woods until you come to the other side, then do just as I told ya."

"Fair enough. But I'm gonna need a nap first. Mind if I sleep here 'side the road? Wake me when you're done with your shift."

"Fine. Whatever. But it's hotter'n a dogs ass on Tuesday out here, I'll tell ya that right now..."

"I can sleep through it. Been in worse."

"I'm sure you have."

And the man went over to the side of the road and slept until the road construction dude's shift was over. At which time, he woke the man and sent him on his way. "Good luck!"

The grizzled man turned, gave a slight wave, and disappeared into the woods.

The road construction dude went home, with the dust going on before him according to the set of the wind, and was soon at *The Fountain*, squeezing down a

Bud with a Miller Genuine Draft chaser.

When the good folks of Reams had eaten their scant dinners (except those employed by Walmart, who ate at the China Buffet out on 19 for a discount), it did not creep to bed as it usually did at that time, but came out of doors again, and remained there. A curious contagion of whispering was upon it, and also, when it gathered together at The Fountain to drink, another curious contagion of looking expectantly at the sky in one direction only was en vogue.

Postmaster Gabriel, having taken up residence at The Chateau after a curious court battle rendered the rightful heir to the place, one Charles 'Bubba' Darnet, wanting nothing to do with it, and turning it over (secretly, as Bunnie would've had his balls had she had known) as a ward of the city of Reams to which, of course, Postmaster Gabriel immediately beset his grubby little paws upon it—with a little legal wrangling, but nothing too complicated—and claiming it for himself.

The night deepened. The trees environing The Chateau, keeping its solitary state apart, moved in a rising wind, as though they threatened the pile of building massive and dark in the gloom. Up the two terraced flights of steps the wind ran wildly, and beat at the great door, like a swift messenger rousing those within; uneasy rushes of wind went through the hall, among the old spears, harpoons and knives hanging on the walls, and shook the curtains of the bedroom where the Postmaster now slept.

Before long, however, The Chateau began to make itself strangely visible by some light of its own, as though it were growing luminous. A faint murmur about the house from its single occupant, and the sound of a revving BMW could be heard racing away.

The Beamer raced down in front of The Fountain and Gabriel poked his head out to those standing round.

"Help! Help! Someone call the fire department.

Now!"

As to help, there was none. The road construction dude, and thirty of his closest friends, stood with folded arms at The Fountain, looking at the pillar of fire in the sky.

"It must be forty feet high," said they grimly; and never moved.

The rider from The Chateau, with the Beamer's fuel most likely now in a foam, or at least in a solely gaseous fume, tore away through town to the location of the fire station itself.

"Help! Fire! Fire! The Chateau is on fire! There are valuable objects in there that must be saved!"

The fireman looked at each and gave no orders. They merely answered with shrugs and biting of lips, "Sucks to be you."

So The Chateau was left to itself to flame and burn. In the roaring and raging of the conflagration, a red-hot wind, driving straight from the infernal regions, seemed to be blowing the edifice away. Not only that; but the townsfolk, light-headed with famine and fire, and bethinking that Postmaster Gabriel had to do with the collection of taxes most of them could not pay (except those who worked at Walmart) decided to chase him into the night on all manner of motorcycle, four-wheeler, big stupid truck with big stupid tires, rust bucket Fords and Chevy's, and even a few two-bit donkeys, until Gabriel was corralled—half-out of his stricken mind from losing the mansion—down the road leading to a place where youngsters gathered to engage their hormonal urges, commonly known to the teenage set as 'Mayker Holler,' also known as a cliff edge above which one mildly raging stream took it upon itself to flow past one hundred feet below.

But instead of parking as one would do to make-out with their significant other, Gabriel in his haste and haze shot right through the parking area and landed his Beamer, which used to belong to one Clay D. Markee, headlong into the stream, in which most of

Gabriel's body, and bodily fluids, now mingled to become as one.

24

To Crash-and-Burn, Or Not to Crash-and-Burn

In such rising of fire and rising of sea—the firm earth shaken by the rushes of an angry ocean which had now no ebb, but was always on the flow, higher and higher, to the terror and wonder of the beholders on the shore—three years of tempest were consumed. Three more birthdays for little Brittany woven together into the madness that was her life and her home.

Many a night and many a day had said home's inmates listened to the echoes in the corner hopped up on 'x' and 'shine, sometimes with guests having heart failure who imbibed a little too much of both, or the incorrect combinations and quantities of said narcotics. The local authorities never questioned the deaths as long as they didn't know about them, and most having been transients or super-impoverished low-life's, they didn't.

Some drunkards and drug abusers continued to swear they heard footsteps, for, the footsteps had become to their minds as the footsteps of a people, furiously spraying their houses with cans of Black Flag, and with their county declared in danger from being overtaken by roaches and termites, changed into wild beasts themselves, and exterminated until their own children were born with three arms and five legs as a result of the fumes.

Father Mossenger, being the ass that he was, had disassociated himself from the phenomena of the abuse of alter boys (thank God), by claiming to have not done anything wrong even though he had *not* repented and had *certainly* not stopped the vile practice

(Satan Be Upon Him). He complained to his parishioners that such accusations evidenced his not being appreciated, and of being little wanted in Coon Spit (save, as said before, for a few willing—but still underage—parishioners) and subsequently leading him to believe he was in danger of dismissal, and possible prison time. Like the fabled rustic who raised the Devil with infinite pains, and was so terrified at the sight of him that he could ask the enemy no question, Father Mossenger flirted with The Father of Lies as if he were Mae West. So, Mossenger, after boldly reading the Lord's Prayer backwards for a great number of years, and performing many other potent spells for conjuring the Evil One, and never coming close to successfully bringing about the true form of Beelzebub, the Almighty One had fun with him in merely conjuring a transfer parishioner from Knoxville by the name of Al Listercrolly, who ironically lead the charge to impeach, and possibly dismember, Mossenger for his crimes against youthful humanity.

The shinning Mayor Bull Scythe was gone, or he would have been the mark for many a Smith and Wesson fanatic stuffing said firearms with anti-Walmart 'patriotic' bullets. He had never been a Scythe for any good use, long a tool of Lucifer, and occasionally the cause of much Demonic pride. The city council, from that exclusive inner pro-Walmart ring, to its outermost rotten ring of corrupt lawmen, was gone as well, and new Walmart fence riders of a less acerbic nature were installed in their stead.

The August of the year two-thousand and three was come, and Father Mossenger had by this time scattered his seed far and wide. As was natural, now the new head-quarters and great gathering-place of Mossenger, was Grouse Gulch's own Tall Tales strip club and Cock-N-Bull Tavern. Spirits are supposed to haunt the places where their bodies most resided, and Mossenger's over-active dick glands seemed to have haunted the place where his over-active dick glands found themselves most alive. Moreover, the third stall on the left was the spot where French Ticklers were most to be relied on, and where F.M., as he was commonly known about the place, seemed to have come the quickest (though I don't know who on God's green earth would have been keeping such comparisons).

Again: Tall Tales was a munificent dump, but extended great discounts to old customers who had fallen hard upon difficult times, the very reason most of them were there to begin with—escape, escape, escape! Again: Some who hadn't seen the coming fall of the mom and pop shops as a result of the invasion of the evil Walmart had run-up extensive—and in some cases—exorbitant, bar tabs at Tall Tales (the worst offender being F.M.), to which they spoke with endless excuses, as dripping faucets never to be impeded, about how they would pay Trip back someday—but not today. To which it must be added that every new customer from Coon Spit who came over as a result of economic conditions so nearly destroying the flow of goods and services into and out of their beloved town, they made sure to hug Trip and give him a high-five for continuing to render the one last remaining service Walmart did not, or could not provide, and that was live, in the flesh, titties, hoochies and *fee*-male butter-cheeks.

For such variety of reasons, Trip's club was doing a booming business, so much so that he was finally able to put a little money into advertising. He put up flyers at banks, barbershops and even pediatric physician's offices throughout the county announcing his Happy Hour specials and times when he would have shows such as a stripper (read: young and not worn out) who'd be stopping by from out-of-town for a one-night-only full nude review, along with the occasional nude midget throw (only now Trip knew they wanted to be called 'little people,' so it was duly noted with an asterik on the flyers).

On a steaming, misty afternoon, Trip sat at his

desk, and Bubba Darnet stood leaning on it, talking with him in a low voice. The penitential den—used mostly for the firing of bar tenders who stole from him and letting old worn-out strippers know their day in the sun had shriveled them beyond recognition and they were permanently being put out to pasture—was now the 'news-exchange,' and was often filled to over-flowing. It was within a half an hour or so of the time of closing:

"But, although you are the youngest man that ever lived," said Bubba Darnet, rather hesitantly, "I must still suggest to you—"

"Is that some back-handed way of saying I'm an old fart?" asked Trip.

"But the horrible economic conditions, the mobs running wild in the street, crime is up nine-thousand percent! It's just not safe! Nor would it be profitable. What I'm just sayin' to you is this: Are you out of your goddamned cotton fluffin' mind? I mean, jeez Trip! Starting a branch club of Tall Tales in Coon Spit proper? You must be joking, or on acid; or joking while you're on acid; or just plain..."

"Ok, I get the point, Syphilis-Lips. Christ...give me a break."

"Just think about it, is all I'm sayin'."

"Look, you bring up some good points, but we're making money hand over fist here, and we're packed to the gills every night as it is. I can't even keep the bar stocked! And if I keep running out of alcohol each night before 10:30, I might as well bend over and kiss my ass goodbye cause I won't be stayin' in business very long that way. Besides—and this is the most important besides—the 'old' club here has been doing nicely keeping its head above water with the clients we have in Grouse Gulch. So that steady income ain't a-goin' nowhere.

"In the matter of all this extra business—they're drivin' over from Coon Spit anyway. And look, since live strippin' shows is the only thing Walmart cain't touch—at least not yet, anyway—it only makes sense that I'd be successful with a branch club over there."

"I cain see you've thought this through..."

"Your damn skippy I have!"

"Then let me suggest...or let me offer, rather...that you hire me to be the manager of that club."

"*You*? Well, you do have a face that probably wouldn't scare anybody away, but the reality is, Bubba...the plain truth about that matter is," Trip glanced at the stage where Candy Stripe-R teasingly lifted her one-piece nurse's outfit; the decibel level of the crowd corresponding to how high she pulled it before letting it slide back down (*Somebody Get Me Doctor* by Van Halen blaring as she did so), "You have no idea how difficult it is to run a club. And Lord knows what a wimp like you—no offense—might do if the place were robbed, or whatnot. You said yourself the crime rate over there was outta control. Bubba, I'm tellin' you, you jus' ain't cut out for that kind 'a work! You're too nice a guy. You'd let people steam roll you for a free drink if they told you their dog had died that day..."

"Like you do?"

"When *I* do it, it's different. I actually *know* these people well enough to know whether or not their dog *had* died that day. And that's another thing: You're a good guy, Bubba, but you ain't no people person. You got to live this job 24/7, and that's why I've been single all these years..."

"And because no woman in their right mind would let themselves be chained to a man that—as they got older—knowin' he could see nineteen-year-old hooch anytime he wanted." As Bubba said this, he flipped a thumb over his right shoulder in reference to Candy.

Trip followed the thumb just in time to see Ms. Stripe-R lift the dress just enough to reveal to the crowd for the first time no panties and a lawn mowed clean to the dirt. A smirk of admiration and a long low whistle from Trip blended with the erupting roar from the crowd that nearly blew the roof off.

Trip looked back at Bubba: "Well, you got a point there, kid. And it's well taken. But look, jus' look, the answer is no, ok, Bubba? And please don't bring it up with me again." Trip put his head down and began mulling over the books again.

"How I admire the gallantry of your 'youthful' spirit, Trip," chided Bubba, not having moved from his seat. "Takin' no risks, everything calculated to the nth degree..."

Keeping his head down, Trip looked up through his eyelids: "You see that hot piece of snatch up there dancing a'fore all them horny pieces of shit? That's only happenin' because of takin' no risks and calculatin' ev'rthing to your so-call nth degree. Now git the fuck outta here 'fore I have Hoss toss you out!"

"You cain have Hoss toss me out, I don't care!" countered Bubba.

"If I have Hoss toss you out, you'll remember that toss from Hoss the rest of your life, I assure you!"

"Hoss wouldn't toss a flea even if that flea was Hoss's boss!"

"What? Jeezus, boy! That don't make no sense! You been tappin' my liquor again? Fuck! I oughta have you thrown out jus' for that...tossed out on your ass...by Hoss."

"Hoss can toss himself off for all I care!"

"What the hell's that mean?"

"I don't know. It's jus' sump'in they say in England. I heard it in a movie once."

Trip sighed heavily and leaned back. "Ok, Bubba, look. You's all talkin' crazy and not watchin' the show out there and you're buggin' me to death—so here's the deal. Tomorrow when I go to scout a location, I'm gonna take Jerry with me, jus' 'cause Jerry's been somewhat my bodyguard these past few years and a trustworthy messenger. Nobody would even think about messin' with me over in Coon Spit as long as ol' Jerry's along, 'cause that bastard's crazier than a leaf-blower in a henhouse, and everybody knows it. But as for you, my dear Bubba, I'll *think*—you hear me? I said I'll *think*—about maybe lettin' you do the liquor runs 'tween here and the new club when it opens, cause God knows I cain't trust Jerry with a box of liquor any more'n I can kick my own dick to Chiner. Now listen closely, cause I'm gonna tell you sump'in; a little secret..."

Trip looked both ways.

Bubba leaned forward intently.

"If all goes well with this little deal, and both clubs are successful for a time, I figure I'll be makin' enough to retire. And if that happens...*if* that happens...and *if* I decide to let you run liquor...and *if* you do a good job...and *if* then I might ask you to run that club for a short while...and *if* you then decide you want the job...and *if* you then decide you *like* the job...and *if* you do a good job at that job in which you told me you liked...and *if* in all that time you somehow manage to grow your pussy-ass a couple 'a solid bangers...*then*...I might *think* about considerin' you for takin' over managership of this here establishment in which we're sittin' right now."

Bubba's eyes got wide and he bubbled over with excitement.

"You mean it Trip? Oh, man! You gotta deal! You gotta deal! That's swell!"

Trip motioned for Bubba to move in closer to his face.

"And Bubba..."

"Yeah, Trip? What, Trip? Anything, Trip! You name it!"

"If you ever use the word 'swell' in my presence again, I'm 'a gonna kick *your* dick to Chiner!"

The dialogue that had taken place at Trip's desk had also been overheard by one Father Mossenger, or F.M. as his bar tab relates, who'd been swarming now and then to within a yard or two of the desk, especially and 'accidentally' during unplanned breaks in the blaring sound.

Bubba Darnet had not yet released himself from the conversation under his own 'recognizance'— meaning under threat of another ass tossin' from Hoss— before having heard Trip tell to hisself aloud that he was nearing a decision to have Hoss rough-up Mossenger if the over-sexed and drunken monsignor didn't start making good on his promise to start paying down his exorbitant bar tab.

Presently, Mossenger had walked away from Trip's office and into the Cock-N-Bull and ordered a Long Island Iced-Tea, where he began loudly spouting scenarios of avenging himself against the opinion of his parishioners that he was a pedophile and a homosexual, and therefore should lose his church. Pedophile he could deal with, but homosexual—he would *not* be labeled anything of the sort!

Darnet walked in and took up a stool beside the brooding Father, and soon, Stryker entered and took up residence on the other side of him, ordering his usual first drink of the night, a white-wine spritzer.

For many a drink following, Darnet listened as the two men spewed hot air about various subjects: for Stryker's part, well on his way to promotion as a state prosecutor, he argued vehemently for the need for Trip to heed the hundreds of 'anonymous' requests of late pouring into *Tale Tales* for the establishment of at least one night of the week to be a men's stripper night, in other words, where men stripped in the fashion of Chippendale's, in other words, a Gay Night.

Mossenger, for his part, thus inflamed against talk of homosexuality, spouted loudly (for all who could hear it above the box of juke blaring *If I Could Turn Back Time* by Cher on constant repeat) his want for blowing up all homosexual people and wiping them from the face of the earth, and from Heaven above, and doing without them. Luckily for him, the box of juke was *extremely* loud at this time, and the only ones who heard him say such invectives were Stryker and Bubba Darnet, otherwise he probably would've lost his life that very night.

Stryker, of course, heard these things with a particular feeling of objection, and the overwhelming want to bash Mossenger's head in. Darnet, divided over hearing such talk, stood and walked away that he might hear no more, not wanting to be associated with any controversy involving Trip or the club from either man in light of it having been suggested to him mere minutes before that he might currently be in a position to inherit the club in the foreseeable future.

Stryker made note of the reaction.

And so did Mossenger.

Stryker himself soon went into the restroom and returned moments later proceeding to engage himself in walking among the patrons of the Cock-N-Bull, having a moments discussion with each of them, nearly all resulting in a nodding of the head and a requesting of a pen. Again, Mossenger closely observed such action with interest.

Within the hour, when the 'House' noticed Trip was away from his desk for a short while, Stryker and a few cronies sneaked into his office and placed a package upon his desk, then scurried from the room absent of worry of detection from the club owner.

Trip returned to his office a moment later to find a crumpled and soiled pair of underwear staining the middle of his desk, with a note written on a cocktail napkin in accompaniment. Trip picked up the note as he tried desperately to formulate a plan for the removal of such stench-encrusted (among other encrusteds) garment from his desk without touching it with his bare flesh. He decided to stab the filth with a pen, and lift it into a nearby garbage can. But in the midst of this motion, this lifting after the stabbing, Trip noticed a matter of immense curiosity. For upon said BVD's, there was written, in many different styles, and many different colors, the signatures of about thirty-five men.

Having filed the foul garment in the can, complete with pen, Trip called Hoss for the immediately removal of such toxically wasted trash to the dumpster out back, and slumped heavily into his seat to read the scratch upon the cocktail napkin:

'Very pressing! We have been requesting a men's Chippendale's-style revue here at Tall Tales for many a moon, and the non-compliance and all out *ignoring* of our persistent requests have pushed us to take harsher and more drastic measures to make our strong voices heard. Enjoy the skivies, chump. And what you say we have a Gay Night here? Maybe once a week? Hmmm?"

-*Confided to the care of Travis 'Trip' Templeton, owner of* Tall Tales *strip club, Grouse Gulch, KY'*

Just then, Trip felt a vibration in his pants, and no, it wasn't from the mention of a gay night at the club. It was a text message announcing its arrival on his cell phone:

'I know you are harboring one Chuck Dunnay, originally of Coon Spit.'

On the marriage morning, Doctor Runyon had made it his one urgent request to Charles 'Bubba' Darnet, er, well—one of *two* urgent requests as it turns out—that the secret of his name should be—unless he the Doctor dissolved the obligation—kept inviolate between them. Nobody else knew it to be his name; his own wife had no suspicion of the fact; Trip could have had none.

Trip scratched his head and took note that he didn't recognize the number of the sender, or the key to unlocking the meaning of its cryptic message, so he took the immediate action of deleting the message. He sighed heavily and leaned back in his chair. *What other kind of craziness am I going to have to put up with tonight?*

But thinking twice about the text message, he figured it must have had some meaning. His circle of acquaintances was simply too small for someone to have sent him the text in error. So, with the hands of the clock verging upon the hour of closing the club, there was still a gaggle of current talkers and drinkers over in the Cock-N-Bull. The noise of the stripping acts out front having long died down, Trip addressed the bar in its entirety.

"First of all, thanks for the skivs," said he in sarcasm, to which arose many snickers and nodding of heads. "I have heard you, and have decided to take action."

Roars of cheers went up, and not a few spilled drinks.

"However," a few boos, "it will take just a bit more time before I can make your request a reality. But I promise you, the day is coming, and not far off."

Cheers and slaps on the back, and pats on the butt, occurred over and under vocalizations of 'I can accept that,' and 'that sounds good to me.'

"Next," said Trip as if moving along in an agenda, he held up his cell phone, to which Mossenger glanced, then quickly looked away, "I'm presuming someone in this room sent me a text message tonight addressing a man said to be hiding incognito or something like that by the name of Chuck Dunnay. Anyone know him?"

One man said, "He's the nephew, I believe, or *was*, of that bastard Clay D. Markee, and was the degenerate rightful heir to The Chateau."

Another man said, "An outlaw of the highest order! A traitor to the anti-Walmart movement!"

"Infected with genital warts!" said another man, which garnered many stares and accusing looks, including the immediate scooting away of his gentleman caller for the night.

"He was opposed to Clay D. Markee, I heard," said

a fourth man, "Gave up The Chateau when he legally inherited it, and left it out to dry so that no good Postmaster Gabriel could snatch it up."

"Hey!" cried the flamboyant and very drunk Stryker, "Did he now? Is that the sort of feller we're talking about? If so, I think he's a goddamned douche-bag!"

Bubba Darnet, unable to restrain himself any longer, touched Mr. Stryker on the feather boa and said, "I know the feller."

"Do you, by Jupiter?" asked Stryker in all manner of Rip Taylor-ness, "I am sorry for that!"

"Why?"

"Why, Bubba Darnet? Did you hear what he did? Don't ask, don't tell in these times, that's what I say!"

"*What*?"

"I tell you again, Bubba Darnet, I feel sorry for you. I'm sorry to hear you know the scoundrel personally. For here is a fellow, possibly infected with genital warts, who, abandoned his property to the vilest tax-gathering scum that Coalmont County has ever known, and I'm sorry that a man who 'instructs' youths knows him."

Darnet moved to correct him: "Uh, I think you're referring to Mossenger there, not me."

"Well, either way," continued Stryker in a huff, "I believe the man is contaminated, genital warts or not."

Mindful of the rumor, Darnet briefly excused himself to the commode to check himself for genital warts, then came back and said to Stryker, "You jus' may not understand the feller."

"I understand how to knock your block off if I need to, Bubba Darnet!" said the effeminate, yet very bullying, and yet still very drunk, Stryker, "and I'll do it, too! If this feller is a 'good ol' boy' then I don't understand him! You may tell him so, with my compliments. You may also tell him, for me, that after abandoning The Chateau to that dick-head Postmaster Gabriel (may his soul burn in Hell) I have to wonder if maybe he wasn't in on the Walmart scheme himself, and possibly the *true* master-mind of it?"

Several in the crowd gasped at such an aggressive accusation.

"But no, gentlemen," continued Stryker, looking all around and snapping his fingers as if attempting to conjure his hero Liberace from the dead, "I know something of human nature, and I tell you that you'll never find a 'feller' like this 'feller,' trusting himself to the mercies of such *proteges* as Postmaster Gabriel (may his soul burn in Hell). No, gentlemen; he'll always show 'em a clean pair of heels early in the scuffle, and sneak away.'

This last comment garnered roars of laughter from the crowd, the irony being lost on them, including Stryker himself, that it was actually a sort of back-handed anti-gay slur. Not to mention that Stryker now sat, in a stool at the bar, himself in heels. However, he concluded these words with a flamboyant one-handed snap of the fingers up over his shoulder as he quickly turned his head to the opposing side, and Mr. Stryker got up, and stumbled his way out of the club, along with everyone else, knowing it was closing time, and being tired of listening to the whole ordeal.

Trip Templeton and Bubba Darnet were soon the only ones left at the bar, in the wake of the general departure from the club.

"Will you tell that Dunnay feller that someone's on the look-out for him?" asked Trip to Bubba Darnet.

"Sure."

"Make sure and tell him that I think I got the message by mistake, and I mean no harm, and I certainly mean not to get mixed up in this whole foolish mess, whatever is going on."

"I will. And are you going to Coon Spit directly from here in the morning when you finish the books?"

"From here. Probably at seven."

"I will come back and see you before you go."

"Not necessary to kiss my ass that badly, Bubba.

You can back it down a notch. It won' reflect on my future decisions, I assure you."

"Then good luck in finding a good spot for the new club," and Bubba slapped Trip on the back.

"Thanks. And you have a good night now, you hear."

Outside the club, and very ill at ease with himself, and with Stryker, and with most other men save for a few, Darnet made the best of his way into the quiet night of Grouse Gulch toward Chickenwell Street.

As it turns out, Trip Templeton was able to find a suitable residence for his new club in Coon Spit, not far located from Saint Antwan's Liquors and Beer itself. In addition, he did decide to let Bubba Darnet make the liquor runs from Tall Tales when the new club fell short of supplies, and Darnet quickly proved himself to be a very capable and trustworthy employee. Thus, he was promoted to club manager of the new club, and Trip couldn't have been more pleased with the way that hill-jack handled the new responsibility.

However, Trip was less than pleased at having come to the point where he felt he needed to threaten Father Mossenger with the removal of each of F.M.'s fingers—by way of a rusty Xacto knife—one at a time until he could so pay on his still outstanding exorbitant bar tab from Tall Tales.

Knowing Trip had been on his tail, and with the impending pressure of outside church councilman coming soon to Coalmont County to hold a public hearing on the fate of Mossenger's job as head of his parish, F.M. had taken to frequenting Trip's new club in Coon Spit, and trying in all manner of craftiness to bilk Bubba Darnet for free drinks and try to pilfer from the club's store of money whenever he could—but to Trip's extreme pleasure and F.M.'s extreme displeasure, Bubba Darnet held fast and firm, and did not give the old sinner an inch.

So it was, and now the time had come for Trip to be in a position to make the decision to possibly retire and turn *both* clubs over to Bubba Darnet for good. And so it was, at around this same time, that on his way home from closing Tall Trees (so named as a marketing ploy to attract young environmentally conscious sorts—and hopefully to attract young environmentally conscious strippers— and let's face it, to shamefully jump on the 'global warming' bandwagon), it was then that Bubba Darnet felt a slight discomfort in his left butt-cheek as it pressed against the torn upholstery of the rusted bucket he was driving. Darnet lifted his left butt-cheek at so slight an angle—as one would do in preparation for a fart—instead reached around and pulled from his pocket a note scribbled crudely on a cocktail napkin:

'To one Charles 'Bubba' Darnet, a.k.a. 'Chuck Dunnay':

Bubba felt his heart skip a beat.

'After having long been in danger of losing my job at the hands of those I have so faithfully served for so many years (and who have so faithfully served me for so many years—*you have no idea!*) and having been chased for some time under threats of bodily harm, the latest of which being the removal of my fingers at a snails pace with an arts-n-crafts knife by Trip Templeton and his goons, I have decided that I have suffered enough!

The crimes for which I have been accused, Mr. Dunnay, and for which I shall be summoned before the public forum—and most likely resulting in the loss of my job and therefore my livelihood, and therefore any means I would have of securing payment for my exorbitant Tall Tales bar-tab (and all this without your 'generous' help so far. And yes, I mean that sarcastically)—the crimes for which I have been accused are that I have acted inappropriately with a male immi-grant (not to mention the many, many years of hot al-tar-boy on altar-boy action, menage a trois's, and trysts the likes of which you cannot imagine, but, *ahem!*, I go astray of my communique...), it is in vain that for years I have defended myself, as those I have faithfully served—and have faithfully served me—now feel I have acted against them, that is, the congrega-tion, as well as the alter boys and the immigrant.

As to the altar boys at the Royal George, yes, this is common knowledge, but the only recourse I have to that very latter charge about the immigrant is that yes, many years ago I rented a room from said immigrant, and yes, I have since managed to procure his proper-ty—but in my defense: Where is that immigrant now? Where has he gone? Ah! Most gracious Chuck Dunnay, where *is* the immigrant? I cry in my sleep not knowing where he is! I demand of Heaven to tell me where he is, but there is no reply. Ah, Chuck Dunnay, I send my most desolate cry out across Coalmont County hoping it may reach your ears through this great club of ours called 'Tall Trees'...'

Bubba blanched that the writer— whom he was sure now was 'F.M.'—had the gall to refer to the club as '*ours*'—

'...For the love of Heaven, and for the sake of keeping that job I know you so dearly value, and keep-ing that lovely wife and daughter of yours maintained in the lifestyle to which they've become accus-tomed...allow me for just a moment to press the point. I imagine you *definitely* ain't gonna wanna hear it from your wife, cause I know that little Philly *must* have *some* mouth on her... that if you don't show up in Rabbit Grove at *exactly* the location I tell you at *exactly* the time I tell you (and you'll be told soon enough), then you'll be in danger of forcing me to expose your true identity before the entire impoverished, angry, and potentially violent and bloodthirsty, citizenry and law-enforcement bodies of the *en*-tire County of

Coalmont!
    'Understood?'

       Your afflicted,

       'F.M.'

The latent uneasiness in Darnet's mind was roused to vigorous life by this letter. He wadded up the paper in his hand and rubbed it against his chin. He wasn't sure *exactly* what the writer meant by the exposition of his true identity...Was it referring to his being Dunnay and Darnet, one and the same? Or could it be...? Could it *possibly* be...the other thing? And God knows there were many locations in Rabbit Grove where he would not want to be seen caught dead.

Either way, he hardly saw how he could take the risk of not going to where Mossenger wanted him to go whenever he told him to do so. Either way, his standing in the community, his standing among Trip, and even his standing among the sheriff, seemed to greatly be at risk of jeopardy if he at all failed to comply in this request.

So the desperate resolution of what to do took all of about three seconds. It was actually a no-brainer. He'd have to show up in Rabbit Grove at the appointed locale and time.

Yes. Like the mariner in the old song by the 80's metal band Iron Maiden, *The Rhyme of the Ancient Mariner*, he knew he was being drawn and he knew he must go. Everything that arose before his mind drifted him on, faster and faster, more and more steadily, to the terrible conclusion that awaited him at that 'meeting.' His latent uneasiness had been that bad aims were being worked out in his unhappy county by bad instruments, and knowing from a surprisingly literate teacher he had back in 8th grade who taught him a saying by the writer Pearl S. Buck: 'The only thing necessary for evil to triumph is for good men to do nothing,' Bubba knew he must stand tall and assert the claims of goodness and justice to humanity. But most of all, he knew he had to save his own ass, and make sure—at all costs—that he spared himself a good tongue lashin' from his wife.

His resolution was made. He *must* go to Rabbit Grove whenever F.M. called him to do so, although he also knew the unseen force of the Iron Maiden song *The Rhyme of the Ancient Mariner* was drawing his ship fast toward possible annihilation upon the rocks of an unseen alcove, the winds and tides were setting straight and strong towards it.

THE END OF THE SECOND BOOK

- *Book the Third* -

The Sh*t Hits
the Fan

1

Shanghai Surprise

The traveler fared slowly on his way, who fared toward Coon Spit from Grouse Gulch by way of the Buckskin Trail in the autumn of the year two-thousand and five. Bubba Darnet was languishing on a liquor and beer re-stock run between Tall Tales and Tall Trees, languishing because though it was nearly leaf changing weather, it was still hotter than a goat's balls on an inflamed porcupine.

And languishing because he was hung-over and strung-out from a massive corporate party of *Home Shopping Network* execs that had for some unexplained reason descended on Coon Spit and Tall Trees the previous night at the very late hour of two-and-thirty in the a.m., to which Bubba Darnet had kept the doors open (illegally) for them, and the beer and strippers flowing, until five o'clock that same a.m., only to be up again for the re-stock run between the clubs at the bright and early hour of eight a.m. in the a.m.

In short, he was plumb tuckered out.

He knew long ago when he accepted the managerial position at Tall Trees that he'd have to keep making the re-stock runs himself, since he found out, just like Trip years earlier, that there was no scoundrel that existed in all of Coalmont County, male or female, two-legged or four, that he could trust to make the liquor runs as far as he could throw *anyone's* dick to Chiner, and he'd have to do it all without the least bit of extra recompense in his salary.

Now ain't that just a kick in the log jam!

And to make matters worse, he was enduring more than enough un-repaired potholes and slippery horse droppings on the Buckskin Trail to make his piece of shit Fiero want to roll over and die. Currently a few leagues before Coon Spit, he blasted a pothole real good, having these results;

One: It shook his car so violently that every bottle of liquor he pulled along in his narrow and pretty much nonexistent back-seat (so narrow he'd have to make three more runs this morning) nearly shattered, and

Two: It made him bang his sore aching head so hard against the shallow roof he thought he saw Orion drinking bad 'shine out of the Big Dipper before he damn near passed out. Thus, he pulled the car over to the side of the road for a temporary respite, and to suck the life out of a soon-to-be ignited tobacco stick.

The obstacles of potholes on the Buckskin Trail not only stopped him damn near twenty times a run to check to make sure the Fiero's oil pan was still attached, but it also had the unfortunate and obvious side-effect of retarding his progress to Coon Spit twenty times a run, to which when Trip Templeton called to make sure the shipment was being handled in a timely manner, he'd have to make up some lies to cover his ass.

And he was running out of lies.

So, of course, stopped by the side of the road *again*, he winced when the ring of his cell phone toned: *'I like big butts and I cannot lie..."*

"E-yell-o."

"That shipment on its way, Bubba?"

"Yeah, yeah, Trip. I'm pullin' into *Trees* right now," he lied.

"Good, good. And good job on that corporate gig last night. We made a shi-*ite* load of money off that. Great job. I like the way you handled it, stayin' open late and all."

"Thanks, Trip, thanks. It was a good time."

"*What?*"

Bubba stiffened and dropped his cigarette. "Er, I mean, you know, *for them,* of course, *for them.* I was...me...I was workin' my ass off."

"Good, good. That's what I want to hear."

"Gotta go, Trip! Gotta put out a fire!"

"What?"

"Er, uh, I mean, I gotta go light a fire under my workers. Gotta have the place ready to go again for tonight."

"Ok, I'll let you go, but just wanted to say again, good job."

"Thanks, Trip. Later!"

Bubba reached down, grabbed the offending cigarette off the floormat and promptly burned his fingers all to hell—"*Shit!*"—before jumping out of his vehicle in a blind rage just as he saw a cloud of leaves, grass, sticks and moss come shooting out of the nearby woods.

Jerry Kracker on his 'Stallion.'

"Dammit!" Bubba cursed at high volume. *Trip's busted me! Sent fuckin' old-ass Jerry Kracker to check-up on me! Fuck! It's all over now! Bunnie's gonna kill me!*

"Hey, Bubba," said Jerry, approaching and throttling down his four-wheeler, "I'm afraid you're gonna have to come with me."

Fuck! Bubba cursed again in his mind. "You know Jerry, I *really* need to get this shit to Coon Spit..."

"With all due respect, Bubba, shut the fuck up and come with me."

"I have no choice?"

"Choice?" laughed Jerry. "You work for Trip Templeton and you think you have a choice? Where the fuck you been, boy? Everything else in the god-forsaken county, 'sept that fuckin' Walmart of course, has dried up and gone to Hell! How do you think Trip's been able to stay afloat all these years?"

"Well, pro'ly 'cause they don't allow strippin' at Walmart, ya dumb-shit."

"Well, yeah, you do have a point there," backed-off Jerry. "But still, you're gonna have to come with me. I really have no choice in the matter. I cain't return without ya."

As much of a dumb-shit Bubba knew Jerry Kracker to be, still, he was a good and long-standing employee of Trip's Tall Tales, and in a round-about way, a co-worker of Darnet's. So he looked down at his boots, considered his options, and decided against getting the old gnarled messenger (who probably hadn't seen goddamned day of good clean fun in his whole pathetic life, Bubba reasoned) in hot water with Trip. He would have to take the fall he knew was bearing down on him like the Enola Gay over Hiroshima. He'd have to do his best to take it like a man. After all, he'd done nothing but dig his own grave. He'd lied to Trip—and it was time to pay the piper.

Darnet complied with Jerry's request and slumped down hard on the back of Kracker's 'Stallion.' With a rip of the throttle, they tore off through the woods.

"Fuck!" Darnet screamed after they hadn't gotten far.

"What?" Jerry shot back.

"I forgot to lock-up the fuckin' Fiero! It's sittin' out there on the side of the Buckskin Trail like a duck to be slaughtered! There ain't gonna be piece of that thing left when I get back, much left any of Trip's liquor. *Fuck*!"

"Don't worry, Bubba, there won't even be a shell when you get back," chuckled Jerry internally, "some fucker's pro'ly gonna steal that bad boy outright!"

"*Shit*!" cursed Darnet again, long and hard and loud, which, although piercingly loud in Jerry's ear, actually had the effect of creating in Jerry a deep sense of joy; for he had to admit, he had never really cared for Bubba Darnet. But care for his wife Bunnie?—that was a different story! She only seemed to get hotter and hotter as she grew away from her teenage years, and away from her twenties and now on into her thirties...And not only that, but she grew in attractiveness and stature the more kids she popped out! (Which was only two so far, but one had died at three years old). Jerry was mystified as to how she did it, seemingly being the only woman he'd ever known who could truly turn back the hands of time. So for his part, he would have loved to just rear back an elbow and knock Bubba Darnet off his 'Stallion,' right then and there, flopping him straight into a tree at fifty miles an hour, leaving his dead-ass out there in the woods to rot. And sadly, Kracker knew he'd probably get away with it, too, since the bears, rabbits, ants, and raccoons'd eat him before he'd get found, and the *po*-lice'd just figure he was car-jacked and kidnapped out there on the Trail which weren't exactly an unheard of occurrence at that time—well, that is, they'd call it a car-jacking if they ever found the Fiero again, which weren't likely.

But no, Jerry put those thoughts aside, as joyous as they were. He was a loyal man, always had been, and had a duty to carry out, and that's exactly, as always, what he would do, for good or for ill.

In this case, he knew it was going to be for ill with Bubba Darnet, so that helped.

"You know," complained Bubba further, "when we see Trip I'm gonna tell him it was all your fault we didn't go back and lock-up the Fiero. He's gonna be *pissed*-off when he finds out his liquor was lifted."

"Yeah, we'll tell him all about that when we see him," answered Jerry, unvexed.

"Yeah, he's gonna be good and pissed. Good— And—Pissed!" said Bubba, trying to drive it in.

"Yep, whenever you see him again, you go ahead and tell him that. Tell him I take full responsibility."

"What do you mean, 'Whenever I see him again'? We's goin'ta see him right now, ain't we?"

"Nope."

2

Thirty Pieces of Silver...and a Case of Jack

"I thought you said we was going'ta see Trip?"

"I never said that. You jus' 'sumed it."

Bubba thought back for a second to their exchange by the Fiero—when he still had feet planted mercifully on the good green ground...well, brown, anyway...and he suddenly came to the realization that, no, no Jerry had indeed not said that.

"Jerry! Where the hells you takin' me?" yelled Bubba, suddenly in a fit, "You better tell me *right now*, or I'll kick your ass! And I ain't playin'!"

Facing forward, Jerry snickered, "For one thing, you couldn't kick my ass even if I were bent over a hog gate and you had a cattle prod. And secondly, I don't have to tell you a goddamned thing seein' as how we're moving through these here woods at a clip that'd kill your dumb-ass deader'n a doorknob if you even 'tempted to jump off, and threedly, I'd a told ya where we're goin' if you would a just asked nicely..."

"Ok," said Bubba calmly, "I'm sorry. Now where we goin'?"

"Rabbit Grove."

A bolt of lightning tore through Bubba Darnet's soul, nearly splitting him in two, leaving him smoldering in a smoking heap right in those back-wood hills of southern Kentucky. He grabbed onto Jerry Kracker a little tighter as he felt his head suddenly swoon like he might blackout and fall off the rushing vehicle, altogether ending his ordeal in a split second by becoming one with the roots and berries that lain upon the forest floor.

After many a mile of twists and turns and ups and downs through the tree and mud infested hills, the firm and resistant limbs of wood seemed to part, and a town came into view.

"This ain't Rabbit Grove," remarked Bubba, "We're in Coon Spit!"

"So I lied," Jerry deadpanned, "Sue me. But me-thinks you'll have a date with Rabbit Grove soon enough my friend—soon enough, if things go where I think they're headed..."

Bubba now did nothing but hang his head, fully resigned to whatever fate, and whatever course, this wild-ass roller-coaster ride—literally and figuratively—had him on.

The two pulled into the parking lot of Saint Antwan's Liquors and Beer, and Jerry and several Harlans accompanied Bubba Darnet into the store which smelled of common wine and chewing tobacco; where some men were asleep on the floor; some were drunk; and a rare few were sober. Some were in various states of being higher than a kite or coming down off a hard bender. The incandescence of the store—dark and gloomy halfly as a result of lights being turned off to save electricity, and halfly from the overcast day—giving the place, along with the strung out drunkards and drug abusers, the feel of one of those 'reality' prison shows on cable, or a Chris Hanson expose on MSNBC.

"Jerry Kracker," said Barge as they walked in, "Is that the guy?"

"Yes."

Barge looked at Bubba Darnet.

"How old are you?"

"What does that matter?" protested Darnet.

"It doesn't. Just curious," replied Barge. "You married?"

"Yeah."

"To who?"

"Bunnie Mancrizie. Only she's Bunnie Darnet now."

"Where'd you get married?"

"At St. Pancreas."

"Ah, good church, that one. I like that church."

Mandy shot him a quizzical look.

Barge continued: "Where's your wife now?"

"What's it to you?" Bubba shot back angrily.

"Yeah," agreed Mandy, looking at her husband, "What's it to you, Dick-Stick?"

"Just answer the fuckin' question!" barked Barge, furious at having his authori-*tie* criticized.

"She's at home with the kid, I guess. Sheesh." Bubba looked round the room, agitated. "I demand to know why I've been brought here against my will! I have the right to know what you're planning to do with me, or *to* me."

"Ass-munchers have no rights," answered Barge calmly.

"*What?*" shot Bubba.

Just then, the little bell over the door tinkled and all heads turned to see an old man enter the store with a box of liquors marked 'For: Tall Trees.' Bubba Darnet immediately recognized F.M.; the notorious Father Mossenger himself.

"Here's you payment," F.M. handed the box to Barge.

Barge's eyes bulged. "That's it? That's all there is? I thought you told me I'd get the entire shipment?"

F.M. looked downcast, yet sincere. "Well, the man's got a piece of shit Fiero and has to make like, twenty trips back and forth 'cause the car ain't got no back seat."

"So this is all I get?"

"That was the deal, wasn't it? Whatever was in the car?"

"Old man, I oughta take you out back and beat the living *fuck* outta you! You tricked me!"

"Look, Mr. Barge, honestly, I didn't know there'd only be this much in his car. Truly. You must believe me. And besides, you're missing the big picture here. Think of what you're contributing to the cause! Don't think just about what you can gain in the immediate term."

"I *have* to think about what I can gain in the 'immediate term,' mutha-fucker, cause I gots to pay my bills! And with this paltry box of shit you're givin' me, I ain't gonna be able to do that!"

"I'm deeply sorry," the old man soothed, and he really was, "Look, I'll make it up to you some other time. I'm good for it."

Bubba wanted to say something, but figured Barge was doing just fine being on the edge of ramming the old fucker's head through the front plate-glass window anyhow.

"Ok, ok, old man, I'm gonna believe you for now..." Bubba sighed.

"But if you don't make good on your promise in the foreseeable future, you and I are gonna have words, and I guaran-*goddamn*-tee you they won't be polite!"

Then Barge thought for a moment.

"Harlans One and Two! Take the 'prisoner' out back to the shed and watch him there."

The Harlans led Bubba out.

Barge looked at the old man.

"Where's the Fiero now?"

"As far as I know, it's still out on the Trail."

Barge motioned Harlans Three and Four forward. "Go get that car, and take it over to the Monkey Nut. I think we have a re-sale on our hands."

The Harlans looked at each other and laughed diabolically. Barge couldn't help but smile too. Mandy just shook her head and went back to her *Digest*.

"Idiots," she said under her breath.

3

Wilderness Wonderings

When the Harlans led Bubba out back and ordered him into the shed, Darnet stepped inside, looked about the dank darkness of the place as he walked back toward the locker, and thought how strangely clouded was this prison in all manner of gloom. When he got to the locker and saw no other path but to sit on the cot and wait, he wondered, nearly aloud, at how spectral the place looked in its inappropriate squalor and misery, and he seemed to sit in the company of the dead. The ghost of beauty, the ghost of stateliness, the ghost of elegance, the ghost of youth—had all taken their leave from this desolate shore long ago, having turned away from him their eyes that were changed by their deaths and now haunting some other location far, far from here.

Barge presently passed the two Harlans standing guard of the shed on the outside, and went in to see the 'prisoner'; head downcast and facial expression reading of resigned disposition.

"So you're the one," said Barge in a low voice, pulling up a nasty old desk chair in storage for some god-unknown reason since it would never see the light of day of use in the real world again, "who married Runyon's daughter, huh? That white-haired old guy who did time in the state pen awhile back?"

"Quite awhile back now," replied Bubba, "but yes, that's him, and it's me, and that's her. Well, the old man did the time, of course, not me—if that's what you mean. I haven't done time of course, I just married his daugh…"

"My name is Barge," said Barge, extending a hand, "and I own this here liquor store. Maybe you've heard of me?"

"Of course," rejoined Bubba, "I manage the Tall Trees strip club just up the way a piece."

"Well, yeah. And about that," said Barge in all manner of pensiveness, "I was gettin' kilt for business even before you jackasses bought that club up 'the way a piece.' And you know, that fuckin' Walmart debacle nearly dug my grave several years back, and then ya'all come along, open that club, and pretty much throw me into my final resting place and toss the dirt over it! And for that, I oughta light your dumb-cracker-ass up right now and throw you into the woods for all the woodpeckers to rip you to shreds."

"Well, that's certainly creative," nodded Darnet, impressed. "But I assure you, I had no idea we were having such a negative effect on your business."

Barge leaned back. "Yeah, yeah, I 'spected you say dat. And you know why?"

"Why?"

"Cause you're a dumb fuckin' cracker and you ain't payin' no attention to what's goin' on in this county, ain't that right?"

Bubba put a rebuffed hand over his mouth and looked down at the floor. Then he looked up, sharply, "Look, Mr. Barge..."

"Jus' Barge."

"Look, Barge, I assure you, if I or Trip would've been aware of your plight, I'm sure we would've worked something out with you. In fact, he's probably wondering where I am right now at this very minute. Maybe we could just go over to Grouse Gulch and talk with him together..."

Barge sniffed loudly. "That ain't gonna happen."

"Why not?"

"Cause as I said, you're a dumb-fuckin' cracker and you have no idea what's goin' on around here. This shit you're in is bigger than just you and me and my business and all your all's business's put together. This shit concerns *EVERYBODY* (he made a grand gesture) in fuckin' Coalmont County! And the whole of the southern hills of Kentucky, and possibly even 'Merica itself!"

Bubba looked worried.

"So what's gonna happen to me?"

Barge mumbled: "Just like a dumb cracker to be only concerned 'bout hisself at a time like dis," ruminated Barge with sadness. Then he leaned forward and patted Bubba on the shoulder in mock reassurance, "You'll see what'll happen to you."

Then Barge left Bubba Darnet alone in the shed to shake in fear and bewilderment. That he had fallen among far greater dangers than those of which he knew when he had left Tall Tales that morning, this of course, he knew now. What perils had thickened about him so fast, and might thicken faster and faster yet, he of course knew not. He could not help but admit to himself that had he not made the restock run this morning, his current station in life would be drastically different than that which he now knew. But with Trip always breathing down his neck, how could he *not* have made the run...?

Trip!

A thought like fire from the sky suddenly slammed down upon him, bringing up even more perplexing questions to torture himself with.

Did Trip know about this? Could he have been *in* on this? Would Jerry have taken this 'job' without Trip knowing it? Would Jerry have risked years of loyalty to go above Trip's head somehow? This Barge fellow was obviously working for, or with, Father Mossenger, but who was Jerry working with or for? One or the other— or both? And what was Jerry getting out of this?

But a new thought occurred to Bubba, a reassuring one, which washed over him like a cold drink of water in a vast dry desert; and that was that if Trip *wasn't* in on this, then he most *assuredly* (and/or Hoss) would be combing the countryside at this very moment trying to locate him—and more importantly, his liquor—while Darnet sat imprisoned in this dark dank dingy locker.

But then again, maybe not.

Who knows?

It was then that he heard another set of footsteps approaching him as he sat on the cot in the locker. He nearly threw up when the outline of none other than Father Mossenger walked in, followed closely by two bodyguards Bubba didn't recognize. Mossenger sat on the chair previously vacated by Barge while the two bodyguards stood menacingly behind him.

"Well, well, Bubba *Dunnay*, I do hope you enjoyed your trip through the woods..."

"Mossenger, you fuckin'...!"

"Tut, tut, my boy," Mossenger held up a hand. "Yours is not to make the rules right now. Yours is simply to sit still and shut up and listen. And God help you if you don't give me the right answers to the questions of which I seek."

Bubba sat quietly.

"Good. Let's begin. Bubba, this is what I want. This is all I want. Are you ready?"

"I guess so."

"First, my bar tab at Tall Tales. I want it ripped to shreds and gone forever. I want it to thrown as far as the East is from the West, and remembered no more."

"Fuck you, Mossenger! You know I cain't...!"

"Tut, tut, *again*, my boy. You have not heard me out."

"Ok, I'm listenin'."

"I want you to call off Trip's spies. I want them to leave me alone *forever*. Is that clear?"

Bubba sat silently.

"Oh, I see you're catching on. And lastly, I want, from your own wallet, or even if you have to steal it—I don't care how you get it, just get it!—enough money to get me to Grand Cayman so I can start a new life. I figure somewhere's in the neighborhood of forty-thousand dollars ought to do..."

"Forty-thousand dollars! You know I don't have that kind of mo..."

"Tut, tut, thrice, my boy! You don't have to answer right away. Take a moment to think it over. Because as you know, if you fail to answer correctly—which would be a resounding 'YES!' on all three counts—then your life as you know it is over. Maybe even literally, depending on how pissed-off these dumb hicks in these hills happen to be with that Walmart situation, and last I checked, they *was* mighty pissed-off."

Bent over and seated on the cot, Bubba leaned his chin hard on clenched fists atop arms with elbows planted on his knees. He stayed like that for several minutes, deep in consideration of what was happening before him.

Then he suddenly perked up.

"The answer is NO, Mossenger. Fuck you!"

Mossenger leaned back and let out a long breathy breath. "Huuuuuuuh. Well, I was afraid you might say that. But I'm telling you now, you have one more chance to change your mind before your world comes crashing down upon the shit heap of your life that it's always been..."

"That don't even make sense, you nasty old pedeofile."

Mossenger winced. "So what's it gonna be?"

"FUCK...YOU!" Bubba said in a drawn out manner, "I got my wife, who loves me, and friends around the county who'd never let anything happen to me, no matter what they found out about my past. So fuck you!"

Mossenger laughed, "A wife who loves you? Friends around the county? Are you out of your mother-fuckin' mind? (He quickly crossed himself and apologized to the Mother Mary). Ain't nobody gonna help you. You's as good as sunk, my boy. And good riddance!"

And F.M. stood, exited with his bodyguards, and left Darnet locked in the locker to rot.

Bubba sat, suddenly feeling again as though he was going to throw up. Because troubled as Bubba knew his future was, it was an unknown future, but in its obscurity there was the tiniest shred of ignorant hope that his wife and friends *might* come through for him.

And he also thought that maybe the frightful deeds that were soon to be done to him by his enemies were probably unimagined at this moment in the brains of such doers. How could the terrible thoughts of such actions raging at this very moment in Bubba Darnet's brain have a place in the minds of such gentle, backwood folk? With his unjust detention and hardship, and in cruel (or maybe not so cruel?) separation from his wife and child, Bubba foreshadowed the likelihood—or the *certainty*—that this wasn't going to end well for him. But beyond that—if there even *was* a beyond that—he dreaded nothing distinctly.

It was all going to be bad for him.

Very bad, indeed.

4

Rumblings

Tall Trees strip club, established on the west end of Coon Spit near Saint Antwan's Liquors and Beer, was in the far flank of a small strip-mall. A place of business in Grouse Gulch like the way Tall Trees was in Coon Spit would soon have driven Trip Templeton out of his mind in its seemingly disorganized organization.

For what would staid analness and attentiveness to detail characteristic of Trip have said about having a Hawaiian night where two tons of sand were dumped on a rickety stage, and everyone in the crowd was naked right along with the strippers at any and all hours? Never would such a thing be allowed in such a dingy old-school mess such as Tall Tales.

And what about the enormous inflatable Cupid over the bar at Tall Trees? And the biggest booty contest? And the Jell-O wrestling? And the two-for-one Margarita and Long Island Iced-Tea night? At Tall Tales—no way, never, ever, ever. Hell's no! Yet such things were allowed at Tall Trees, which thrived by drawing in the younger crowd, and was outrageously successful, and all done under the auspices of one general manger: that being Charles Chuck 'Bubba' Darnet. So there you have it. Trip had badly, badly underestimated the man.

Go figure.

Straight across the street from Tall Trees was where Father Mossenger had—as revealed in his threatening letter to Darnet—taken over the property of the afore mentioned 'missing' immigrant (who could by the way, with a few short picks of the ax, be found six-feet beneath the surface in the *Serenity Gardens* of one church of St. Pancreas). Having lost the faith of the tribunal and having been voted out of his church the afternoon of Darnet's 'imprisonment,' a quick investigation by a member of the tribunal with a wild hair up his ass uncovered that the Holy Father had also not taken possession of the house legally, and therefore was instantly evicted and the residence was immediately remanded to the City of Coon Spit.

Having taken up residence an hour later at the home of the one single altar-boy who didn't want to remove Mossenger's balls and cram them up the old sinner's ass, and knowing he was being tailed more heavily than ever by the secret spies of Trip Templeton (to make sure the old sinner didn't skip town without paying down his bill), Mossenger knew it was time to ratchet up the stakes and set things in motion to derail attention from himself and throw a possible monkey wrench into many a man's plans, many a powerful man's plans, and possibly enjoy a little payback in the process.

All this being as it was, Mossenger, under an assumed identity that reflected innocence instead of guilt—helpfulness instead of harm—hastily convened another meeting of the combined Coalmont County Chambers of Commerce the very next day—otherwise know as the *'Walmart, Shmall-Mart'* gathering—by sending invitations by way of texts and emails to everyone he knew who would be interested in his fantastical scheme.

And so, early on the day of the meeting, the day following Darnet's early morning imprisonment, Mossenger arranged for the transfer by the Harlans of one Bubba Darnet from the back shed of Saint Antwan's to the basement of The Rebel Yell Bowling Alley in Rabbit Grove, where Bubba would once again face hard, angry rednecks—a so-called jury of his 'peers.'

So after the texts and emails had been sent out—and before the Harlans had fully fulfilled their entrusted duty to move Bubba—Barge and Mandy Debarge showed up at the Rebel Yell, as did each of the Harlans, The Vengeance, Stryker (with a small contingent of his buddies from the Cock-N-Bull), and a good chunk of the citizenry of Coon Spit who'd embarrassed the palsied grass-eater outside the Horse Chaw and Vittles restaurant on that fine summer afternoon a few short years ago.

Trip Templeton, just a few short hours ago—about sixteen to be exact—had been sitting in Tall Tales, having not left the place since the disappearance of his trusted manger—and his liquor. The previous afternoon he had sent Hoss to stand guard at Tall Trees, as Trip had most assuredly had it shut down for the day pending the appearance of its trusted manager.

Late that morning Trip had called frantically around, having completely forgotten to check in with Bunnie and Doctor Runyon first; mostly because of the fact that he was more concerned with his missing liquor, and a night of blank Tall Trees receipts, than he was with the feelings of his friends.

The nervousness and dread that were upon him inspired that vague uneasiness respecting the two clubs, and whether or not he would meet his goal of early retirement in the next month. Even with Hoss over in Coon Spit, Tall Tales was well guarded, for Jerry had immediately taken up his rightful roost outside the club (along with Little Jerry) after performing his most dastardly of deeds, and Ellsworth the ancient bartender was there too, along with a few ragged-out truck drivers and several of the huskier and more grizzled strippers, who were hanging about with nothing better to do before the hour was upon them to again perform their blood and semen stirring acts.

Trip had got up from his desk, and his calls, in order to stretch his back and clear his mind, and went out front to mingle among his trusted customers and employees, keeping his eye on things out front. It was then that the front door crashed open and two figures had rushed in, at the sight of which Trip exclaimed:

"Oh, fuck. I forgot about them."

It was Bunnie and her father. Bunnie running at him with her arms outstretched, ready to choke his little chicken-shit neck to death right then and there. She had the look of hatred so concentrated and intense, that it seemed as though she'd kill every last one of them goddamned losers in that dank hole of a club with two arms tied behind her back.

"Where's my fuckin' husband!" shrieked Bunnie at top volume. "What have you done with my fuckin' husband?"

Trip had decided his only course for staying alive past the next several seconds was to play dumb.

"What? What's this? What do you mean 'where's your husband'?"

"Don't play dumb with me, cock-sucker!" exploded Bunnie, "I know you know where he is! I called Tall Trees last night, *all* night, and no one answered! I knows it was closed! I tried callin' over *here*, but your fuckin' phone was busy all night. And you didn't return my texts or nothin'! So, are you gonna tell me where he is, or am I gonna have to shoot Botox up your crack 'til you 'splode like the Hindenberg?"

With her fiery eyes fixed upon him—in all their bloodshotness and wildness—she panted for breath, but because of the stress of it all, instead of choking him to death, she tenderly fell into Trip's arms in honest surrender.

"Oh God, Trip," she said calmly. "Where is my husband? Do you think he's all right? I know I don't always show it—well, almost *never*— but I don't think I can go on if anything's happened to my lovely man."

That was just about the time Trip's cell phone vibrated, and on the tiny screen lay a text inviting himself, Doctor Runyon and his daughter Bunnie to the basement of the Rebel Yell Bowling Alley for an emergency meeting of the 'council.'

5

Things Begin (?) to Get Nutty

And so, now, Trip, sitting next to his messenger Jerry and still completely in the dark as to his trusted employee's involvement in the whole debacle, was very vocally asking if anyone knew where the *fuck* his club manager was, and where all his *goddamned* liquor had disappeared to.

Not any more less concerned as to the whereabouts of Bubba were a man, a woman, and small child in the back of the room. Doctor Runyon, with his white hair and haggard complexion, frowned and looked forward over the crowd, sensing that something very bad was about to take place, while for her part, Bunnie did her best to entertain and calm a bored second-hand-smoke-gagged little girl, rubbing her bloodshot eyes with one hand, and clutching a plain manila folder in the other, whining piercingly as to why they 'had to stay one more minute in this rotten stinkin' place!'

In a few minutes, a large African-American man came and sat down beside Trip, and with a keenly observant look about him, he addressed Trip by his real name.

"'S'up, Travis."

"Hey, Barge," said Trip, somewhat taken aback upon hearing his real name. "Hey, do you know where Darnet is?"

"Perhaps at my liquor store," chided Barge, pulling double-duty of avoiding lying to Trip *and* knowing he wouldn't be taken seriously.

Trip laughed. "Yeah, right. That would mean you would also know where my liquor is then?"

"Sure," said Barge straight-faced.

Trip laughed again, then sighed deeply. "Well,

fuck, Barge. So what do you make of all this?"

"Don't know. But seems like somethin' crazy is comin' down the pike. I don't think all this is happenin' just for some crazy bitch to tell us how to get rid of that Walmart. Don't believe it for one second."

Struck by Barge's manner, Trip looked dubiously at him. Then he tapped a single finger repeatedly on his chin as he scanned the room and said, "Me neither. Somethin' jus' don't seem right here..."

In the meantime, Father Mossenger had entered the basement rather surreptitiously, brilliantly disguised as a woman (and a horrendously unattractive one that that, so no one thought to question her much less look too carefully at her) having been let into the meeting under the pretense of being an out-of-towner who chaired a committee from a small Midwestern town that had successfully taken on, and taken down, an established Walmart near her home.

Under such pretense, 'she' was to be the guest speaker—the reason given for today's hastily convened meeting in the hastily sent texts and emails, Mossenger well aware this would get everyone's immediate and undivided attention.

And that's exactly what it did.

'Judge' Donny Ray Judge called the meeting to order, and Father Mossenger, aka—F.M.—was introduced as Fanny Mae Terwillicker from Rabbit Hash, Indiana. As 'she' walked forward to speak, Trip sat back and scowled, his only concern his unsuccessful gathering of any information as to the whereabouts of his manager, and more importantly—to his missing liquor. Holding fast to 'her' pretense, F.M. began in a falsetto voice:

"Thank you all for coming. As this handsome gentlemen ('she' pointed to Donny Ray, and he blushed, despite her being so inhumanely ugly) so stated, my name is Fanny Mae Terwillicker from Rabbit Hash, Indiana...so of course, I'm happier'n a hyena trapped in a fiddle to be in Rabbit Grove, Kentucky!"

Several in the crowd chuckled at the attempt at humor, but most simply sat struggling, having to look upon her hideous countenance as 'she' spoke.

"I want to share with you how my small and humble committee over in Indiana managed to get rid of the corporate behemoth and stealer of livelihoods, better known to you as Walmart..."

Boos showered the place like 'shine at a Kentucky AA meeting upon the mention of the accursed store.

"...and how you can get rid of them too right here in your own home-town..."

As the behemoth 'woman' prattled on with made-up stories and lies, Mandy Debarge, having long since buried her face in the latest copy of *Soap Opera Digest*, didn't stir one iota when her husband looked to the back of the room and noticed Doctor Runyon was no longer to be found.

Barge nudged Trip, who looked at him, then Barge merely signaled toward the back of the room with a flip of his head.

Trip turned.

No Runyon.

Trip looked back to Barge, who nodded and both men got up as quietly and stealthily as they could to make for the back of the room, Mandy Debarge joining them with her head still buried in her *Digest*.

Just as Trip gathered the breath in his lungs to inquire of Bunnie, 'Where's your Pa?,' Doctor Runyon returned down the stairs, walked up to the group, and handed a note to Bunnie. She unfolded it in the manner of 'for her eyes only,' and scratched on the back of the bowling-shoe rental receipt were these words:

> Dearest Bunnie—Don't cry for me, I am well. Your father can tell you I am well for he is standing right here with me. I have every confidence that whatever is going on here will be cleared up soon and our lives will get back to

normal. Kiss our child for me.'

-Your darling Bubba

Bunnie folded the note without showing it to any-one, and she was so overcome by emotion that she leaned over and grabbed Mandy Debarge's arm to steady herself. It was a passionate, lovingly warm and womanly outreach, but Mandy Debarge ignored it and let Bunnie's hand fall from her graces like a flopping fish fast approaching death, and went immediately back to scouring her *Digest.*

There was something in this rebuff that gave Bunnie a start. She stopped in mid act of tucking the note into her bra and looked at Mandy Debarge with a terrified look, to which Mandy Debarge looked up and met her stare with a cold impassive stare of her own, and coughed loudly and rudely in Bunnie's face.

Barge looked gloomily at his wife, and said, "Why you always got to be such a bitch?" Then he turned with a shrug of resignation back to the two men stand-ing nearby.

"So where'd you go?" asked Trip to the Doctor.

"I went upstairs to take a piss, cause contrary to them fuckin' commercials on the T-V about those old men who gotta leave the ball game, the golf course, and finish sex with their wives early—them pills don't fuckin' work."

Trip blanched at the old man's frankness.

Runyon continued: "But when I was up there, these two roughneck rednecks hustled in Darnet, and they got rental shoes and started bowling a game. I went over and asked what the big idea was, and they says, 'Step off, old man! We's got business here!' And I says, 'What business? To bowl a game or two?' and they says, 'No, business with the boy here, down-stairs.' And I asks, 'When? After you bowl a game or two?' and they says, 'Whenever we're called to take him down there.' So's I says, 'When do 'spect that will be?' and they says, 'Pro'ly after we bowl a game or two.'"

Trip blanched again, this time at the idiocy of the whole transaction.

"This is idiotic," said Trip sternly. "Let's just go up there and get him!" And he moved to go upstairs.

Doctor Runyon put a hand on Trip's chest.

"No, no, my boy. Those goons up there mean business. I don't have the slightest clue in a raccoon's wiener what's a goin' on around here, but my best advice, from the looks of them two's Smith and Wesson's, is that we should just sit tight here and see how this whole thing's gonna play out."

Trip thought for a moment and decided it best to relent. After all, he figured if the old man and Darnet's wife weren't too concerned about taking action, then neither would he.

"Is that the little shit?" asked Mandy Debarge to Bunnie, stopping her reading for the first time, and pointing the *Digest* at little Brittany as if it were the finger of the Wicked Witch of the West herself.

"If you mean 'is that my daughter?' corrected Bunnie with a shake of the neck, "then yes, yes it is. And you better stay away from her, you mangled piece of toad shit!"

The shadow attendant on Mandy Debarge seemed to fall so threateningly and dark on the child that her mother instinctively kneeled on the ground beside Brittany, and held her to her gloriously huge breasts. The shadow attendant on Mandy Debarge seemed then to fall, threateningly and dark, on both mother and child.

"I've had enough of those losers," said Mandy to her husband. "Let's go back to our seats."

But the suppressed manner had enough menace in it—not necessarily visible and presented, but indistinct and withheld, which was even worse, that it alarmed Bunnie into standing and saying, "I mean it,

Bitch-On-Fire! You better leave us alone!" and then she reached out and grabbed the hem of Mandy Debarge's mini-skirt.

"Oh, no you di'nt!" called out Mandy.

Bunnie fired back: "You *will* leave me, *and* my child, *and* my husband alone! You hear what I'm sayin', Bitch?"

"Your skank-ass husband is not my business here," returned Mandy Debarge, looking down her nose at Bunnie with perfect composure.

"Eat fuckin' puke and choke on it, Bitch!" reacted Bunnie, ready to throw down right then and there, not having bothered to listen one bit, or tried to give one ounce of thought, to the cryptic message Mandy had just given her.

Mandy, for her part, after her husband picked her up bodily and pulled her away in all manner of the bald bouncers on *The Jerry Springer Show*, smugly took what Bunnie had said as a compliment—in the same way the dredges of humanity who appear on *The Jerry Springer Show* are wont to do.

Mandy shot to Bunnie as she was being carried away: "What was in that note you stuffed in your over-sized silicon-filled balloons just now, Bunnie? Huh? What was it?"

"You mother-fucker!" Bunnie simply yelled back. "These bitches are real!"

Mandy Debarge looked coldly as ever at her in-sulter, and said, turning to her friend, The Vengeance, who Barge plopped her down next to: "That Bunnie, *she's* the mother-fucker! Have we not all known every-one's husbands, and even laid their father's while they were in prison, and kept it all from their wives and mother's often enough? Have we not all had enough weenie in this melting pot of V.D. and incest known as the southern hills of Kentucky to last each of us a thousand lifetimes? It's a wonder we're alive and not all talkin' out of our belly-buttons at this point!"

"Yep, we have seen nothing else," agreed The

Vengeance.

"We've *all* been playin' this game for a long time," said Mandy Debarge, turning her eyes again upon Bunnie. "Fuck you!" she shot at her, "You think I'm gonna give a shit about one wife and mother now?"

Bunnie just stuck her tongue out at Mandy, and Mandy thought with sarcasm, *oh, that's real mature!* then resumed reading her *Digest*, under the auspices of many a 'shut up and quit disturbin' the meetin'!' dirty-look from her husband and others around the room.

Having put up with the disturbance for some time, F.M., or Fanny Mae, finally stopped and said, "Ok, in the back there, chill out ya'all before I have to come back there and whup some ass!"

The manner and delivery with which this comment was released garnered a smattering of applause from others nearer the front who were trying their best to listen to the guest speaker unimpeded. But having finished his, or 'her,' made-up stories and lies about having run a Walmart out of town, Fanny Mae Terwillicker changed gears in mid-stride and said, "I am nearing the conclusion of my talk today, but before I do, I have for you a very special guest I've brought with me who has some very important and worthwhile news to share with you."

And that was the signal to the two roughneck rednecks at the top of the stairs, who'd been waiting there since finishing their second game of bowling, to bring Bubba Darnet into the room. They escorted Darnet down into such dingy and smoky pit of despair, and heads nearly snapped off from whiplash and gaped-mouthed surprise as Bubba Darnet went and stood at the front of the room, a 'prisoner' for the second time in his life.

6

And Nuttier

"I give you, Charles Chuck 'Bubba' Darnet Dunnay! One and the same!" announced Fanny Mae, as he pulled off his wig and exposed his true identity just as he had now exposed Bubba's.

Trip caught a quick glance back at Doctor Runyon, and watched the face of his friend—now sixty-two years of age—and a misgiving arose in him that they shouldn't have waited to get Darnet out of the Rebel Yell, because the old man looked in this moment as if he were going to keel over from a heart attack. Of course, he didn't exactly know what the old man would look like if he were *really* having a heart attack, because he had never seen him in this present aspect either, all worried and shriveled on someone's else's behalf instead of his own.

He had never seen the Doctor in such a present character—selfless and not selfish, hoping for someone else's best instead of looking after his own interests first. Maybe he had indeed found Jesus? Trip wondered.

Mandy Debarge, without looking up, but turning her head ever so slightly, had also chanced a glance at the 'good' Doctor, and took notice of the changed demeanor. She decided that somehow in the near past, this family had, for all its dysfunctional fights and outright inability to communicate with each other, that they had somehow grown to be *tight*, almost as if they were a real, American, Normal Rockwell family.

But how could that be? Mandy Debarge wondered, *The man's a frickin' idiot and a monster!* and then she went back to her magazine.

Among the brood of terrors belonging to this

basement this day, the Doctor continued to stand in the back of the room with a steady frame, never doubting that once again his son-in-law would get out of this with his innocence being cemented for all time. At least, that is what he hoped, as he caught a quick glance at the manila folder in his grand-daughter's flapping hand.

Bubba Darnet's 'jury,' the same one he faced before, sat near the bar in feathered red hats; and that is when Bubba realized it was wild turkey hunting season (the actual *bird*, that is—they already had the whiskey set before them, as usual). But looking at the 'jury' and the turbulent audience, Bubba might have thought that the usual order of things was reversed, and that the felons were trying the honest man—and most likely, he was right.

The lowest, cruelest, and worst populace of the town, never without its quantity of low, cruel, and bad, were the directing spirits of the scene: Noisily commenting, applauding, disapproving, anticipating, and precipitating his fate without checks and balances. Of the men, the great part were armed in various ways, this being the southern hills of Kentucky, of course. Of the women, some wore knives, some .22's, and all ate corn dogs and drank beer as they looked on, many managing to chew dogs and spit tobacco all at the same time.

Among these last, was one, with a copy of the latest *Soap Opera Digest* buried before her nose. She was in the middle of the room, by the side of a man Bubba recognized as Barge Debarge, the man responsible for initially holding him against his will. Bubba noticed that she once or twice whispered something in Barge's ear; and though Bubba knew her to be his wife, they had a contentious air about them that was less than agreeable to being in possession of a 'perfect,' or even a 'good,' marriage.

But that was neither here nor there.

What mattered at the moment was Bubba observing that though Mandy Debarge sat relatively close to him, she never looked towards him. She seemed, with a dogged determination, to be waiting for something. Or maybe she was just truly engrossed in the fake lives of those empty-headed actors. The only time she did look up from her magazine was to steal a glance at the 'jury' as if reading their moods and trying to gauge their propensity to decide Bubba's fate one way or the other.

F.M. continued from the front: "Charles 'Chuck' 'Bubba' Darnet Dunnay is hereby officially charged with being a co-conspirator in the fiendish plot of one Clay D. Markee (May Satan Burn His Soul), a plot to destroy your livelihoods and the economy of this great county, and possibly even this country, by allowing the evil empire that is Walmart to set up shop in your own backyards after having first—masterfully, I must admit—bilked your resources in fighting such a plan by having them wasted on a wild goose chase over in Coon Spit proper."

Boos showered the room, as well as flying chew, having been spit from the mouths of many of the less couth, which was pretty much everybody.

"And, you might ask," furthered F.M., "what evidence do I have to connect Mr. Darnet Dunnay to such crimes?"

"Yeah, what?" interrupted the less than couth, which was almost everybody.

"It is that he is nothing more than the very nephew of the vile Clay D. Markee (May Satan Burn His Soul), and so, by nothing more than that association alone—and I believe no other evidence is needed—he is guilty by association, either by direct commission, or omission of stopping it—either way—he must have known of the plots of the evil Clay D. Markee (May God Burn His Rotting Soul)."

Shouts of "Yeah!" "Fuck yeah!" and "That's right!" spattered the room, along with more chew-filled spittle.

"Shoot the fucker with a cross-bow!" one especially gnarled redneck called out. "He's an enemy to the small-businessman's, and woman's, association!"

'Judge' Donny Ray Judge banged the heel of his boot on the bar to silence these cries, and asked the prisoner if it was not indeed true that he was the nephew of one Clay D. Markee (May Satan Skewer His Soul Like A Shish-kabob).

Bubba responded that undoubtedly he was.

Then, was he not aware and involved in the evil plots of his uncle?

No, he was not aware or involved. He was competely unaware. And speaking in truth, he hoped a sense and spirit of justice would soon prevail in the hearts and minds of those assembled.

Donny Ray desired to know: And how was that possible—not to know?

Because he had voluntarily washed his hands long before the plot was ever dreamed up of anything involving his uncle, and of anything involving his uncle at all, going so far of late as to relinquish his inheritance of The Chateau, and other monies and things associated with such an association, when his uncle had passed from this earth. Not only that, but he found the association of his uncle so distasteful that he left Reams, the town of his childhood, to go make a life for himself as a self-reliant and working-class stiff in Grouse Gulch.

And what proof had he had of this?

He handed over the names of Postmaster Gabriel (who had a copy of his birth certificate, with his birthname, stored in the tax records office now taken over by someone else, but it's still there), and Doctor Paul Runyon.

And he had been married in Grouse Gulch?

Yes, at St. Pancreas.

To a citizen of Grouse Gulch?

Not by birth. She was born in Coon Spit.

Her name?

Bunnie Runyon Mancrizie Darnet.

Jeezus, that's a lot of names!

Yes, I know. She's the daughter of Doctor Paul Runyon, now of Grouse Gulch. He's sitting right back there, next to my wife and child. Hi, honey! I love ya!

This statement had an ooooo-ing and ahhhing effect on the crowd, for they rarely saw a family as seemingly loving and functional as this one appeared to be, on the outside at least. But no matter, it was a refreshing departure from the norm that this husband and wife were willing to admit in public to knowing and being with one another.

So capriciously were the people moved, that the gnarled redneck who minutes before had called for Bubba to be shot through with a cross-bow now had tears rolling down his big gnarled cheeks.

Donny Ray continued: "Trip wants to know where you stashed his fuckin' liquor, Bubba. Do you have it? And if not, where's it at?"

Bubba looked at Mandy Debarge, who still would not look at him, but kept her face disinterestedly buried in her *Digest.*

Then Bubba looked at Barge, and said, "I don't have it, and I don't know where it is. It was probably stolen from my car when I left it broken down on the Buckskin Trail."

"And why did you leave your car out there on The Trail instead of calling for help?"

Bubba looked directly at Jerry. "Because I didn't want to disturb the lives of any of my friends that day, and figured I'd take care of it myself."

Jerry almost fainted.

"Take care of it yourself?"

"Yes, I walked back into town."

"All the way back into town? By *yourself?*"

"Yes."

At that point, Donny Ray put the question before the combined chambers of commerce: "So do we think this man is our enemy?"

"No!" the populace cried enthusiastically, led most

loudly by Barge and Jerry.

For the first time in the meeting, Stryker and his small contingent of buddies from the Cock-N-Bull rustled fitfully. They had only reacted to the meeting thus far by showing stone-faced complacency.

But suddenly, as if a bear had been startled in its cave and is now pissed-off with all the anger of Hell, Mandy Debarge cocked back her head and yelled, "Let's hear from the witnesses!"

The crowd slowly murmured to a hush, and heads nodded in agreement all around.

"Fair enough," said Donny Ray. "Let's call the witnesses."

It being common knowledge that Postmaster Gabriel fell to his doom at the top, and the bottom, of 'Mayker Holler,' it was taken for granted by all present that Bubba Darnet-Dunnay's birth certificate was indeed on record at the county house of the collection of taxation (which, as mentioned earlier, doubled as the post office), and that it would prove, were anyone to look at it, that both names were indeed to prove Bubba to be one and the same man.

So in lieu of such a missing witness, the only other witness mentioned during testimony still converting oxygen to carbon-dioxide was one Doctor Paul Runyon, who was quickly hustled to the front of the room by F.M.'s two henchmen.

Doctor Runyon's horrendously disheveled appearance and the slurredness of his answers (from years of being smoked on 'shine), surprised no one. What did surprise them, however, was his genuine concern and lack of hostility concerning the Accused.

He decried Bubba Darnet as a man he called his son-in-law, as well as a friend, and as you can imagine, this garnered much astonished gasping throughout the current patronage of this meeting-house. He went on to describe Bubba as a man who had come to Grouse Gulch from Reams, a seeming slacker, a loser if you will; who, though always faithful to his daughter (well, sort of) had made good after the birth of their daughter to became a responsible and industrious member of the Coalmont County community by being selected manager of the Tall Trees strip club in Coon Spit, and now currently being on the verge of taking over the storied Tall Tales strip club in Grouse Gulch, as well as continuing to oversee Tall Trees.

Now nothing, *nothing*, could have prepared the crowd for *that* little drop of an A-bomb, most of all Travis 'Trip' Templeton himself, who, figured no one outside of himself—and possibly Bubba if he had un-knowingly alluded to it in front of his manager at some point in a drunken sess—could have known of such a plan.

Added to this, audible gasps and wary shakes of heads from the old-guard patrons of Tall Tales—so resistant to change that they had the bull-headed ignorance to pine away for the 'good old days,' otherwise known as anytime in American history before the 1960's, otherwise known as the days of African-American oppression—and added to that, sparks of amazement continued to ignite throughout the crowd like drops of yeast being dripped, slowly then quickly, into leavening loaves of bread, that Travis 'Trip' Templeton was prepared to trust such a respected county icon of filth and disgust known as the Tall Tales strip club to just any old Tom, Dick or Bubba who came along. And certainly not to one whom Trip had clearly failed to give a thorough background check.

But in all this milieu of shock and amazement, the most visibly shocked were Stryker's small contingent of Cock-N-Bull regulars, seated on the far side of the room. After all, they were so...oh, so close!...after many years of threats and wrangling, were so *close* to talking Trip into giving them a men's gay night; and this little bit of news felt to them like their progress had been set back forty years. For they were well aware of Bubba Darnet's negatory position and disparaging remarks now and then toward 'homer-seckshuls.'

It had been stated just now that members of the Cock-N-Bull contingent were shocked at the news, but one member of such 'club' was not; that being Mr. Stryker himself. For he had the insight and foresight to have foreseen this little hand-over of the club coming down the pike, and without having been told about it directly. After all, he was a very loyal and long-standing frequenter of the club, and if anyone could give its history backwards and forwards, as well as predicting its future to within a millimeter as to where the ship was headed, it was Mr. Stryker himself.

Presently, trickles of sweat drolloped down each side of Stryker's pudgy temples as he envisioned in his mind's eye his future pleasure-time he'd worked so hard to gain for himself—not to mention his only reason for continuing to live—slowly sliding away. He had to take action! He *must* take action!

With the present instability of the crowd blowing at full mast, Stryker stood up and shouted: "I vote Guilty! He's an enemy of the people! And he should be run out of the county on a rail!"

A peppering of nods began to emerge throughout the room, none having the slightest realization that what Stryker meant was not that Bubba was an enemy of the anti-Walmart movement, but was, in fact, accusing him of being homophobic. The majority of those nodding their ignorant heads didn't care much about such matters anyway, their only concern was they simply didn't want to see things change, or 'youthanized,' at Tall Tales, in the same way things had been done at Tall Trees.

The folk began to stand and yell, "Guilty! Guilty!"

And that is when Bunnie Runyon Mancrizie Darnet quietly took the manila folder from her daughter's precious hand, and placed the child in the capable arms of a nearby mother, and walked calmly to the front of the room with her father at her side, amidst all the ruckus.

Grasping her father's hand for courage, she gave

her husband a warm embrace when they reached the front, then lovingly and tenderly whispered into his ear, attached to a fearful and trembling frame: "Grow some balls, honey. You look like a frickin' puss up here."

Then she turned her beautiful head toward the near-brawling crowd, and with the help of Donny Ray—furiously banging the heel of his boot on the bar—they finally got everyone to shut the fuck up, and sit the fuck down.

7

Things Get Even Nuttier
(if that's at all possible)

Bubba Darnet's wife at present trembled, a vague and heavy fear having just come upon her as she stood to face the 'council.' All the air in the place was so thick with smoke and so dark—the people so slowly but consistently killing themselves on chew and cheap cigarettes and bad 'shine—but it was impossible for her to forget that she and her husband were not blameless in such an endeavor, for they too were heavy smokers and chewers, not to mention frequent imbibers of large quantities of bad 'shine.

Her father, despite their troubled past, stood and secretly cheered for her, picturing the baby Jesus at that moment doing the exact same thing. However, as if these proceedings could not possibly have gotten any stranger, there was a loud commotion at the top of the stairs as two 'attendants' struggled mightily, without success, to block a wild-braying jackass from entering the basement. Said jackass turned out to be, once she got to the bottom of the stairs and in sight of all, Miss Priss!

"There you are, Jerry Kracker!" she sluthered, her black and red bloodshot eyes filled with ferocity, "If you are ready to go, then so am I!"

Jerry leaned over to a startled and caught off-guard Trip and said hoarsely, "Well, I guess I gotta go."

For it had been for some months back that Miss Priss and Mr. Kracker had begun having an affair, which one would think too horrifying an action to actually be true (on both their accounts), but her being crazier than a shit-house rat, and him being uglier'n a human corpse left to rot in the Sahara sun, they both figured, equally and separately, 'what have I got to lose?'

It was far from a smooth engagement, their affair—as one would probably figure. For though he had somehow managed to rid himself of his ass-cheese before hooking up with her, nothing could file down his spiky pubic-hair, and she complained of it often, and often bitterly.

However, at the present time and place, Mr. Kracker bowed his head low in embarrassment as he made his way to meet her at the staircase, as she spouted whatever cockamamie thing came into her unbalanced mind at that moment.

"There's all manner of things wanted!" yelled Miss Priss in Jerry's direction. "And we shall have a precious time of it! We want wine, among the rest! Nice breasts these redheads have right here in front of me! We will be drinking, whenever we buy it!"

"Yes," retorted a beyond humiliated Jerry Kracker, faking like he understood the slightest bit of sense of her random prattlings, "We will soon drink to your health, and to the older un's."

"Who's he?" said Miss Priss, looking right at Jerry. Mr. Kracker explained himself as, "It's me. Old St. Nick."

"Ha!" said Miss Priss, "it doesn't need an interpreter to explain its meaning to these creatures!"

Jerry took her by the arm. "Come on, Gollum, let's get you out of here. That's a good girl. Hush, now, and watch these steps on the way up..."

"Yes, yes, yes, I'll be cautious!" barbled Miss Priss, looking out over the crowd once more, "But I may say among yourselves that I do hope there will be no onion-y or tobacco-y stains on my carpet you all are setting upon." Then she suddenly caught sight of Bunnie standing up front, and immediately stopped on the bottom stair. "Now, Ladybug, never you stir from that fire 'til I come back, ya hear? Take care of that dear husband and don't remove your pretty head from his lap as it is now, or you'll be seein' me again!"

Sadly, it was the most lucid thing Priss had said in months.

"Hush! Go on home now!" called Bunnie after her.

"Well, my sweet," continued Priss, "the short and long of it all is that I am a subject of His Most Holy Gracious and Royal King George the fifth," she motioned to Jerry, "and as such, my maxim is to confound his politics, and maybe lick his balls now and again, but also to frustrate his knavish tricks—though on him my hopes are fixed—God save the King!"

Many in the crowd began to audibly snicker.

Mr. Kracker, in a most unbearably awkward manner, growlingly reproached her for such comments made aloud at a public gathering of county-wide proportions and influence, and tried again to tug her on her way up the stairs.

But she was having none of it.

"I am glad you have had so many Englishman, Mr. Kracker...!"

The audible snickering now became guffaws.

"...though I wish you had never taken that cold dildo out of my refrigerator..."

Peals of laughter.

"Heigh-ho-hum!" said Miss Priss, cheerfully, it becoming apparent that not only was she crazier than an intelligent person watching '*Keeping up with the Kardashians*,' but she had probably also gotten hold of someone's stash of 'X.' "Ladies, we must hold our legs up high and kick them low, that is what my brother Solomon used to say, though come to think of it now, I have no idea in God's name why."

Thunderous laughter.

"Now, Mr. Kracker! Take me away! But don't you move, Ladybug!"

They finally went out, and everyone ever associated with Miss Priss, and even Jerry Kracker, held hot faces of excruciated embarrassment.

It had, early in the proceedings, dawned on Runyon that the man who was once before a 'prisoner' of this tribunal was now his dear relation, his son-in-law. 'Prisoner' again before a group of people—some asleep and some awake, some dirty with grease stains and chew dripping from their chins; some sober (yeah, right) and some not (make that: *all* not)—who held his life and liberty in their hands.

As he set his face toward his mission: preserving life and liberty not only for the sake of his son-in-law, but also for the future happiness of his daughter, the dear Bunnie. Greater things than the Doctor had at that time to contend with—such as checking the chemical balance of his latest batch of 'shine—would have to be yielded before this preserving purpose. This 'new life' of Runyon posed its questions in the minds of those who knew him, no doubt; but the sagacious Trip Templeton now saw, as Runyon stood before all, that there was a new sustaining pride in him. Nothing unbecoming of a man of Jesus, mind you; it was a natural and worthy pride, and one Trip observed with much curiosity.

The Doctor knew, up until that moment, that he had in the minds of his daughter and his friends been associated in all manner with the basest of ex-cons in his unfortunate, and unwarranted, imprisonment; and with his personal afflictions and weaknesses that had caused those around him so much deprivation of emotions and needs gone unmet, now that he was changed, he knew himself to be invested with forces that looked after Bubba Darnet's ultimate safety and deliverance. So he took the lead, and required of the weak—as he perceived his daughter to be in that moment—to trust him as the strong one. The preceding relative positions of himself and Bunnie were suddenly reversed, as only the liveliest of forgiveness and acceptance of that forgiveness could reverse them, the hated becoming the loved, and the failure becoming the bold rescuer of the tender hearted (or at least, somewhat tender hearted—but she was trying).

All curious to see, thought Trip, in his amiably shrewd way, *and all natural and right for a man who truly found Jesus; so take the lead my dear friend, and keep it! It couldn't be in better hands.*

As for the crowd at this moment, there was no pause (except for Priss's freakish scene), no pity, no peace, no interval of relenting rest, and no measurement of time in their scoffing hatred of Bubba Darnet as far as they were concerned. Calls for his banishment came forth again:

"Guilty!"

"Kick him out of the bowling leagues!"

"Kick him out of the county!"

"Kick him out of the *state!*"

"Kick him in the jimmy!"

The Doctor tried hard to calm the drug and alcohol soaked tribunal, and never ceased trying. Finally, Donny Ray shot his pistol in the air, a puff of plaster settling down upon his hair as Old Man McMillian upstairs was hurried to the hospital for a random gunshot through the foot.

Doctor Paul Runyon now had the floor.

"I know many of you at this moment are upset with my son-in-law..." began Runyon.

"Damn straight!"

"Got that right!"

"Shit yeah!"

"Yee haw!"

"...And you think that since his kin were pro-Walmarters, *he* must be a pro-Walmarter too, and knew of, or at least failed to prevent, the fiendish plot of his uncle, Clay D. Markee..."

"Damn skippy!"

"Got that right!"

"Shit yeah!"

"Yee haw!"

"...But I have here in my hand evidence that will show he is not at all the man you think he is."

"Huh?"

"Whatchu you talkin' about, Willis?"

"Shit...what?"

"Yaw?"

And Doctor Runyon reached into the manila envelop and retrieved an item he held high in the air. It was a nametag which stated, 'Hi! My name is Bubba Darnet. I'm your friendly Walmart greeter!'

A shower of boos and booze and chew and vomit spewed forth from the crowd.

"Hells no!"

"Burn the sun-bitch!"

"Not fit to live!"

"Let's fuck his goats!"

The Doctor patiently let this diatribe continue for two or three minutes, then he pulled several 8 x 10 black and white photographs from the very same envelope and held them high for all to see.

Most of the crowd leaned forward to get a better look through their alcohol and drug induced haze, and many reached for reading glasses and bifocals.

When the full impact of what they saw finally registered, the crowd gasped and went silent in a collective shock.

"That's right!" shouted Doctor Runyon loud enough for all to hear, even a few Witnesses upstairs. "*This* is your anti-Walmart 'prisoner'!"

The pictures revealed a man looking at a group of people carrying away merchandise from beneath a loading dock as a gust of wind came up and took off his disguise, revealing a fake mustache, wig and beard—in split second photographic increments—peeling from the face of Bubba Darnet, revealing him to be the heretofore unknown 'Loading Dock Thrower.'

"There! There is your 'prisoner'! But he should not be your 'prisoner,' indeed, this man should be your *hero*!"

The silent shock slowly turned to smiles and a few initial shouts of *'hooray!'*

A slow clap was begun in the middle of the mob, which eventually morphed into a full standing 'O.'

Donny Ray banged his boot on the bar in lieu of reaching for his pistol—to the unbeknownst relief of those upstairs who had feet—to restore order. And once order was thus regained, Donny Ray called out, "So, is this man—Bubba Darnet—a criminal in the eyes of the counsel?"

"No!" the populace cried enthusiastically, followed by:

"Hells no!"

"Fuck no!"

"Let him go!"

"Do I still get to fuck his goats?"

I have saved him, thought Doctor Runyon with satisfaction, *just as surely as Jesus saved me!*

It was not another of the dreams in which he had often never come back; he was really here. And yet Bunnie did not seem relieved. She trembled, and a vague and heavy fear was upon her. She just didn't believe it to be true.

Not yet.

Her father, cheering for her and her husband, showed a compassionate superiority to her seeming nonchalance, which was wonderful to see.

"My dear!" said Runyon, "Why so glum? Did you not see what just happened? Our photos...?"

"Oh, Pa! Pa! Hide Bubba! Save him! He's ray-taded'r than an onion-flavored stick of butter, but I do love the bastard! I truly do!"

"Bunnie," said the Doctor, laying a soothing arm around her shoulder, "I have saved him. What is this weakness in you? I have never seen it before. I thought I'd beaten it out of you when you was a wee child..."

Stryker, an ever-worried look upon his own stricken face—the only man in the room not standing and clapping—rose slowly.

"Not so fast, Bubba Darnet!"

The air in the room became thick and dark once again, and the people who were moments before jubilant and excited now cowered at the base of Stryker's extreme girth and supreme cock-suredness.

"This man claims to be our hero? Well, he may be *your* hero, but he is most certainly not mine! Unless...unless..."

Several of the more extremely inebriated nodded their heads along with what Stryker was saying even though they had no idea what they were nodding too; they were simply three sheets beyond the wind and swayed by the forcefulness of the attorney's dissent.

"We—those of us faithful customers and consumers of much beverages over the years at the Cock-N-Bull in the back of the Tall Tales club—are concerned that in the same way this man disguised himself before the 'thorities of this county, and the 'thorities of Walmart (even if it was a noble cause) also might be disguised as a friend of us loyal consumers of beverages who have made progress in certain dealings at Tall Tales of late, the culmination of our own hard fought battle for many a year to which much sacrifices have been made, and we are concerned for the security and the well-being of our future inebriatic, and otherwise, enjoyments!"

Much of the crowd by this time were nodding along, still having no idea what Stryker was *really* talking about, but having much sympathy toward fellow drinkers whose seeming future enjoyment of the alcoholic arts might soon be in jeopardy.

And we can't have that now, can we?

Many in the crowd were heard to whisper: "Bubba's plannin' to take away that man's right to drink and smoke doobage! That ain't right, now, is it?"

"Hells no!"

"Shit no!"

"Where's them goats?"

Stryker's contingent now began a slow clap of

their own, this time for *Guilty!*, and chants of 'throw him out of the state!' beginning again in earnest.

The Doctor looked down, dismayed, as if seeing all his hard work and clandestine activities going quickly down the drain.

But Bubba, for his part, alert to what was *really* happening with Stryker's crew, acted quickly and decisively to head off the wily attorney.

"Stryker," said he, "I'll do whatever it takes to show you, and your little group there, that I'm serious about preserving the security of the well-being of your future enjoyments—and you have my word on that."

This simple statement relieved the notion in the worried minds of the crowd that someone would be prevented from exercising their right to drink, and again, the crowd immediately turned toward the opposite pole and chanted 'Free him! Free him!'

Stryker seemed satisfied. "I will take you on your word for it for now, Bubba Darnet. But you better come through! Or else...!"

Stryker slowly sat back down, his contingent pacified, at least for the moment.

Then, as if anyone could stand much more, especially Bunnie and the Doctor, a faint voice was heard from the middle of the room.

"Do you know me?"

Bubba squinted to locate the origination of the voice.

"Yes, I know you," Darnet answered in recognition.

"Not you, dill-weed! I'm talkin' to your putrid father-in-law!"

Doctor Runyon placed a hand over his eyes though no glare was present, and located the voice.

"No, I can't say I've ever seen you before," said he.

"Well, I know *you*, Doctor," the voice seethed. "And if the anti-Walmart counsel demands that you sacrifice your son-in-law on account of what you've done, then you'd do it, wouldn't you?"

Nods all around in the crowd.

"He better!"

"Hells yeah!"

"Shit yeah!"

"Haw!"

"If I may get a word in edgewise," scrambled Doctor Runyon, "Who is it that accuses me?"

"I," said the voice, "I of Saint Antwan's. Oh, I almost forgot—and someone else accuses you as well."

"Who? Who else accuses me?"

"I will tell you soon enough, because right now I have forgotten the name."

"Dumb bitch," muttered a redneck near the back.

8

The Spy Who Didn't Love Her

Happily unconscious of the calamity she caused at the Rebel Yell, Miss Priss threaded her way through the bumpy streets of Rabbit Grove in her rusted-out Datsun, crossing over the Gizzard River on her way to Coon Spit, reckoning in her disturbed mind the number of indispensable purchases she had to make. Soon, she and her companion pulled into Saint Antwan's Liquors and Beer and Mr. Kracker, armed with a basket, got out and walked by her side.

They both looked to the right and to the left before entering the store; she because she thought space aliens were about to swoop down and decapitate her; he because he didn't want to be seen in public with such a crazy old coo-coo, especially with one in which he was having a lurid affair.

It was a raw evening, and Jerry—having just purchased a razor (soon to be dulled by his full beard) at the dying Rexall drugstore in downtown Coon Spit, and some oil from the Monkey Nut just after having left the bowling alley—now shopped the aisles of Saint Antwan's with Miss Priss for the wine they wanted. After peeping several times into the women's bathroom (and the mens?) while Jerry looked over the beer selections, Miss Priss stopped at the sight of 'The Good Republic' black label wine, not far from 'The National Pleasure' red label wine. 'The Good Republic' had a quieter look, thought Miss Priss, and was not as red as the other. Yelling to Jerry to ask his opinion, Kracker grumbled back, "Get whatever you want, you old decrepit antique!"

Slightly observant of the smoky lights, and of the people: some with pipes in mouths, almost everyone chewing chaw, or chawing chew; some played with soggy playing cards and yellowed dominoes; one shirt-less tattooed single-armed soot-begrimed lazy good-for-nothing read a *Ladies Home Journal*—aloud—and some others listened to the poor bastard; two or three 'customers' had fallen asleep in pools of their own vomit and urine—the outlandish couple approached the counter, and showed what they wanted to pur-chase.

The clerk filling in for Mandy Debarge rose from his game of dominoes near the back and walked to the front of the store. In doing so, he had to pass by Miss Priss. No sooner did he face her than Priss uttered a scream and clapped her hands like a kindergarten teacher. In a moment, the whole store was on its feet. Everybody looked to see who had fallen, possibly in one of the random pools of vomit or urine—or both—but only saw an extremely embarrassed man standing with and a whacked-out bitch who stood facing the clerk; the clerk with all the outward appearance of be-ing from south of the border, and the bitch evidently of Grouse Gulch.

What was said in this disappointing anti-climax—since everyone now realized someone had *not* slipped and fallen in the urine and vomit—would have been Greek to Miss Priss anyway since she was battier than Dracula's castle at midnight. But everyone stood silent in their surprise, for, it must be recorded, that not on-ly was Miss Priss lost in her own world of the Lollipop Guild, but, Mr. Kracker's head, though lost as well on his own separate account, but living very much in the real world; was also in a state of wonder.

"The fuck's the matter wit' chu?" said the man who had caused Miss Priss to scream; speaking in a vexed abrupt voice (though in a low tone), and in Spanish; without a trace of hillbilly accent.

"Oh, Solomon, dear Solomon!" cried Miss Priss, also in Spanish, clapping her hands again in the man-ner of a kindergarten teacher. "After not setting eyes on you or hearing from you for so long, I find you here!"

"Don't call me Solomon! Do you want to be the death of me? Call me Garcia," said the man, in a furtive, frightened way.

"Brother! Brother!" cried Miss Priss in Spanish, bursting into tears. "Have I ever been so hard with you that you treat me in such a cruel way?"

"Shut your fuckin' mouth!" said Solomon, again in Spanish, "and come out to the parking lot with me if you want to speak to me. But pay for your wine first—I know how you are!—then lets go out. By the way, who's the gringo fucker with you?"

Miss Priss, shaking her loving, dejected and psychotically demented head at her long-lost brother, said through tears, "Mr. Kracker."

"Seems appropriate," replied Solomon. "Bring his dumb-ass out too. Does he think me an illegal?"

Apparently, Mr. Kracker did, to judge from his look. He said not a word, however, and Miss Priss, exploring the depths of her dementia through tears with great ease it seemed, paid for her wine. As she did so, Solomon turned to the slackers in the store and offered a few words of advice in English:

"Mind your own fuckin' business!"

Solomon turned back to his sister and her 'companion' and said, "Now," again, in Spanish, "What the hell do you want?"

"How dreadfully unkind in a brother nothing has ever turned my love away from!" cried Miss Priss.

"Are you trying to talk like Yoda or something, or has it just been that long since you've spoken Spanish?" asked Solomon in English.

"She's just having a rough time right now, for some reason," helped Jerry.

"Hey! Chez Whitey!" charged Solomon. "When I want your opinion, I'll ask for it. Kapeesh?"

Jerry cowered before the mean-looking Latino, who seemed most likely capable of anything.

"Oh!" Miss Priss belly-ached again, "To give me such an awful greeting! And to show me no affection!"

"Confound it!" Solomon spoke in Spanish. "There!" and he made a dab at Priss's lips with his own. "You happy now?"

Kracker turned and vomited on the side of the building.

Miss Priss only shook her head and wept in silence. Jerry did the same.

"If you expect me to be surprised," said her brother in Spanish, "I am not surprised; I knew you were here, just as I know of most of my people who are here. If you really don't want to endanger my existence—which I half-believe you do—then get away from me as soon as possible and take that fuckin' hill-jack with you! Let me get back to my work. I'm busy."

"My half-brother Solomon," mourned Miss Priss, casting up her tear-fraught eyes. "He had the makings in him of being one of the best and greatest of men in his native country, a god among foreigners, and such foreigners! I would almost sooner have seen the dear boy lying in his-!"

"I said fuck off!" cried her half-brother, interrupting. "I knew it! You want the death of me! I shall be rendered a possible suspicious illegal, and by my own half-sister! Just as I am getting on!"

"The gracious and merciful Heavens forbid!" cried Miss Priss. "Far rather would I never see you again, dear Solomon, though I have loved you truly forever, and forever will. Say but one affectionate sweet nothing to me, and tell me there is nothing angry or estranged between us, and I will not have you detained by immigration!"

Good Lord! Priss was groveling at his feet as if the estrangement between them had come of any culpability of hers. As if Trip Templeton had not known it for a fact, years ago, in the quiet corner of Chickenwell Street, that this precious half-brother had spent her money and left her!

He was saying the affectionate sweet-nothing, however, with a far more grudging condescension and patronage than he could have ever shown if their skin-colors had been reversed (which is invariably the case the world over), when Mr. Kracker, poking him on the shoulder, hoarsely and unexpectedly interposed with the following singular question:

"You ever done your sister?"

"No, you gross hick! Never!"

Kracker took this information in.

"Might I ask a favor?" asked Jerry. "Is your name John Solomon Garcia-Priss, or Solomon John Priss-Garcia?"

The Latino turned towards him with a sudden distrust, for Kracker had not uttered a word in awhile.

"Come now!" said Mr. Kracker, "Speak! John Solomon Garcia-Priss, or Solomon John Priss-Garcia? She called you Solomon, and she must know, being your half-sister and all. And I know you are John. So which of the two? And regarding that name of Priss, that weren't your name down south now, was it?"

"What the hell do you mean, Kracker?" barked Solomon.

"Well, I ain't the sharpest tool in the shed, I'll admit, and I'm having trouble remembering what your name was that you originally brought up here with you from down south o' the border."

"You can't remember?"

"No, but I'd swear it was something der'ogatory..."

"Yeah?"

"Yeah. The alias you used was one syl'a-ble. Yeah, I know you! You was a witness at the Rebel Yell! Hey, now! What in the name of the Father of Lies, your own father (which got a smack from Priss, who shared said father), was you called at that time? And come to think of it, you must've been wearing a bit of pancake make-up to blend in..."

"Bastard," another voice said, striking in.

Jerry turned to the voice. "Fuck you! Call me a

bastard, will you…?"

"No, you country-fried sheep-fucker!" returned the voice. "His *name* is Bastard!"

"That's the sixty-four thousand dollar answer!" cried Jerry.

"He's right! You are Bastard!"

The speaker who struck in was Bubba Cotton. He had his hands behind him tucked under a skirt he wore over his blue-jeans, and he stood at Mr. Kracker's elbow as nonchalantly as he might have stood at the Rebel Yell itself.

"Don't be alarmed, my dear Miss Priss. I was at Trip Templeton's—to his surprise—yesterday evening; and we agreed that I would not present myself in public until all was well, or until I could be of use. I present myself here, to have a little chat with your half-brother. I wish you had a better employed brother than Mr. Bastard. I wish for your sake Mr. Bastard was not a frequenter of farmer's sheep." For 'sheep-fucker' was a derogatory referral at that time in the hills of southern Kentucky for a 'spy', or an illegal. The 'spy', who used to be pale, but without the pancake make-up was now dark, asked him how he dared—.

"I'll tell you," said Cotton. "I saw you, Mr. Bastard, while I was parked in a stall in the liquor store bathroom an hour or so ago, contemplating the graffiti on the door in front of my face. You, my friend, have a face to be remembered—and a small mole on your man parts—and I remember faces and man-parts well. The chalky residue from the pancake make-up sprinkled on your shirt didn't hurt either. It was curious to see you in the bathroom, then to see you working the front counter of this liquor store, and I associated you with the misfortunes of a friend now very unfortunate, and I spied on you myself from behind the cardboard Ripple ad near the back of the store. I had no difficulty, deducing by the rumor-mill swirling in this house of swill, the nature of your calling. And gradually, a random dump seemed to shape itself into far greater purpose, like a Play-Doh Fuzzy-Pumper Barbershop."

"And what purpose would that be?" asked the 'spy.'

"It would be mighty dangerous to talk about it here in the parking lot. Would you trouble yourself to join me in my car for a ride to the Tall Tales strip club and we could talk about it there?"

"Under a threat?"

"Oh, did I threaten you?"

"No, but why should I go there with you?"

"Mr. Bastard, I can't say if you won't go."

"Do you mean to say you won't tell me unless I go?" the 'spy' irresolutely asked.

"You understand me very well, Bastard. I won't say unless you go."

Cotton's negligent recklessness of manner came powerfully in the aid of his quickness and skill, in such a business as he had in his 'secret mind', and with such a man as he was seeking to do it with. His 'practiced' eye saw what he wanted, and made the most of it.

"I'm blaming this all on you!" said the 'spy,' casting a reproachful look at his half-sister; "If I have trouble from this, I'm blaming you!"

"Come, come, Bastard," exclaimed Cotton. "Don't be such an ungrateful fucker toward your sister. But for my great 'respect' for your sister, I might not have so gracefully presented my offer. Will you go with me to the club then?"

"I'll hear what you have to say by going. Yeah, I'll go with you."

"I propose that we first tell your sister to get her coo-coo ass straight home, with the help of this fine gentleman here. Mr. Kracker, if you would?"

Jerry reluctantly took Priss's arm, for he had had enough of her hokey horseshit for one day.

"Are we ready now, Bastard? Let's go. Priss and Jerry—bye bye now, take care then!"

Miss Priss recalled in the one moment of lucidity

she enjoyed at the very last instances of her physical life that as she pressed a hand upon Cotton's arm and looked up into his face, imploring him to do no hurt to Solomon, there was a braced purpose in the arm and a kind of inspiration in the eyes, which not only contradicted his light manner, but changed and raised the man. She was too much occupied then with fears for the half-brother who so little deserved her affection, and with Bubba Cotton's friendly reassurances and her mind being gone further than one-hundred laps at Daytona, she failed to heed what she observed.

They left the couple outside the liquor store and Cotton drove them to Tall Tales—which was many a minutes drive—while John the Bastard, or Solomon Priss, rode shotgun.

Only they didn't go to Tall Tales, but to the Rebel Yell Bowling Alley to which John the Bastard protested greatly, but Cotton's Smith and Wesson convinced him to abandon any plan for escape he might have hatched in that moment.

They went inside and had a runner go down and pull Trip Templeton from the meeting. When Trip came up for fresher stale air, and to see who had called him from such a three ring freak show downstairs, he showed great surprise when he saw Bubba Cotton sitting at the public bar with the stranger, and with Bubba's S and W poking him in the side.

"Miss Priss's half-brother," said Cotton. "A Mr. Bastard."

"Bastard?" repeated the aging strip club owner. "Bastard? I have a friend, er, um, an associate, with that name—and with that face; only if it were white…"

"I told you you had a remarkable face, Bastard," observed Cotton with a wink.

Then Bubba proceeded to supply Trip with the link he was desperately searching for, by saying to him with a frown, "Witness at the first trial." Trip immediately remembered, and regarded his new visitor with an undisguised look of abhorrence.

"Bastard here has been recognized by Miss Priss as the 'overly affectionate' brother you have long heard of, and has acknowledged the inappropriate relationship."

Trip gagged a little and threw up in his mouth. Struck with consternation, the aging club owner exclaimed, "Why do you tell me such things? You know I have a sensitive gag reflex!"

"Just wanted you to know, Trip. I also intercepted a communication between Bastard and a friend of his over a bottle of Jack at Saint Antwan's that something crazy is about to go down concerning Bubba Darnet, Doctor Runyon, and Mandy Debarge."

Trip's 'business' eye read in the speaker's face that it would be a loss to question his integrity on the point. Confused, but sensible that something might rely on his having a clear and sober mind, Trip resolved to quit drinking at least for the duration of the downstairs proceedings.

"I trust Doctor Runyon has been working to get his dear son-in-law freed, so he can go back to that dear and precious bangin' hot wife of his; and even *after* she had kids, for chrissakes!"

"He tried, but a few other things have come to light that have thrown wrenches into the works. Just before you called me up here to tell me what I already know as far as Mandy, the Doc and Darnet, she was about to drop the bomb."

"Bastard here and I have some business to discuss, if you will excuse us for a moment."

Cotton nodded to Trip.

Trip nodded back. "Certainly."

Then Trip got up to go back downstairs just as Jerry Kracker again entered the scene.

"What's up, Trip?"

"Jerry! You're back!"

In the time Cotton was in discussion with Bastard the 'spy,' Templeton filled his messenger in on the dealings in the basement that had taken place since he last taken leave with Priss.

Then Cotton and Bastard returned, and with an 'Adieu, Bastard!' by Bubba, John the Bastard, now Solomon...er, uh, Garcia-Priss, or whatever; was sent on his way.

"What was that all about?" asked Trip to Bubba Cotton.

"Oh, nothing. I have only secured for myself Bastard as a spy—a true spy that is—in my employ, under threat of tuning him over to immigration. He will keep me abreast of the doings in the Debarge camp since he works at Saint Antwan's for next to nothing, and in case things get at all ugly downstairs, and we, or I, should have need of him in future matters, possibly dealing with the future of your clubs..."

Trip was now astonished, and didn't attempt to hide it. "My clubs?" he interrupted. "What could possibly be happening downstairs that could interfere with my clubs?"

"Maybe nothing," replied Cotton coolly, "We'll just have to wait and see."

"You have no right to speak to my boss that way!" interjected Kracker. "Scaring him for no good reason!"

Cotton stared at him calmly. "Speaking of 'scaring,' you good-for-nothing bastard yourself, Jerry Kracker," Bubba began, "I believe I have it on good authority that you've been out moonlighting on Trip, pretty much literally I'd say..."

"What?" shot Jerry, "What are you spewin' about?"

"You're a grave robber, are you not? You and two of your buddies?"

"That's not true...!"

"What?" exclaimed Trip, staring at Kracker. "Is that true?"

"Well..." began Jerry, unsure of the authority of Cotton's information; after all, it might be good. "...not exactly."

"And you have the balls to not share your findings with me? Me! Your good and faithful boss of all these years! Have I ever let you down?"

"No."

"Have I ever treated you unfairly?"

"Well, no."

"So what's the hold up, Jack? Share the wealth, man! Give me a take! I'll be expecting it in the future, so from now on you better cut me in on your 'winnings,' or maybe the sheriff and the tax man would like to hear about your 'other' occupation?"

"Ok..." was all Jerry could squeak out, and he sheepishly turned and went back downstairs to the proceedings.

Upstairs, Trip turned to Cotton. "Jeezus, Bubba. Is there anything that happens in this county you don't know about?"

"Not much, my friend, not much."

And he slapped Trip on the back, and they both went downstairs to listen in on the end of the 'trial.'

9

More Reviling Reveal-ations

"Ok, people, break's over!" Donny Ray smacked his heel on the bar. "And let's remember to thank Grandma Johannsen for them sweet corn dogs she's provided for everyone today, seein' as how the meetin' is goin' longer than expected. Thank you Grandma Johannsen," he nodded to a blue-haired old woman who was all smiles and hopped up on a mason jar full of gratitudinal 'shine.

"So," continued Donny Ray, "where were we? Oh yeah, some woman in the middle of the room had re-accused Bubba Darnet, or his father-in-law, or something like 'at or other..."

"It was me!" volunteered Mandy Debarge, in the middle of the room. "Mandy Debarge! I accuse Bubba Darnet and his father-in-law, and so does one other!"

"And who may that be?" asked Donny Ray.

"One Paul Runyon, veterinarian!"

A great uproar took place in the 'council,' and in the midst of it, Doctor Runyon was seen, pale and trembling, standing again in the front of the room next to Bubba and Bunnie.

"Donny Ray," said Bubba Darnet when the crowd finally quieted once more, "I violently protest this here hearing as a forgery and a fraud! How cain a man be accused of himself? It jus' ain't possible!"

"Chill out, Bubba," said Donny Ray calmly, "If you fail to put yourself under the submission of this council we may be forced to kick you out of the state without finishing this fiasco. As it is, we need to pick things up a bit and get this thing going cuz it's getting late in the day. Now, Mandy, just what in tar'nation has gotten up your crack?"

Eldridge 'Barge' Debarge silently, and seemingly reluctantly, stepped to the front of the room and related the history of his dealings with Doctor Runyon, and keeping him safe at his shed out back Saint Antwan's after his release from prison. Then he added, "For all I knew, the Doctor was a good man."

Someone then said to Barge, "You did good service by taking the Bay Steel, you know that?"

"I believe so," Barge said hesitantly, not knowing where this was going.

Here, an excited woman screeched from the crowd: "You were one of the best 'patriots' there! Why not say so? You were a leader of the first order that day, and you were among the first to enter the bank yourself before we burned it to the ground. Patriots, I speak the truth!"

Shouts of 'hooray!' went all around.

It was The Vengeance who, amidst the warm commendations of the audience, thus assisted the proceedings. Donny Ray smacked his boot on the bar to restore order again; but, The Vengeance, warming with encouragement and bad 'shine, shrieked, "Fuck you, Donny Ray, and your goll-derned boot!" wherein she was much commended by the audience.

"Tell the counsel what you did within the Bay Steel that day, Barge." It was Mandy Debarge, a smirk on her face and a twinkle in her eye.

"I knew," said Barge, looking at his wife, who sat in the middle of the crowd, looking steadily up at him over top her *Digest*; "I knew that Doctor Runyon, of whom I speak, had interviewed at the Bay Steel Bank and had made it through all his interviews but one, the one in which Clay D. Markee sat in, and against all other votes, turned him down. And not only that, he framed the good doctor for a crime he did not commit and had him sent away from his family to the state penitentiary for eight long years. The Doctor told me so himself. When the Bay Steel was about to be burned, on a hunch, I looked on the new president's computer to see if I could find evidence of the Doctor's being framed. But what I found was even more disturbing. I found a reference to a note by Doctor Runyon which was found buried in a field out back Tower Liquors when he was part of a chain-gang clearing litter. That paper no longer exists, because it turned to dust when the jar was opened, and yet, through the assistance of a 'spy' I know, I tracked down that paper—an exact copy of which was retrieved from the 'good' doctor's former mattress in his cell—and examined it closely. Comparing it to the other notes in the Doctor's handwriting, I have concluded that it was written by one and the same man, the Doctor you see here before you today."

Barge pointed to Runyon, and many in the crowd ooh'ed and ahhh'ed, for some reason. Then he pulled the note from his pocket.

"This is the note."

"Let it be read," ordered Donny Ray in a bored tone.

And in a dead silence and stillness—the 'prisoner' under 'trial' looked lovingly at his wife, his wife only looked from him to look with solicitude at her father; Doctor Runyon kept his eyes fixed on the reader, Mandy Debarge never took her eyes from the 'prisoner', Barge never took his eyes from his beastly wife, and all other eyes there intent upon the Doctor, who saw none of them—the paper was read, as follows:

10

An Effrontatious Confession

'I, Paul Runyon, unfortunate veterinarian, native of Coalmont County, and long time resident of its cities therein, write this unholy note in my doleful cell in the state pen. At this moment, I don't think I'll make it out of here alive, because I cannot take one more beating from Carl Brennan and his henchmen, and the guards do not seem to care anything about helping me. I am going to put the note in a jar and bury it in the ground, and maybe one day, some poor unfortunate bastard will dig it up again and read it...'

Barge smirked at this, his seeming incrimination at being said bastard. Some in the crowd snickered.

'...when I and my sorrows are turned to dust.

'These words are formed by the rusty iron point of a spring from my bunk mattress, written with great difficulty using urine, human feces, spit and drops of blood...'

At this point, Barge dropped the letter as if it were toxic waste and said, "Oh, yeah, I forgot about dat..." and continued reading the note as it lay on the ground.

'Hope of ever feeling a breast again, and other things, has departed from me. I know from terrible warnings I have witnessed in my brain that reason will not long remain in my mind unimpaired, but now, be-ing solely in possession of my right mind, I write the truth, and my confession, for all to judge, whether it be by man, or simply by Him seated at the Eternal Judgement seat himself.

'One rare sun-drenched summer morning in the third week of my veterinary practice, after just having received my license from the state by mail, I was walking back to my house from the mailbox when a fast moving car sped up my small driveway and skidded to a stop in a cloud of dust.

'Two men got out of the car and I observed that both looked about my age—or what I *would've* looked liked had I not smoked, whiskey'd and 'shine'd the youth right out of my dumb ass by that time—and they looked very much alike, and sounded very much alike when they talked, almost like twins.

"'Are you Paul Runyon?" said one.

"'I am."

"'Formerly of Nashville, Tennessee?" said the other; "The one who's been working on his veterinary license?"

"'I just got it. I have it right here in my hand..."

"'The one who used to have a traveling strip show, something about Paul Runyon and a Babe with a big blue box?"

"'Yep, that's me."

"'We don't have time to get a real doctor, and we want to keep this real quiet anyway, so get in the car."

"'What if I don't want to go?"

'One of them pulled out a gun.

"'How 'bout now?"

"'Let's go!"

'They threw me into the back seat and off we roared over the country side.

"'Gentlemen," said I, "pardon me; but I'd like to inquire as to who does me the honor of being my first clients, and who, pray-tell, will be my first patient—or patients?"

'The reply to this was made by him who had spoken second. "Doctor, your clients are people of considerable wealth. As to the nature of the case, or 'patients' as you say, we have every confidence in your skills that you will diagnose the situation by seeing it better than we can describe it."

'I could do nothing at that point but sit back and ride along to wherever they were taking me.

'I have repeated this conversation exactly as it happened, word for word. I describe everything exactly as it took place, constraining my mind not to wander from the task. Where I make the broken marks that follow here, I leave off for a time, and put my paper in its hiding place in my cell. * * * *

'The car left Coon Spit behind and raced across Rabbit Grove and then on to Reams and out the other side. We came over a long hill and pulled into a very large driveway leading to a great mansion with stables behind it. There was oppulate and ornate stone work and carvings surrounding the house, and much wrought iron lattice-work flowing from balconies and staircases.

'There was a neglected fountain out front of the main entrance, and we walked past it and went back to some sort of utility shed near the stables where a common redneck came out to meet the men, to which the first man who spoke jacked the man across the jaw with a ruthless right-hook, knocking the man to the ground out cold.

'"Jackass!" commented the ruthless man, spitting on him.

'The look and bearing of the two men I was with was so similar in that moment, that I definitely took them to be twins.

'Next we walked toward the stable and I heard cries—mortified cries as if someone were being killed—getting louder and louder as we approached. We entered the stable and went up into the loft, at which time I saw a woman, probably the wife of one of the men, holding a small girl with bloody towels wrapped around her feet, though the true condition of the feet was hidden by the towels. The young girl continued to cry bloody murder, even more so when she saw me, and I could tell she was on the verge of fainting, if she hadn't already done so many times already, only to wake up and howl in misery once again.

'For the purpose of this narrative, I shall call the

brother who hit the maintenance man, the elder, and the other, the younger. The elder said to me, "Are you ready for this?" and I said, "I guess so," and he bent toward the writhing girl and unwrapped the towels from her bloody feet only to reveal there were no feet at all! Just two bloody stumps, and blood pouring out of them.

He quickly wrapped the towels around the stumps again to try to contain the bleeding and the girl passed out once more.

"What happened?" I exclaimed.

The younger brother told me, "She was out sunbathing on the lawn—we don't know who she is or where she came from. We didn't even know she was out there, not even the maintenance man, and since he didn't see her, he accidentally and stupidly ran over her feet with the riding mower."

"Good Lord!" I exclaimed.

Then I told them: "Well, you see, you should not have brought me here. I'm an animal doctor, not a people doctor."

"There is another patient," said the woman calmly, as she lightly rubbed the unconscious girl's cheeks.

The men then lead me down from the loft, and it was at that time that I asked the elder man, "Was that your wife up there?"

"Yes," he replied.

"She's got a nice ass," I told him.

"Yes, she does."

"I bet that thing could win some awards at the state fair."

"It already has," he informed me.

"Oh? She lets other people touch it?"

The man smiled slyly, "I assure you, that thing has been *heavily* petted."

Then we walked to a stall at the very end of the stable where we found a young donkey calf inside, struggling to stand.

"The donkey you saw lying next to my wife and

daughter upstairs," the elder man said, "this is it's off-spring. The mother is in here too, somewhere."

'The younger man then moved to a corner of the stall where the mamma ass lay, void of movement.

'The man bent down to check on her.

"'She's already dead," he said grimly, but with compassion, obviously shaken by the discovery that the donkey had not survived childbirth.

'So we closed the stall door with reverence and walked back outside.

"'Well, good luck with the girl," I told them. "And I'm truly sorry I wasn't here in time to save your ass."

'That is when the elder brother again pulled out the gun.

"'You're not going anywhere until something is done about the girl! Can you imagine the scandal it would cause this family if it got out that our mainte-nance man mowed over some common little girl's feet? We have too much at stake in this community to let something like that happen!"

"'I have an idea," continued the elder, more ruth-less brother. He lead us up to the big house and we went inside. We walked up a rather astoundingly large staircase and entered a room where a little boy was drawing pictures quietly at a table. On the other side of the room, I noticed two beautifully whittled wooden feet, the exact size that would fit the little girl.

'The elder twin said, pointing to the wooden feet: "Put those onto the girl's ankles somehow. That should be good enough."

'I went to grab them, but "No!" the young boy squealed, obviously oblivious to the young girl's plight outside in the stable.

"'But we must!" the ruthless man insisted, harshly tossing the boy aside.

"'But that's my 4-H project for the state fair next month!" protested the boy. "I worked for months whit-tling those! You can't take them!"

'And the boy threw such a heart-rending fit that

the younger twin, obviously the boy's father, stood between me and the feet and would not let me touch them.

'The younger man looked down at his own feet for several minutes. Presently, his boy finally calmed, but still heaved deep breaths as he wiped away tears.

"I have an idea," his father finally told us. * * * * *

'I am weary, weary, weary!—worn down by my misery and shame. I cannot read what I have written thus far, much less think straight enough to write the final chapter! But know, for all those involved, I did what I did because I was held at gunpoint; and I did what I did under threat of the powerful brother's threat to revoke my veterinary license for all time before I even got started in the practice; and in no way did I feel, or do I feel now, that what we did—what *I* did—was justified in the eyes of any man, and least of all before God (if there is one). But know this also, to whoever finds this note one day, I will go to my dying bed regretting what was done that day, and if there is any way I could change places with anyone involved, so as not to have to deal with the scenes that go round in my noggin' each night before I lay my head upon my pillow, I would gladly do so, *gladly*, and seal some other poor bastard to the doom I carry around each second of my waking days.

'If it had pleased God (if he exists) to put it in the hard heart of either of the brothers not to make the horrible choice we made; to not do that horrible deed we did on that frightful day—to grant me one moment's peace from the torment that lives within me day and night—then I might have had a whole different life! I might have been a completely different person! Who knows? But what I do know is that I, Paul Runyon, unhappy prisoner in reality—and in thought and in deed—do this very night, denounce what was done that day for all time when all things shall be answered for. I denounce them in Heaven (if it exists) and on Earth (which I'm fairly certain exists)!'

11

A Reveal-ation to End All Reveal-ations

A terrible sound arose when the reading of this document was done. A sound of craving and eagerness that had nothing articulate in it but blood. The narrative called up the most revengeful passions of all time, and there was not a head in the room that wasn't green with nausea over the statement that was just read about the girl with no feet. It was little wonder the Debarges had kept that paper from the public, biding their time until just the right moment. And all the worse for the doomed man, Bubba Darnet, that the subject of the paper was the very own father of his wife.

Mandy Debarge got slowly out of her seat and walked to the front of the room with that wobbly but oh-so-sexy walk of hers. She reached down, slowly unzipped her boots, and ripped them off to reveal two donkey hoofs where even the most half-witted of 'tards would've expected to find feet.

"Holy Crap!" yelled Bunnie.

"I need to make shoes! I need to make shoes!" screamed the doctor, suddenly thrown into a robotic trance, and scratching around on the ground for his tools.

The crowd, as you can imagine, was thrown into a frenzy. Many a woman—and not a few men—fainted right then and there in their chairs. And those who didn't faint had to turn over those who had fainted to help them not choke on their mouths-full of chew.

Even Barge tottered backward as his eyes rolled back in his head, smacking his head off the concrete since he'd never actually seen the 'feet'; since Mandy'd never taken off the boots in front of him, not even in bed. He'd always just bought her excuse that her feet were unnaturally smelly—and now he knew why.

"He did this to me!" screamed Mandy Debarge, pointing to the Doctor. "And *he* did this to me!" she screamed again, pointing to Bubba Darnet. Then Mandy reached into her blouse, grabbed something from her bra, and pushed it in Bubba Darnet's face.

"Does *this* look familiar, Bubba? Huh? Huh! Does it?"

An oversized blue ribbon with the words printed:

First Place
4-H
Wood Carving Contest
Kentucky State Fair

Bubba stammered, "B-b-but I had no idea, I had no idea...!"

"*You* are the reason I started having to wear these knee-high boots to cover the grotesque 'hooves' that gave me such a sexy swagger—unintentionally of course—so that the kids at school made fun of me, and eventually I drove even the most E.D. of old men into frothy lathers! That was the very day I vowed my revenge!"

The Doctor had since hurried over to wave a hand in front of poor Barge's face to give the big man some air. He patted Barge's cheeks lightly in an attempt to resuscitate him.

"Do you know where I can get some materials to make shoes?" the doctor asked Barge frantically, still in a trance, "I need to make shoes! I need to make shoes, right now!"

Bunnie, the wretched wife of the innocent man doomed to be kicked out of the bowling leagues; Nay, kicked out of the county; Nay! kicked out of the *state!*—he may even lose his job!—she couldn't bear the thought of moving out of the southern Kentucky hills. After all, she'd never known anything but its hillbilly lifestyle, and the thought of being pulled from it made her want to shrivel up and die. But however mortally stricken she might have been from such a thought, she uttered no sound; so strong was the voice within her, representing that it was she of all the world who must uphold her husband and her father in this time of their misery, and not augment it.

If I might embrace my husband just once! she thought tenderly, *it just might give him the balls to carry on...because I sure as hell ain't moving out of these Kentucky hills! No ma'am! No way!*

She looked at her husband who had turned white with shock at the recent turn of events.

Farewell, dear darling of my soul. My parting blessings on you, my love! We shall not be separated long. I feel that this will break my heart by-and-by, and maybe yours too, but I will do my duty as your wife while you are still here, and when you leave here, maybe my father's Jesus will raise up for us both new friends, and maybe new lovers...hmmm...wouldn't that be exciting?...No, no! My husband! My dear husband! We shall meet again some day...maybe...where the weary are at rest!

She stole a glance at her father, who had helped Barge to his feet, and now stood wringing weary hands through his bright, white hair. She glanced again at her husband.

*I can bear it, dear Bubba, I will be supported somehow by father's Jesus up above. So please don't suffer for me, dear Charles...A parting blessing for our child...*And she held darling little Brittany up for Bubba to kiss, one last time.

But Bubba Darnet put a hand on his anguished father-in-law's shoulder.

"This is not your fault, old man. At least we know now what a struggle you have gone through, what you underwent when your conscience made you—against your will it seemed—to make shoes and boots day and night in some strange attempt to right the wrongs of the past. But you worked hard to help clear me, with the photos and all, and for that, you have earned Bunnie and I's hearts, love, and duty to take care of you for as long as we are together as a family; no matter how dysfunctional that may be."

At these words, the white-haired old man broke out of his trance and let out a shriek of anguish, knowing they probably wouldn't be allowed to be a family much longer, for he too was only going to move out of Coalmont County over his dead and shriveled up body.

Meanwhile, Donny Ray had taken once again to banging his boot heel to restore order.

"Order! Order!" he called, as people scooted chairs around to let the Rebel Yell janitor begin the unenviable task of mopping up pools of corn-dog saturated vomit splattered all over the floor when Mandy Debarge had had the gall—and the balls—to take her boots off.

"I said, Order!" yelled Donny Ray once more, and pulled out his gun in a threat to shoot it again. Everyone instantly shut-up and covered their ears.

But he didn't shoot. Instead, he said: "Ok, good. Now that I have your all's attention, I'd like to try and take a frickin' vote on this so's we cain all git home at a goll-derned decent hour tonight! All who are with me, say 'I'!"

Many 'I's echoed back to him.

"Nays?"

He shot a look at Mandy, who scowled and sincerely failed to appreciate the joke, and Barge reached to restrain her as she screamed like a banshee and leapt to release Donny Ray of his testicles.

A couple garbled but true 'nays' of objection from a few folks in the middle of the room now coming round from having fainted—their hair having long since soaked up as much vomit as it could afford.

"The 'I's have it!" barked Donny Ray, slamming his heal on the bar and taking note that he owed Barge one helluva good Christmas present this year. "Now, the question before us is are we gonna hold this man, Bubba Darnet-Dunnay, and his father-in-law, Dr. Paul Runyon, responsible for what happened to this here poor woman with the ass's feet? Yes or no?"

"Hell no!"

"Fuck no!"

"It's her fault!"

And finally: "Those men are heroes for making her walk that way!"

Of course this was heard from all the men, the women didn't really give much of shit and just wanted to get the hell out of the now horrendously smelling basement 'afore they all throw'd up or fainted again.

"Ok!" Donny Ray banged his boot. "They cain go free! Now let's go bowl some fuckin' ball!"

"*What*?!" Mandy Debarge shrieked, but her weary husband merely helped her put her boots back on, then took her by the arm and led her up the stairs and back to her rightful position at the counter at Saint Antwan's Liquors and Beers.

Soon everyone else had left the Rebel Yell basement, along with a dejected F.M. and the toughs that came in with him.

Bunnie hugged her husband, then released him, and hugged her father, then released him. She did this in an attitude of prayer, thankful that their family would not indeed be broken up, and her husband would not indeed lose his job, and her father would probably not touch another fuckin' pair of shoes for the rest of his life.

Then, issuing from an obscure corner from which he had never moved, Bubba Cotton came up and hugged Bunnie as well. It was an extra long full-frontal hug, one that made even the most sex-addicted so uncomfortable Bubba Darnet had to step in and break them apart.

Trip was there too, congratulating his club manager for beating the rap, *again*, and asked him, "Ok, now, really, what the fuck happened to my liquor?"

Bubba Darnet told him, and Trip left to go hire F.M.'s toughs to get his liquor back from Barge.

Bubba Cotton, the Doctor, Bubba Darnet and his wife Bunnie—with Brittany in tow—all left the bowling alley and went back to Chickenwell Street for some smokes, some 'shine, and some R-N-R after another brutally rough day.

"Cotton! Cotton!" cried little Brittany, wanting to play with the man once they were sufficiently hopped up on 'shine (not Brittany, of course—she only got a few drops with dinner).

"I can't play now child, I must go," Cotton told her. "You and your family are safely in tact once again, and there's nothing more I can do here. But before I go," he looked at Bubba Darnet, "May I kiss her?"

Darnet looked at his innocent child as she lovingly gazed up at Bubba Cotton.

"Sure, what the hell."

And Cotton walked over and planted a kiss (tongue included) on Bunnie that lasted, again, a little bit longer than anyone else in the room was comfortable with. Again, Bubba Darnet had to walk over and pull Cotton from his wife.

"Ok, Cotton," he said drolly, "I think she gets the point."

And Cotton made his exit.

When the over-affectionate man was gone, Bubba Darnet turned to his father-in-law and said, "Do you think Stryker was serious about that stuff about makin' me do something to prove I wouldn't interfere with him and them queers' men's night at Tall Tales when I take over?"

Runyon exhaled deeply, then coughed a short fit as he poured a bit of 'shine down his gullet.

"Well, for as long as I been around these parts," he coughed and wheezed, "Stryker has always been a serious man with a serious plan. He usually backs up everything he says. So if I were you, I'd keep my eyes out, I'm sure he'll be up to sump'in."

12

"You Want Me To Do *What?*"

Bubba Cotton paused, sitting in his car, not quite decided where to go.

"To Tall Tales at nine tomorrow," he told himself, with a musing face. "But should I do well in the meantime to show myself around the county on a drinking binge? I think so."

He started the car and drove to the Skinned Hare, the same dive he'd had drinks with Bubba Darnet after saving him the first time; but not before first stopping to have a short consultation with Mr. Stryker at his home in Rabbit Grove, the contents of which shall remain unrevealed at this time.

Having met with Stryker, and now walking from the parking lot to the Skinned Hare, Cotton tended toward an object and took a turn or two toward it, in the already darkening street. He traced through his mind the possible consequences of following his hunch, but having decided to throw consequence to the wind, he followed the dark shadow, otherwise known as John Solomon Priss-Garcia-Bastard, into a back alley where dumpsters reigned supreme, and the smell choked the life out of the biologically sustainable.

Having thus emerged from meeting with Bastard without consequence, except the shaking news he just learned, and being in a stupor as to the effect of how news traveled like lightning around the county he loved so much; he dined at the dive and soon fell asleep with his face in the mashed potatoes, though he hadn't touched a drop of drink all night.

At seven in the morning, Cotton crawled again from the back dumpster and decided to make a trip to

Saint Antwan's Liquors and Beer.

Before entering the liquor store, Cotton spied his reflection in the glass of the door, and arranged his clothes and hair to look as much like Bubba Darnet from the day before as he could possibly could. Then he entered.

There happened to be no customer in the store except Harlan Three, he of the restless fingers and the croaking voice. This man, whom Cotton had seen at the 'council' meeting the day before, stood drinking a sample of wine at Mandy's counter; one in which he undoubtedly didn't pay for. Cotton noted he was probably making up the cost in some other manner—most likely a dubious one. Harlan Three was locked in quiet conversation with the Debarges, man and wife. The Vengeance also stood nearby, like the regular member of the establishment she now was.

Cotton walked in and took a seat at an empty dominos table near the front of the store, thinking to buy a bottle of wine to drink on the premises.

Mandy Debarge cast a glance at him and did a double-take that nearly gave her whiplash. But then decided there was no way it could be *him*. However, the coincidence was uncanny.

She walked over to him herself and asked what he wanted.

He said he wanted a particular wine and wanted to drink it there.

"You sure you want a whole bottle of 'Old English Leather'?" she asked. "That stuff tastes like shit!"

Cotton repeated that it was what he wanted.

"Ok, it's your intestines, buddy," said she, and walked to get it. "But I ain't payin' your fuckin' ambulance bill to get you outta here."

Mandy Debarge soon returned with the wine, and gave him the bird for being a no-good out of towner.

"I swear, Mandy!" shouted Barge from behind the counter, having seen the action. "Could you *please* be a little more respectful of the customers? Please!

Fuck!"

Barge brought over a medium size Dixie cup for Cotton, and said, "I'm sorry my wife's such a bitch, but she's like that with everyone. Don't let it bother you."

"Thank you," replied Cotton. "I won't."

Barge went back to the counter and said quietly to the others, "Yeah, I see what you mean. He does look a *little* like him."

Mandy snorted. "A good deal like him! *Just* like him if you ask me!"

The amiable Vengeance added with a laugh, "Fuck yeah! He looks just like that bastard you said made those wooden feet..."

Cotton followed their conversation by reading their lips, with such a nonchalant expression they thought he was staring off into space instead of reading their moving mouths. They were all leaning with their arms close together on the counter, speaking in low tones. After a silence of a few moments, during which they all looked towards him without disturbing his outward attention, they resumed their conversation.

"Is it true what Mandy says?" observed Harlan Three. "Is that him? Is that the guy?"

"No way," reasoned Barge. "What kind of fool would take the kind of beating he took before us yesterday and then come all up in here like he don't know us or nothin'? That'd be just plain idiocy!"

The Vengeance highly agreed, "Damn straight, I'm tellin' ya."

"But he does look just like him," Barge had to admit. "Freakishly so."

Other customers soon entered and the little group was broken up. Cotton polished off his wine and got up to ask directions of the married couple to the nearest Walmart, just to fuck with 'em.

"Get bent!" retorted Mandy, and Cotton went on his way.

Without having gotten an outright confirmation of what the Bastard had told him the night before, Cotton had gathered enough information from that little informal stopping-in that he knew what his 'spy' had told him was spot-on.

Yes, things were a brewin' in Coalmont County, about to come to a head. And Cotton needed some time to think things over and clear his head before putting into motion a plan he had conceived while sipping that god-awful shit-swill wine at Saint Antwan's.

"You want me to do *what*?"

Bubba Darnet was enraged.

"No deal, Stryker! You got to be out of your fuckin' mind!"

"I'm deadly serious young fellow, and if you refuse, I and my loyal contingent of Cock-N-Bull'ers will take our patronage elsewhere for all time. Is that what you want?"

Darnet looked at Trip, whose expression hadn't changed.

"Come on, Trip. Help me out here. You can't be taking this shit seriously, can you?"

Trip leaned forward and put his elbows softly on the desk. "I think the man is deadly serious, and I also think you ought to do what he says. Besides, I'd like to know just how dedicated you are to your loyal customers before I decide I'm gonna turn this place over to you."

Stryker smiled and raised an eyebrow up and down.

"Awww, come on, Trip! Come—On! Jeezus!" exclaimed Bubba, leaning back in his chair, flipping his legs up in disgust, pounding his boots down on the desk. Trip eyeballed him over top his bifocals and Bubba immediately removed the boots from the desk.

"Sorry, Trip. But look, what's my wife gonna say? What're my friends gonna say? What's my fuckin' *child* gonna say?"

Trip was unmoved.

"Well, young man, what's it going to be?" posed Stryker, holding out his hand. "Do we have a deal or don't we? Will you do it?"

Bubba exhaled hard, then slapped a palm into the big man's hand.

"Oh, all right! I guess. Jeezus! But I ain't gonna enjoy it! I'll tell ya that much! I ain't a gonna enjoy it one bit!"

"Not askin' you to enjoy it," said Stryker with satisfaction as he turned to go, "Just askin' you to do it. That's all."

"Jeezus fuckin' Christ, Trip!" Bubba whined to the club owner when Stryker had gone.

Trip merely shrugged his shoulders.

13

The Moment Finally Arrives

Two months later, the doomed night awaiting Bubba Darnet's fate had finally arrived: The first 'Men's Night' ever was held at Tall Tales strip club, Grouse Gulch, Kentucky.

As per Bubba, Stryker and Trip's agreement, the first ever Tall Tales Men's Night was to see Bubba Darnet slated as the first ever male dancer—*and stripper*—of the evening.

Before it had set in dark on this night of his condemnation, backstage the old haggard and wore-out female strippers had a ball makin' ole Bubba up with a bit of stage rouge, some black eyeliner, and penciled in abs. They stepped back to admire their handi-work and decided to a one of them that Chippendale's this redneck was most certainly not—he was more like Chris Farley in the Saturday Night Live *Chippendales* sketch.

Well...maybe not that bad—that was pretty awful.

Anyway, as that was going on amongst the cramped background, in the cramped foreground, seventy-two people crammed into an area the local fire officials said could only hold fifty-two maximum; legally, that is.

Not everyone in the crowd was gay of course, and not all were men. Some came out simply as a result of morbid curiosity. Others from the sheer force of the controversy. Others came to see the historic change to such a long and storied institution of heterosexualism that Tall Tales had always prided itself on. Others were simply there because they had seen that *Queer Guy for the Straight Guy* show on the Tee-Vee, and wanted to see just what all the 'rage in city culture' was they was hearin' so much about.

Some were there, of course, in protest. And they stood around the back of the room, holding signs.

As show-time grew close, the crowd chanted louder and louder and the protesters protested louder and louder until the 'regular' crowd threw beer on the bashers and decided to chase them from the club. The few police on hand, including the sheriff himself, did nothing to stop it, figuring with the protesters out of the way it'd be a smoother evening.

The protesters picked themselves out of the mud puddles of the recently rain-deluged parking lot, as Stryker and his companions—who were parked inside the velvet VIP rope with 'reserved' tagged on it coarsely with a black Sharpee—sat up front against the stage and clapped and hollered in anticipation with every click of the second hand that ticked from the Elvis hip-swivel clock above the bar.

Ten minutes before scheduled show-time, Trip, standing off to the side of the bar, was surprised to see Mandy and Barge Debarge, The Vengeance—and a short nervous-ticky man known to a select few as Harlan Three—walk in and quietly sit at a table near the back. Never having stepped foot in the dirty dingy and dungy Tall Tales before (as far as Trip knew), the trio looked around in bewilderment as if they were females suddenly finding themselves in the male commode, or vice-versa.

Trip decided it best to go over and greet them personally, to make them feel more comfortable, and told them warmly he was glad to have them here at Tall Tales. He took their drink orders personally, and welcomed them to sit back and enjoy the evening.

"This is a gay thing, right?" asked Barge to Trip just as he walked away.

"Yeah, that's what I understand," said Trip.

"S'what I thought. So no, no, I ain't gonna enjoy the show."

In contrast to this, Mandy looked as jacked as she

could be—ready to go!—and with a smile on her face as big as Barge's gut. She looked forward with great— no, *huge*—anticipation to what was to come.

The Vengeance merely ordered a double side of Nachos (with extra cheese) and sat quietly in drool-soaked anticipation of the arrival of her artery-incinerating treats.

As the crowd milled about and murmured its less than enthralling conversations, there were several prominent citizens of Coalmont County that were conspicuously, and inconspicuously, *not* in attendance.

Conspicuously absent: Bunnie Darnet, her father, and his granddaughter.

Inconspicuously absent: Bubba Cotton.

The former by special request, nay, *by demand!* of Bubba Darnet; the latter, well, quite honestly, who gave a shit?

Bubba Darnet was at this moment completely oblivious to the scene out front and found himself now left alone of the strippers and sitting solely by himself in the back dressing room, sustaining himself with several shots of whiskey and no flattering delusion that this was actually going to be an enjoyable show for anyone, save for maybe Stryker and a few of his cronies. In every line of the narrative in his head about how the night was about to be played out, he could only think of hearing the clanging bell of his own personal condemnation for what was about to happen.

But there was no turning back now.

Only moving forward, forward, forward, into an unknown destiny. He had fully comprehended that no personal—or otherwise—influence could save him now, and if he chose to run out the door, the place would surely riot and be burned to the ground. He couldn't do that to the innocent and hard-working Trip, no matter how much he dreaded what was about to happen. He was sentenced by the masses that chanted and clapped for him now, and nothing could avail him of his dread.

Nothing.

Not even several shots of whiskey.

Nevertheless, with the image of his beloved Bunnie before him, he tried to compose his mind to what he must bear. His hold on life as he knew it was strong, and it was very, very hard to loosen; by gradual efforts and degrees it was unclosed a little here, unclenched a little there. His mind was in a hurry, too; all his thoughts a turbulent and heated working of his heart, which contended between fight or flight—or all out resignation. If, for a moment, he did feel resigned to quit and run out, then the image of Bunnie and her future happiness came forth, and he knew backing down would be a selfish thing.

But, all this was at first. Before long, the consideration that there was complete disgrace ahead in his fate grew to titanic proportions within him, and the danger of what was about to happen began to scare him out of his mind. But the next thought was that much of the future peace of mind enjoyed by the dear ones depended on his quiet fortitude to go through with such humiliation, so, that by degrees he calmed himself into a better state. And when he finally decided to fully resign himself to his fate, he drew comfort from the fact that he was locked into this path once and for all time, and there was no turning back.

He wrote a long letter to Bunnie and shoved it up inside the drop ceiling for her to find one day, or maybe one of the skanky-ass strippers would find it soon enough and give it to her. But if not, such was life. No big deal. He only wanted to communicate to her on this side of the act—in case things went terribly wrong—or worse—if things went terribly right. He wanted to tell her what he felt for her in the moments before the act was to play itself out—in the moments before life as he knew it might be—and most likely would be—irrevocably changed for now and evermore.

He had only mere seconds to finish the letter before the chanting grew louder and louder and the lights went dim—the signal that the house DJ was ready for him to come out onstage. It shook him from his fantasy world that what was about to happen was really, *actually*, going to take place. He was shaken from the fantasy that at that moment he was free and happy, back at Chickenwell Street, drinking 'shine and bullshitting and hallucinatin' with the boys (and Bunnie) until the wee hours of the night.

A pause of forgetfulness from another shot of whiskey, and then he came back to her. To Bunnie. And the thought that he may go back to her unchanged by what was going to happen tonight. But that was unlikely. Another pause, and another shot of oblivion, and he awoke in a sombre mourning, unconscious where he was momentarily, until it flashed upon his mind, 'This is the day of my death!'

Thus, he had come through the hours, minutes and seconds, to the moment when the seventy-two heads were to see his bare naked naughty-bits out there in the ether for all to ogle, and most certainly (except for Stryker and his cronies) for all to ridicule until the end of time.

And so with the lights having gone dimmed, and the music starting up, he stood, composed, and hoped he could meet the end with quiet heroism. It seemed like hours as he walked the five paces from the cramped dressing room to the cramped stage to face the cramped crowd, and he walked and retreated the first three paces two or three times before gathering up the nerve to go further.

*One step gone forever, two steps gone forever, three steps gone forever, four...*and so on until as if lifted and carried up by a cloud, he seemed set down on the stage from above, as if by angel, as the first notes of *Macho Man* rang throughout his ears. Then he realized it wasn't an angel at all, but big fat Stryker having given him one monster shove forward.

"Get on up there, for fuck's sake!"

At first, Bubba walked up and down the stage,

softly repeating in his head the names of folks he recognized in the crowd. He came out in an outfit of skimpy gold lamé wrestling shorts, with a gold lamé cape around his shoulders and nearly knee-high gold lamé wrestling boots. He felt he was barely wearing enough to shield himself against the judgment of his shame by the crowd, and yet, he would soon be made to undergo the task of taking more *off*, not putting more *on*; to shield him from the gawking, and partially drooling(?), mob.

With the striking of the initial chords of Frankie Goes to Hollywood's *Relax*, Stryker and his contingent sprang to their feet and danced and cheered as they clapped and partied to the beat.

Bum-Bum-Bum-Bum-Bum-Bum-Bum...RELAX!
Don't do it! When you want to su...!

Bubba walked to and fro upon the stage like a frightened deer—or a horrified chicken. He held his arms folded across his chest, palms flat against his nipples as if he were fighting against the deepest of arctic freezes. One yelp of *'take it off!'* from a participant of the roped-off 'reserved' section was enough to send a bolt of dread sizzling through Bubba with enough force to split him in two.

14

I Gots To Go

It was in the hours soon after the second trial that the plan was hatched.

After having quickly gotten wind (by John the Bastard, the double agent) of Stryker's plan to humiliate and test Bubba Darnet on the very first night of the Tall Tales once-weekly men's nights to come, Mandy Debarge held a darkly ominous council with The Vengeance and Harlan Three. Not in the wine shop did Mandy Debarge hold such council, no, she did so in a shed on the outskirts of Reams, which also happened to be the current residence of a particular road construction worker. The road construction worker did himself not participate in the conference, but held his distance from the shed, like an outer satellite who was not to speak until required, or to offer an opinion until invited, as the others plotted.

"But this Bubba Darnet," said Harlan Three, "Will he even go through with it?"

"Absolutely!" the voluble Vengeance said in her shrill notes. "It's a good job, he'll want to keep it. Besides, he wants to take over them clubs real bad when that Trip Templeton decides to retire."

"Please, my little Vengeance!" said Mandy Debarge, "Would you shut your frickin' hole for five minutes? Please? Let me frickin' speak here!"

Mandy smiled sadistically as she saw a slight frown cross her lieutenant's lips.

"Now look, you two. Though my husband can be a dick, he's also a good man—most of the time—and he'll want no part of the plot I'm about to unveil here, I'm sure of that. My husband has his weaknesses—and oh, they are many!—but one weakness I'd swear on my grave that he has no stomach for is murder..."

"Murder?!" cried the Vengeance. "Didn't nobody say nothin' 'bout no murder when I signed up for this!"

"See now, Vengeance," said Mandy disgustedly, "didn't I tell you not to come? Didn't I? Didn't I ask for you not to be here? But what'd you say? 'Oh, no! I gots to come! I gots to be part of this! Count me in!' Is that not what you said back at the store? Isn't it?"

"Yeahhhh," said the Vengeance slowly and with much meekness.

"Then shut your yap before I shut it for you!" barked Mandy Debarge. "You're in this show now whether you like it or not, and unless you want to end up like our dear friend Bubba Darnet is going to end up, then I'd like to advise you to shut up and keep what you're about to hear to yourself! Am I clear?"

"Crystal," replied the Vengeance lightly, her large tummy suddenly very upset and screaming in protest at the whole macabre scene.

"In a word," continued Mandy, "I cannot wholly trust my husband in this matter. Not only do I feel, since earlier today, that I dare not confide to him the details of my little 'project,' but I also feel that if we delay it beyond the next couple months, there is a danger of his being given warning, and then Darnet might be prepared for what is coming. Or worse—my husband might try to stop us."

"Can we go now?" butt-in Vengeance nervously.

"No! I said chill!" answered Mandy.

"That must never be," said Harlan Three. "No one must ever find out! We probably have only half the balls to pull it off as it is..."

Mandy slapped him in the face, hard. "*You* may only have only half the balls Harlan *Pee*, but I'm tellin' ya, mine are strapped in, hard, and ready to go; bigger'n the fuckin' heads on Mt. Rushmore! You hear me?"

Now it was Harlan Three's turn to cower nervously, wondering what the hell he had gotten *him*self into.

Mandy continued: "Now Harlan, this is what we'll do. You'll do the deed, and for that, you'll be duly compensated. After the deed is done, I will wash my hands of the whole situation, so however you want to escape future incarceration as a result of what you're about to do, well, you figure that out your own damn self. I only need you so far as the deed. So..."

"Can we please go now? Please...?" begged the Vengeance, now shaking slightly.

"No, godammit! No!" Mandy shot at her. "We ain't through yet! Cain't you see?"

The Vengeance demurred, but shook harder, as if in an after-shock of an 8.0 on the Richter Scale.

"Now Harlan," continued Mandy, "this will be the signal. When I raise my hand to my mouth, and you see me put two fingers in each side of my cheeks like this..." She put two fingers in her cheeks, then pulled them out. "...that is when you should get ready. And then, when you hear me whistle real loud, like this..." She put the fingers back in her mouth and blew an ear-shattering *tweet!*

The Vengeance and Harlan Three nearly toppled over.

"...just like 'at, like I'm cheerin' for Bubba or something—that is when I want you to do the deed. Got it, Harlan?"

"Yes ma'am. Hand—fingers—mouth—whistle—I go."

"Right. Perfect. Good. Now let's go. Let's get the fuck outta here."

The three exited the shed and Mandy gave the road construction dude a slight wave of thanks for letting them convene privately in his shed.

He waved back, and they went on out to their car.

"We better get outta here quick!" shot the Vengeance, her large frame shaking convulsively now.

"Why?" asked Mandy. "For fuck's sake, Vengeance! What's the matter?"

"I gots to take me a monster dump!"

15

A Final Shock to the System

RELAX! DON'T DO IT! WHEN YOU WANT TO...

The music was pumping at excruciating decibels as the 'reserved' section sufficiently lathered themselves to a hot and heavy froth, ready for the clothes to fly off the slow and shuffling man, currently timidly moving back and forth upon the stage in front of them like some kind of human pendulum.

"Take it off, honey!"

"Don't be shy!"

"We won't look! We promise!"

And all of a sudden, without warning, and with the duly married Debarges, The Vengeance, and Harlan Three looking on in amazement, Bubba Darnet seemed in a flash to be transformed, as if by the yanking of an invisible lamp string, going from a shy modest prude into a raging male stripping lunatic in one second!

Fuck it, Bubba decided in the deepest recesses of his mind in that moment, *I'm already fuckin' committed, so if we're gonna do this thing, we might as well turn this bitch out!*

Bubba began to strut and prance, to the unfathomable glee of the 'reserved' section, like he had trained for this moment at Julliard. He made naughty faces and poses, like he'd seen the girls do plenty of times, and slowly unzipped his gold wrestling boots and let them flap around awhile near his ankles, as he'd seen the girls do plenty of times.

He kicked one boot high over the crowd, then the other, nearly shattering the mirror behind the bar had Ellsworth not caught each projectile with football-like dexterity (much to the relief of Trip). Bubba followed with wrapping and unwrapping himself in the cape, until dragging it along the stage until finally giving it release.

He now turned to high-stepping, chest hair bristling forth and fully exposed, to the final notes of *Relax* in nothing but his gold lamé wrestling shorts. Stryker's crew howled and moaned, dripping with sweat as their temperatures rose in accordance with the rising temperature of the overcrowded room, the whole scene spinning before them like the cinematic motion-sickness that is *Goodfellas*.

The sound, the visual, the veri-lights moving, swaying, slashing through the night; the fog machine belching its magical dry ice; the disco ball dropped from the ceiling and swirled and twirled as if Olvia Newton-John had been risen from the dead—oh, wait, she's not dead—it was at that very moment, for the very first time, just as *Relax* came to a close, that Bubba Darnet onstage, as well as Mandy Debarge and Harlan Three to the right of her out the crowd, knew for the gods-honest sure first time, that they were truly and fully committed to going all the way with their individual and sordid plots.

No turning back.

Never say die.

Remember the Alamo.

Tucked away in his jacket, no one but Harlan Three had seen the instrument that was to end Bubba Darnet's life. And tucked away beneath those gold lamé wrestling shorts, no one but his wife, Bunnie, and thirty odd other girls—and a few select men— had seen the instrument Bubba Darnet was about to spring forth upon the crowd.

At that very moment, Mandy Debarge emerged from the restroom and sashayed her sexy walk back toward her table. Many heterosexuals in attendance threw her an appreciative glance, happy to be distracted for a time from what was taking place up on the stage, and the monkey show directly in front of it.

There were many women in the room, upon whom time had laid a dreadfully disfiguring hand; but, there was not one among them more to be dreaded than this ruthless—and ruthlessly disfigured—woman, now taking her seat near the back.

Mandy Debarge's face was of a strong and fearless character, of shrewd sense and readiness, of great determination, of such unattractive proportions which not only seems to impart to its possessor firmness and animosity, but also strikes into others an instinctive recognition of what The Devil's butt-hole must look like. And if Satan himself had tried to eat her flesh in that moment, he surely would have heaved her up, so vile was her heart and soul toward the man prancing about onstage before her now.

Imbued from her childhood with a brooding sense of wrong, and an inveterate hatred for Bubba and his father-in-law, opportunity had developed her into a demon of her own making, one absolutely void of pity. If she ever had virtue in her, which wasn't likely, it had quite gone out of her long, long ago.

It was nothing to her that an innocent man was to die for the sins of his father-in-law. She saw, not them as individuals, but as one. It was nothing to her that his wife should be made a widow and his daughter an orphan; that was insufficient punishment, because they were her natural enemies and her prey, and as such had no right to live. To appeal to her would have been made hopeless by her having no sense of pity, even for her own damn self. If she had been laid in the streets, out there in the open, just as she was in the backseats of many a car in any one of her many encounters in which she had been 'engaged' in her youth, she would not have pitied herself any more than she did now.

Such a heart Mandy Debarge carried underneath her rough exterior. Carelessly worn, it was becoming rough, callused and leathery, like the skin of an overexposed twenty-five-year-old Florida woman who now looks ninety-five.

As the opening notes of *Y.M.C.A.* blasted forth from the sound system—lights still going crazy and the fog machine gushing out the last of its wares—the entire room stood and cheered; the 'reserved' section was absolutely out of its mind in anticipation of what was oh, so near to come...er, uh, so close to happening soon...

Bubba Darnet did a few quick passes at faking like he was going to pull down his britches, and a small part of the room ooh'ed and ahh'ed in steamy anticipation of such blessed event.

Lying hidden in Harlan Three's jacket was a pistol he reached in and massaged in anticipation of a forthcoming blessed event of his own.

Young man!...

Mandy Debarge looked coldly at Harlan, and he nodded slightly to signal he was ready. Her dark eyes followed from his eyes to her hand being raised from her lap to her jaw, two fingers jutting out above the others, ready to engage her mouth in their dastardly work.

But as the hand was raised to chin level, Barge looked at them as a stray offshoot from a veri-light hit the disco ball and landed squarely inside the jacket of Harlan Three, sending a reflected glint of light through Barge's retinas; the unmistakable image of steel impressed itself upon his brain.

Y—M—C-A!...

"What the fuck you two doin'?" inquired Barge harshly just as it hit him that they were obviously fixin' to assassinate Bubba Darnet before all the world to see, on the very birth of Tall Tales' very first Men's Night.

It's fun to stay at the Y—M—C-A...

With no time to think, Barge quickly reacted, reaching past his wife to grab at Harlan Three's jacket, knocking over all three drinks and causing Harlan to drop the gun; it clanked noiselessly to the ground, drown in the thump and circumstance of the ear-splitting Village People standard.

Satisfied he had bought some time, Barge grabbed his wife and said to her face. "What *are* you, the wife of Lucifer?"

Mandy quickly shook loose from his grasp and bent down, scrambling for the gun along with Harlan Three.

The Vengeance, seated in front of the table and oblivious to what was happening behind her, tapped her foot to the music and sat face-forward, contentedly munching her nachos.

...you can hang out with all the boys...

Barge dove under the table, and his wife addressed him as all three scrambled for the gun.

"If I'm the wife of Lucifer, jackass, I guess that makes you The Devil!"

Barge shot back at her: "Woman, you done gone and lost yo' damn mind! The fuck is wrong with you?"

Y—M—C-A!...

Mandy Debarge looked at him scornfully, but only for a second, since she was presently keyed in on the location of the gun, but could do nothing but watch as the hand of Harlan Three snatched it up before her. What ensued then, as Harlan rose to regain his previous seat, was a wrestling match between an infuriated wife and her equally infuriated husband, underneath the table.

...it's fun to stay at the, Y—M—C-A...

"You're a wiry bitch, ain't ya?" Barge spat at her, amazed at the strength his wife had so effectively kept shielded from his cognizance all these years.

"If those eyes of yours weren't so beady and squinty, I'd shove a splinter into 'em right now!" Mandy shot back.

"I know your intentions are evil," observed Barge, "and you can count on this— that as long as I'm alive, you ain't gonna kill that boy up there!"

"Watch me!" Mandy spewed, and wrestled from his

grasp, popping back up in her seat right beside Harlan Three, who had the gun cocked and ready to go, concealed by the flap of his jacket.

Barge bopped back into his chair, badly heaving to catch his breath, just as Mandy shoved two fingers into her mouth and Harlan concentrated the gun on Bubba's heart. The amateur stripper twirled forward from the back of the stage, and approached the audience to perform his final opus.

Y—M—C-A!...

With both hands, Bubba grabbed either side of his gold lamé britches and slung them to the ground just as Mandy blew down hard on her fingers, whistling for all she was worth.

...it's fun to stay at the, Y—M—C-A!...

"Sweet Mother of God!" Harlan Three yelled, frozen in time, still as a statue, along with the rest of the seventy-two patrons of Tall Tales, presently engaged in inhaling the entire contents of the room's oxygen into their lungs with one collective gasp. Which is exactly the same moment Barge's hand came down hard atop the gun, startling Harlan into squeezing the trigger, but, firing a shot not at heart level, but at *crotch* level; releasing a bullet that whizzed forth smacking Bubba Darnet square in the...*vagina*?

"He's a frickin' woman!" some redneck shouted atop the shocked and silent crowd, a revelation which, sadly, took precedence in their reeling and dumbfounded minds over the fact that a human being was bleeding to death onstage from a gunshot wound to his—er, her—woman parts.

* * *

The following day, an anonymous man in the Horse Chaw and Vittles restaurant in downtown Coon Spit put his coffee cup down, picked up *The Coalmont County Gazette*, and read the lead story. It stated that Charles 'Bubba' Darnet-Dunnay had bled to death onstage at the Tall Tales strip club on the first of what was to become a weekly 'Men's Night' at the club; a death died in plain view of ten or fifteen confirmed gay men, and thirty or so still en-wardrobed ones; Mr. Darnet having died before emergentary help could be rolled beyond the flimsy overhead door of the outdated and under-budgeted Grouse Gulch fire station. The article went on to state that of the dead man—well, now woman—many said it was the peacefullest they'd ever seen Charles 'Bubba' Darnet as he—she—died. Many others added that she looked sublime, though mostly pathetic.

The man set the newspaper down next to his plate of uneaten scrambled eggs and discarded toast crumbs to reflect on the last time he had ever seen Charles 'Bubba' Darnet, the man the article claimed had died last night at Tall Tales.

It was when he'd been sitting alone in the Tall Tales dressing room, after the last wannabe Hollywood make-up artist stripper had left the room before the show.

That is when he heard a knock at the door.

The door was quickly opened and closed, and there stood before Darnet, face to face, quiet, and intent upon him, with the light of a smile on his—now her—features; a cautionary finger on her lips, one Sydney 'Bubba' Cotton.

There was something so bright and remarkable in his look, that, for the first moment, Bubba Darnet misdoubted the figure to be an apparition of his own imagining. But, he spoke, and it was his voice; he took Bubba Darnet's hand and held it tight within his grasp.

"Of all the people of the earth, you least expected to see me, I presume?" Bubba Cotton had said.

"I couldn't believe it to be you. I can hardly believe it now. You ain't..."—the apprehension came suddenly into his mind—"gonna strip tonight too, is ya?"

"No, I'm accidentally possessed of a power that

drives me, a power known to you, I'm sorry to say, as—your wife."

"The *fuuh*...?"

"Yes, I know. I've probably been guilty of making you seethe with jealously on more than one occasion, but know that it was harmless—mostly—and that nothing between your wife and I ever transpired beyond what you saw before your own eyes...mostly."

Darnet turned his face aside.

"I know, for jealously's sake it sucks to have such a hot snatch for a wife, but I tell you, I just couldn't help myself. I'm in love with her. I thought I'd just admit that outright since I'm here to do you, and her, a great service."

"And what would that be, asshole?" retorted Bubba Darnet to him in disgust.

"I'm going to secure yours, and her, future happiness for all time."

"And jus' how you gonna do that, numbnuts?"

"Hurry! Take the make-up kit in front of you and make up my face exactly as yours is now. And give me fake abs, too."

"But..."

"Just do it! Now!"

Bubba Darnet did as he was told, but the true reason and meaning for what was happening before him remained lost.

Quickly, but with hands as true to the purpose as his heart was to Bubba Darnet's wife, Cotton pulled the gold lamé clothing from Darnet's body and left him standing there naked and shivering in the middle of the room.

"Sorry," said Cotton, "I guess I forgot to bring clothes for you..."

"That's ok, I can just use your clothes..."

"Nope! Back up the bus! Off limits, Buck-o! Sorry."

Bubba Cotton then pulled a large manila envelope from under his jacket and said: "Have no fear, Bubba Darnet!"

"Well, I wasn't really scare't anyway..."

"...you shall soon be getting on with your normal life even better than you had it before. Here are the documents you're going to need; some birth certificates and such...," Cotton handed him the envelope, "...and some instructions inside. Follow them and be happy. Peace be with you!"

And Cotton shoved a startled and bewildered Darnet from the dressing room where he escaped buck-naked out the back door of Tall Tales and into the dark night, shivering and shaking as he ran.

That was the last time Bubba Darnet had ever seen Bubba Cotton, now known to all the world, in his death—well, *her* death—as Bubba Darnet-Dunnay. The man in the restaurant booth retained a haunting image that still lingered in his brain for a good part of his days—along with the guilt he carried like a ton of bricks—that he didn't think to question the odd forest of seemingly artificial chest hair springing forth from the top unbutton of Cotton's flannel shirt that fateful night. No, instead, he left Bubba Cotton in the dressing room alone to melancholically ruminate over 'her' love for Bunnie, and the impending cessation of her own life; reflecting on how much she would sacrifice to secure the future happiness of the one human being on earth she loved more than life itself.

As far as the outside world was concerned, the man in the back booth at the Horse Chaw and Vittles nonchalantly got up from the table, took one last sip of his now cold coffee, gathered his 'new' bride, his child and his father-in-law in his wake, and failed to exit the storied greasy spoon without first signing the merchant's copy of his credit card receipt: *Sydney 'Bubba' Cotton.*

Epilogue

(Many years later...)

Minutes after the wrecking ball slammed its final pass into the back wall of what used to be known as the Tall Tales strip club, an unsuspecting demolitioner walked through the rubble and noticed at his feet a yellow, folded-up piece of paper. He bent down, picked-up the object, and unfolded the crisping pulp ever so carefully, then deciphered:

'Tall Tales strip club, Grouse Gulch, Coalmont County, Kentucky—on one random nasty night inside an equally nasty dive strip club...

'To the dear, dear One who will always be with me in my heart, soul and mind:
'Soon I will look out into the crowd and see John the Bastard, and Jerry Kracker, the Debarges, and that shaky Harlan fellow I saw sucking down gallons of wine free of charge at Saint Antwan's; and probably Donny Ray, and most certainly that fool Stryker, and oh, yeah, that study in morbid obesity, that hideous ignoramus who calls herself 'The Vengeance' (like she's some wannabe rock-star or something).
'But in spite of all these losers, I see a beautiful county with a beautiful people one day rising up from the corrupt shit-hole it now most certainly is. I see the evil of this time gradually making expiation for itself and wearing itself out.
'I see the lives for which I now lay down my life, peaceful, useful (maybe?), prosperous (??), and happy, in that Coalmont County which I shall see no more. I see Her with another child suckling at that glorious rack, who bears my name, or at least, the middle

name—of 'Cotton' (And I can only hope that they spell it right, for chrissakes...).

'I see that child's father, aged and bent, yet as dopey and noble as he ever was, and at peace.

'I see the 'good' old man, well...the old man that was once a mother-fucker, but is now 'good' since it'd been confirmed that he really did come to Jesus...enriching all their lives with all he has, and by eventually perfecting that shit swill 'shine of his (that nearly drove us all out of our minds on many a night), and I wish tranquility and a clean drunkenness to be his long and final reward.

'I also hope that after this night I might hold a sanctuary in all their hearts, and in the hearts of their descendents, generations hence.

'I see Her, an old woman—but still with that bodacious rack—weeping for me on the anniversary of this night. I see Her and her husband (that fucking prick that ended up with her and not me!) lying side by side in their bed, she thinking of me instead of him! Ha! Wouldn't that be poetic justice...? But I digress...

'I see him with Her, taking the millions in lottery money I won last month and building an extraordinary life which I might have led, and telling their children my story, with a tender and faltering voice.

'It is a far, far better thing that I do, than I have ever done; it is a far, far better rest that I go to than I have ever known.'

Signed,

Yours Truly For All Time,

The Swab

The great-great grandson of the Coalmont County coroner of several generations past, now Coalmont County's foremost expert in the demolition arts, crumpled up the note and watched it turn to dust. But as he continued shuffling through the rubble, like an old retiree scooting a metal detector over some random beach he can no longer enjoy for its flesh flashing purposes, he couldn't help but wonder if the words just put forth into his brain were penned by the same she-male stripper that his father, and his father's father before him, claimed had a small but distinguishable tattoo of a bunny rabbit—portrayed with a singular tear-drop dripping from its right eye—affixed above her left hip.

(MERCIFULLY) THE END

About the Author

D. Harold is an international journalist who divides his time between the Middle East, Colorado, Florida and the Great State of Ohio.